Love and romance brighten the air every Valentine's Day. And what better way to celebrate than with three charming stories set in Regency England by three top-notch Zebra Regency writers.

Sara Blayne presents a Valentine's Day gala where hearts are lost and won. Jo Ann Ferguson tells the tale of a Hart winning her true love heart. And Lois Stewart brings lost lovers together forever.

Hearts and flowers, hugs and kisses— romance is the order of the day and love is the order of the heart. Indulge yourself with a token of our affection and enjoy **VALENTINE LOVE.**

ZEBRA'S REGENCY ROMANCES
DAZZLE AND DELIGHT

A BEGUILING INTRIGUE   (4441, $3.99)
by Olivia Sumner

Pretty as a picture Justine Riggs cared nothing for propriety. She dressed as a boy, sat on her horse like a jockey, and pondered the stars like a scientist. But when she tried to best the handsome Quenton Fletcher, Marquess of Devon, by proving that she was the better equestrian, he would try to prove Justine's antics were pure folly. The game he had in mind was seduction — never imagining that he might lose his heart in the process!

AN INCONVENIENT ENGAGEMENT   (4442, $3.99)
by Joy Reed

Rebecca Wentworth was furious when she saw her betrothed waltzing with another. So she decides to make him jealous by flirting with the handsomest man at the ball, John Collinwood, Earl of Stanford. The "wicked" nobleman knew exactly what the enticing miss was up to — and he was only too happy to play along. But as Rebecca gazed into his magnificent eyes, her errant fiancé was soon utterly forgotten!

SCANDAL'S LADY   (4472, $3.99)
by Mary Kingsley

Cassandra was shocked to learn that the new Earl of Lynton was her childhood friend, Nicholas St. John. After years at sea and mixed feelings Nicholas had come home to take the family title. And although Cassandra knew her place as a governess, she could not help the thrill that went through her each time he was near. Nicholas was pleased to find that his old friend Cassandra was his new next door neighbor, but after being near her, he wondered if mere friendship would be enough . . .

HIS LORDSHIP'S REWARD   (4473, $3.99)
by Carola Dunn

As the daughter of a seasoned soldier, Fanny Ingram was accustomed to the vagaries of military life and cared not a whit about matters of rank and social standing. So she certainly never foresaw her *tendre* for handsome Viscount Roworth of Kent with whom she was forced to share lodgings, while he carried out his clandestine activities on behalf of the British Army. And though good sense told Roworth to keep his distance, he couldn't stop from taking Fanny in his arms for a kiss that made all hearts equal!

Available wherever paperbacks are sold, or order direct from the Publisher. Send cover price plus 50¢ per copy for mailing and handling to Penguin USA, P.O. Box 999, c/o Dept. 17109, Bergenfield, NJ 07621. Residents of New York and Tennessee must include sales tax. DO NOT SEND CASH.

VALENTINE LOVE

Sara Blayne
Jo Ann Ferguson
Lois Stewart

ZEBRA BOOKS
KENSINGTON PUBLISHING CORP.

ZEBRA BOOKS are published by

Kensington Publishing Corp.
850 Third Avenue
New York, NY 10022

First Printing: January, 1996

Printed in the United States of America

Contents

Cupid's Arrow

Sara Blayne

One

It was February 13th, a Friday. Hardly an auspicious day to undertake a journey one had not the least wish to make, Lady Letitia Treadwell reflected humorously, even one of only five or six miles across the valley. Resolutely she ignored the insistent chimes of the hall clock striking the hour of nine, the unmistakable rattle of harness and the snort of a carriage horse outside her window, and, most of all, the fashionably attired figure of her Aunt Eleanore, poised inside the door, her arms akimbo and the toe of an elegantly shod foot tapping the flowered Wilton carpet in an ominous, measured rhythm. Letitia had other matters to attend before she allowed herself to be bundled off to the Duke of Vail's house party.

"You may inform Chalfont that I have no intention of selling Treadwell Textiles," Letitia dictated to her secretary, Charles Warren. "The mills are beginning to flourish while providing the workers a decent wage and a safe environment in which to work. I have no intention of allowing Chalfont to have them. Not now, when the improvements as well as the policies I instituted have proven both sound and profitable. Healthy workers are industrious workers. Furthermore, they are loyal. There will never be a strike at Treadwell Textiles, you may be sure of it."

"I should never again argue that point with you, Letitia," replied Warren with a reminiscent quirk of the lips. "You have more than demonstrated that an initial investment in improvements and the modernization of equipment is more than compensated for by greater production. I simply doubt that you will win many converts among your fellow factory owners."

"Fortunately, I do not require their approval. Nor do I seek it. I have taken the modest competence left me by my Great Aunt Felicity and turned it into a fortune that allows me to do exactly as I choose without waiting until I am thirty or married to gain control of my father's trust."

"You will not be so free to choose, Letitia dear," interjected Aunt Eleanore in dire accents, "if it ever becomes known that L. Treadwell, the mysterious nabob with a Midas touch, is in reality Letitia Treadwell, the eccentric spinster. You will not have a shred of reputation left you."

Letitia laughed. "But I haven't the least need for a reputation," she declared. "Except for Charles and you, my dearest aunt, my family, what is left of it, long ago washed their hands of me. Certainly Mama and Papa are beyond being affected by anything I might do."

"They would roll over in their graves," averred Eleanore. "And you haven't the least notion what it would mean to have your reputation ruined. It is bad enough that you choose to absent yourself from society in order to pursue your various exotic interests. But were it to become known that the only offspring of the late Marquis of Clarendon had taken up trade, it would mean every door would be closed to you. Letitia, I said nothing when you decided to try your hand at investing or even when you studied acting, then dancing, and finally sculpting. I did not even object when you undertook to master fencing and that dreadful Oriental boxing."

"It is not boxing, Aunt Eleanore," Letitia objected. "It is kung fu, the ancient Chinese art of self-defense."

"It is barbaric and unladylike, and that is all I need to know," replied Eleanore firmly. "I cannot hold my tongue any longer. My child, you are five and twenty. It is past time you ceased all this nonsense and thought of settling down to a home and a family."

At last it seemed that Eleanore had penetrated her niece's formidable composure. The young woman visibly started. "Good God, Aunt, I have a home, three of them, in fact. What the deuce should I wish with a family?"

Eleanore, throwing up her arms in an eloquent gesture, turned to Warren for support. "Surely you have *some* influence over her, Charles. Tell her what she is flinging away."

"Oh, no," replied that worthy, putting away his notes and rising from his chair. "I may be her cousin and the closest thing she has to a brother, but acquit me of having the least sway over her. I leave that to you, Eleanore, and wish you every luck. I shall be on my way now, Letitia. With any luck I shall be back in London in time to celebrate the birth of my new son."

"Who might very well be another girl," Letitia said, laughing. "After three daughters, you would seem to have set a pattern."

"Oh, no, not this time. My dearest Anne has given me her promise." Dropping a buss on Eleanore's cheek, he winked at Letitia and left them to carry on without him.

"He is utterly hopeless where you are concerned," Eleanore observed with disgust. "I daresay he is as incorrigible as you."

"Nonsense. Charles is perfectly unexceptional. He simply learned long ago that there was nothing to be done with me. Something you would do well to accept for yourself, Aunt Eleanore. I had my fling at Society, and I made a mull of it. I have not the least desire for a repeat performance."

"But you were seventeen, Letitia, a mere bud on the point of blossoming," Eleanore entreated. "It was an unfortunate incident, but it was not your fault. You simply were not ready."

The younger woman's eyes softened with sympathetic amusement, a look that her Aunt Eleanore knew all too well, having had this discussion on numerous previous occasions with as little success. "My dearest, best loved aunt. Whether I was ready or not has little to say to the matter," Letitia declared. "What is done is done, and nothing can change it."

Eleanore stared in mounting despair at her niece. Gowned in the first stare of fashion in a deep burgundy morning dress that perfectly complemented her dark brown hair and golden brown eyes even as it subtly drew attention to her regal height and soft feminine curves, Letitia was a more than strikingly beautiful woman. One love-stricken Prussian count had been moved to call her a goddess. And, indeed, she was possessed of a flawless ivory complexion that not even an abiding passion for the outdoors could alter, and finely molded, delicate features belied somewhat by a hint of stubbornness about the lips. She was the sort of woman whose air of elegant poise and calm self-assurance must draw attention wherever she went. Unfortunately, she had been a rather late bloomer, having come into her own after the age most girls usually reached the flower of perfection. With the result that her come-out had been something less than a success. It had, in fact, thanks to the Unfortunate Incident, proved an utter disaster.

Not every ingenue, after all, had the distinction of tripping over her own feet and practically ripping the dress off the Reigning Beauty, who just happened to be Princess Esterhazy's protegee. Had it not been for the

Marquis of Ulverston's timely intervention, Letitia would very probably have been laughed out of London. As it was, the child had insisted on returning home that very night to Clarendon Hall, and she had never gone back for a second Season.

Eleanore could not blame her. Letitia had not been ready then. Indeed, Eleanore had done her best to persuade Letitia's mother to put off the girl's curtsey in Society. To no avail. It was almost as if the marchioness had foreseen the boating accident that would make the only offspring of the Marquis of Clarendon an orphan at eighteen. The loss of both parents coupled with her disastrous first Season had changed Letitia practically overnight from a bubbling, vibrantly lovely child to a woman—calm, resolute, and irrevocably set upon a course of stubborn independence. And that was why Vail's invitation had come like a gift from heaven. Letitia must not be allowed to fling away this last chance at claiming her rightful place in the Society to which she had been born. And, besides, Letitia owed it to Vail to make her appearance. Though neither he nor the girl knew it yet, they had a great deal in common.

"That was then, Letitia. You are eight years older now," Eleanore persisted. "In that time, you have become a beautiful woman endowed with grace and charm. You have traveled the world and won the admiration of foreign princes and nobility. You must remember the Russian prince, what was his name?"

"Mikhail Andreyev," supplied Letitia, her lips curving faintly in a smile of reminiscence. "But he was only a boy, Eleanore."

"He was a year older than you and head over ears in love with you. Furthermore, you, my dear, were fond of him. Do not deny it."

"No, I do not deny it." Letitia sighed. "I was sorry to leave him to his little Russian princess. Unfortunately I could not countenance the thought of seeing him exiled for what amounted to little more than an amusing interlude on my part. And that has nothing to do with what we were discussing."

"It has everything to do with it," Eleanore insisted. "It is a reminder that you are far from being that green girl who made her come-out eight years ago in London. You have nothing to fear in the duke's house party, my dear, I promise you."

Instantly Letitia's head came up. "But I am not in the least intimidated at the thought of facing your precious English fashionables," she asserted. "I confess I am surprised that the duke and his mama have condescended to invite me to their valentine celebration. I cannot, in fact, imagine how you managed it."

"It was not I," said Eleanore with an air of triumph. "*You* managed it, Letitia—when you befriended a little girl in the woods."

"A little girl! Why, you cannot mean Sally," exclaimed Letitia, calling to mind an incident that had occurred little over a se'nnight ago. After two years abroad, she had only just arrived at Beechcote, her country cottage in Buckinghamshire, when she gave in to the irresistible impulse to don breeches and boots and put Brierly Tuck, her newly acquired Thoroughbred stallion, through his paces. Letitia had come upon the child in the woods, sitting, legs asprawl on the ground, her eyes filled with tears of humiliation and her pony grazing a short distance away.

"My poor dear," Letitia had exclaimed, quickly swinging down from the saddle, "are you all right?"

"I-I think so," replied the child as, with Letitia's help, she gamely climbed to her feet. "Little Bit shied at a pheasant, and the next thing I knew I was flying over his head." She made a wry grimace. "I guess Uncle Giles was right. I was not quite ready to ride out on my own.

He will be dreadfully angry at me when he learns I am gone."

"If you stole out without leaving word where you were going, he will have every right to be," observed Letitia, dusting the child off. "He will undoubtedly be worried."

"I daresay you are mistaken. Uncle Giles is not the sort to worry about anyone, least of all about me. I am an inconvenience that he would rather be without," said the girl with a shrug that not only had struck a sympathetic chord somewhere deep inside Letitia, but had caused her lips to thin ever so slightly.

"And what about your mama? Surely she will be worried," she gently suggested.

"There's only Uncle Giles," confessed the child frankly. "And Grandmama. My name is Sally. I haven't seen you around before. I expect you're Lady Treadwell of Beechcote."

"As a matter of fact, I am," confirmed Letitia with a bemused arch of her lovely eyebrows. "How did you know?"

"Easy. Everyone in the village knew a letter had come to Mrs. Parker from London. Mrs. Hicks told Mr. Pettigrew, who told the parson, and so on. It was plain as a pikestaff that the new owner of Beechcote had sent word she was coming. Especially as Mrs. Parker immediately initiated a thorough housecleaning. The rest was a simple matter of deduction."

"You are obviously a very astute young lady," observed Letitia. "And I am happy to make your acquaintance. It occurs to me, however, that you had better be on your way back home before your uncle has the entire county out combing the woods for you."

"Yes, I suppose I should, though I should much rather stay and visit with you. For if you must know," she confided, whether Letitia really wished her to have done or not, "Grandmama is determined to make a proper young

lady of me and consequently will allow me to do only
the things a proper young lady would do. And though
Uncle Giles is a bit of all right, he is far too busy to have
time to spend with a schoolroom miss. It is hardly any
wonder that I am constantly in the briers when I have
nothing to do and no one with whom to do it. Do you
come out riding often, Lady Treadwell?"

"Letitia. And yes, I plan to do a great deal of riding.
I have been cooped up on a ship for all of six months,
you see."

Speculative blue eyes, fringed in dark lashes, lifted
guilelessly to hers. "Is that why you have not married?
Because you are always traveling?"

"That, my dear, is none of your business."

"I was afraid you would say that. Grandmama is always
confining me to my room for what she calls my impertinence, but how else is one to find anything out if one
does not ask?" Then, to Letitia's patent amusement,
Sally continued with hardly a breath between sentences,
"My Uncle Giles has never married either, though he is
ever so good-looking. He was almost legshackled once,
but something happened to put him off; and now he
has set his mind on marrying Miss Adeline Pemberton."

She said it with such comical dislike that Letitia could
not but laugh. "I take it you do not approve of Miss Pemberton."

Sally's face screwed up in a grimace. "Everyone must
approve of Miss Pemberton. She is quite unexceptional,
like a Dresden doll without an ounce of real blood in
her veins. Do you always wear breeches and sit astride
when you ride?" she asked with a sudden keen interest
that inexplicably sounded an alarm in Letitia's head.

"Only when I am certain to encounter no one but
overinquisitive girls not yet out of the schoolroom who
should know better than to ask."

"Of course I know better, but you are not really offended," declared Sally, looking for all the world like a miniature sage in spite of her red hair and freckles.

Letitia, who had earlier been on the point of placing the youthful stranger in the category of Sweet Young Innocent, quickly revised her opinion. Indeed, if she were not mistaken, she was in the presence of an overly precocious twelve-year-old who would never be molded into anything so prim as a proper young lady.

Letitia laughed in spite of herself. "No, I am not offended. On the other hand, I have no intention of being quizzed. I believe we were discussing your predicament."

"You *would* have to remind me. Everything would have been all right today had I not lost my way in this wretched forest. I should have been back in my room before ever I was missed." She glanced sideways at Letitia. "Indeed, I shouldn't be at all surprised if I have at least another thirty minutes left before someone thinks to release me from my unjust confinement."

"Nevertheless," Letitia said dryly, "I suggest we catch your pony and see if we cannot find the way home before your absence is discovered. I may be new to the valley, but I have an unerring sense of direction, which tells me the main road lies directly before us. I shall be glad to see you as far as your drive."

"Splendid," said Sally, beaming her approval. "I knew you were a right one the moment I laid eyes on you."

"And you, I doubt not," Letitia replied, smiling, "are a complete hand. Now, up with you."

With Sally once more in the saddle, Letitia had mounted and, true to her boast, led her young friend straightaway to the village high road. Once there, Sally had insisted she could find the rest of the way without any further help, and that was all there had been to it. Or had it?

"What," Letitia demanded suspiciously of Eleanore, "has Sally to do with the duke's Valentine party?"

"Why, everything," replied Eleanore, "when one takes
into consideration the fact that your little Sally is none
other than Sarah Emberly, Vail's niece."

"Good God," breathed Letitia, "it needed only that.
No doubt the duke and his mama are firmly convinced
I contrived the entire affair with Sally in order to wangle
an invitation. In which case, they will be exceedingly
gratified to receive my regrets. I believe I have just been
called away to London."

"You have been no such thing, Letitia. You gave me
your promise that you would attend the duke's house
party, and I mean to hold you to it. Besides, it is too
late. I have already dispatched Winifred and Julia in the
coach with the trunks, and the chaise is waiting in front
for us, since you insist on driving us yourself. It is high
time we were going."

"You are a conniving woman, Aunt Eleanore," observed Letitia, in dire accents.

"I am a woman who is exceedingly fond of her only
niece and who would do anything to insure that niece's
happiness," Eleanore retorted, ushering Letitia out of
the study into the hall where Carstairs, the butler, waited
to help them on with their pelisses.

Letitia, who considered herself more than contented
with her life as an independent spinster of a deal more
than moderate means, bit her tongue to keep from delivering her aunt a caustic retort. She owed her mama's
sister too much to ever wish to hurt her.

Upon the untimely demise of the marquis and the
marchioness, Eleanore had not hesitated to give up her
quiet existence in Bath in order to take her orphaned
niece under her wing. Since that time, she had put up
with Letitia's sudden starts with a seemingly endless re-
serve of patience, accompanying the younger woman on
any number of sea voyages, including an extended tour
of the Orient. In spite of the fact that Eleanore cared

very little for junketing about, usually at a moment's notice, and probably would very much have preferred to take up her old life at Bath, she had never uttered a word of complaint.

Letitia would have done anything for her aunt short of marrying to please her. Indeed, she had been motivated to accept the duke's invitation more in the hopes that Eleanore might meet someone who could engage her affections than for any other reason. And why not, when at thirty-nine, Eleanore, with her blond hair, blue eyes, and trim figure, was an extremely attractive woman. As for Letitia herself, *she* certainly had no wish to enter the lists of marriageable females! The last thing she wanted was a man, who would wish to curtail her freedom, usurp her will, and rule her fortune. She had not the least need for a husband, she vowed, stepping lightly up into the chaise and taking up the ribbons.

Letitia had been to Hambleden on numerous occasions with her parents to enjoy the water meadows and boating on the Thames. She had never forgotten the charm of the Chilterns in the summer with their wooded slopes of beech and silver birch. No doubt it was out of some small wish to recapture those enchanted days of her childhood that she had purchased the cottage, sight unseen. Nestled in a wooded vale among hollyhocks, clematis, and lilacs, it was exactly the sort of secluded retreat that she had hoped it would be—a place to rest after the lengthy sea voyage and to indulge herself in long rides through the woods while she took stock of her life and decided what course of action she would pursue next. Indeed, Charles had outdone himself in finding it for her, for she was heartily tired of foreign courts and the sort of intrigues to which she had been subjected as soon as it was discovered that not only was

she an English noblewoman, but that she was both
wealthy and single. Had she had her wish, she would
have shut herself away from all but the members of the
household during her planned month's stay at Beechcote. As it was, she found herself committed to a whole
week of just the sort of thing she had wished to avoid.

Resigning herself to the inevitable, she occupied herself with driving to a shade along the quaint country
road that wound through trees that had been mature
when Good Queen Bess had ruled. Absently, she wondered if the duke's ancestors had hunted deer and boar
in these woods in the company of the queen. Vail's prin-
cipal holdings were in the north of England, she knew,
having taken the precaution of quizzing Charles about
her host and his mama when the unexpected invitation
had first arrived. His family, however, had maintained a
country house in Buckinghamshire for as long as anyone
could remember. Indeed, there were rumors that it had
been variously used by earlier dukes of Vail for political
intrigues, romantic interludes with various married mistresses, and even as a place of rendezvous for members
of the Medmenham Hell Fire Club before and after their
infamous meetings at the abbey.

As for the present duke himself, she had never laid
eyes on him and knew very little about him, save only
that possessed of a large fortune, a title, and the reputation of an Arbiter of Fashion, he had long been the
Catch of the Marriage Mart. At five and thirty he had
never married and was considered dangerous by mamas
of unwed daughters, whom he could either make or
break with little more than a word or the condescension
of his notice. He was known to have maintained a long
line of barques of frailty whom he treated generously.
He made a practice of gambling often and heavily, but
won more often than not, and he was noted for his racing
stable, his cattle, and his unparalleled skill at driving.

He was, in short, a Nonpareil, a top of the trees Corinthian, and a rake—all the things she had come to distrust most in a man of their class.

At least, she reflected, glancing over her shoulder at the Thoroughbred tied behind and following, she had thought to insist on bringing Brierly Tuck with her. Whenever the company became too tedious, she would have the means to get off by herself for a time.

Marshgate, the duke's Elizabethan country manor, was set charmingly at the base of a forested hill. Its three high-gabled wings in the pattern of an *E* boasted a southern front laced with stone mullioned windows. These overlooked a decorative pond graced with swans and Muscovy ducks and fed by a brook spanned by a gracefully arching stone bridge. Letitia's initial impression was of tall chimneys, great bay windows, and stone walls covered with clinging vines of clematis and ivy. In spite of herself, she felt an immediate affinity for the sprawling house, as she neatly feathered the turn into the graveled drive, bordered on either side by pollard beech trees, and skirted a well-manicured lawn laid out with flower beds of blooming daffodils and Dutch tulips. No wonder it had served as a favorite retreat for the dukes of Vail for over two hundred years. She thought perhaps she herself could have ceased her restless rambling and settled down quite contentedly here were it not for the fact that it belonged to the duke.

As she brought the chaise to a halt before the portico with a flourish, a groom appeared to hold the horse's head while a footman helped the two women down from the carriage.

They were instantly admitted at the door by a staid-faced butler, who, bowing stiffly, informed them that

Her Grace was with her guests on the Summer Porch.
"If you would care to accompany me, mesdames."

Letitia, following in the measured steps of the very
superior servant, delighted in high beamed ceilings, mu-
raled walls, and coral damask wallpaper, brass chande-
liers and a mahogany staircase. Potted plants and
sunshine streaming through tall windows brought the
outdoors most charmingly inside. It occurred to her that
perhaps she had been too hasty in her judgment. She
had always believed that a house reflected the personality
of its occupants, and she liked the homey intimacy of
the duke's country house. But then, a homey intimacy
no doubt served very well for entertaining one's secret
amours, she reflected, dimpling naughtily.

A bemused smile touched Letitia's lips as she indulged
in a brief fantasy of herself in the role of the duke's inamo-
rata. In spite of the fact that she was hampered by not
being personally acquainted with His Grace, the mental
picture she conjured was sufficient to bring a delicious
warmth to her veins and a wry twinkle to her lovely eyes.
She thought perhaps it would be vastly more entertaining
to be a mistress than a wife. A mistress, after all, especially
one of independent means, would have all the advantages
of enjoying an intimate relationship with a man she found
charming while still retaining her freedom.

They were greeted by the sounds of gaiety and laughter
before they stepped out on to the paved verandah, which
in another month or two would be shaded with vines. The
verandah seemed crowded with elegantly clad people,
conversing in small groups over an alfresco tea or partak-
ing in an impromptu game of Pall Mall on the lawn.

"Lady Letitia Treadwell and Miss Eleanore Freeman,"
intoned the butler, bowing before dutifully withdrawing.

Their arrival, noted Letitia dryly to herself, was apparently not considered a particularly momentous occasion. Other than a curious glance or two and, in the case

of two languorous beauties seated on a marble bench beneath a cherry tree and attended by four gentlemen, a low-voiced colloquy promptly followed by a twitter of laughter, they appeared not to have made any impression at all. It occurred to Letitia that Eleanore was wrong. Eight years had made little difference. She had been made to feel as little welcome then as she was now. Only this time, she was neither naive nor vulnerable. She did not care a tinker's damn what anyone thought of her.

"I believe, contrary to your expectations," she murmured to Eleanore, "that nothing has changed in my absence, except, perhaps, that we are to be inconspicuous rather than an embarrassment. In which case, I believe I should prefer to remain unnoticed in the comfort and privacy of my own house. No one will be the wiser if we leave now, dearest aunt."

"I wish you will not be absurd, Letitia," Eleanore retorted with a censorious frown. "You are hardly a green girl. You know as well as I that no one has as yet remarked our arrival."

"You are not attending, Eleanore." Letitia smiled wickedly. "I believe that was the salient point I just made."

Eleanore was startled into a reluctant chuckle. "Incorrigible child. I cannot imagine why I put up with you."

"No doubt it is because of my lamentable habit of making you laugh," Letitia quipped fondly. "Come, if it will make you happy, we might as well mingle with the other guests, though I fear you are to be disappointed. No gentleman here will wear my heart on his sleeve. You may be sure of it."

"I am sure of no such thing," replied Eleanore, who had not failed to observe the sudden keen-eyed glances of a group of four likely specimens of the male gender who were just leaving the Pall Mall playing field. Not only was it obvious they had spotted Letitia, but unless she was very much mistaken, they were demonstrating every manifestation of interest. Indeed, one in particular, a well-made gentleman somewhat above forty with dark hair touched most intriguingly with silver over the temples, was regarding them with a singularly arrested air.

Apparently someone else had not failed to notice the newcomers still poised on the threshold. A vision of loveliness gowned in blue-violet velvet disengaged herself from the company of an elderly female, seated rigidly erect in a wicker chair, and a trio of young women, ranged picturesquely before a gurgling fountain graced with a plump, winged cupid at its center. The young woman in blue-violet glided toward the new arrivals.

"I beg you will forgive what must seem an incivility on our part," said the fair-haired beauty with eyes the deep blue of harebells. "I'm afraid, in all the commotion, we did not hear Biddles announce you. You are, of course, Lady Treadwell and Miss Freeman, are you not? I am Miss Adeline Pemberton."

Confronted with the female who was destined in all likelihood to be the next Duchess of Vail, Letitia could not but note Sally had failed to mention that besides resembling a Dresden doll, Miss Pemberton was a diamond of the first water. She was perhaps nineteen or twenty and built on dainty proportions. Her complexion was flawless and fashionably pale, her features classically regular and beguilingly childlike, and her manner gentle and meant to be pleasing. Altogether, she promised fair to make His Grace a wholly agreeable, conformable wife.

"There is nothing to forgive, Miss Pemberton." Letitia smiled, extending her hand. "It is a pleasure to make your acquaintance."

"Likewise, I am sure, Lady Treadwell," replied Miss Pemberton, delicately pressing Letitia's hand before releasing it. "Vail has yet to return from his morning ride. Lady Honoria, however, has asked me to bring you to her. She regrettably suffers from inflammation of the joints and experiences some difficulty getting about. If you would care to come with me, I should be only too glad to present you to her."

"You are very kind," murmured Eleanore, smiling.

Lady Honoria Sinclair, the Dowager Duchess of Vail, was tall and spare, with iron gray hair beneath a black tall bonnet tied firmly beneath her chin. Whatever beauty she had once possessed had long ago given way to an uncompromising strength of character. She had the look of a fierce old dragon, bound to earth by swollen, misshapen joints.

Eyes the steel blue of rapier points lifted to survey Letitia when Miss Pemberton had completed the introductions to Miss Gilcrest, Miss Tilberry, and Lady Margaret Windholm.

"So you're Clarendon's gel," she said in a voice which, though raspy with age, retained undertones of rich vibrancy. Letitia recalled Charles's having mentioned the dowager had once been a noted coloratura. "You have the look of your paternal grandfather, Edward. A wastrel and a womanizer, who was notorious for his gambling and his duels. You did not take at your come-out. I trust it was not because you take after him."

"I should be greatly surprised if you did not know why I failed at my come-out. And if I in any way resemble my grandfather, I should only be grateful," replied Letitia, a sparkle in her eye. Eleanore stifled a groan. She had seen that look before. "Grandpapa was not only a man of great wit," Letitia continued, unabated by a startled twitter from Miss Gilcrest, "but he had the gift of knowing how to enjoy life. Even from a wheelchair."

"Letitia was very fond of her grandfather, Your Grace," Eleanore hastened to interject. "They were practically inseparable, especially after the carriage accident that left him incapacitated."

"Were they indeed," murmured the dowager, one

steely blue eye grotesquely enlarged as she surveyed the
unfortunate Eleanore through a black-handled quizzing
glass. "Miss Freeman, is it?"

Eleanore flushed, but held her ground. "Indeed,
ma'am. I daresay you do not remember, but we met years
ago in London."

The dowager's gnarled hand clamped on the gold
head of her cane. "I'll thank you not to be impertinent,
gel. I may be old, but I am not in my dotage. I remember
you very well. You were to be married. A young naval
officer, considerably beneath your station. What happened? Were you persuaded not to go through with what
was obviously a mesalliance?"

Letitia's lips thinned as she saw Eleanore's cheek grow
pale. "I daresay no one could ever have done that," Letitia answered for her aunt. "He was killed, Your Grace,
in the Battle of the Nile."

The elderly woman lowered the quizzing glass. "I see.
And now you think to have my sympathy."

It was on Letitia's lips to retort that they cared for nothing from the dowager, save perhaps to take their leave of
her at once. She was silenced by her aunt's hand on her
arm.

Eleanore smiled gravely. "It was a long time ago, Your
Grace. And this is a time of festivity. I should do better
with a dish of tea than with sympathy."

The dowager gave what sounded very like a snort.
"And with that you think, no doubt, to have put me in
my place. Very well. Miss Pemberton, if you and the others have nothing better to do, you may send for a fresh
pot of tea. And take Miss Freeman with you. Make her
known to our other guests. As for you, Lady Treadwell,"
she added, in the wake of the flurried departure of the
Misses Pembroke, Gilcrest, Tilbury, and Lady Windholm, who swept a reluctant Eleanore away, "I suggest
you learn to bridle your temper. You made a bad begin-

ning eight years ago, perhaps through no fault of your own. You would do well to amend your image of brash impertinence before you fall deeper into disrepute."

"No doubt I shall take your advice into consideration, Your Grace," replied Letitia, wondering what the old dragon would think if she knew the impertinent Lady Treadwell was quite the rage in Russia, Greece, and the Orient.

"You will not, Lady Treadwell," predicted the dowager. "On the contrary, you will do exactly as you choose. More's the pity. That, however, is neither here nor there. The fact of the matter is you have made something of an impression on my granddaughter, who unfortunately is of a similar disposition to yours. Indeed, if she is allowed to continue in her present vein, she will undoubtedly come to an equally bad end."

"A hideous prospect," Letitia commented mildly.

"Indeed," confirmed the dowager, unimpressed by her guest's attempt at levity. "In the absence of her mother and father, I have tried to do my best by the child. I, however, am an old woman. I cannot possibly provide her the constant guidance she requires."

"And you wish me to do what, Your Grace?" Letitia queried, at a loss as to where the old woman was going with her train of logic. "Take her under my wing and instruct her as to how she should go on in polite company?"

"On the contrary, Lady Treadwell. Such an office will naturally fall to Miss Pemberton, who is clearly better qualified for it. I should prefer that you have as little to do with Sarah as possible. In view of your past performance, I cannot allow you to exert what can only be an unwholesome influence on the child."

Letitia stared at the dowager with a stunned sense of disbelief. Good God, she thought. Eleanore could not have been farther from the truth when she reasoned that the Unfortunate Incident had long been forgotten. Clearly the Dowager Duchess of Vail was in possession of all the sordid details, whether real or the mere product of the wildest speculations that had raged in the wake of Letitia's disappearance from the scene of infamy. After all, it had variously been rumored that she was under the undue influence of spirits at the time or that smitten with the gentleman who had figured in effecting her escape, she had deliberately set out to discredit her rival—all of which had been patent nonsense. She had always comforted herself with the thought that she vastly preferred the unsavory explanations for her exceedingly odd behavior over the rather more mortifying judgment that she was merely a blunderhead. That none of them were the truth had been her secret alone—hers, that was, and Ulverston's.

She had willingly suffered ignominy rather than reveal the whole of the incident eight years before if only to save Ulverston from sharing her disgrace, and nothing had occurred since to change her mind. Certainly not the realization that she had been naive enough to indulge in a foolish romantic fantasy involving the most sought after man in London. The Marquis of Ulverston had not even known she existed before that night, and she fervently hoped his knowledge of her had afterward receded into the farthest recesses of his mind. The last thing she wished was to ever be remembered to him.

"I am afraid I do not understand, Your Grace," she said when she had got herself perfectly in hand again. "If you had no wish to inflict my unsavory influence on Sally, then why did you invite me to your Valentine celebration?"

"Pray do not flatter yourself," the dowager replied dampingly as the fresh tea tray arrived. "It was not I who issued the invitation. Sarah has apparently prevailed upon Vail to make you a part of the company."

"No, did she?" Letitia's eyes lit with sardonic amusement. "But how very enterprising of her. I am Sally's guest, then, and Vail's, one must presume. In which case, I fear I cannot make you any promises. I should be clearly sunk beneath reproach were I to snub my host and hostess. And now, Your Grace, shall I pour, or do you prefer to do the honors?"

The dowager's blue-veined hand tightened on her cane. "You are impertinent, Lady Treadwell, and a fool if you think to cross swords with me. I might have known it was a waste of effort to appeal to your better nature."

"Indeed you might, Your Grace," returned Letitia, reaching for the tea server with an unruffled, impossible calm. "You may be sure that I haven't one. One lump or two, Your Grace?"

"None, Lady Treadwell. I am afraid I haven't the stomach for tea at the moment."

"Understandably so. I shouldn't wonder if you had a bitter taste in your mouth," remarked Letitia, adding cream to her cup. "And you are obviously in no little discomfort. Might I suggest frequent doses of birch tea? I understand it has a soothing effect. And if that does not give you relief, I should recommend a poultice of the bark, leaves, and catkins for your rheumatism."

"Rubbish. Old wives' cures. I suppose you will next recommend that I wear a toad about my neck or swing a black cat nine times about my head. I am not such a fool, Lady Treadwell."

"I did not suppose that you were, Your Grace," Letitia replied, imperturbably sipping her tea, which, having come some distance from the kitchens, was already little better than lukewarm. "I have made a study of old folk remedies, however, and it is my experience that birch does indeed have many beneficial effects. I should be glad to send home for some if you change your mind and wish to try such a treatment."

"No doubt you may save yourself the trouble," grumbled the dowager. "Indeed, I fail to see why you should do anything of the kind. If you think by this pretense of concern for my well-being to soften me toward you, you are doing it much too brown."

It was only with a deal of effort that Letitia did not choke on her tea at the dowager's insistence that she was some despicable creature intent, no doubt, on feeding her poison. The old dragon might indeed drive a saint to commit murder. "Oh, you are quite right to question my motives, Your Grace," Letitia bitterly retorted. "I am, after all, an unsavory character with a deplorable temper and a total lack of scruples. And you will admit that in our short acquaintance you have given me little cause to feel in the least charitable toward you. Nevertheless, you may be sure that I have no intention of putting myself out to win your good opinion. I am, I fear, of a contrary disposition and very likely should not wish to afford you that gratification."

In spite of her anger, she had spoken quietly, even pleasantly, as if she and the dowager had been engaged in a mere exchange of the latest on-dits from London. Now she rose from her chair, oblivious to the cup in its saucer still clutched in her hand. Only she knew that she was shaking inside with indignation at the incivilities to which she had been subjected since arriving at the duke's abominable house party or that she was furious with herself for having given in to the temptation to unleash her unruly temper. It was time to make a graceful exit before she thoroughly disgraced herself.

"And now I must ask you to excuse me, Your Grace," she said and even managed to smile quite credibly. "I believe I have enjoyed enough of the pleasure of your company."

"Sit down, Lady Treadwell," snapped the dowager. "I have no intention of excusing you. On the contrary, I wish to introduce you to your host." Letitia's glance narrowed sharply as she glimpsed a curious gleam in the old woman's eyes that if she did not know better, she might have supposed to be something very nearly resembling satisfaction.

"Lady Treadwell, my son, His Grace, the Duke of Vail."

Letitia, caught off balance, was made suddenly and acutely aware of a looming presence. She turned, half-smiling. And instantly froze.

He was exactly as she remembered him. Tall and magnificently proportioned, his broad, powerful shoulders encased in a perfectly tailored coat of blue Superfine that could only have been cut by Weston, and his skintight breeches of an immaculate dove gray seemingly molded to muscular thighs above gleaming brown Hessians. His hair was as black as midnight, just as she remembered it, and the lean, tanned face and hard, chiseled features wore the same expression of arrogance and pride that had never quite ceased to haunt her—as had his eyes. Hooded behind drooping eyelids of fashionable ennui, they were the penetrating steel blue of rapiers.

"Ulverston!" Letitia gasped, as the teacup slipped from her suddenly nerveless fingers and spilled its contents over an exceedingly startled dowager duchess.

Two

Lady Honoria gasped and went alarmingly rigid, even as those nearest to the scene of debacle froze in various attitudes of disbelief, their eyes fixed in morbid fascination on the lapideous aspect of the dowager duchess. It was like finding oneself thrust suddenly into the grips of a nightmare that was all too dreadfully familiar, thought Letitia, fighting the insane urge to give in to a fit of the giggles.

Only the duke appeared to take all in stride.

Signaling to a footman, he bent calmly over his stunned parent.

"Mama, I fear you are not looking at all well," he observed smoothly. "And why should you, when I have caused your dress to be ruined? How very clumsy of me to precipitate so regrettable an accident."

"Don't be a fool, Giles," snapped the old dragon, allowing Vail to assist her to her feet. "If it was an accident, it was not at your instigation."

Letitia's head came up, a wry gleam of appreciation in her eyes. "You are quite right, Your Grace," she stated flatly. "It was all my fault."

As if freed from the spell that had held them all in thrall, the rest of the company appeared galvanized into action. Heads moved and a tinkling laugh sounded above the renewed drone of conversation. A slender gentleman whom Letitia recognized as Lord Eppington, one of the duke's intimates, knocked Lady Trowbridge's wooden ball across the lawn into a thicket. And Miss Pemberton, excusing herself to Eleanore, glided to the dowager's side.

"Lady Honoria, pray let me help you," she crooned in her unaffected, well-modulated voice. "Naturally, you will wish to go inside at once. It is not yet so warm that you do not risk a chill in those wet things."

"Nonsense. I am not so old and feeble as to perish from having a dish of tea flung in my lap, though there might be some who'd not be disappointed at seeing me struck down with the ague," rasped the dowager, her look baleful on Letitia.

"On the contrary, Your Grace," Letitia objected, "I should never wish any such thing. Indeed, I should not have had this happen for the world. I am sure I do not know what got into me—except," she added, casting a fulminating glance at the duke, "that I was taken unawares."

"Harumph!" was the dowager's only comment as, with Miss Pemberton in tow, she turned and hobbled toward the house.

Vail, left alone with Letitia, lifted his eyes to hers. "I beg your pardon—er—Lady Treadwell, is it?" he murmured. "It was never my intent to startle you."

If he had thought by that to put what he obviously considered an ill-mannered upstart in her place, he had not reckoned on his subject, mused Letitia darkly. Incensed at his toplofty manner to one who had once rendered him a service at no little cost to herself, she straightened to face him squarely. "Oh, was it not," she demanded, bridling with indignation. "And just exactly how did you think I should react?"

A single, arrogant eyebrow arched imperiously toward the duke's hairline. "I am sure I could not say, only just having had the pleasure of your acquaintance."

"Only just having had . . ." Letitia's eyes widened,

then quickly lowered to conceal her dismay. The devil, she thought. He meant to pretend as though there had never been anything between them. She might have known it. What a fool she had been to imagine that he had brought her to Marshgate to make up in some small way for eight years of ignominy! And yet she had, for a single, wild moment, when it had first registered that Vail and Ulverston were one and the same. Letitia's eyes flashed golden sparks of resentment. If that had been his reason for inviting her there, he had obviously changed his mind in the face of her newest debacle.

Met by that magnificent blaze of fury, quickly doused, the duke narrowed his gaze sharply on her face. "Or am I mistaken," he drawled, lifting his quizzing glass the better to observe her. He could not recall a Lady Treadwell on the guest list that he had requested his secretary to draw up and which he had briefly scanned before the invitations were sent out. Obviously, she must be a friend of the dowager's. Or perhaps Miss Pemberton had issued the invitation. Whatever the case, he could not deny that there was something vaguely familiar about the woman, though for the life of him he could not say why she would seem to have struck a distant chord of memory. Surely he would recall having made the acquaintance of this tempestuous, exceedingly ill-mannered young beauty. "You called me Ulverston just now. Have we met somewhere before, Lady Treadwell?"

Letitia, staring incredulously back at him, was suddenly stunned by the realization that he was not pretending. Hell and the devil confound it, he had not the least idea who she was! He truly did not remember her, and she would be dashed if she would oblige him by jarring what must be a most lamentably faulty memory.

"No, Your Grace," she answered, smiling sardonically at the absurdity of it all. "I am sure *I* should remember it if we had."

Vail's black eyebrows snapped together. Now, what the
devil? She was lying, he was sure of it, and what was
more she had obviously found something in that fact to
amuse her. The ungrateful little baggage. He had taken
the blame on himself for what could only be described
as a social blunder of the first water; he had even gone
so far as to offer an apology for what was clearly not his
fault, and she had had the temerity to fling it back in
his face. And now this! Clearly, she was either totally
lacking in social graces or she was up to something. In
either case, she would soon catch cold if she thought to
cross swords with him. He had a particular aversion to
scheming, unprincipled females.

"Quite so," he responded with the air of one fast suc-
cumbing to an advanced state of ennui. "No doubt we
shall have the pleasure of becoming better acquainted
in the next few days, Lady Treadwell."

"I suppose anything is possible, Your Grace," Letitia
agreed archly. The rogue. Getting better acquainted was
undoubtedly the very last thing he intended.

Vail's gaze snapped to the lovely countenance. The
impertinent wench. If he did not know better, he might
imagine that she had just called him a liar. Never mind
that she was perfectly in the right of it. He had every
intention of quashing whatever pretensions she might
have toward him with a ruthlessness well known to his
intimates.

"Williams," he said to the footman who had been
standing at attention, his expression carefully impassive,
"see that our guest is brought a fresh pot of tea and
anything else that she might require."

"Very well, Your Grace," intoned the footman.

"Lady Treadwell," murmured the duke dismissively,
bowing at the waist.

Smiling, Letitia inclined her head. "Your Grace."

For a moment she watched him go, stopping here and

there to exchange words with various of his guests. Then recalling the presence of the footman, she said with a thoughtful air. "Tea will not be necessary, Williams. Thank you. I believe I have had my surfeit of that beverage. Perhaps you would be so good as to direct me to my room instead."

"This is all my fault," groaned Eleanore some fifteen minutes later, dropping her head into her hands. "I knew Ulverston and Vail were one and the same." She lifted accusing eyes to Letitia, who stood at the bedroom window, her back to the room. "As would have you had you not deliberately cut yourself off from the world to which you were born. Letitia, I could swear no woman who had made her curtsey in Society could be ignorant of the fact that Ulverston was heir to the Duke of Vail, except that I know you. You have never paid the least attention to anything that did not interest you."

"I know, Aunt Eleanore," Letitia said quietly. "You must not blame yourself."

"But I do blame myself," Eleanore insisted, feeling quite miserable. "I should have told you who Vail was. I did not because I was sure you would not come if you knew."

Letitia's slender shoulder lifted in a shrug. "No doubt you were in the right of it, dearest aunt," she replied. "It is a trifle late, however, to weep over spilt milk. The damage has been done. And in truth, I cannot find it in myself to be overly grieved for what happened." At last she turned to face the other woman. "After all, it was only what was expected of me," she said, straight-faced, her eyes meeting Eleanore's, "and I should have been terribly sorry to disappoint Lady Honoria after she was so kind as to let me know exactly what she thought of me."

They stared at one another in a long look of dawning

mutual understanding. Then Eleanore gave a choke, and they both burst into helpless gales of laughter.

"Oh, good God," breathed Eleanore when the first spasms had passed, leaving them both weak and gasping for air. "It-it was dreadfully funny in a terrible, nightmarish sort of way. His Grace looked absolutely thunderstruck, and I-I was afraid for a moment that Lady Honoria would go off in an apoplexy."

"She recovered quite well, however," observed Letitia, reflectively. "I daresay Lady Honoria is as tough as shoe leather. A pity she has taken me in aversion. I believe I could actually like the old dragon under different circumstances."

"Unfortunately, the circumstances cannot now be altered." Eleanore sighed, her previous mirth quite forgotten as she was brought back to the reality of the moment. "I shall tell Winnifred and Julia to pack. No doubt you will wish to be leaving at once."

Letitia came about. "Leave?" she declared, as if such a notion were utterly preposterous. "But why? I vow I am quite looking forward to the week's festivities. Indeed, I intend to have the time of my life. Now go along with you and freshen up," she added bracingly as she guided her aunt to the door. "I have a few things to take care of, but I shall see you at the archery contest at two."

"But, Letitia—" Eleanore hesitated in the doorway. "I'm afraid it will not be enough that the duke took the blame on himself. Even if he did startle you, the whole world will recall only that Letitia Treadwell was the one who spilled her tea on the Dowager Duchess of Vail."

"Never mind the duke, Aunt Eleanore," Letitia said, her gaze going beyond the other woman with a peculiar fixity. "His Grace has chosen not to remember me or our previous brief encounter eight years ago." At last she looked at Eleanore. "So far as he is concerned, it is as if it never happened. Consequently, it cannot matter if I have managed to play the fool again. Can it?"

"Well," Eleanore faltered, still reluctant to go, "if you are quite certain—"

Letitia smiled. "But of course I am certain. Indeed, I believe I have never been more certain of anything in my life." She was still smiling when she pushed the door closed.

Unaccountably, Eleanore experienced a shiver of apprehension.

Letitia paused beneath the arched trellis that covered with grapevines served as a gateway into the garden, and viewed the assembled company. The weather being particularly fine, everyone was gathered outside where a game of bowls was in progress on the short-cropped lawn and a target in the rather whimsical form of a heart had been set up in readiness for the archery contest. As if drawn, her gaze went unerringly to a tall, languorous figure who stood with Miss Pemberton beneath the spreading boughs of an oak tree observing one of the guests roll the bowl toward the white porcelain jack. Vail, she noted, was being properly attentive to his bride-to-be.

A blush invaded her cheeks at the memory of her own earlier encounter with the duke. How cool and insufferably arrogant he had been! And how dared he impale her with an eye grotesquely enlarged by the lens of a quizzing glass as if she were some particularly rare and curious specimen he had never encountered before. What an odious creature he was, to be sure. It had come as something of a shock to conclude at last that he was telling the truth and that apparently he had not the smallest recollection of her. Indeed, it had been unutterably lowering. To think that the incident that had ruined her had meant so little to him that she had failed to make even the smallest impression on him!

It was like having the rug swept out from under one. And, indeed, it was true that the entire rationale upon which she had sustained herself over the years had been rendered null and void all in a single moment. She had willingly made a laughingstock of herself eight years ago in order to save the Marquis of Ulverston a greater humiliation. After all, she had made sure the female to whom he had been betrothed did not keep her assignation to elope with another man. In return, Letitia had had every right to expect that he might be just a little bit grateful to her. Enough to at least remember who she was, she told herself, and was immediately reminded that only a few hours earlier it had been her sincerest hope that he recalled none of it.

Well, she had gotten her wish, and in a curious sort of way she felt suddenly freed of a burden that she had carried, unbeknownst to herself, since that fateful night when she had overheard Miss Harriet Willet plotting to elope with a gentleman who most certainly was not the Marquis of Ulverston. Aside from Eleanore and Charles, she did not owe anything to anyone. Furthermore, she could not have cared less whether anyone at Marshgate, or anywhere else for that matter, approved of her or not. It gave her a wondrous feeling of power to know that she might obey any whim with perfect impunity. She, after all, was already damned in the eyes of those present.

No doubt it was one of those very whims that had prompted her to don the cherry red cassinette walking dress, which, while perfectly suited for an afternoon of alfresco sporting events, was bound to raise more than a few eyebrows. It was quite daringly short, after all, in the very newest style. The flounced hem, in fact, reached above the ankles to reveal red jean half boots and cambric stockings that matched the red and black stripes of her sleeves. It was a wonderfully outrageous costume, made even more so by the wholly fetching conversation hat of red felt, trimmed in black ribbons, the broad brim turned back and cocked to one side to conceal the left side of her face from any would-be eavesdroppers on her intimate chitchat.

Not that she was likely to be afforded the opportunity for an intimate tête-à-tête with anyone, she reflected with sardonic amusement. Not after having managed to sink herself beneath reproach in her first twenty minutes at Marshgate. The duke's house guests would far sooner consort with a pariah than one who had committed the supreme folly of spilling tea on the dowager duchess.

No sooner had that thought crossed her mind than a gay, young voice shouted her name. "Letitia! Letitia, you came!" Sally, rushing to Letitia's side, clasped her new friend's hand in both of hers. "I am so glad. I was dreadfully afraid you would not."

"Were you?" Letitia smiled. "But of course I came. How could I not when I learned you were Sarah Emberly. Why did you not tell me the duke was your uncle?"

"You didn't ask me," Sally pointed out, her blue eyes dancing. "Besides, I didn't suppose you would be interested. You made it perfectly clear you had no intention of ever marrying, and Uncle Giles, after all, is promised to Miss Pemberton."

"Little devil," exclaimed Letitia with obvious feeling. "I could not care less about your uncle's marital plans, and I am definitely not on the lookout for a husband."

"Well, that's what I just said, isn't it?" Sally shrugged, spreading wide her hands. "Never mind about Uncle Giles," she hastened to add at sight of the warning light in Letitia's narrowed glance "I'm glad you came for my sake. At least I shall have someone to talk to who does not treat me like somebody's pet pug inconveniently underfoot. You cannot know how lowering it is to have people forever patting one on the head and telling one how simply adorable one is when they are actually thinking how very unfortunate it is that the duke's only niece should have red hair and a face full of freckles."

Letitia laughed in spite of herself. "Come now. Surely it is not so bad as that?"

"Oh, but it is. Miss Pemberton assures me, however, that there is every hope my freckles will eventually succumb to assiduous application of oatmeal and cucumber packs and that should they not, I need not worry that I shall be doomed to remain on the shelf. After all, I am very well connected and shall have, besides, a not inconsiderable fortune."

"Sally, she did not!" exclaimed Letitia, horrified that anyone should be so unfeeling as to say such a thing to the child. "I daresay you misunderstood her."

"There is nothing wrong with my understanding, I assure you," Sally retorted, screwing up her face at the memory. "I daresay she sincerely meant to offer me comfort for what she considers my unfortunate disfigurement. Miss Pemberton, you see, is well connected, but she hasn't a feather to fly with. Which is why Uncle Giles's offer of marriage was so extremely fortuitous." Assuming a demure pose, her hands clasped before her and her expression tranquil, she presented an all too recognizable caricature of the future duchess as she recited, "While it is true they have no very great affection for one another, sentiment plays little part in marriages among our kind. Vail requires an heir, and Miss Pemberton must consider the futures of her three impoverished younger sisters. It is thus clearly her duty to marry Uncle Giles."

"Miss Pemberton is perhaps to be pitied," Letitia mused aloud, chilled to think that Vail had entered into so passionless an arrangement. This was not at all like the Ulverston she had known. Eight years ago, it had been rumored that he was head over ears in love with

Miss Willet and consequently must have been deeply disappointed when she proved unworthy of his affection. That was no reason to determine on a loveless marriage with the insipid, but conformable, Miss Pemberton merely to avoid the risk of making the same mistake twice. Indeed, she had thought better of him than that. "Still," she added, reminding herself that she could not care less what the odious duke might choose to do with his life, "she would very probably be just what your uncle looks for in a wife, and it is, after all, none of our affair."

With a wry grimace, Sally abandoned her pose. "Well, I think it is too dreadful. I should rather die than marry out of a sense of duty. Indeed, I should rather be like you, a Woman of the World, who has no need of anything so mundane as marriage and a family. I cannot but think such an existence would be ever so much more adventurous."

"And *I* think that you would do better to wait until you are older before you make so momentous a decision. One day you will discover that you have grown into a beautiful young woman for whom any number of gentlemen would be proud on Valentine's Day to wear your heart on their sleeves."

"Perhaps," said Sally, clearly unconvinced and still romanticizing over the image of herself as a female excursionist of great renown. "Who, I wonder, will be wearing yours after the names are drawn from the valentine box tomorrow?"

"Some poor unfortunate who will be wishing himself at Jericho rather than to have to claim me for his valentine, I shouldn't wonder," Letitia speculated, laughing. "Is there to be a valentine box, then?"

"Oh, yes." Sally nodded, making her red curls bob. "Miss Pemberton insisted on it."

"Did she? It is a rather old-fashioned custom. I should

not have expected the duke's betrothed to be of a sentimental disposition."

"But then, you probably didn't know that Miss Pemberton brought two of her sisters with her."

"I see," said Letitia, marveling at the child's sagacity. "Miss Pemberton, besides being of a practical nature, is not one to miss a chance, is that it?"

"Well, she has planned 'Kiss-in-the-ring' for one of the evening entertainments," Sally supplied with a guileless air. "And a game of 'Heart-to-heart' for determining who will be partnered with whom for the evening meal. What do you think of that?"

"Why, only that it sounds as though Miss Pemberton is very much in the valentine spirit," Letitia observed lightly. "I myself am quite looking forward to the archery contest, which, it appears, is about to begin. Shall we?" she said, gesturing toward the small group gathering in the area of that scheduled competition.

As the bowling green lay between them and the designated field of archery, Letitia and Sally had perforce to pass within close proximity of Miss Pemberton and the duke.

"But *I* did not invite her, Giles," drifted to Letitia and her young companion as they approached, unnoticed by the duke and his bride-to-be. "Indeed, I had never met Lady Treadwell before today. Good heavens, if neither you nor the duchess invited her and I did not, then who did? Surely you cannot think she is a gate-crasher."

"I cannot venture an opinion at this time as to what Lady Treadwell is or why she is here," replied His Grace darkly, his handsome features exceedingly grim. "But I intend to find out."

Letitia, who could not but take exception to being thought the sort who would force herself on the duke's house party, or anyone else's for that matter, especially in light of the fact that she had had no wish to come there in the first place, felt the first flush of anger slowly recede to be replaced by a fierce, icy calm that would have been readily recognizable to her intimates. *They* no doubt would have suffered a sudden frisson of warning at the sight.

After a single, pointed glance down at Sally, who wore an expression of sublime innocence, Letitia had no need to ask who had sent the mysterious invitation. The sly little puss, she thought to herself, little knowing whether to be angry or amused at the child's maneuvering. Squeezing Sally's hand in warning, she nodded pleasantly to Miss Pemberton and the duke, who returned a civil, if somewhat stiff, acknowledgment, and continued on without the smallest break in her stride.

Indeed, not until they were safely past the duke did she brace her youthful companion. Arching a single, dampening eyebrow, Letitia observed in exceedingly dry tones, "You might at least have approached your uncle and obtained his permission rather than place me in so untenable a position."

"Pray don't stop. Not here," Sally evaded, then groaned as Miss Pemberton called out, "Sarah, dear. Your grandmama was asking for you. I am sure she wished your immediate attendance."

"There. See what you have done?" whispered the child in dire accents. "Now I shall miss seeing the archery contest."

"Never mind that now. First, I shall have an answer. Why did you do it, Sally?"

Sally, to her credit, did not pretend not to know what Letitia meant by that pointed question. "After Grandmama refused to alter the guest list, I couldn't take the chance Uncle Giles might refuse me. It was ever so much easier to send the invitation myself. As to why, it's quite simple really," she said artlessly. "Uncle Giles's house party promised to be dreadfully dull. I thought perhaps it could use some livening up."

"Little miscreant. And you thought my presence here would serve that purpose?"

"I daresay it has already," replied the miscreant without a visible shred of remorse. "You are already the topic of every conversation."

"Of that, I have not the least doubt," Letitia responded feelingly, staring after the child, who was fleeing toward the house, presumably in search of her grandmama.

The archery contest, it soon developed, had apparently been designed for the sole purpose of allowing the gentlemen to perform for the benefit of the ladies, who, while perfectly willing to arrange themselves picturesquely in the lawn chairs provided for spectators, demonstrated not the least inclination to take up the bow and arrow in armed competition.

"Oh, dear no," Miss Ingersol, a dainty, golden-haired beauty with green, roguish eyes, replied to Anthony Clevenger's invitation to try her hand at the sport. "I am not in the least athletically inclined. I should not know the first thing about it."

"But there is nothing to it," protested Clevenger, who, thus far, had shown himself to be the ablest bowman among the gentlemen. Bending his head over Miss Ingersol's shoulder in an intimate proximity to her fair cheek, he extended the bow of sturdy yew in front of the lady and, with his other arm about her slender person, tested the string. "I should take great delight in instructing you in the rudiments."

"Should you indeed, Mr. Clevenger." Laughing, Miss Ingersol slipped from beneath his embrace and settled prettily in the lawn swing. "But to whose benefit, I wonder," she said with a wink over her fan at Miss Olivia Pemberton, who sat on the seat opposite hers.

"Oh, come now," Clevenger challenged when the general merriment had subsided. "I require a worthy opponent, since Cousin Giles has determined to take himself out of the competition. Or at least a pretty one. Come now, there must be one devotee of Artemis among you."

Letitia, who had been staring in a peculiarly studious manner at the gentleman, experienced a sudden shock of recognition. Good God, she could not be mistaken in either his voice or his mannerisms. It was Harriet Willet's secret lover. The next instant, carried on an irresistible impulse, she stepped forward.

"Not Artemis," she said, masking her instinctive dislike of Mr. Anthony Clevenger behind a mask of civility. "Not on the Eve of St. Valentine's Day. But another bowman, surely." Coolly, she took the bow from his hand. Then, selecting an arrow and fitting the nock to the bowstring, she pulled back and let fly the dart. "Cupid, Mr. Clevenger," she added with no little satisfaction, as the arrow, sent true to its mark, thudded home at the center of the heart.

"Heigh-ho, madam. A bull's-eye," cheered Lord Eppington. "It looks as if you've found your worthy opponent, Clevenger. And she is not only pretty. The lady has beaten your mark."

"An excellent shot," agreed that worthy, eyeing her with a sudden narrow-eyed interest that Letitia could not quite like. "But confess, Miss . . ."

"Treadwell," Letitia completed for him. "Lady Letitia Treadwell."

"Yes, well, now. It was only beginner's luck, was it not?"

"I should admit nothing of the sort, Lady Treadwell," came in cool, drawling accents that inexplicably caused a quickening of Letitia's senses.

She glanced up to meet Vail's hooded gaze beneath heavily drooping eyelids. "Indeed, Your Grace? And how, then, would you have me answer the gentleman?" she queried.

"With the truth, naturally, Lady Treadwell," the duke replied. "Obviously you are no stranger to the sport of archery."

"Damme if I don't think Vail is in the right of it," drawled Eppington. "I'll wager the lady could outshoot you, Clevenger, a good three arrows out of five."

"Make it four out of five and a hundred pounds, and it is done, my lord," said Clevenger, his eyes going to Letitia. "Well, Lady Treadwell? What say you? Have we a match?"

Letitia, who had not anticipated finding herself the object of a wager, and especially one of so outrageous a sum, parted her lips to protest, when Vail pointedly interjected, "You need not feel in any way obligated to answer, Lady Treadwell. I fear my cousin, in his enthusiasm, has forgotten himself. Naturally a wager is out of the question." Instantly she closed them again.

The devil take the duke! Naturally he knew as well as she that she would be thought forward and headstrong were she to allow herself to be the object of a wager. Nevertheless, obviously having already judged her something less than a lady of refinement, he had expected her to do that very thing. A plague on the man! What His Grace needed was a good shaking.

Instantly her head came up, her eyes sparkling dangerously. "On the contrary, Your Grace, I am not in the least adverse to a friendly wager. I shall put up a hundred pounds against yours, Mr. Clevenger. I fear I could never resist a challenge, you see."

"You make that indisputably clear, Lady Treadwell," the duke replied grim-faced. "The question is, are you perfectly aware of what you are doing?"

"You may be sure of it, Your Grace," Letitia smilingly assured him.

Letitia, avoiding her Aunt Eleanore's eyes, firmly refused to accept the advantage of ten yards that the gentlemen urged upon her in deference to her feminine gender. "You are all very kind, but I assure you I am not such a poor creature. I daresay I shall do very well at forty paces. Indeed, I should think fifty would make for a more interesting competition, do not you, Mr. Clevenger?" she added recklessly.

"Your wish is my command, madam." That gentleman bowed, his glance sweeping her slender figure in a manner that could only be described as bold and quite odiously familiar. "I fear, however, I am taking an undue advantage."

"You are, indeed, sir," Letitia instantly retorted. "But pray do not let it concern you. You will find that what you have taken advantageously will in the end prove of little profit to you."

A guffaw went up among the gentlemen at the expense of Mr. Clevenger, and Miss Ingersol was heard distinctly to remark that Lady Treadwell would seem to be a spirited female of lively wit.

"Indeed," replied Miss Adeline Pemberton, delicately pressing a perfumed lace handkerchief to her nose presumably to ward off a faint in the face of such unseemly behavior in one of her sex. "Gentlemen of distinction, however, must naturally prefer ladies of a quieter, more refined disposition, would you not agree, Mr. Wickum?" she inquired of a moderately attired gentleman of perhaps five and twenty, who, apparently solicitous of her comfort, had, with a deal of effort, fetched a wrought-iron chair from no little distance for her to sit upon.

"Oh, indeed, Miss Pemberton," agreed that worthy, mopping at his sweat-dampened brow with a linen handkerchief. "I most wholeheartedly agree."

"You have only to look to His Grace to see that I am right," Miss Pemberton added, glancing as if for further proof of her stated position to the undeniably compelling example of her future husband.

Letitia, who had been doing her best for the past ten minutes *not* to do that very thing, had perforce to bite her tongue to keep from delivering Miss Pemberton a stinging rejoinder. Good God, the thought of Vail legshackled to such a paragon of virtues would have been comical were it not so patently foredoomed to failure! Vail would not last a week with his insipid bride before sheer boredom drove him to seek solace in all his former London haunts.

To Letitia's annoyance, telling herself that such a fate was no less than what he deserved did little to quiet the small whisperings of a persistent voice that reminded her she had played no small part in the events that had hardened his heart against Cupid's arrow. The devil take him! Even if there were something she could do to avert such a disaster, he was hardly likely to thank her for it.

Buoyed by the fatalistic sense of power engendered by the realization that she had already placed herself utterly beyond reproach and comforting herself with the knowledge that she had been instructed by some of the finest archers in the Orient and, further, that she had been known to hit the ace of spades dead center nine times out of ten at an even greater distance than fifty yards, Letitia followed as Vail stepped off the additional ten paces.

The truth was, however, that she was already regretting the impulse to give the duke the proof of the pudding by demonstrating she cared not a whit what he thought of her. Indeed, she could only suppose it was some hitherto unsuspected quirk in her nature that had prompted her to launch herself on so decidedly unwise a course. She had been much better to follow her Aunt Eleanore's instincts to depart without further roundaboutation

from Marshgate—or her own, for that matter, never to
have come in the first place.

Again, at Letitia's insistence that a contest between two
equals must of necessity obviate the customary deference
to females, it was agreed on a drawing of straws to determine who should have first go at the target. With the
result that Letitia's short straw put Clevenger up first.

Mr. Clevenger at thirty-two was a well-made specimen
of the male gender, with the muscular build and easy
grace of one endowed with a natural athletic ability. That
he was also of a profligate nature, indulging himself
freely in drinking and vice, and had long since tossed
down the River Tick whatever resources he might once
have commanded had not yet served to alter his manly
appearance. He was possessed of fair hair and handsome,
boyish features, marred only by a hint of petulance about
the well-molded lips. Letitia had recognized after a very
few moments one who must in the very near future come
to be accounted a gazetted fortune hunter. In the meantime, he no doubt served very well in the capacity of a
charming ne'er-do-well who might be depended upon to
even the lists between male and female guests at the
houses of note to which he was frequently invited.

Whatever the case, he was more than merely proficient
with the bow and arrow. His first arrow sped true to the
mark, and the subsequent four clustered in and about
the area encompassed by the bull's-eye, ranging no farther than a mere handspan one from another.

"It would seem, Lady Treadwell," Lord Eppington
confided in his drawling fashion, "that we have given
you no small feat to perform. Rest assured, however, that
I have complete confidence in you."

"You are very kind, my lord. I shall endeavor not to
disappoint you," replied Letitia, who, had she not been
studiously trying to ignore Vail's disturbingly compelling
presence, might have noted with interest that Eppington

would seem to be paying a flattering attention to her Aunt Eleanore. His lordship had taken up station beside Eleanore, and his dark head, intriguingly touched with silver over the temples, was bent near to Eleanore's in what gave every manifestation of a lively exchange of conversation.

As it was, however, Letitia was far too distracted by other things going on around her to notice that Eleanore's cheeks were most becomingly tinged with color or that her lovely eyes sparkled with an animation that made her appear a deal younger than her thirty-nine years. As Clevenger, bowingly, surrendered the field to Letitia, various of the gentlemen offered her good-natured encouragement, Chester Chadworthy even going so far as to assert Lady Treadwell should have his undying affection did she but take Clevenger down a peg or two.

"Haven't forgot the pony you took off me, Tony, old boy," he called out. "Ain't likely to either. Who'd have thought a duck would swim twelve times in the same circle? Unnatural, that's what it is."

"There was nothing unnatural about it, Chadworthy. Dame Luck just happened to be on my side," Clevenger sneered. "A pity you haven't a hand with the lady."

"I shouldn't take it too seriously, Mr. Chadworthy," spoke up Letitia in instinctive defense of the florid-faced youth for whom she had felt an immediate sympathy. "If it was luck with a lady upon which Mr. Clevenger's wager depended, I suggest, Mr. Chadworthy, that his Dame Luck was nothing more than a lame duck."

"Oho, did you hear that?" chortled Chadworthy. "A facer, if ever I heard one. Never claimed to be in the petticoat line m'self. I daresay, however, that Lady Treadwell might change my mind."

"It occurs to me," laughed Miss Ingersol, clearly delighted with the manner in which Letitia had turned the tables on Anthony Clevenger, "that Lady Treadwell might well make a convert of anyone."

Clevenger's eyes flashed with cold fury, quickly concealed behind a charming mask. "Brava, Lady Treadwell," he murmured, smoothly saluting her hand. "I fear if your aim is as unerring as your wit, my purse shall soon be made the lighter for it."

"My wit notwithstanding, I am accounted a dead shot with more than a bow and arrow, Mr. Clevenger. Perhaps I should have warned you," she added, tugging her hand free of his prolonged grasp. "I have received an exceptional education for a female."

"That much is obvious, Lady Treadwell," growled the duke, taking her by the arm and escorting her to the mark from which she was to shoot. "Apparently, however, you were not instructed in the perils of crossing swords with a man who is considered dangerous when it comes to green girls with more bottom than brains."

"Am I to assume the man to whom you are referring is yourself?" Letitia queried, glancing innocently up into Vail's grim countenance.

"Little devil," replied the duke feelingly. "You know very well to whom I am referring."

"Indeed, Your Grace, I do—*because* I am neither green nor a girl," Letitia did not hesitate to point out. "I am a woman of five and twenty and have seen something of the world." Coming to a halt, she gently disengaged her arm from his and, drawing an arrow from the quiver he carried, fitted the nock to the bowstring. "Pray do not concern yourself, my lord duke," she added quietly. "I am well able to look after myself."

"You will pardon me, Lady Treadwell, if I have seen little evidence of it. Or is it your usual practice to introduce yourself by spilling tea on your hostess, only to progress to making a spectacle of yourself by engaging in a wager with a gentleman for an outrageous sum?"

"Gammon!" Letitia laughed, and, pulling back on the bowstring, sighted down the arrow to the target, preparatory to sending the dart flying. "You would think nothing of it were I a man instead of a woman." With a twang of the bowstring, the arrow shot through the air. "As for the sum, I can well stand the nonsense," she added, as the arrow struck the bull's-eye well within Clevenger's cluster of shots. Amidst the spate of applause, she calmly drew forth a second arrow and fitted it to the string.

"No doubt I am comforted by the knowledge that you will not have recourse to consult a cent-per-cent," Vail observed bitingly. "Unfortunately, the same cannot be said of my Cousin Anthony."

"Can it not, Your Grace?" murmured Letitia, and let fly the dart true to the mark.

"He is a man who lives by his wits. It would be wise were you not to allow yourself to be alone in his company." Letitia, sighting down yet a third arrow, could not but wonder if His Grace was in the least aware that she had thus far bettered Clevenger two shots out of two and was about to make it three. With an amused smile, she released the dart.

"No doubt I am moved at your concern, my lord duke," she said complacently as the arrow thudded home, forming with the others a triangle within the bull's-eye no greater than two inches on any leg.

"I pray you will be moved to heed my warning," Vail replied, as Letitia prepared for her fourth and winning shot. "I cannot be accountable for his actions should you persist in flinging yourself at him." Bowing curtly on that austere note, he turned on his heel and with long, quick strides left her.

"Flinging myself at him!" Letitia exclaimed, astounded that he should have put such an interpretation on her actions. "The devil!" Turning swiftly, she let fly the arrow.

* * *

No doubt His Grace was made to feel the slight breath of wind against his cheek, and it was fairly certain that he heard what must have been a faint, somewhat chilling, whoosh quite close to his ear, followed by a solid *thump*— as Letitia's arrow embedded itself in the tree trunk not more than twelve inches from his head.

"Oh, dear, Your Grace," came Letitia's voice, sounding femininely ruffled and quite charmingly flustered. "It just seemed to slip out of my fingers. How very clumsy of me. Thank heavens you were not hurt."

For an awful instant Vail stood in his tracks, his eyes fixed with dawning comprehension on the feathered projectile still quivering from its abruptly halted flight. Then with a preternatural calm, he deliberately came about to view the perpetrator of his near demise, looking ridiculously charming in her outlandish red cassinette walking dress and matching red felt conversation hat tilted at a garish angle. The little baggage. She was not, he was instantly certain, either ruffled or in the least flustered at having come within a foot of cutting his stick for him. Nor had the arrow "slipped" out of her fingers. By God, he would wager his life on it.

Drawing himself up to his full six feet, two inches in height, he ironically inclined his head to the lady. "Think nothing of it, Lady Treadwell. I count it a distinct honor to have been *missed* by one of your barbs. I can only trust that your having so unfortunately wasted one will not cost you the wager."

"How very kind of you to be concerned, Your Grace," replied the lady, irrepressibly dipping him a curtsey. "I should not dream of disappointing you."

And drawing forth an arrow, she proceeded to hit the target dead center.

Three

The last thing Letitia might have expected when she agreed to attend the duke's house party was to find herself suddenly much sought after, and not only by a flattering number of the gentlemen present, but by a goodly portion of the ladies as well. This peculiar circumstance, she attributed to the fact that she had come to be considered something of a novelty for her ready wit and her skill with a bow and arrow—and for one other, far more cogent reason.

Embarrassed at having won a wager of a hundred pounds off a gentleman, she had graciously suggested that as she was quite comfortable and consequently had no need to further add to her purse, Mr. Clevenger might choose to donate the sum to some worthy charity of his choice. In a society noted for its gambling, it was one thing to hazard losing a hundred pounds on a wager. It was quite another, having won, to blithely consign one's winnings to the devil, or to charity, which, in Anthony Clevenger's point of view at least, was tantamount to the same thing. With the result that she unintentionally broadcast to the entire assembled company that not only was she a woman of an independent nature, but one of considerable, independent means.

Apparently, Letitia humorously concluded, it was perfectly acceptable to spill tea on the dowager duchess, embroil oneself in a ruinous wager, and come to within a

hairsbreadth of impaling one's host with an arrow so
long as one had the excuse of being eccentrically wealthy.

Whatever the case, she was met upon her entrance in
the withdrawing room before dinner that evening by a
chorus of greetings altogether different from her earlier,
unheralded arrival at Marshgate. With a gay flutter of
silk skirts, the ladies converged on her, exclaiming over
her Turin gauze gown over burgundy satin. Cut rather
lower at the neck than she was normally used to wear,
the bodice was covered in tiny seed pearls and had
ruched sleeves that left her arms and shoulders bare.

"It is an exquisite creation, Letitia. I may call you Letitia, mayn't I?" Laura Gilcrest fairly gushed. "After all,
we are all friends here, are we not? Pray tell, who is your
modiste? I really must know."

"I should be only too glad to share her name with
you," replied Letitia, no little bemused at her unexpected popularity. "Unfortunately, I fear it would little
serve you. You see, I had the gown made up in Turin."

"Turin?" queried Lord Eppington, cocking a startled
eyebrow at Eleanore, who, smiling somewhat flusteredly,
lowered her gaze. "Never say you were there?"

"Indeed, my lord, I was. Some months ago with my
aunt," Letitia replied. "During the Peace of Amiens. Unfortunately, the peace, as everyone knows, was of an unconscionably short duration. We had hardly settled in in
a lovely villa overlooking the city before we were forced
to flee for fear of our safety."

"It would seem, Lady Treadwell," the dowager observed loftily from her seat before the fireplace, "that
you have chosen an adventurous life for yourself. One
must suppose the impropriety of a young unmarried female jaunting about alone in foreign places never once
entered your mind."

"But you are mistaken, Mama," drawled the duke.

"Not alone, surely. Lady Treadwell said she was traveling in the company of her aunt."

Surprised at what would appear his championship, Letitia met Vail's eyes, unreadable behind drooping eyelids. "As a matter of fact, Your Grace," she said in answer to the dowager, "such a thought did not occur to me. I have done a great deal of traveling the past several years. Foreign places have always held an appeal for me. And, since there was little enough to hold me in England, I have not hesitated to indulge my passion to see some small part of the world."

"Well, I think it is a grand notion," Miss Ingersol applauded with no little enthusiasm. "Indeed, I should jump at the chance to do it myself. Unfortunately, my parents would certainly never agree to it."

"I, for one, should hardly blame them," pronounced Miss Pemberton, evincing a small shiver at the very prospect of doing anything so unfemininely daring. "Traveling the world may sound adventurous, but I daresay it is fraught with extreme peril and discomfort."

"Certainly it is not the sort of thing for females of delicate sensibilities," kindly asserted Mr. Fredrick Wickum, tenderly laying a grenadine silk shawl about Miss Pemberton's shoulders.

"In my day, young women did not indulge their passions," declared the dowager. "They got married, just as they should."

"And *then* indulged their passions," quipped Anthony Clevenger with a sidelong glance at Letitia, which she pointedly ignored. "Very discreetly, of course."

The dowager, in the ensuing laughter, thumped the floor with her walking stick, which commanded an almost instant silence. "It is appallingly evident, Nephew, that neither your manners nor your character has improved since you came into your majority. I am fast losing patience with you, I warn you."

"Losing patience? But how can you say so, my dearest Aunt Honoria?" Clevenger exclaimed, smoothly bending over the elderly lady to place a buss on her withered cheek. " 'Tis true I forgot myself, but only because I know you, like most women of beauty and charm, have ever been secretly fond of rogues. Of course I shall behave myself if you are quite certain that is what you want, but only think how very dull that would be."

"Gammon!" declared the dowager, surveying the self-declared rogue with a sapient eye. "You are more like your father every day. One can only hope that one day I do not cease to find *you* amusing."

Apparently the duke was of a similar opinion. Propping one elbow casually on the mantelpiece, he favored his kinsman with the faintest of smiles. "Doing it a bit brown, Anthony?"

"I do try my best—Cousin," Clevenger asserted, ironically bowing.

"Quite so," agreed His Grace, apparently unmoved by the mocking light in his cousin's eyes. "And now that you have managed to redeem yourself with your customary adroitness, perhaps we should proceed to the next order of business. I believe, my dear," he added to Miss Pemberton, "you have prepared a small entertainment for us before we go into dinner?"

"Indeed, it is nothing very grand," Miss Pemberton replied. "Only a small game of 'Heart-to-heart' before we go in. Each of you was handed a colored heart when you entered the withdrawing room this evening. I ask you now to take it out and seek the heart that yearns for yours. When you have found your match, you are free to proceed to the dining table with your newfound partner and be seated according to the gentleman's place name."

Letitia, who could hardly claim any great familiarity with the other guests present and who was, as a consequence, in no hurry to discover the identity of her dinner partner, contented herself with merely observing the general merriment as each maid went in search of her heart's desire. The young Misses Pemberton, she noted with no little interest, were fortunate enough to find themselves paired off with the two most (with the exception of Lord Eppington and the duke himself, that was) eligible bachelors present—one to Viscount Windholm, who in addition to being Lady Margaret's brother was heir to an earldom, and the other to Sir Reginald Cavendish, who was not only young and well to look upon, but was in possession of a more than respectable fortune. Miss Ingersol laughingly claimed Chester Chadworthy, who seemed more than pleased with his good fortune, while Lady Margaret seemed perfectly happy to link arms with Oliver Stanhope and Eleanore had the extremely good fortune to find herself paired with so charming a personage as Lord Eppington. Suspecting that the game was not entirely on the up and up, Letitia watched with something less than anticipation as Anthony Clevenger gravitated toward her with the obvious expectation of discovering that their two hearts must be made for each other. Fortunately, to Letitia's relief, Laura Gilcrest, who, while no great beauty and with no claim to nobility, was the sole daughter of a nabob who had made his fortune in the West Indies sugar trade, intercepted Clevenger with a pink heart trimmed in Valencienne's lace that thankfully was a perfect match to his.

It was only then, as the withdrawing room grew noticeably empty and as Miss Adeline Pemberton tranquilly departed on the arm of Mr. Fredrick Wickum, that Letitia was made suddenly and acutely aware that there remained only one other person in the room besides herself.

"Well," she proclaimed, robbed, no doubt, of originality by the singular circumstance of finding herself alone with the odiously expectant Duke of Vail.

"Just so," replied Vail sympathetically, still standing with his arm propped on the mantelpiece.

Letitia only just managed not to choke on an unwitting burble of laughter. "Oh, how very abominable you are," she exclaimed, awarding him a moue of mock displeasure. "I cannot but wonder what quirk of mischance places us alone in this room together. Can it truly be that you are in possession of a crimson heart, shot through, as it were, by Cupid's errant dart?"

"It would seem something of a monumental coincidence, would it not?" whimsically speculated the duke, as he held his crimson, arrow-impaled heart up for inspection. "Almost metaphorical, as it were."

"Let us hope it is in no way prophetical," Letitia retorted dryly. "I, apparently, sir, am your dinner partner."

"Indeed, ma'am. Shall we go in?"

"I confess, Your Grace," Letitia murmured a minute or two later, "that I had not expected, after my inauspicious introduction to your house party, to find myself seated in such close proximity to the head of your dinner table. I fear it may prove unpalatable to your mother to be forced to dine with me in her constant view, enthroned, as it were, in the seat of honor."

"My mother, you will discover, is not so feeble as she appears, Lady Treadwell," replied His Grace, seating her in that most favored place, to the right of the ducal chair. "You may be certain she will survive the experience."

"Good God, I should hope so, Your Grace. I did not suppose it would be the death of her. But then, I did not plan to drench her in tea."

"Any more than you planned to loose your arrow at me, one must presume. I suspect, Lady Treadwell, that you are a female of irresistible impulse."

"I prefer to say I am a woman of strong instincts, Your

Grace," Letitia replied with an imp of laughter in her eye. "Or inspiration, perhaps. Both have been of immeasurable aid to me in ways that you could not possibly imagine."

"Have they, indeed, ma'am?" drawled the duke, who, having seated himself, leaned negligently back in his chair. "You will no doubt pardon me if I find that curious in light of today's series of events. I should be interested to hear how this propensity of yours for impulsive behavior has been of use to you."

Letitia, keenly aware of Vail's studied gaze on her face, did not disbelieve that for a moment. No doubt he considered her fortunate in the extreme merely to have survived twenty-five years of what gave every manifestation of having been a life ruled by mischance. And yet how much less must he think of her did he but know the acute instincts she so implicitly trusted had thus far netted her a sizable fortune!

"Unfortunately, I am not in the least inclined to enlighten you, Your Grace," she answered, spreading her linen napkin over her lap. "For now, suffice it to say that I am enjoying a most peculiar popularity that must be the result of that series of events you felt obliged to bring up again. Surely, it cannot be due to anything *rational* I have done since arriving at your house party."

"Can it not, Lady Treadwell?" Vail said, swirling his dinner wine slowly about in its crystal goblet. "I wonder."

Fortunately, Lord Eppington, who sat to her right, chose just then to remark that he had had occasion at one time to know the Somerset Treadwells and to ask if she were any relation to the Marquis of Clarendon.

"He is, as a matter of fact," she replied, grateful for the excuse to turn away from a pair of disturbingly penetrating blue eyes, "my uncle. Do you know the marquis, my lord?"

"Only as a passing acquaintance. I used to be on

friendly terms with his brother, the previous marquis. A
good man, Wilfred. I was saddened by his untimely demise. A boating accident, I believe."

"They were sailing off Minehead when they were over-
taken by a sudden storm. The marquis and the marchioness were both lost when their boat was flung onto the
rocks." Letitia smiled gravely. "It was a very long time
ago."

"Not so long that they are not sorely missed," replied
his lordship kindly. "I was just telling Miss Freeman that
you greatly resemble him."

Letitia laughed. "My Grandfather Edward used to say
that I should have been the spitting image of my father
had I not had the supreme misfortune to be born a female.
Even so, I believe Grandpapa was not displeased with my
boyish accomplishments. He taught me how to fish when
I was five and how to shoot when I was ten. Furthermore,
he was used to boast that I could outride any boy."

"Edward Treadwell was a grand gentleman of the old
school" Vail interjected quietly. "I believe Lady Honoria
was quite fond of him."

"Was she, Your Grace?" Letitia queried, furious to
feel the blood stain her cheeks as she turned to find Vail
staring at her with a curiously fixed intensity. Hell and
the devil confound it! Caught off guard by Eppington's
sympathetic reminiscences, she had completely forgotten
to guard her tongue. Too late, she realized she had revealed a deal more of herself than she might otherwise
have wished to have done. She had all but caused Vail
to apprehend who she was. "I fear it did not seem so
this afternoon when she mentioned him," she added,
determined to retrieve her error. "I believe she was no
little concerned that I might have had the ill fortune to
take after him."

"The dowager duchess was, regrettably perhaps, plain-
spoken," Vail said, contemplating Letitia over the lip of

his glass. "She is also a woman of great subtlety, a facet of her character that is recognized only by those who know her best. My mother, Lady Treadwell, was undoubtedly baiting you."

"Your mother, Your Grace, is a fierce old dragon," Letitia baldly retorted. "If she did not so obviously disapprove of me, I believe I should like her enormously."

She was rewarded with a quizzical arch of a single imperious eyebrow. "And you, Lady Treadwell, are obviously a female of no uncommon perception. It occurs to me that you and my mother would deal exceedingly well."

Letitia was startled into laughter at the very notion of herself on intimate terms with the dowager duchess. "On the contrary, Your Grace," she said, her eyes alight with merriment. "We should undoubtedly soon find ourselves at loggerheads. I suspect Lady Honoria and I are far too much alike ever to suit."

"Perhaps," murmured Vail, watching her. Then, inquiring about her foreign travels, he smoothly turned the topic of conversation.

Vail, it soon transpired, was himself extensively well-traveled, having made the Grand Tour in his youth followed by numerous other excursions to foreign places. Furthermore, he was a gifted conversationalist. With him to guide her, Letitia soon found herself relating any number of humorous anecdotes concerning the places she had visited, the methods of travel she had been forced at times to endure, and the peculiar customs of peoples she had encountered along the way.

Vail, she came to realize, was not only quite as charming as he was reputed to be, but every whit as subtle as he had accused his mama of being. They had progressed through the chestnut soup, the poached salmon steaks, the asparagus souffle, and the veal galantine before Letitia realized that not only was she enjoying herself immensely, but she had been masterfully drawn into talking about herself for all of an hour and twenty minutes.

Protesting at last that he was allowing her to monopolize the conversation, she adroitly turned the tables on him.

"Tell me about your European travels, Your Grace. Did you visit Rome? Marseilles? Paris? Lisbon or Madrid? Did you navigate the Rhine?"

Vail had seen all these places. Without the hindrance of war, he had followed in the tradition of earlier generations, who sent their sons on the Grand Tour of Europe for the purpose of rounding out a gentleman's education. He was, consequently, vastly more knowledgeable of the European Continent than she, but he knew Greece and Constantinople as well and had traveled up the Danube and taken walking tours through the Alps. Only in the matter of the Orient did her firsthand knowledge exceed his.

Long before the jellies and sweetmeats were served, Letitia had succumbed to the pleasure of the duke's company. So much so, in fact, that she failed to notice the long, studied glances the dowager duchess cast her way down the length of the table. Or the manner in which Miss Adeline Pemberton grew more subdued as the dinner progressed with stately magnificence toward its eventual conclusion.

Others, however, did not fail to notice them or to draw their own conclusions. Chief among them was Anthony Clevenger, who appeared anything but pleased to witness Letitia holding forth in great animation with the duke, her lovely features alight and her eyes sparkling with enjoyment. No doubt he was even less gratified to note that far from his customary expression of ennui, His Grace wore the aspect of a man presented with a vision something on the order of a sublime revelation.

Letitia, who had never, until that evening, encountered a man with whom she held so many interests in common or with whom she could converse with the full certainty that she would not receive either a blank look of incomprehension or a condescending one of male superiority, was conscious of a sharp pang of regret when the dowager duchess rose to announce it was time to leave the gentlemen to their port. The realization that she could not recall having enjoyed herself so much in a very long time was more sobering than comforting. Indeed, she could not but be more than a little disturbed to discover herself on the very brink of repeating history.

Eight years before, she had allowed herself to become enamored of the Marquis of Ulverston, who was betrothed to another woman. To allow herself to fall all over again for the Duke of Vail in similar circumstances would be foolish in the extreme. It was, in fact, simply out of the question. Or was it? she mused, an impish gleam in her eye.

"You seem to be enjoying yourself," Eleanore observed dryly to Letitia as, arm in arm, they proceeded to the withdrawing room. "Do you have the least idea what you are doing?"

Fully aware that her dearest aunt must have been thinking along the same lines as herself regarding any possible involvement with the duke, Letitia laughed. "Indeed, Aunt. I am creating something of a stir among the duke's house guests and a deal of speculation as to my intentions. No doubt I can look forward to a summons from the dowager in the very near future during which she will take it upon herself to instruct me on the inadvisability of carrying on a flirtation, light or otherwise, with Vail. I find the prospect of such an encounter fraught with amusement."

"I, on the other hand, see nothing amusing in watching you cast your chances away. The dowager duchess is not one to be taken lightly. My dear, you will only end up getting hurt if you let it seem that you are flinging your bonnet at a man who is already promised. Surely you must see that?"

"I see only that you are truly upset," exclaimed Letitia, instantly filled with remorse at her lighthearted teasing. "Forgive me, dearest. I thought you knew I was only roasting you. I am not flinging anything at the duke, least of all my bonnet, I promise you."

"Are you not? You will forgive me if I say it looked very much like it this evening, Letitia," Eleanore replied doubtfully. "You may be sure Lady Honoria thought so, too."

"Stuff and nonsense. I did not choose to be partnered with the duke, but once the thing was done, I could hardly be rude to him. I wish you will cease to worry, and concentrate instead on enjoying yourself for a change. I am, as you are so fond of pointing out, a grown woman. I can well look after myself."

"Can you, Letitia?" queried her aunt, who had not failed to note that the duke had seemed to be paying more than merely a polite attention to her niece. "Sometimes I think you have not the least notion what a devastating effect you have on members of the opposite sex. You are a vibrant, beautiful woman. A man would have to be dead or blind not to fall head over ears in love with you."

Letitia was startled into laughter. If she thought about it at all, which was not often, she had never been one to be greatly impressed with her looks. These, since petite blondes with china blue eyes were all the fashion, she considered only passable at best. "I wish you will not be absurd, my dearest of aunts," Letitia gurgled in amusement. "Vail cut his wisdoms long ago. You may be sure he is perfectly capable of guarding his own heart. And that, he has set on Miss Adeline Pemberton."

"Which is why you should not allow yourself to be overmuch in his company," insisted Eleanore, who was a deal older than Letitia and knew rather more about the vagaries of that unruly organ. "One can never tell when Cupid's arrow will strike. You may be sure, however, that Miss Pemberton has no intention of releasing Vail from their arrangement, and a gentleman, after all, does not cry off."

"Which leaves me at *point-non-plus,* I must suppose," Letitia replied fondly. "In that case, you will no doubt be relieved to learn that far from entertaining any marital designs on the duke, I wish him only the best of good fortune with his promised bride. I daresay he will need it. Or a flesh-and-blood mistress when the thing is done and he is properly legshackled. And so you must see there is no need for your concern. Cupid may shoot his arrows where he will, and none shall prove the sorrier for it."

"Letitia Treadwell!" exclaimed Eleanore, coming to a sudden halt. "You cannot mean what I think you mean!"

"Then of course I must not, if you say so, Aunt," replied Letitia, and with her eyes dancing, she dropped a buss on the other woman's cheek and blithely took her leave, saying she was just going upstairs to wish Sally a quick good night before the gentlemen condescended once more to join them.

A few moments later, having earlier taken the precaution of learning its whereabouts from one of the maids, Letitia knocked lightly on Sally's door before slipping noiselessly inside. Closing the door behind her, she softly called the child's name.

"Letitia! It *is* you," whispered thrillingly through the darkness, which was relieved only by the glow of embers in the fireplace. "I had so wished to see you. Uncle Giles said I should be completely free of my lessons tomorrow

if I promised to work very hard to make them up after
everyone is gone. He said he might even take me out
riding if the weather stays nice. Is that not simply marvelous?"

"It is very kind of him," Letitia answered, groping her
way across the room to the child's bed. "I daresay your
uncle takes more notice of you than you have been used
to thinking."

"I do think he has a certain fondness for me," agreed
the child, "in spite of the fact that I was more or less
left on his doorstep when Mama made up her mind to
accompany Papa on his diplomatic mission."

"His diplomatic mission?" Letitia exclaimed in no little surprise. "But then, they are not. . . . And you are
not. . . . Sally, why did you not tell me?"

"But I did tell you. The first time we met."

"You told me there were only your uncle and your
grandmama," Letitia answered dryly. "I thought your
parents were dead."

"Well, they might be, for all I know," Sally replied
practicably. "I have not heard from them since they set
sail over a month ago, and they will not be back for me
before the end of the summer. So it is very like being
an orphan," she added gruffly, turning her head away
from Letitia.

"It is nothing like," Letitia said sternly. "You may take
the word of one who knows. Still," she added, staring
thoughtfully at the child's averted profile, "I daresay you
are feeling just a trifle abandoned. Would it perhaps
make you feel better if we pretended—just for tonight—
that I am your mama and I have come upstairs to kiss
you good night?"

"It might." Sally swallowed and turned her head back
to Letitia. "I'm not a child, you know," she declared.
"You mustn't think that I am. It is only that I have been

missing them lately. And though Marshgate is very nice, it is not quite the same as home, is it?"

Smiling, Letitia gently smoothed the girl's tousled curls back from her forehead. "No, I daresay it is not. No place is quite the same as home. Still, home will be there, waiting for you, and in the meantime you have your new pony and the picnic tomorrow. And I shall be at Beechcote for a few more weeks. Perhaps your uncle may be persuaded to allow you to come and visit. Before you know it, the summer will be over, and you will be back at home with your mama and papa. Just think of all the marvelous adventures you will have to tell them about."

"It is not all that adventurous doing lessons and learning how to tat and do needlepoint," Sally replied doubtfully. "And Uncle Giles will be off to the north country to see to his estates before very much longer. I shall be alone with Grandmama. Still, if you say I may come and visit, perhaps the spring will not be entirely lost. And there is still Valentine's Day tomorrow," she added, noticeably brightening at the prospect.

"Yes, of course there is," Letitia said in accents of encouragement. Then bending over, she kissed Sally lightly on the forehead. "Good night, my dear. I must be getting back before I am missed. I shall see you in the morning."

Sally halted her as she rose from the bed to leave. "Letitia?"

"Yes?" Letitia turned back to the girl.

"Letitia," Sally said, plucking at the counterpane, "you are not sorry you came, are you? You are enjoying yourself?"

"Why, indeed I am. More than I thought I should. Though I fear your grandmama may soon be wishing me at Jericho. Especially if she catches me talking to you when you should already have been asleep ages ago."

"She won't. Very likely she is in bed by now. She always

retires immediately after dinner. I wish you did not have
to go."

"No more than do I. Still, you do need your sleep,
and I shall soon be missed." Leaning down, she tucked
the girl's hand beneath the bed covers. "Pleasant dreams,
Sally, and thank you. It was very sweet of you to invite
me to your uncle's house party."

"You do like him," Sally said unexpectedly. "Now that
you have met him? I know he can seem dreadfully toplofty
and proud, but, underneath, he is really quite different."

"But of course he is. And I am sure I like him well
enough. How could I not, when he is your uncle?" Letitia answered, deliberately sidestepping the question.
Then, crossing to the door, she opened it and looked
back at Sally. "You may be sure that Miss Pemberton
likes him, too," she gently added, "and that is what really
matters, is it not?"

Softly, she closed the door behind her and for a moment
stood with her back to it, a faint whimsical smile playing
about her lips. The little minx to lure her there for the
sole purpose of promoting a match between herself and
the duke! And how very fond she must be of her uncle
to go to such lengths. Nevertheless, fond or not, the child
was clearly out of her depths. Furthermore, she had
placed Letitia in a wholly untenable position.

It had been one thing to assume Sally's manipulations
had been for the child's own sake. It was quite another to
realize she had done it for altogether different reasons.
Indeed, it changed everything. It robbed her of that sense
of freedom that came in knowing she did not owe anything to anyone. Faith, it would be nigh unto impossible
to behave with any naturalness in the duke's presence,
knowing she had been brought there for ulterior purposes. In truth, Letitia did not see how she could remain
a moment longer at Marshgate under false pretenses.

Her earlier pleasure in the evening quite vanished,

Letitia pushed away from the door and made her way thoughtfully down the hall. The logical course, she told herself, was to plead a headache and retire to her room. In the morning, it would be a simple enough matter to take her leave before anyone else was up and about. A note to Eleanore explaining she had received an urgent summons from Charles on a pressing matter of business would relieve her of any embarrassing questions and might even be sufficient to persuade Eleanore to stay on until the end of the week. Yes, it was the rational thing to do.

Her plans laid, she should have experienced a measure of relief. After all, she had never wanted to come to Marshgate in the first place, and though the notion of becoming the latest in the long line of the duke's mistresses was enticing, it was not really the most practical idea she had ever had. Why, then, did all her instincts cry out at her that she was taking the coward's way out?

Letitia was brought up short at the withdrawing room door by the sounds of music and hilarity, which left little doubt that the gentlemen had rejoined the ladies or that a parlor game of some sort was in full progress, the most likely candidates being "Heart March" or "Kiss-in-the-ring." For a moment she hesitated, tempted to fling caution to the winds and join in the merriment. After all, it challenged the laws of chance to suppose she might be paired a second time in one night with the Duke of Vail. And what harm could it really do to allow herself a few more hours of light-hearted fun?

Could she help it that Sally had decided to usurp the role of Cupid on behalf of her uncle? It had certainly never been Letitia's intention to cast lures at the undeniably compelling duke. Still, she could not like the thought of filling Sally with false hopes any more than she could abide the prospect of being accused, no matter how falsely, of having set out to entrap a duke.

Reluctantly and with no little disgust at herself, Letitia drew back from the door. The earlier charm of the evening was gone, at any rate, she consoled herself, and it was highly unlikely that it could be recaptured. She would do much better to cut her losses and simply walk away while she was still ahead.

Feeling little inclination for bed, Letitia snatched up a decorative shawl flung over the back of a settee and made her way through the house to the Summer Porch where she had earlier made her memorable debut. The cold blast of January was already well on its way to relenting before the first incursion of spring, and the night, though moonless and chill, was not unbearable, considering it was mid-February. Letitia pulled the shawl closer about her shoulders and stepped out onto the pave-stones to stroll aimlessly beneath the barren vines. Inhaling deeply, she savored the scent of mist in the air, which was somehow so distinctly English. She had carried its memory with her wherever she went, along with the mingled aromas of her mother's garden with its poppies, delphiniums, pinks, hollyhocks, phlox, and roses. Even in the grandeur of tropical rain forests, she had not forgotten the domestic simplicity of the English garden, nestled beside every English house and country cottage. Indeed, there were many things that she had carried with her, like hoarded treasures to be contemplated in the strictest privacy. Memories of her mother, fairy-light and beautiful in pale blue gossamer, seated before a dressing table as she affixed glittering diamond and sapphire earrings to her earlobes. Or her father's booming laughter, his strong hands, which had been remarkably gentle, his tall, reassuring presence.

Letitia swallowed hard around a lump in her throat. For the first time since setting foot once more on English soil, she felt as if the lid to the treasure trove had been thrown open, so that she was overwhelmed all at once with its poignant memories. No doubt this was why she had put off coming back to England for so many years. Certainly it had been the cause of her leaving. That, and her unalterable resolve that she would never be ruled by her uncle, especially in the matter of her marriage. She would rather live in exile the rest of her life than wed her Cousin Albert to keep her inheritance in the family. Indeed, for all she cared, they could have the money, if it meant she need never set eyes on any one of them again.

She had not sent word to her loving family that she was arrived in England for that very reason, and she had every hope that they would not learn of it before she was once more far from English shores.

She halted suddenly in her perambulations, struck by the realization that she had without conscious thought come to a decision. So, it was not to be England after all, then, but another extended sea voyage. Where? she thought with an odd sort of pang. To the Americas perhaps?

It was one of the things that had drawn her to Beechcote, the need for privacy and seclusion in which to sort out her thoughts and make some determination about her future course. Strange that it should all be made clear to her in the midst of the duke's valentine party. Or perhaps it was not so strange, she reflected wryly, but only ironic. After all, she had fled the first time in the wake of an ill-fated encounter with the Marquis of Ulverston. This time, however, she could not but be conscious of the fact that she felt an unfamiliar reluctance to be parted from England.

The awareness that she was not alone came hard upon that realization.

No doubt it was the sudden prickling at her nape that warned her. Or perhaps unconsciously she had detected

some barely perceptible sound or movement. Whatever
the case, she went quite still, her every sense attuned to
the mist-laden night. Someone was there. She knew it, in
spite of the impenetrable curtain of darkness that en-
shrouded the grounds. She had not, after all, undergone
months of intensive instruction in the art of self-protec-
tion without having developed an intuitive instinct about
such things. Whoever it was, she could think of no good
reason why anyone should be playing at Peeping Tom in
the dark. Indeed, she was on the point of calling out to
demand the villain show himself, when a light step
sounded at her back. All in a single movement, she spun
on her heel and dropped into a crouch, her hands up
before her in the posture of *tan-gun*, the first position of
self-defense.

"Hold, sir!" she declared in no uncertain terms to the
tall, unmistakably masculine figure that loomed, large
and forbidding, out of the shadows. "Should you be
thinking of trying anything, I should warn you that I
am well equipped to fend off any would-be attackers."

"I must naturally find that knowledge enlightening in
the extreme, ma'am," drawled a mortifyingly familiar
voice in exceedingly dry tones. "Rest assured, however,
that I have not the least inclination to dispute the matter
with you. Strange as it may seem, I have never made it
a practice to force myself on females, defenseless or
otherwise."

With a wry grimace, Letitia instantly dropped her de-
fensive stance.

"I wish you will not be absurd, Your Grace," she retorted, torn between relief and annoyance. "Indeed, had
you the least notion how near you came to finding yourself thrown ignominiously flat on your back, you would
realize that this is no laughing matter. You might have
been hurt. At the very least, your clothes would have
been ruined. And never mind that it would have been

all your own fault for sneaking up on me in a manner
wholly unbefitting a gentleman, you may be sure that *I*
should have been the one to take the blame."

"You are quite right, Lady Treadwell," drawled the
duke, properly grave. "In such an event, I should indeed
find little that was amusing. As it happens, I am particularly fond of this coat."

"As well you might be. It is obviously cut by Weston,"
Letitia bitterly rejoined. The devil! He clearly did not
believe for an instant that she could do any such thing,
but, worse, he was laughing at her! "Would you be so kind
as to tell me just how long you have been standing there?"

"No more than a moment or two. As a matter of fact,
I had just stepped out for a breath of air, when, becoming immediately aware of your presence, I came forward
with the express purpose of making myself known to
you." A smile that was singularly devoid of mirth twisted
at his lips. By God, he had been nothing *but* aware of
her since she had all but hurtled herself to his attention
that morning. No doubt she would have been no little
amused to learn that, indeed, having become unreasonably concerned at her unexplained absence from the festivities, he had come expressly in search of her. "You
will no doubt pardon my curiosity, but is it your belief
that I was spying on you?"

The question was couched in dangerous, velvet soft
tones that should have been a warning to anyone, apparently, but the mettlesome Miss Treadwell. Far from being
in the least intimidated, she gave every indication of having forgotten he was even there.

A wry gleam flickered behind the duke's heavily
drooping eyelids at sight of his companion, her lovely
lips pursed in a frown of seeming concentration, as she
stared with apparent fascination at the shrubs along the
far end of the verandah. Unused to being ignored by

young beauties, Vail's first leap of anger was swiftly supplanted by an ironic amusement at himself.

In spite of the fact that considered the Catch of the Marriage Mart, he had spent his bachelor days evading the toils of a host of matchmaking mamas and their simpering offspring, he had never fooled himself into thinking that they were not more interested in his worldly station and possessions than in himself. Never, that is, save for his one, unfortunate miscalculation in the matter of Miss Harriet Willet, whose angelic appearance had served to hide a calculating female with a heart of jade. At eight and twenty, he should have known better than to open his purse strings to a woman, but there had been no accounting for love. By the time he had discovered her true nature, he had already settled her considerable debts, leaving her free to attempt an elopement with her secret lover. The timely intervention of a mysterious angel had averted a scandal, but he had been left with a cynical view of the fairer sex that had hardened his heart against Cupid's dart. Only the necessity of setting up his nursery had at last prevailed upon him to abandon his bachelor state in favor of a purely business arrangement without the least pretense of any romantical involvement.

He had not thought then to meet a woman who, far from having designs on either his title or his fortune, took advantage of every opportunity to demonstrate a total disregard for him. If Lady Treadwell had deliberately set out to capture his interest, she could have found no better way of doing it.

"Lady Treadwell?" he gently prodded, goaded at last by an overwhelming curiosity.

"What?" Letitia, jarred out of her distraction, turned startled eyes on the duke. Instantly realizing he must have been speaking to her without her being aware of it, she furiously blushed. "Oh, dear, I do beg your pardon. I'm afraid I was not attending. What was it you said? Something about spying."

"Never mind that. I am more interested to know if there is something troubling you. You would seem to be uncommonly distracted by the yew hedge."

"As a matter of fact, Your Grace," Letitia said frankly, "I am convinced that there was someone lurking behind that very hedge. Oh, you needn't investigate. He is gone now. You undoubtedly frightened him away. I should be careful, however, to lock the doors and windows. Very possibly he was plotting a burglary."

Had Letitia's intent been to allay her companion's misgivings, she was to fall far short of the mark. Far from being comforted by the thought that a female guest in his house had been ogled by a possible intruder, he was made furious at her failure to remove herself immediately to a place of safety.

"Little fool," he growled, closing fingers of steel about her arms. "Did it never once occur to you that his intentions may have been a deal more serious than robbery? He might very easily have preferred to abduct an unaccompanied female witless enough to present him with the opportunity. If you knew someone was there, why the devil did you not go inside?"

"I am not such a-a poor creature, I assure you," retorted Letitia, a trifle breathless and more than a little unsettled at finding herself so unexpectedly in the duke's clutches. Even worse, she was swept with an almost overwhelmingly irresistible impulse to simply allow herself to melt against him. Her eyes widened on his, and she stood, stunned by the realization that she wanted nothing more than for the odious duke to take her in his arms and kiss her.

It was an exceedingly startling revelation, and it was some time before she became aware that he was staring back at her with a strange, piercing intensity that she found altogether entrancing.

"I really feel I must warn you, Your Grace," she said, feeling that very soon she would be lost in those magnificently compelling orbs. "Whether you choose to believe me or not, I am well-versed in the art of defending myself. And if you do not unhand me at once, sir, you will discover just how proficient I am at disabling a man improvident enough to lay hold of me."

She was rewarded for her efforts with a smile that could only be described as grimly amused.

"Do not, Lady Treadwell, tempt me," Vail warned, showing not the least inclination to unloose his hold. "You will find I am perfectly capable of throwing you over my knee and beating some sense into you."

Letitia felt her pulse unwittingly quicken, as it seemed he might give in to an entirely different temptation. "Are you, sir? I, on the other hand, cannot advise you to try it."

She felt his hands tighten on her arms, and her knees went ridiculously weak at sight of the fierce light that leapt into his eyes. Then just as suddenly it was as if a shutter had dropped over his face, and she found herself staring into the wholly impenetrable, slightly bored mask of the Corinthian once again. Dazed, she felt his hands drop away.

"No doubt I should find it amusing to disabuse you of any misconceptions you might have concerning the outcome of such an experiment," he said, insufferably sure of himself. "I suggest, however, that we should both be better served to rejoin the festivities before we do something we shall later regret."

Letitia, still reeling from the momentous revelation that she was far from being indifferent to the detestable duke, wished only to be away from his disturbing presence.

"You may join the festivities if you wish, Your Grace," she replied testily, wishing him without remorse to the devil. "I, however, have had enough amusement for one day. I, sir, am going to bed."

"Why, I wonder, am I not surprised?" Vail drawled acerbically.

At that, Letitia came around, her eyes sparkling dangerously. "I beg your pardon. I'm afraid I fail to see the point of that observation."

"On the contrary, Lady Treadwell, you know precisely to what I am alluding. It is your custom, is it not, to retreat in the face of any unpleasantness. No doubt you will pardon my curiosity, but I cannot but wonder what drove you to absent yourself from England for an entire seven years."

"How dare you presume to know anything about me. Nothing drove me, unless it was a curiosity to see the world."

"You will pardon me if I find that difficult to believe. One does not deliberately choose exile from everything one has known unless there is a reason more compelling than curiosity. You will find that I know you better than you think, Lady Treadwell. I am, in the norm, an infallible judge of character."

"How very nice for you," Letitia bitterly retorted. "No doubt I am devastated to discover you think so little of me as to imagine I run at the least little thing."

"And yet, I suspect that you have already made up your mind to leave us in the morning. It would seem, after all, to fit the pattern, would it not? What excuse shall you leave behind? An urgent message perhaps, calling you away to London?"

Seething at the accuracy of his hateful speculations, Letitia turned on him with glorious, flashing eyes. "I am sorry to disappoint you," she said witheringly. "I should never give you that gratification, Your Grace. Or your mama. You may be sure that I am staying. I am, after all, Sally's guest, not yours, and, despite what you think of me, I am not in the habit of running out on my friends. Now, if you will excuse me, I find I have a splitting headache. Good night, Your Grace. I am retiring to bed.''

Letitia, gathering her dignity about her, retreated in the grand manner, her head up and her back rigidly straight.

Consequently, she did not see the duke staring after her with a faint smile of satisfaction.

Four

"I must have suffered a momentary aberration," declared Letitia to her Aunt Eleanore, who, seated on the settee, was observing with no little interest her niece's furious perambulations about the bedroom. "I was irrevocably set on leaving in the morning in order to avoid the very complications that have now perversely led me to declare to His Grace that wild horses could not drag me away. Good God, I should be confined to Bedlam for allowing myself to abandon all rationality. I vow I have never met a more infuriating specimen of the male gender. I daresay he even rivals my uncle for sheer perversity of character."

"Are you not being just a trifle harsh in your judgment?" Eleanore queried mildly. "It seems obvious to me that His Grace was merely acting out of concern for your welfare. One can hardly blame him, after all, for doubting your ability to fling a grown man over your head and pin him to the ground. It is hardly the sort of accomplishment one would normally look for in a female of refinement."

"No, but then I am not in the usual style, am I, dearest aunt?" Letitia pointed out, flinging herself down in the wing chair. "I have tried to live my life as Grandfather would have had me do—with relish, an inquisitive mind, and a keen sense of adventure. And with honor, Eleanore. Always with honor. I have never departed from these precepts until tonight. Honor dictates that I leave this house, since I have been brought here under false pretenses."

"Oh, stuff and nonsense," declared Eleanore, out of all patience with the younger woman. "You received an invitation, and in all good faith, you accepted it. That, my dear, is all there is to it."

Letitia, however, was in no mood to be dissuaded from her own interpretation of events. "Oh, if only it were that simple," she exclaimed, jumping up from the chair and beginning to pace again. "I shall not have it said that I have twice plotted to come between Vail and his promised brides. With the eye, no doubt, of usurping the duke's coronet for myself. It is too humiliating to contemplate."

"Are you quite certain that is what has set you off, Letitia?" Eleanore asked, studying her niece. "Or can it be that you find Vail more than a little attractive."

"Faith, Eleanore, you have an absolute knack for understatement," exclaimed Letitia, flinging up her hands in resignation. "I find him irresistibly attractive. Indeed, he is everything I have ever wished for in a man. And I should not scruple to become his mistress, were it not for one insurmountable obstacle."

"Good God, only one?" Eleanore demanded incredulously. "I can think of any number without even trying."

"Oh, but you are wrong. When you go straight to the heart of the matter, there is only one—Uncle Clarence." She turned to look at Eleanore. "I will not make Vail the object of Clarendon's rancor. Indeed, I should not wish that on anyone."

"I see," said Eleanore, suppressing a sigh. "Then I must presume that you have come to a decision regarding our future. Where is it to be this time?"

Letitia turned to gaze blindly out the window at the thick curtain of darkness. "The Americas, I think. There are numerous business opportunities there, and I have always entertained a curiosity about our colonies, both former and present."

"Ah, the Americas." Eleanore nodded, her facial expression studiously neutral. "I am sure they will prove—interesting."

Eleanore seemed uncommonly preoccupied in the wake of that pronouncement, and Letitia, feeling a trifle downpin, was not sorry when her aunt took her leave of her. She was equally glad that she had had the foresight to instruct Winifred, her abigail, not to wait up for her. She was in no mood for company, especially Winifred's on this night of all nights.

The abigail, a Welsh girl, was positively enamored of Valentine's Day and had not hesitated to instruct Letitia in the Welsh tradition of spooning. She had even brought forth the wooden spoon that her papa had long ago carved for her mama to wear on a ribbon about her neck upon the occasion of their having become betrothed to be married. It had all been very entertaining, hearing about the various customs that prevailed, but the last thing Letitia wished at that moment was to dwell on the one day out of the year devoted specifically to the pairing off of sweethearts.

Nevertheless, she could not suppress an amused smile when she found four bay leaves pinned to the corners of her pillow and a fifth to the middle. It occurred to her that it would be extremely unlikely that she would be able to sleep at all with the absurd things pricking her in the night, and even more farfetched that she might be moved by them to dream of her valentine.

Still, she had no wish to injure her abigail's feelings, she told herself. Turning the pillow over without removing the leaves, she laid her head down, only to discover that no matter how she plumped the feathers or positioned her head, it seemed she could not make herself comfortable. Indeed, it was well into the night before she at last succumbed to an exhausted slumber, disturbed by dreams of rapier blue eyes and hair the color of midnight.

She awoke early the next morning feeling tired and irritable and unable to bear another moment in her torturous bed. Impatiently flinging the bed covers aside, she rose and hurriedly donned her riding habit with the intention of going out for a gallop before the other guests began to put in an appearance at breakfast. The other unmarried females in the house might be peeping through their keyholes in the expectation of casting eyes on the first man to come along, but she had no wish to encounter anyone, least of all the duke or his cousin. Very likely, the former would demand she remain in the safety of the house, while the latter would insist on riding out with her.

It was easy enough to slip out of the house and around the back to the stables. She was even fortunate enough to find Brierly Tuck and her riding equipage without encountering a stable lad or groom. No stranger to saddling her own mount, she was soon mounted and well out of sight of the house on a trail that wound through the woods.

Though Brierly Tuck had not a mean bone in his body, the stallion was fresh and wanted to run, a sentiment with which Letitia was in full accord.

"Soon, Tuck," she crooned, holding the Thoroughbred to an easy canter until they both might work the chill from their muscles and joints.

Letitia loved the early morning better than any other part of the day. It was the time when everything was at its freshest and one's problems loomed rather less large and insurmountable. She inhaled deeply, glorying in the feel of the horse beneath her and the invigorating sense of being free of the house. The air was brisk, and the mist still hung like a gossamer veil over the forest of denuded beech trees and silver birch. The scent of mold-

ering leaves and rich, damp earth filled Letitia's nostrils.
Somewhere overhead a meadow pipit sang in flight, and
the stallion snorted and sidled as a startled hare bolted
almost from beneath its hooves to vanish into the gorse.
It was truly a glorious morning, she decided, wishing
she might ride on forever.

Inevitably, however, the irresistibly attractive Duke of
Vail impinged once more on her consciousness. She saw
him again as he had been the previous night at dinner—
charming, his marvellous eyes alight with interest and a
keen intelligence. And then again, later, those same orbs,
thrillingly piercing and altogether dangerous. She had
suffered a tumult of sensations not unlike what one
might feel standing on the brink of a precipice with a
strong wind at one's back. She could not recall ever having felt quite so gloriously alive before. And then the
sudden awakening to reality.

She, Letitia Treadwell, was hopelessly attracted to the
very same nobleman who had been the inadvertent cause
of her social ruin eight years before and under the very
same circumstances, and there was nothing she could do
about it. Nothing, after all, had really changed. Indeed,
she had been foolish beyond permission to imagine that
it had. It was the one thing Vail had done for her. He
had made her see she had been living in a fool's paradise
to suppose for one moment that it would be sufficient
simply to barricade herself away from the world. The
world, after all, had a nasty habit of impinging itself on
one in the most unexpected manner.

Hell and the devil confound it. It really was too bad
of fate to present her with the one man with whom she
might gladly have shared her life, only to erect insurmountable obstacles between them. What a waste it
would be to fling it all away, when it was so obvious that
she and Vail were ideally suited. Nevertheless, she could
not see any alternative.

And then, too, there was the matter of her Aunt Eleanore, who, though she would never confess it, was whole-heartedly weary of foreign travels. In all conscience, Letitia could not allow her aunt to go on sacrificing her own happiness for Letitia's sake. Letitia suffered a sharp pang of loss at the thought that when she embarked for the Americas, she would be going alone. Still, she vowed to make sure of it, and that Eleanore was provided with a more than comfortable income when she took up her life once more at Bath. It was the very least that she owed her aunt for all her years of devotion.

The thought gave Letitia very little comfort. Indeed, she was left feeling that the future looked rather more bleak than it had before. No sooner, however, did that thought cross her mind, than she immediately straightened in the saddle. How her grandfather would have scoffed at her for indulging in anything so blatantly absurd as self-pity! In all the years, she had never once heard him complain at the fate that had landed him in a wheelchair without the use of his legs. Nor had it curtailed his enormous enjoyment in life. Quite the contrary. He had made a celebration of it. Surely she could do no less!

Carried on a wild impulse, Letitia leaned forward and, calling into his ear, let the stallion out.

It was a wonderful, glorious ride. Brierly Tuck had been bred to run and required no urging. They raced through the trees, Letitia riding recklessly, her cheek pressed nearly to the stallion's neck to avoid low-hanging branches.

When at last she pulled the magnificent Tuck to a walk, she was glowing with excitement, her face flushed from the wind and the cold. She bent down, her hand going to the stallion's neck in affection and gratitude. Her lips parted to say his name, when suddenly she froze, her every sense instantly alert to the distant crash of underbrush and the pound of hooves behind her.

Letitia stiffened to attention, her nerves tingling. Just as suddenly as they had come, the sounds had ceased. Now, what the devil? Deciding that discretion was perhaps the better part of valor, she set Brierly Tuck in motion and, pausing now and again to listen, cut a wide arc through the trees that would gradually take her back in the direction of Marshgate.

Twenty minutes later, having succeeded in back tracking so that she pursued a course parallel to the trail to Marshgate, Letitia pulled her mount to a halt. Every muscle tensed, she listened for the telltale signs of her mysterious stalker. She heard it at once—the muffled thud of hooves brought swiftly to a halt, followed by silence. She felt the hairs rise on her nape, followed swiftly by the cold leap of anger.

The stalker had gained on her, indeed, was perceptibly closing in on her. The next instant she brought her reins down sharply across the stallion's rump.

Unused to such treatment, Brierly Tuck bolted.

A harsh curse rang out, and, apparently having abandoned all attempts at stealth, Letitia's shadower came after her in full pursuit.

The man at Tattersall's who had sold her the Thoroughbred had sworn there was not the stallion's match short of Vail's racing stables. Apparently he had not lied, reflected Letitia, her admiration for the gallant steed increasing by leaps and bounds as he left the other horse behind.

Nevertheless, Letitia felt a swift surge of relief when, some ten minutes later, the Thoroughbred thundered out of the woods into full view of Marshgate. Indeed, she was sure nothing had ever looked so beautiful as the steeped roofs and gables of the duke's country manor did at that moment. Less welcome, perhaps, was the sight of the duke himself in the act of dismounting from a handsome hack in the stableyard.

Faith, it needed only that, thought Letitia, fighting to check the stallion's headlong flight. She saw Vail turn, frowning. Then the Thoroughbred thundered into the yard and came to a plunging halt.

For an instant brown eyes met rapier blue across the distance, and the next, Vail strode forward to catch the stallion's bridle.

"Softly, my lad." Running his hand over the horse's sweat-dampened neck, Vail lifted his eyes to Letitia's with every expectation of an explanation for her manner of arrival.

Letitia, resisting the urge to glance over her shoulder to see if her pursuer was still behind her, drew in a long, tremulous breath and assayed a brilliant smile.

"Well, *that* was invigorating," she announced.

"Yes, no doubt," Vail agreed acerbically. "Putting your fate to the touch in a harebrained stunt, like riding neck or nothing through a forest, generally has that effect on one. Are you going to tell me what the devil you thought you were doing?"

"But it is obvious, is it not?" reflected Letitia with twin imps in her eyes. "It is Valentine's Day. I must surely have been hastening back to Marshgate so that you could have the honor of being the first man upon whom I might lay eyes. I believe, sir, that that makes you my valentine."

"I am naturally touched, Lady Treadwell, but hardly amused," Vail replied dampeningly. "I have, in fact, at the request of your aunt, spent the last hour scouring the woods for you. If I am to be your Valentine, I shall at least have the truth from you."

His Grace, it seemed, was in a devil of a mood, noted Letitia in no little bemusement. And what in the deuce was Eleanore about to send Vail out looking for her? Surely her aunt, of all people, must know she was well able to look after herself. Still, it seemed that she was to be given no choice in the matter save to tell Vail the details of her little adventure. "Oh, very well, Your Grace. If you insist." Dropping her reins, she held out her arms for the duke to help her down. Then, as strong hands spanned her waist and lifted her with ease from the saddle, she added, "As it happens, I was being followed."

The duke froze momentarily as he was, Letitia held at the end of his arms above his head. "Not that it is of any great significance," Letitia gasped, attributing her sudden feeling of light-headedness to the lofty altitude at which she hung suspended. "I was never in any danger of being taken."

"Naturally I must find that comforting," replied His Grace, acerbically. Deliberately, he lowered her to the ground. "I believe, however, I really must hear the whole of it."

Letitia shrugged and slapped Brierly Tuck fondly on the rump as a stable boy appeared to lead the stallion away. "Yes, somehow I expected as much, though there is really not that much to tell. I never got a look at him and so can neither describe nor identify him."

Letitia, insisting that she had not the least notion who the man was or why he was following her, related the morning's events in humorous detail, which revealed nothing of the fear that she had felt. After all, nothing had happened. She had kept a level head and was back at Marshgate none the worse for wear.

The duke, it soon proved, however, was not disposed to dismiss the affair so lightly. Clearly he blamed himself for not having foreseen such an eventuality in light of the previous night's intruder. Indeed, he was positively grim by the time she had finished.

"I suggest, Lady Treadwell," he said, with a singular lack of humor, "that you think twice before you take it into your head to go off riding by yourself without bothering to inform anyone. Had I known you desired an outing, I should have seen that you had an escort."

"But of course you would. I never doubted it," Letitia answered reassuringly. "Which is why I did not mention it. The last thing I wished was company."

A single imperious eyebrow arched toward the duke's hairline. The devil, he thought. She had not seemed so displeased last night with his company.

"I believe, Lady Treadwell," he pointed out, greatly tempted to throttle the impertinent little wretch, "that you had company nevertheless. If you find the thought of mine distasteful, at least you may be sure that you would have been safe in it."

"Oh, dear. Now I have hurt your feelings," Letitia exclaimed apologetically as they turned to stroll along the rail fence toward the house. "I never said I found your company distasteful, Your Grace. On the contrary, I think you are quite possibly the most attractive man I have ever met; and, if you are offering me your protection, you may be sure I should be greatly tempted to accept it. As to my safety, however, you really need not concern yourself. I am well able to see to that myself."

Had she meant to elicit a response from him, she was not to be disappointed. A muscular and wholly masculine hand planted itself on the fence rail in front of her, effectively impeding any further forward progress.

"I beg your pardon, Lady Treadwell," Vail drawled in deceptively mild tones, "but I believe I must make sure I understand you perfectly."

"Naturally, Your Grace," Letitia rejoined, not in the least put out to find herself impaled by eyes like glittery points of steel. "Indeed, it is what I have come to expect in you."

"You flatter me, Lady Treadwell," said the duke ironically.

"Not at all, Your Grace," replied Letitia reasonably.

"We are both highly intelligent, rational beings, after all. I daresay there is nothing we dare not discuss."

"Indeed, it would seem not," His Grace agreed with obvious feeling.

Upon which, Letitia smiled encouragingly. "But of course there is not. How absurd it would be to suppose otherwise. Now, what, exactly, is it that you wish to have clarified?"

Vail, gazing down into remarkably beautiful, guileless eyes, wondered if he had lost a grip on his sanity. "Am I to understand, Lady Treadwell, that you have just declared yourself amenable to an offer of carte-blanche?"

"Not at all, Your Grace. I believe I am not such a fool. I should never enter into an arrangement based on unlimited authority. I have my independence to consider, and while I might enjoy the pleasures of your company, I should detest being made to feel I was your rented property. Indeed, in such a case, I might as well be your wife, whose distinction of being property that has been purchased, no matter how properly, is hardly any distinction at all. I should think a liaison between two equals of independent means would be a better term for what I had in mind. In such a case, I should far prefer to be your mistress than your wife."

"Should you indeed?" murmured Vail, who considered the distinction he would incur upon a wife rather more than insignificant. "I am, as you so readily pointed out, on the verge of matrimony, Lady Treadwell. What makes you think I shall be on the lookout for a mistress?"

"But it is obvious, is it not? You, sir, have made a business contract, and while it is true a marriage can be conducted on the lines of business, I can think of few business partners with whom I should enjoy climbing into bed on a regular basis, can you?"

"You would seem to have an intriguing aptitude for analogy," observed His Grace, apparently much struck

at her originality of thought. "No doubt you will pardon
my curiosity, Lady Treadwell, but I cannot help but wonder if you are speaking hypothetically or from the benefit
of worldly experience."

"Oh, come now, Your Grace," Letitia answered, laughing, as she ducked beneath his arm. "You need not beat
about the bush with me. What you really want to know
is whether or not my virtue is intact. And that, my dear
Valentine," she added, flashing a look at him over her
shoulder as she strode blithely away, "you will simply
have to discover for yourself."

The little rogue! thought Vail, keenly appreciative of
the lovely eyes, which had been alight with devils of laughter. He was not and never had been, with the exception
of his one error in judgment, normally prey to a pretty
face. He had, in fact, had his surfeit of eligible young
beauties. It was not, however, Lady Treadwell's undeni-
able beauty that piqued his interest or even her outrageous flaunting of the proprieties that made him want to
take her by the arms and shake some sense into her. He
suspected that despite her unquestionable originality of
thought, she was exactly what she took great pains to
hide—a green, innocent girl, who, no matter how vehe-
mently she professed to be able to take care of herself,
was not nearly so invulnerable as she wished others to
believe.

It was that indefinable air of mystery about her, indeed, the unshakable feeling that in some sort of trouble
though she might be, she would never ask his help, or
anyone else's, for that matter, that threatened to drive
him to the brink of distraction.

Damn the woman and her blasted pride! Who the devil
was she and why should someone be spying on her?

That she was, of course, the daughter of the former
Marquis of Clarendon, he had learned at dinner the
night before, and his mother had not hesitated to further

enlighten him as to the nature of Lady Treadwell's disastrous come-out some eight years before. In spite of her inauspicious introduction to Marshgate, he found it difficult to believe that this could be the same female who had disgraced herself at Almack's by stumbling into his erstwhile bride-to-be. He recalled that evening with an ironic appreciation of that fateful incident, which, in ruining Lady Treadwell, had spared him the humiliation of a public scandal. It was the same night that his mysterious angel had taken it upon herself to broach him outside the card room with the information concerning the deceitful Harriet's intention to elope.

Wrapped in an absurdly oversized cloak that had made it impossible in the dimly lit foyer to distinguish either her face or her form, she had obviously been on the verge of tears, and yet she had managed to retain her composure long enough to tell him about the coach in which Harriet's lover waited. Swept with a cold rage, he had only just had enough presence of mind to bundle the distraught child into her carriage and send her on her way before her involvement in the farce could be discovered. Indeed, in his haste to reach that other, waiting coach, he had forgotten even to ask for his angel's name.

In retrospect, he could only be grateful he had arrived in the alley too late to discover the identity of Harriet's mysterious lover, he reflected grimly. No doubt sensing something amiss, the villain had bolted, leaving Vail with only a glimpse of the coach before it vanished around the corner.

In the aftermath of the fiasco, Harriet had been bundled off to Ireland, where she had been induced to wed an elderly squire, and Vail, after placing a brief notice in the *Gazette* that the marriage was off, had offered his services to British Intelligence. It was the one excuse he had for his failure to apprehend the night before that it might be Lady Treadwell who was in danger from the intruder and not himself. Attempts, after all, had been made before on his life. It was hardly reasonable to suppose that he should have had any expectation that this time it might be one of his guests the intruder was after.

He would not make that mistake again. Indeed, it was time he took advantage of his not inconsiderable resources to discover why the little baggage had lied to him.

It was hardly to be expected that her luck could hold out forever, Letitia reflected sardonically an hour later as she read the name on the billet she had just drawn from the valentine box. Good God, it would have to be Clevenger. No doubt she should have been more trusting and taken Sally up on her offer to draw the billet for her. Indeed, in retrospect, it was foolish to suppose that the duke's niece could contrive to pick out Vail's billet from all the others. Sally was precocious, but she was no magician.

"Pray do not keep us in suspense," Lady Margaret called thrillingly, waving her own billet about in one hand as though it were a victory flag. And why should she not, Letitia reflected dourly. Lady Margaret had not drawn Anthony Clevenger.

"Oh, very well," Letitia said at Felicity Ingersol's further urging. "If you must know, it is Mr. Anthony Clevenger."

"Oh, you poor dear," exclaimed Miss Ingersol. "I do not wonder that you wished to keep it to yourself. I suppose, however, if someone must have him, I am glad it is you and not I."

"Felicity! How perfectly dreadful you are," said a scandalized Miss Hortence Melcourt, who, no doubt because of her insistence on wearing her spectacles, had been preserved from any intimate contact with the gentleman in question. "Surely he is not so bad as that?"

"Oh, no," agreed Miss Ingersol, rolling her eyes at Lady Margaret, her bosom bow. "I daresay one would be perfectly safe in his company—if one were excessively plain and utterly without a feather to fly with."

The ladies, who had gathered in the downstairs withdrawing room in order to draw names from the valentine box without the gentlemen in attendance, broke into appreciative laughter at this pointed observation from Miss Ingersol. All, that was, save for Miss Adeline Pemberton, who could not feel quite comfortable gossiping about her future husband's cousin, and Miss Laura Gilcrest, who, far from being amused, took immediate exception to hearing Mr. Clevenger castigated.

"Well, I think you are being horribly unfair," she declared heatedly, her color high with indignation. "Mr. Clevenger may indeed be a gambler, a womanizer, and a rake, but I cannot think he is wholly without his merits. I find him to be handsome, witty, and thoughtful and charming and-and—perfectly delightful as a dinner companion," she ended defiantly.

"Laura Gilcrest! You have a *tendre* for him!" exclaimed Lady Margaret, suddenly enlightened.

"And, if I do, what of it?" Miss Gilcrest demanded. "It is not, after all, as if I were one of you. I do not have to be so nice in my tastes. After all, I cannot hope that a Lord Eppington or any of your other fine gentlemen will be moved to offer for one whose father is tainted by trade. I am, if nothing else, practical, and if Mr. Anthony Clevenger were by some miracle to return my admiration, I should be proud to accept him just as he is. I daresay all he needs is a woman's steadying hand to bring out the best in him."

An uncomfortable silence fell over the room in the wake of Miss Gilcrest's rather too frank declaration. It was true, after all. She might indeed have had the good fortune to attend the same ladies' academy as had Miss Pemberton and, having befriended the younger girl when no one else demonstrated the least inclination to have done, had gained an admittance into the exalted company of her betters that would not otherwise have been accorded her. The fact remained, however, that not having been born to it, she could never hope to be what she was not, except, perhaps, that she married a gentleman with the credentials she lacked.

Letitia, herself guilty of having judged Miss Gilcrest on face value, was made suddenly to see the young woman through Laura's own eyes, and it struck her that while she rather liked the clear-sighted, unassuming person beneath the gushing facade of one thrust in the role of nouveau riche, she was not at all sure she liked herself very much at that moment.

"You are quite right," she said, smiling gravely at Miss Gilcrest. "We have perhaps been unfair to judge Mr. Clevenger harshly. I daresay anyone who has someone like you to champion him must have more to his credit than immediately meets the eye."

"He is, at the very least, a man blessed by good fortune," surprisingly observed Miss Adeline Pemberton. "I pray for your sake, Laura, that he will one day be made to realize it—before he tosses his one real chance at happiness away."

She said it with such gravity that Letitia could not doubt that she had meant it sincerely. Indeed, if one did not know better, Letitia soberly reflected, one might assume Miss Pemberton was speaking from her own experience.

It had long been the tradition that though both the ladies and the gentlemen drew names for valentines, only the lady's name that fell to a gentleman was accounted as binding. Miss Adeline Pemberton, however, had suggested the rules be changed, solely for adding to the entertainment. The gentlemen would draw separately from the ladies, and neither revealing to the other whose name they held, they would each attempt to guess at their valentine's identity based on hints and anonymously sent valentine messages.

Letitia, who had not the least intention of wooing her secret valentine with hints or messages, could only be grateful for the gift of anonymity. Indeed, she was even moved to suggest privately to Laura Gilcrest that no one would be the wiser should a lady choose to send a valentine to one who was not, strictly speaking, her valentine. No doubt the truth could be made known at a later date, purely at the discretion of the sender.

She was left feeling that Miss Gilcrest understood her meaning perfectly and that furthermore, the unfortunate victim of love would not hesitate to act on the suggestion.

Mr. Clevenger having thus been happily disposed of, it never occurred to her to consider the other side of the coin—the fact that her name had been drawn by one of the gentlemen. It was consequently with no little surprise that she arrived at her room some time later to discover a paper heart hanging on the door handle and, thrust beneath her door, a card from her anonymous valentine.

Constructed on paper embossed by pinpricks of varying thicknesses, it was a lovely "flower-cage" valentine, sometimes called a "cob-web" because of the delicate thread, which, when pulled, caused the figure on the front to be raised to reveal a message of love underneath. In this case, the figure was of two plump red apples surrounded by basil leaves, iris, and dill, and the message read:

> "Though forbidden fruit,
> It doth me suit
> To dare a bite
> For love's delight
> And thee, Valentine.
> My heart divine."

It was, she saw, a message within a message, cleverly
wrought, for the herbs themselves were obviously chosen
to convey a particular meaning. Basil might mean love,
good wishes, or hate, which, had it not been for the iris
and the dill, she might have taken to mean the gentleman,
though he wished her only good, was uncertain as to his
true feelings toward her. The other two herbs, however,
would seem to make little sense in such a context. An iris,
after all, denoted a pure heart, courage, and faith, while
dill conveyed a message of good cheer and survival in the
face of odds. All of which led her to deduce that the gentleman meant her to apprehend that his good wishes
stood between her and the ill will of another. Having
perceived that her heart was pure, he desired her not to
despair of her safety in the face of odds, but to be of
courage and good faith.

It was an astounding message, one which would seem
to make little sense when one got right down to it, she
reflected, sinking down onto the settee. Indeed, unless
one took into account her morning's adventure, she
could not think why anyone would suppose she was in
any sort of danger. Of course, if it were because of the
events in the wood, then it would seem to eliminate all
of the gentlemen save for one. Only Vail had been privy
to the incident.

But, no, it was preposterous to think that Vail had sent
her the valentine. It was far too obvious a clue. He might
as well have signed his name had it been he. Obviously
she had misread the message. No doubt she had been
right in the first place, and her anonymous admirer had
meant to convey the ambiguity of his feelings for her.
As for the rest, he considered her pure of heart, coura-
geous and faithful and consequently wished her to be
of good cheer, though it was unlikely his affection would
survive in the face of odds. That would not, however,

seem to explain the peculiarity of her valentine's last line: "My heart divine."

Or perhaps it was not peculiar at all. The word *divine*, after all, used as an adjective, could mean something so very unexceptional as that she had been enshrined in his heart as a goddess or some such thing. The period, however, at the end of the preceding line must surely make *divine* a verb, in which case the meaning would be entirely different. Indeed, the first time she had read it, she had seen it as a command or a plea to divine the gentleman's intentions, to understand his heart in this matter. She had, in fact, taken it almost in the context of a warning. But a warning of what? That though it was forbidden fruit to love her, he meant to have her? That though she was in peril from one who wished her ill, she could depend on him to protect her?

"Good God!" she exclaimed, springing in disgust to her feet. "It is only a silly valentine, hardly worth the effort of trying to decipher it. And certainly not worth driving oneself to the brink of distraction over it."

Determined to banish all thought of it from her mind, she thrust it out of sight in a bureau drawer, only to draw it immediately out again. Telling herself that silly or not, it was pretty to look at, she propped it against the vanity mirror. Unfortunately, she found she could not keep her eyes off it. Indeed, no matter where she went in the room, the cursed thing inevitably drew her back to it to speculate who had sent it and with what intent.

At last, in a sudden fit of temper, she slammed it down on its face on the vanity and, flinging a cashmere shawl around her shoulders, fled the room as if pursued.

The earlier mist had turned to rain when Letitia made her way downstairs again to the withdrawing room, which she was not displeased to find deserted. The other guests, she surmised, were either in the card room pursuing their favorite pastime or were about constructing valentines for their secret sweethearts. She stood for a moment before the fire, grateful for its warmth, and toyed with the notion of summoning the carriage. She felt restless and vaguely discontented, as though she were a prisoner in the duke's country manor; and she could not help but wish herself snug in her own cozy cottage with a cup of hot chocolate close to hand and a book in her lap.

What she most heartily did *not* wish was to turn at the sound of a step and discover Anthony Clevenger limned in the doorway and looking inordinately pleased with himself.

"Lady Treadwell," he declared, coming the rest of the way into the room. "I confess I am not surprised. Indeed, you will be pleased to know that I should have been surprised only if it had been someone other than you."

"I'm afraid, Mr. Clevenger," Letitia informed him, "that 'pleased' does not begin to describe what I am. It occurs to me, however, that you must be laboring under a misconception. I am here purely by chance, while you, it would seem, are not."

Undeterred, Clevenger drew insidiously near her. "Come now, Lady Treadwell. There's no need to play missish with me. I have been perfectly aware since the first moment I laid eyes on you that you are not altogether indifferent to me."

The coxcomb! fumed Letitia. If only he realized the source of her interest in him, he would not be so bloody sure of himself. "How very perceptive of you." She smiled, moving casually away so as not to become entrapped between the wolf and the sofa. "I daresay, however, that you do not even recall the first time you laid eyes on me. I, on the other hand, recognized you at once."

"I do seem to have that effect on women," preened the coxcomb. "On the other hand, I should not be so sure, if I were you, that my memory is so faulty as not to recall the memorable event of our first encounter."

Letitia, staring at him, wondered just how much she could believe him. He would seem to be remarkably unmoved by the reunion, considering the nature of that encounter—and what had come of it, thanks to her. "Should I not?" she hedged. "Eight years, however, is a long time, and I believe I should not be mistaken were I to say I have changed a great deal since then."

"Has it been so many?" the gentleman smoothly countered. "How time does fly. If the years have worked their change in you, you may be sure it is only the transformation of a bud into a full-blossomed flower. You are even more beautiful than my memory accords."

"You are too kind, sir," replied Letitia, neatly maneuvering a potted palm between them. "You, I should venture to say, have not changed at all."

"Then you would be mistaken, my sweet," the gentleman said, sidestepping the obstacle with the ease, no doubt, of long practice. "I am, if anything, more impatient than ever to take up where last we left off."

Letitia, backing before his determined onslaught, did not doubt it for a moment. Indeed, it occurred to her that it was time to resort to more forceful means of dissuasion. "Hold, sir. I believe I must warn you not to come a step closer."

The gentleman, observing her with no little bemusement assume the first position of *Chun-gi*, her knees slightly bent and her hands up before her, chose not to heed her warning.

"On the contrary, Lady Treadwell. You did, after all, invite me to this assignation. I not only intend to come closer, but I promise to make you pay dearly for the eight years you have eluded me."

The thought flashed in her mind as he made a lunge for her that she had undoubtedly found her stalker. Catching hold of his arm, she shifted her weight and, using his momentum, sent him flying, head over heels, over her shoulder. Before the dust could even settle, indeed, before the bric-a-brac had ceased to rattle in the wake of Mr. Clevenger's resounding landing, she moved to pin him, facedown on the floor, one arm clamped painfully at the small of his back—just as Miss Laura Gilcrest chose to make an appearance through the hall doorway and Vail, apparently having made the same decision, entered, utterly soaked and streaming water, through the French windows that opened on to the rose garden.

"Lady Treadwell!" shrieked the lady, horrified to behold Mr. Clevenger spread eagle on the floor with Lady Treadwell crouched over him in a manner that could only be described as highly improper. "And Mr. Clevenger. Faith, what have you done to him!"

Five

"Why, nothing very much, Miss Gilcrest," drawled the duke, a suspicious gleam in the look he bent upon Letitia. "I believe my cousin tripped and Lady Treadwell was looking to see if he has hurt himself. Is that not right, ma'am?"

Letitia, meeting Vail's eyes, only just managed to quell an unwitting choke of laughter. "You are most perceptive, Your Grace," she replied. Hastily, if somewhat belatedly, she released the downed man's arm and rose to her feet.

Miss Gilcrest eyed them both with obvious skepticism. "But I am sure I saw Lady Treadwell—well, for want of a better word—*grappling* with Mr. Clevenger," she insisted in a scandalized tone. "Indeed, I should almost say she flipped him in the air as if he were little more than a rag doll, upon which she proceeded to pounce on him in a most unseemly manner."

"No, did she?" murmured the duke, turning his gaze with apparent acute interest on the furiously blushing culprit. "Really, Miss Gilcrest. I daresay you are mistaken. Only look at her. Does she appear to you as if she could flip a grown man over her head?"

Letitia, finding herself the object of an intense scrutiny, resisted the urge to add another masculine victim to her list of infamies and instead assayed a demure attitude in keeping with one unjustly accused. Vail, she vowed, would pay for his entertainment at a later date, no matter that he was attempting to salvage the last shreds of her reputation.

Laura Gilcrest, who could not but question Letitia's verisimilitude in light of the peculiar circumstances attendant in the room, visibly faltered nonetheless. "Well, I suppose I could have been in error."

"But of course you could," applauded the duke. "It was, in fact, only another of those unfortunate accidents which seem to attend Lady Treadwell with distressing regularity."

It was at that point that the unfortunate victim, who until that moment had lain stunned and for the most part forgotten, quite audibly groaned and began to show signs of life.

Instantly, Laura Gilcrest dropped to her knees beside him and tenderly lifted his head to her lap. "Mr. Clevenger, you poor dear," she crooned, smoothing the tousled hair from his forehead. "Pray tell me you are not seriously injured."

The gentleman, considerably shaken and not a little distracted, stared up at his ministering angel with a distinctly dazed expression.

"Ecod, what hit me?" he demanded thickly.

"Why, nothing but the floor, sir," Letitia kindly informed him. "You tripped, it would seem, and all but knocked yourself unconscious."

Unconvinced, Clevenger frowned in what could only be described as a ferocious manner. "The devil, you say. I never tripped before in my life. Indeed, I seem to recall—"

"I suggest that you do not try to talk," the duke was quick to advise before Clevenger could finish whatever he had been about to say. "You have sustained a nasty fall and should no doubt lie still until you have your wits once more about you. I daresay you will put everything in its proper perspective when you are able to think more clearly."

The wisdom of Vail's speech could hardly have been lost on Clevenger, who, after all, could hardly have wished to have it bandied about that he had been thrown by a woman. "Exactly so, Cousin," he grumbled, running a hand through his hair. "I confess I am feeling a trifle dizzy. I suppose it is not inconceivable that I might have tripped." Shifting his glance to Letitia, he eyed her with what might have been a reluctant, if wary, admiration. "Perhaps when I have recovered, Lady Treadwell, you would not mind setting me straight on some of the finer points of what happened. It would seem to be a trifle vague in my mind. For instance, the truth is I cannot recall at all where we might have met before or under what circumstances. You were quite right about that."

"I see," replied Letitia, who was indeed enlightened by the gentleman's confession. If he in truth had not recognized her, he could hardly have been her pursuer in the woods. What motive would he have had, after all? "And of course I should be only too glad to discuss it sometime with you, except that there really would be no point in it. It was all a very long time ago and very likely better left forgotten. I suggest, instead, that you turn your attention to more pertinent matters. Whom, for instance, were you really supposed to find waiting in this room?"

Perhaps something in her voice or her manner convinced him that it was, indeed, better left alone. It was certain, at any rate, that he showed no inclination to pursue the matter further. On the contrary, Miss Gilcrest's solicitous presence seemed to loom suddenly with new and intriguing possibilities. Rather than accept the duke's offer to help him to his feet, Clevenger declared he was as yet far too unsteady to attempt anything so very arduous as that must be and that no doubt he would do better right where he was. He was in the process of making inquiries about Miss Gilcrest's admirable papa when Vail firmly led Letitia out into the hall and, from there, straight to his study.

It was only then, upon finding herself disturbingly alone with Vail in the cozy confines of his private sanctum, that she was brought to an abrupt awareness of his sodden state. Demanding to know what he was thinking to stand about in his wet things, she proceeded to strip him of his many-caped greatcoat and curly-brimmed beaver and, turning these over to a bemused butler, ordered Vail to go at once and warm himself before the fire.

"It is the shabbiest thing," she said, unreasonably annoyed at his careless lack of concern for his own well-being. "Very likely you will catch your death, and everyone will say it was all due to the fact that Miss Letitia Treadwell was in attendance at your house party. Another of the unfortunate accidents like the one that befell poor Clevenger."

"Very possibly, Lady Treadwell," drawled the duke with a suspicious twitch at the corner of his lips. "By the way, what *did* you do to my unfortunate cousin? I confess I am prey to an overwhelming curiosity, having only myself just escaped what I believe must have been a distressingly similar fate."

"Well, I did warn Clevenger," Letitia said virtuously, "just as I warned you. *He,* however, preferred a demonstration. I employed the ancient Chinese art of self-defense known as kung fu, a little something I picked up in the Orient."

It occurred to Vail as he watched the remarkable Lady Treadwell cross to the grog tray and pour a brandy that it might be wise to inquire at a later date what other little oddities she might have picked up in the Orient.

"Grandfather was used to say that there was nothing

like brandy for what ails a man," she informed him a moment later as, handing him the glass, she waited for him to down a swallow.

"Your grandfather sounds a wise man," Vail observed, swirling the glass and testing the aroma before raising it to his lips. "I'm sorry I never had the chance to know him."

Letitia smiled and turned away to gaze into the fire. "I daresay he would have liked you. In some ways you remind me of him. I miss him frightfully sometimes."

Vail, observing the play of firelight in her hair, propped an elbow on the mantelpiece. "And your parents?"

Letitia's eyes grew clouded. As though chilled, she hugged her arms across her breast. "Of course I miss them, too. I thought the world must surely come to an end when I lost them. And then, when Uncle Clarence—" She stopped. Then shrugging, she confessed with a twisted smile, "I'm afraid I do not get on at all well with Uncle Clarence. He and the family do not approve of me, and I cannot bring myself to care." At last she looked at Vail. "Does that shock you terribly?"

"No, should it?" Vail asked, watching her over the rim of his glass.

Letitia laughed. "I suppose nothing I might do or say after the past two days would shock anyone, except, perhaps, Aunt Eleanore. I am gloriously sunk beneath reproach."

Carefully, Vail set his glass on the mantelpiece. "For which you no doubt think to be congratulated."

Letitia glanced at him, suddenly wary. "No, hardly that. Difficult as it may be to believe, I did not set out to disgrace myself."

"I never supposed that you did. And if you had, you failed abominably. You are, if anything, an unmitigated success, Lady Treadwell. I daresay if you were to put your fate to the touch in London, you would soon find you were all the rage. Contrary to your expectations, the world is always eager for novelty, and you, my dear, are an Original."

He had spoken strangely, with an odd sort of cynical twist to his lips, and Letitia, unreasonably hurt by what she perceived to be his sarcasm, reacted in a manner best calculated to arouse his anger.

"Then it is fortunate," she retorted, "that I have no intention of wasting my time in London. Far from wishing to be the rage, I should sooner be what I was judged before. Not an Original, Your Grace, but an absurd little misfit whose only redeeming virtues were my name and a more than generous inheritance. Even they were not enough, however, to compensate for my obvious defects or to redeem me in the wake of the Unfortunate Incident."

"The world can be cruel," Vail conceded. "I should never dispute that."

Abruptly, Letitia turned on him. "It is people like you who make it so. A single word from you, a glance even, is enough to make the difference. Do you, I wonder, even consider the feelings of those you deem beneath your notice?"

An arrogant eyebrow arched toward Vail's hairline. "No, Lady Treadwell," he admitted evenly, "but then, I did not make the rules. Nor do I trifle with the affections of young, unmarried females. To do so would serve only to raise false expectations. Is that what I did to you, Lady Treadwell? Did I fail to notice you?"

It was a trap, and she only just recognized it in time. The devil, to bait her! "If you did, Your Grace, it was only what everyone else did, and therefore you can hardly stand accused. Besides, you were already promised. I was speaking in generalities."

"You, Lady Treadwell, are a liar." He watched with

interest as the color flooded her cheeks. He had landed a blow beneath her guard, but she was holding herself well in hand. It was time to try a new tack while she was still off balance. "Tell me why someone would wish to have you followed. Oh, no, do not bother to deny it." He smiled grimly as she furiously clamped her mouth shut. "You have not asked me why I should have chosen to go out in a rain storm. Are you not in the least curious?"

Letitia shrugged with a fine show of indifference. "Should I be, Your Grace? It is hardly my affair what you choose to do."

"But in this case, it is, you see. I was tracking your mysterious stalker to his lair. Unfortunately, he gave me the slip in the rain."

No doubt he was gratified to see her face drain of all its earlier color. "Why the devil should you do any such thing, Your Grace?" she demanded, furious at him for taking such a risk. "I never asked you to. Indeed, I should vastly prefer that you not put yourself out on my account."

It was a mistake, she realized, almost as soon as the words were out.

Vail's face set with grim certainty. "Then you admit the villain was after you."

Letitia turned away, her heart pounding unreasonably beneath her breast.

"I admit nothing of the kind. It seemed that he was after me, but perhaps it was only because I was the one who was there. It might have been anyone," she pointed out. Her temper snapped, and she came about to face him. "Why are you quizzing me? Had I known I should be submitted to a Spanish Inquisition, I should have remained in my room."

"No doubt, Lady Treadwell," Vail agreed, insufferably sure of himself. "You are here, however, and I will know why you are lying to me. You may start by telling me where we have met before. Was it in London, when you made your come-out?"

"I do not know why you persist in thinking I am some low creature who delights in telling falsehoods," Letitia flung coldly back at him, "but you may be sure I do not intend to stay here and be insulted."

"Oh, no, Lady Treadwell, not yet." Vail's hand on her wrist stopped her from bolting from his presence. "First, you will tell me what I wish to know."

Letitia stiffened, furious that his very nearness was enough to make her feel suddenly weak and giddy. Even worse, however, she had the most lowering thought that in another moment she would betray herself utterly by flinging herself into his arms.

"Trust me, Lady Treadwell," she heard Vail saying, his face a disturbingly scant few inches from hers. "You will not be hurt by it, I promise, and I have decided, you see, that I really must know. We have met before, have we not?"

"You attended my coming out ball," she said in flat, unemotional tones. "Lord Wiggenton, who was a particular friend of my father's, formally introduced us. I should not refine on it, however, Your Grace," Letitia added bitterly. "There was little reason for you to remember it or me. You may be sure I should never hold it against you."

Vail stared at her, obviously not satisfied. "And that was all? We never met again under different circumstances?"

"It was the Season, Your Grace. We had occasion to come together in the normal course of events. You were kind enough to dance with me once at Lady Trowbridge's ball. I did not distinguish myself, however, except that you were moved to advise me that the floor was perfectly safe and did not require my constant vigilance."

A wry smile twisted at his lips. "No doubt that explains

it, then," he said. "I should have remembered had I seen those eyes."

Letitia, who had no answer to that observation, stirred at last, restively. "Yes, well, who can say what will stick in one's memory. I should not dwell on it, were I you." Deliberately she looked into his eyes. "You may be sure that I do not."

The next moment, she turned and walked out the door.

Vail stood staring after her; then at last, frowning, he seated himself before the desk and drew what appeared to be a square, folded envelope from a drawer. Leaning forward in his chair, he carefully unfolded the four doubled flaps, each bearing an intricately worked design so that when the whole lay flat on the desk before him, it gave the appearance of a kaleidoscope of hearts, Cupids, and arrows, with at its center a single lock of dark brown hair.

Softly he cursed. The puzzle purse, for so it was, had already occasioned him a deal of perplexity and promised more. He had been convinced that he had correctly deciphered the cryptic messages, but now he was not so sure. And yet what other meaning could they have? he asked himself, reading again the bewildering jumble of verses.

As in every valentine of this sort, reading the verses in the proper order was the key to solving the puzzle, and he had already wasted a deal of time on the solution that lay before him. Taken at face value, it was a rather silly piece of jumbled rhymes, but he could not persuade himself that they did not contain a pertinent message, as once again he read over them in the order he had settled upon.

> "A Cupid's arrow, misfired, darts.
> A gallant knight a love forswears.
> A lady fair a sorrow bears.
> Lonely hearts in a sea of hearts.
> A Cupid's arrow darts.

Sea to sea, a harbor sought.
Heart to heart, a message brought.
A Valentine of joinéd hearts."

He had no doubt, at least, who his anonymous valentine
was. The lock of hair identified her beyond question.
Lady Treadwell, after all, was the only woman at
Marshgate with hair that shade of deep, rich brown. From
which he could only deduce that she had intended him
to know at once she was his valentine and that furthermore, she saw them both as the objects of Cupid's cursed
"misfired" darts. The theme, moreover, would seem altogether too coincidental not to be deliberate. She *had*
come within an inch of piercing him with an arrow only
the day before, with the result that he had not, from that
moment on, been able to banish her from his mind. It
had seemed to follow, then, that the first few lines must
necessarily refer not only to his own earlier, aborted wedding plans, but to the distinct possibility that he had somehow been responsible for causing Letitia Treadwell a
sorrow so deeply felt that she had chosen exile from England rather than face him again.

Suddenly everything had seemed to fall into place—
her violent start of what could only be recognition of a
man she knew, but had hardly expected to discover was
her host. She had called him Ulverston, a circumstance
that he had found singular even then. She had lied about
knowing him very probably out of wounded pride and
because he so obviously had no recollection of her. It
even explained her wager with Clevenger, which was no
doubt made in order to prove she was just as outrageous
as she believed he, Vail, thought her to be. A wry grin
tugged at his lips as he recalled her even more outrageous proposal to become his mistress.

Damn the woman! There *must* have been something
more significant between them than the innocuous

events she described—significant, that was, at least in
her own mind. As for himself, he had been a bloody fool
in love with Harriet Willet. He had been far too blinded
by his own obsession to even look at another female.

Well, he was no longer blinded. He saw exactly where
his happiness lay. It remained only for him to resolve
the puzzle that was Letitia Treadwell.

Letitia fled the duke's study, her heart pounding. Intent on reaching the safe haven of her room, she was
less than pleased to hear herself peremptorily sum-
moned by the dowager duchess.

"Your Grace?" she said, assaying a somewhat less than
convincing smile as she turned to behold the elderly lady
making her way down the hall toward her.

The dowager, who had been conspicuously absent that
morning from the valentine drawing, appeared surprisingly spry, considering the rumor that she had taken to
her bed the night before feeling somewhat under the
weather.

"You are deucedly hard to find, Lady Treadwell," Lady
Honoria announced without preamble. "Where the
devil do you take yourself off to when you are not spilling tea on your hostess or shooting arrows at your host?"

"No doubt I am off plotting murder and mayhem or
some equally pleasant pastime, Your Grace," Letitia announced airily. "Forgive me for not being where I apparently was supposed to be. It is a lamentable fault of mine."

"One of many, Lady Treadwell," the dowager did not
hesitate to inform her. "Impertinence being not the least
of them. You caused a package to be delivered to me,
the contents of which were curious, to say the least. And
pray do not deny it."

"That the contents were curious, Your Grace?" Letitia

queried innocently. "I should never dream of it. What, may I ask, were they?"

"You know very well what they were," the dowager snapped. "A revolting mixture of leaves, roots, and stems. With written instructions as to how to prepare them, presumably for consumption."

"I see, and did you consume some small portion of them?" Letitia asked.

"You must know very well that I did, thanks to the manipulations of my granddaughter, over whom you have worked your influence. No doubt you will be equally glad to know that I have, as a result, detected some little improvement in my indisposition, for which I thank you. That is all I wished to say, Lady Treadwell. Unless you would care to join me for tea in the withdrawing room. I believe the others are already gathered there."

"You are very kind, Your Grace," replied Letitia, resisting the urge to smile. How greatly that grudging expression of gratitude must have cost the old dragon! "Perhaps in a moment or two. I was just going to my room to freshen up a bit; then I shall be pleased to join you."

"As you wish," grumbled the dowager. "Only don't be too long. Sally will be particularly disappointed if you fail to put in an appearance."

Letitia stared in startled disbelief after the retreating dowager. In her gruff manner, she had let it be known that Letitia was no longer persona non grata. "You may be sure that I shall come, Your Grace," she called after Lady Honoria, who was already halfway to the stairway. "I should never wish to disappoint Sally."

Well over half an hour had passed, however, when the dowager duchess was finally compelled to order the tea tray to be brought, and Letitia had yet to keep her promise. It was another ten before the duke strode into the withdrawing room and, immediately noting the conspicuous absence of three of his guests, was moved to inquire after Lady Treadwell. Indeed, well over three quarters of an hour had managed to slip by before Vail had satisfied himself that the elusive Lady Treadwell was nowhere to be found.

Eleanore, trying gallantly not to look as worried as she felt, was moved to point out that Letitia could not have gone far. "She has taken nothing with her, Your Grace. All of her things are in her room, just as she left them. Surely she stepped out just for a breath of fresh air."

No one, and especially not Lord Eppington, who, taking her hands in his, hastened to reassure her that she was undoubtedly in the right of it, could bring himself to mention the one glaring fault in Eleanore's line of reasoning. None, that was, save for Anthony Clevenger, who waited until he had drawn Vail into the hall out of the earshot of the others.

"Does it not occur to you, Cousin," he said quizzically, "that the weather is damnably unpleasant? Somehow I cannot think even the redoubtable Lady Treadwell would choose to go for a stroll in such a torrent."

"No more than I believe she would choose to leave her window wide open to the elements," Vail replied, grimly ringing for the butler. "I believe it is safe to assume she was made to leave against her will."

"In which case, might I suggest we delay no longer in mounting a search for the lady?"

"Not we, Cousin." Vail gazed straight into Clevenger's eyes as the butler arrived with the duke's greatcoat and curly-brimmed beaver. "I have already ordered my horse brought around. I suggest that Lady Treadwell would be best served if we made as little of this as possible."

Clevenger's grin was decidedly lacking in mirth. "You have, as a matter of fact, been called out on a matter of some importance and do not expect to be back before dinner. In the meantime, we shall continue with the festivities. Oh, and, Giles," he added as Vail reached for the door. "See that you bring her back, will you? It seems that I find myself in the lady's debt. Miss Gilcrest, you see, has consented to be my wife. She is a rare gem, my dearest Miss Gilcrest, and, far from decrying my embarrassing lack of the ready, she assures me she is rich enough to settle any number of debts and still keep me in the lifestyle to which I shall no doubt look forward to becoming accustomed. You may well wish me happy, Cousin."

Vail looked away from his kinsman. Briefly he nodded. "You may be sure of it, Anthony. I wish you both happy." Then flinging the door open, he stepped out into the storm.

Vail, who had not been strictly honest earlier with Lady Treadwell, did not bother to look for tracks, which would have been washed out by the rain in any case. He headed his mount south, along the valley road, which led to the village. Plagued by the grim awareness that a great deal could have happened to Lady Treadwell in an hour, he spared neither himself nor his horse, with the result that he arrived on the outskirts of the village in relatively short order. He wasted little time discovering the drive to Lady Treadwell's secluded cottage, a feat made easier by dint of his already having been down it once that day.

Bitterly he cursed the arrogance that had led him to believe the villains would never dare to touch her in Marshgate itself. He had known she was in danger the moment he had seen the coach in the stableyard behind the cottage that morning. There was no mistaking the coat of arms that it bore.

Dismounting, he led his horse into the stable and proceeded on foot the short distance to the cottage.

The fools were damnably sure of themselves, he

thought, as he boldly let himself in the house. They had bothered neither to bolt the door nor to post a sentry. But then, it was reasonable to suppose that Lady Treadwell's own house would be the last place anyone would think to look for her abductors. It had been the merest chance, after all, that he himself had stumbled upon the old fool, Pettigrew, that morning in search of a milch cow that had providently strayed into the woods. A mirthless smile touched his lips at the thought that impatient with the old man's garrulous ramblings, he had almost missed the importance of what Pettigrew had to tell him.

British Intelligence might well have been envious of the village network of communication. Pettigrew, it seemed, had got it from Pippin, the butcher, who had it from Mrs. Endercott, who in turn had been told by her sister, Mrs. Hicks, who worked as housekeeper for the reverend, who himself had heard it straight from Mrs. Parker's own lips that a gentleman of noble pedigree had taken up residence at Beechcote in anticipation of Lady Treadwell's return. What they had learned had been sufficient to clarify much of what had been puzzling about Lady Treadwell, not the least of which was the identity of the man responsible for her present difficulties.

It was Saturday, the servants' day off, and Mrs. Parker, Vail was reliably informed, would be in the village with her sister and invalid mother, while Carstairs, the butler, was down to Clivedon indulging in his passion for billiards. The house was still, save for the drone of voices issuing from behind double doors that presumably opened to the downstairs sitting room.

Vail slipped his hand into the greatcoat's deep pocket and curled his fingers around the checkered grips of a pistol. His face went grim as a woman's voice, distinctly familiar and unmistakably defiant, drifted through the twin oak barriers. Without bothering to knock, Vail reached for the door handle and slid the door open.

He was not altogether certain what he expected to find on the other side of the doors. Certainly it was not the cozy impression of coral damask wallpaper, Oriental rugs, a great fire leaping in a marble fireplace—and Lady Treadwell, seated on a dimity sofa pouring tea from a silver tea set for three gentlemen guests.

Letitia, looking intriguingly dishevelled and little the worse for her harrowing experiences, abruptly paused in her pouring, her lips parted in startled surprise, which was just as swiftly altered to a dazzling smile.

"Your Grace," she exclaimed, relief flooding her face. "How *good* of you to come. And just in the nick of time, too. Perhaps you are already acquainted with Lord Chalfont, who was just informing me that he would be obliged to publicize my identity and ruin me socially if I refuse to relinquish control to him of certain holdings he desires. And this, sir, is my esteemed Cousin Albert, who has been so generous as to demand my hand in marriage. In exchange for control over my father's trust fund, which would come to him in such an eventuality, he promises to restore me to a state of respectability. Otherwise, it seems I may look forward to being confined in an institution for the insane, since I should obviously be judged mentally incompetent to reject so magnanimous an offer. And finally, Your Grace," she said, turning to regard the third of her guests, who visibly writhed at being thus singled out. "My Cousin Charles, whom I have always loved as a brother, my trusted confidant and only friend." Letitia's eyes darkened with pain and an expression of profound pity. "He was the bait to draw me out."

With a groan, Charles lunged to his feet, his face pale and gripped in anguish. "Oh, God, Letitia. I had no choice. I had to do it. Chalfont said there were men watching the house. He said one night, when Anne and the children were asleep, he would have the house set to flame. You must believe me, Letitia, I should never have allowed anything to happen to you. I only needed time to remove Anne and the children to someplace of safety."

Albert Treadwell, who, resplendent in a teal morning coat without pocket flaps, a makada waistcoat of pale apricot with a neckcloth dyed to match and exquisitely tied in the "Waterfall," and buff short trousers that revealed apricot gaiters over black patent-leather shoes, resembled nothing so much as a sleek peacock with pomaded blond curls, waved a deprecating hand. "Oh, come now, Charles. Such an outrageous accusation. No one will believe it. You might as well own up. The truth is you were dipping in the till, and Lord Chalfont was kind enough to cover your indiscretion with a handsome bribe."

"That's a lie!" Charles rounded on Letitia, like a desperate animal. "Letitia, you cannot believe that I would ever—"

"Silence, you fool!" hissed Chalfont, heaving his big frame out of the chair. Something above forty, he was solidly built with only the beginnings of a slight paunch at his middle to show he had begun to allow the luxuries of life to impinge on his more active pursuits. Brown, thinning hair framed a face remarkable for its ruthlessness. "It would seem, Your Grace, that you have called at a most inopportune time. Lady Treadwell and I were on the point of completing a small business transaction. I don't suppose you would care to withdraw until we are finished?"

Vail shrugged eloquently, keenly aware that Letitia stood perilously close to the line of fire between himself and Chalfont. "I'm afraid not," he replied apologetically. "As a matter of fact, I have long looked forward to this meeting. You may not realize it, but you have been the subject of great interest to me for some time now. You *were* responsible for the shipyard riots in Liverpool, were you not? And more recently, the attempts to provoke a strike among the textile workers in Manchester and Bolton. Curious." His gaze shifted to Letitia (who paled ever so slightly), held, then returned to Chalfont. "The latter was put down before it ever had a chance to start—by the mysterious nabob, L. Treadwell, was it not?"

"The lady has proven an embarrassment on more than one occasion," Chalfont answered, making it a point to reveal the pistol he held in one beefy fist. "You would seem to know a great deal about me, my lord duke. I am flattered."

Vail smiled coldly as he tightened his grip on the gun cocked beneath his thumb in his pocket. "I am, by nature, a curious man, my lord. Tell me, Chalfont. How much does Napoleon pay these days to traitors willing to sabotage their country's war efforts?"

"Enough to make me a very wealthy man, Your Grace. And you a dead one, I'm afraid. A pity. I shall probably have to disappear for a time—when your body is discovered in suspicious circumstances with that of Lady Treadwell."

It was at that moment, as Chalfont raised the pistol to fire, that the entire room appeared to erupt in a bewildering flurry of motion. Albert, who, though he was not averse to confining his cousin to a mental institution, drew the line at murder and treason, lurched to his feet and cried, "Now, hold on, Chalfont!" Letitia, thinking that she was about to see Vail shot dead at her feet, took the opportunity to fling the contents of the silver tea server in the villain's face, and Charles, intent only on protecting Letitia, hurled himself at her as Chalfont, roaring in pain, discharged his pistol blindly.

Vail saw Letitia go to the floor, pinned beneath her cousin. His blood went suddenly cold at the sight of the crimson stain forming a pool on the Oriental rug beneath her. The next instant he was swept by an icy rage.

"*Chalfont!*" he uttered chillingly.

Six

"Well, I must say," declared Letitia, some moments later and just a trifle shakily, as she gazed down at Chalfont, sprawled unconscious on the Oriental carpet, "kung fu, notwithstanding, there is something to be said for a handy pair of fives."

"No doubt your Chinese art of self-defense would have stood you in just as good stead had you not had a sack thrust over your head," observed Vail, who was in the process of tying the bandage off on Charles's shoulder. "There," he added, covering the wounded man with a quilt. "I believe he is not seriously damaged. The wound, fortunately, was high and consequently hit nothing vital. We shall know for certain when Albert returns with the doctor. In the meantime, I suggest we bind our friend there, before he has time to gather his wits about him."

Letitia could not quite quell a shudder. "To think that all the time he was a French saboteur. Poor Charles. What he has been made to suffer! It was all a lie, you know. Charles would never steal from me. He had no need to have done. Thanks to L. Treadwell's various enterprises, he is a wealthy man in his own right."

Vail, having made certain that Chalfont was rendered harmless, led Letitia to the sofa and, ordering her to be seated, placed a cup of tea in her hands. "No matter what he may or may not be guilty of," he said sternly, "I should say Charles has more than redeemed himself today. Now, drink that while I see about putting things to right."

Letitia, however, who could not have cared less that her sitting room had been made a shambles, caught his sleeve. "Vail?"

A single look into her eyes, and Vail sat down beside her, his arms gathering her strongly to him.

It was sometime later before Letitia, stirring, bent her head up to look at him. "How did you know?" she said. "I was never so glad of anything as when I saw you standing there."

Vail, stroking her tousled curls, smiled reminiscently.

"You might be surprised to learn that British Intelligence does not compare to the intelligence gathering capabilities of a quaint English village. Suffice it to say, I chanced to meet a Mr. Pettigrew in the woods this morning when I was tracking your would-be assailant. By the time I managed to make my escape, Mr. Pettigrew had informed me of every pertinent fact concerning the local population in its entirety, not the least of which was the news that your cottage had been invaded by two lords and a gentleman of quality."

"I might have known," Letitia said, smiling. "And, though I could never really bring myself to believe that you were my anonymous valentine or that I had correctly deciphered the message you sent, I could not keep myself from hoping you would somehow come riding *ventre à terre* to rescue me." Vail's hand stopped in her hair. "You did send me the cob-web, did you not? With the basil, iris, and dill clustered about two apples that opened up to reveal the verses about forbidden fruit and divining your heart and . . . my God, you didn't, did you," she exclaimed, seeing it in his face, carefully devoid of expression. "Then who—?"

"The same prankster, I must suppose," replied the duke, no little bemused at this new conundrum, "who sent me a puzzle-purse containing a lock of your hair and a damned piece of nonsense about Cupid's misfired darts. Which, you will no doubt be glad to hear, served to convince me that you had been a deal more to me eight years ago than you were willing to admit."

"Oh, but you were," Letitia confessed, her cheeks assuming a wholly becoming tinge of color. "I was hopelessly head over ears in love with you. So much so, that I could not bear to have you hurt when I chanced to overhear Miss Willet planning to elope with—" She stopped, clapping a hand to her mouth. "With—with a gentleman, who was—"

"My Cousin Anthony," Vail interrupted, saving her from what was doomed to become a hopelessly convoluted sentence. "Harriet told me before she was shipped off to Ireland."

"And you did not mind?" Letitia blurted before she thought. "I mean—all those years, you said nothing. You allowed him to run tame in your house."

"And how not? He is my cousin and, for reasons known only to herself, a favorite of my esteemed mama's. Besides, I could hardly blame Anthony for falling prey to the artifices of a woman who was as adept as Harriet Willet at manipulating men to her own purposes, when I had been no less a victim. A man does not like to admit that he has been made a fool," he ended, studying her with an odd little glint in his eye. "I believe I owe you an apology, Lady Treadwell, and a somewhat belated expression of gratitude."

"For what, my lord duke?" Letitia queried, her lovely face wearing an expression of profound innocence. "For causing you no end of trouble from the moment I spilled tea on your mama?"

"No, my dear little termagant. I believe I must thank

you for sacrificing yourself to save me from embarrassment and then going so far as to warn me my erstwhile bride was on the point of eloping with another man."

"Oh, I see," said Letitia, not in the least disconcerted at having been found out at last. "And the apology, Your Grace? Am I to assume it is for having taken so little notice of me at the time that you failed utterly to recognize me yesterday on the verandah?"

"No, Lady Treadwell," Vail answered in no uncertain terms. "I hardly need apologize for not recognizing someone I glimpsed only for a few seconds in a dimly lit corridor and who, furthermore, chose to conceal herself in a hooded cloak that all but covered her face."

"Oh, dear!" Letitia exclaimed, suddenly greatly enlightened. "I never thought about that. I was so afraid someone would see me talking to you in the wake of my having utterly disgraced myself that I snatched up the first cloak I saw and wrapped myself in it. I do beg your pardon, Vail. I promise I should not have shot that arrow at you had I realized it was not your lamentable memory that caused you to forget me after all that I had done for you. But what, then, were you going to apologize for?"

"For not having taken you over my knee and beating you for lying to me," he said, fiercely drawing her to him, "when everything might have been simply resolved in a matter of moments had you only brought yourself to trust me. For that my infuriating little love, I intend to punish you dearly."

Letitia, who quite naturally took exception to the notion of being thrown over anyone's knee for such a purpose, started vociferously to object, only to find herself summarily silenced by the duke's mouth covering hers in a manner that proved not only pleasurable, but gratifying in the extreme.

Indeed, when no little time later he released her, she felt curiously dizzy and not a little dazed at the experience. With a long sigh, she allowed her head to fall back against Vail's shoulder and gazed dreamily up at him. "I believe, my dearest lord duke, that I shall have to contrive in the future to find new ways to earn your punishment. Indeed, it occurs to me that I shall enjoy very much being your mistress."

"No doubt I am sorry to disappoint you," murmured Vail, taking advantage of her weakness to nibble at one of her earlobes. "Delightful as it might be, I have no intention of making you my mistress. I should never have any peace from match-making mamas and their simpering offspring, and there is the matter of an heir to consider. My mother never ceases to remind me that it is long past time I set up my nursery. No, I'm afraid, my dear, that as much as I should enjoy having you for my mistress, what I really must have is a wife."

Letitia, who was having difficulty thinking at all clearly with all the unfamiliar and pleasurable sensations Vail was arousing in her, blinked at him in no little confusion. "Your wife? But you have a wife," she murmured. "Or at least you are about to have. Miss Pemberton—"

"Is by now being married by special license to Mr. Wickum, who has worshipped her from afar for far longer than I should ever have done. No, do not look so surprised. It was you, after all, who inspired her to 'indulge her passion' and snatch at her one chance at true happiness, or so she wrote in the note she left behind informing me she had decided to break off our engagement."

"Oh, my poor, dear lord duke," Letitia exclaimed, her eyes alight with a glad warmth and an irrepressible laughter. "You have been jilted again."

"It would seem," admitted His Grace in a manner that could only be described as philosophical, "that I have had yet another narrow escape. For which, since I find that I am hopelessly in love with a mysterious nabob, I can only be fervently grateful. My dearest L. Treadwell, would you do me the honor of becoming my wife? You will undoubtedly wish a double wedding with your Aunt Eleanore and Eppington, who are patently made for one another. I must warn you, Letitia, I am in no case to take another rejection and shall undoubtedly be forced to resort to desperate measures if you do not soon answer in the affirmative.''

"Well, I do think it would have been grand to be a duke's mistress," Letitia reflected, "and ever so much more adventurous. On the other hand," she hastily added at sight of her beloved valentine's thunderous expression, "I should not wish to disappoint a certain overly precocious Cupid, who, besides being your niece, possesses a considerable talent for poetic composition. Oh, yes, my lord duke, I will marry you," she said at last, flinging her arms about him. "How could I not when she has, it would seem, gone to a great deal of trouble to bring us together.''

Game of Harts

Jo Ann Ferguson

One

"Is this it?"

Lucinda Hart drew her heavy cloak more tightly over her shoulders as she glanced up from her book and out of the carriage. The trees were growing as close as a miser's fist, and their thick branches scraped together like an anatomy's bones. Through them, she could see a stone building. The roof tipped at a peculiar angle, and shutters were missing from one window. Smoke came from one of the chimneys, and she saw the hint of lamplight before the trees loomed over them again in the late afternoon twilight.

Sitting back, she said, "It looks rather primitive."

Beside her, her great-aunt Jennie Benedict chuckled. "It is nothing but a hunting lodge, Lucinda. You should not have expected more."

She smiled, in spite of herself, as she looked at her great-aunt, who was nearly a head shorter than she. As always, Aunt Jennie's linen white hair was poking out from beneath her bonnet in every possible direction. With her favorite cape, which was lined with rabbit fur, tucked beneath her chin, she could have been a wise gnome perched on the seat of the carriage.

"I did not expect more," Lucinda said, "but you must own that Terence has become renowned of late for his love of luxury."

"It seems even your brother prefers the informality of

grassville before rushing into the propriety of the Season."

Lucinda's smile faded. She would be anticipating the upcoming whirl of soirées with much more eagerness if Terence had not prattled endlessly about them since his return from Cambridge. Her brother was anxious to toss aside the austere life of his studies and surround himself with every pleasure offered in Town. When she had left Hart's Priory for this journey across the shire, he had been packing cards in his saddlebag in preparation for his hours at the table of green cloth. He hoped to hone his skills before joining the other young bachelors at Father's club in St. James's.

"Dear aunt, I pray that you will not speak that dreadful word in my hearing until we are forced to go to London."

"Dear child," her aunt returned in the same tone of voice, "one would think you have no interest in going to Town."

"I have been to Town." She stroked the cover of her book and pressed it against the thick wool of her blue cloak which was only a shade darker than her eyes. "I have been to balls and to assemblies and to teas."

"But those were events here in the country. You shall find the Season in Town is like nothing you have ever experienced."

"How can anything be so different? The people who have joined the family at Hart's Priory will be the same ones who call in London." With a laugh, she said, "I know I am being want-witted, but I don't want to be fired off into the Season as Verna and Edna were."

"Your older sisters made excellent matches."

"Boring matches, you mean," Lucinda answered with a raised eyebrow.

"A viscount and an earl are excellent matches for a baron's daughters, especially a baron who has three daughters."

Rolling her eyes, she said, "Oh, no, Aunt Jennie, not you, too. Is there nothing more I should want in life than to buckle myself to a titled husband?"

"A titled *and rich* one?"

"Oh, do please cut line."

"Such language." The carriage lurched as it turned onto the rough road leading to the cottage. Aunt Jennie put one hand on her bonnet and wagged her finger at Lucinda with the other. "You spend too much time reading books and believing those fairy tales that every maiden will have a knight in shining armor. Whatever are you reading now? Not another one of those atrocious novels by Mrs. Radcliffe, I hope."

"I agree those novels are silly." Wrinkling her nose, she lowered the book to her lap and smiled. "I do so love this story. It is by a Mr. Parsons."

Aunt Jennie tilted the book to see the spine. *The Haunted Cavern?* What type of story is that for an impressionable young woman?"

" 'Tis a love story of a man who would do anything to save the woman he loves from marrying the wicked man her father has chosen for her."

"Something you need not worry your head about." She sighed audibly. "I fear Jerome has spoiled all of you children beyond repair." She glanced out the window. "Not only does he allow you to become far too involved in reading such unseemly novels and not in life, but he grants your brother leave to plan this absurd gathering."

"You know you were eager to come."

The smile stripped years from Aunt Jennie's face. "I own to that, for Terence promised us a Valentine's Day weekend we would not soon forget. What surprised me was that you chose to come."

"What was the choice? To stay home for that silly Valentine's Day lottery Constance insists every young bachelor and miss participate in?" She shook her head. "I shall not let my life be steered by blind chance. Let my cousins enjoy that excitement as my sisters did."

The old woman smiled. "You have been avoiding the Valentine's Day lottery for as many years as you were eligible to participate. There is talk throughout the shire that you have not set aside your saucy minx ways and have no wish to find yourself a husband."

"I shall find myself a husband, dear aunt, but not by drawing his name out of a hat on the eve before Valentine's Day. More likely, I would be forced to endure the company of the greatest gaby in the shire." She stuck her hands back into her fox muff and shivered. "This must be the coldest winter ever."

"It does look like snow."

"Again?"

Aunt Jennie laughed. "Listen to yourself! You sound like an old tough bemoaning what cannot be changed."

Lucinda smiled and hugged her aunt, being careful, for the old woman's bones appeared as fragile as a bird's. An illusion, Lucinda knew, for, if Jennie Benedict had been the one facing Napoleon's troops on the other side of the channel, the war would be over by now. Aunt Jennie simply smiled and let people argue with her until they gave in to her. She ruled the family with a kind smile and the occasional glance which was cold enough to freeze the garden pond at ten paces.

"I should be happy it is snowing," Lucinda said as she leaned back against the seat and stared out at the trees. "A blizzard would be perfect for the day Father plans to close the house and take us to London."

"You should be pleased you have this opportunity, Lucinda."

"Why is everyone telling me how I should feel? Why will no one listen to how I *do* feel?" She sighed. "Forgive me. That was my frustration speaking."

"I know." She patted Lucinda's hand. "Be aware that

you shall get little sympathy from those you know. Few people will understand why you would wish to turn your back on a London Season with Lady Constance Kenyon as your sponsor."

She smiled with irony. "I know people will say I am an ungrateful wretch to denounce such generosity, but accepting Constance's offer will put my family even more in her debt. Deuce take it!"

"Lucinda, your language."

"I have heard you utter far worse, Aunt."

"But I am an old woman who has no need for society's approval." She took Lucinda's hands. "Dear child, it distresses me to see you in a flutter."

"Do not let it concern you, for I have accepted Terence's invitation to come to this gathering and, by doing so, shall avoid both the lottery and my cousin's wife."

The carriage slowed as the road grew steeper. Lucinda could not think of one good reason why her brother had chosen this place for his party. Not only was it out of the way, but not far from the sea, so the wind blew harsh and cold through the carriage.

She smiled, recalling how Terence had pleaded with her to come here today. Her fun-loving, jokester brother was the only one who could wheedle her to do such madcap things as leaving the comforts of the Priory and riding here. How she had missed him while he was away at school! Only to herself would she own that she wished to delay leaving for the Season primarily because she wanted time to reacquaint herself with her brother's bizarre sense of humor that was the match for her own. No one else in the family, save Aunt Jennie, understood it.

"Finally," Aunt Jennie said as the carriage slowed to a stop. "Lucinda, do make sure the tiger gets our bags out of the boot. I have no interest in spending the whole weekend in this heavy dress, although I suspect the cottage will be as cold as the Black Prince's heart." As the door opened, she grasped her gold-topped cane and added, "And do leave that book here. I shall not have you sneaking off somewhere and reading all weekend. It would not reflect well on our family if you were to shun polite society so openly."

"Yes, Aunt Jennie," she answered obediently, but slipped the book into a pocket sewn within her cloak as her great-aunt looped the bag with her embroidery over her arm. Although she had read the novel several times already, she was nearing her favorite passage. She would enjoy it this evening after she retired at a respectfully late hour that would satisfy her great-aunt.

Snow crunched under Lucinda's high-lows, and she raised the hem of her cloak to keep it from getting wet. Even the oldest servant in the Priory spoke of this being the coldest winter in living memory. She did not doubt that for it was lasting into February when, in other years, spring warmth had begun to sneak in from the sea to lure the first flowers from the earth.

"Oh, my!"

At Aunt Jennie's gasp of dismay, Lucinda turned to look past the carriage at the cottage. It was in even worse repair than it had appeared from the road. The steps leading to the front door were crooked, and she doubted if anyone had attended to the gardens during her lifetime. Two trees had fallen against the roof and been ignored. Their branches dripped over the eaves, covering the uppermost windows like a naughty child hiding his face.

A shiver coursed along her back. This house would be the perfect setting for one of the heinous plots Mr. Parsons favored in his books. She was sure more than the steps would creak ominously, and the wind would whistle its secrets around every window.

"How did Terence find this place?" Aunt Jennie asked.

"He told me it belongs to a gentleman he knows from Cambridge."

"Clearly the gentleman has invested all his time in his studies as lief attending to the upkeep of his property." Her nose wrinkled as she slipped her arm through Lucinda's. "As we have come all this way, it seems senseless to return to the Priory."

Lucinda steered her great-aunt up the path to the front door with the coachman, who was carrying their bags, following. Her eyes widened when she saw the brass knocker. It had been recently polished. Mayhap the situation within would not be as appalling as the exterior suggested. Mulled wine and a crackling fire would revive her spirits in no time and perhaps give her the chance to sneak a few more pages of her book.

The door opened only a few inches. A woman peered out, and her eyes grew wide.

With an imperious motion that surprised Lucinda, for her great-aunt was usually the pattern-card of graciousness, Aunt Jennie pushed the door aside and walked into the entry. Lucinda rushed after her. The coachman dropped their bags on the floor and strode away without waiting for her to speak. Frowning, Lucinda looked from his retreating back to her great-aunt, who was appraising the entry.

It was not large. Dark wood covered the walls, swallowing what light there might have been. The stone floor was nearly as cold as the ground outside. A single lamp had been lit against the darkness, but light spilled from a passage to the left. The muted resonance of men's voices flowed out from it as well.

When the woman who had opened the door closed it, Lucinda offered her a smile. Instead of returning it, the woman cried, "Thank the good Lord you are here!" The woman pressed her hand to her generous bosom. "Will you help?"

"Help?" Lucinda stared at her in astonishment. The

woman must be nearly hysterical, for her voice was choked. "Whatever is wrong, Mrs.—?"

"Mrs. Chaplin." She rubbed her hands together and glanced fearfully toward the passage. "Oh, alack! Who would have thought such a fate could befall this house?"

"What fate?"

"Those horrid men."

Lucinda bit her lip to hide her smile. What prank had Terence created now? It must be a grand one if this poor woman was so distressed. Lucinda would have to remind him to apologize to Mrs. Chaplin at the earliest opportunity. Unlike the staff at Hart's Priory, this woman had no way of knowing Terence's heart was gentle and that he never meant to upset anyone . . . too much.

"Is Mr. Hart here?" she asked as she removed her gloves.

"Mr. Hart?" The woman looked at Aunt Jennie for an explanation. "Who is Mr. Hart?"

"Mr. Terence Hart," Lucinda answered, slipping her bonnet off her head. She smoothed her dark brown hair and wished for a looking glass so she could be sure she did not appear a complete rump before her brother and his other guests. "He left Hart's Priory at the same time we did, but should be here because he rode while we took the carriage."

"I am not sure . . ."

Aunt Jennie pushed a stray strand of Lucinda's hair back over her ear, then turned to Mrs. Chaplin. "May we assume Mr. Hart has not arrived yet?"

"Didn't none of them give their names, madam." She swallowed roughly and said in a more cultured tone, "Forgive me, madam. Not one of the men gave his name."

"This may be more than a bit uncomfortable," Aunt Jennie said as she loosened the bright yellow ribbons on her hat. "Come along, Lucinda. We shall have to make the best of this situation. I do wonder what has delayed

Terence. It is unlike your brother to be late for any gathering. I hope his horse hasn't pulled up lame."

"We would have seen him when we passed him on the road."

"True. This is most peculiar."

Lucinda reached for the frogs closing her cloak at her throat. "I do not like this one bit. I hope we have the right house. It would be . . ."

She stared at the man who was coming along the passage. A lion. That was her first thought. Tawny hair and green eyes and powerful muscles that flowed as he moved. The caramel color of his coat and his subdued gold waistcoat added to her fanciful thoughts. Riding boots clung to his brawny legs, their heels striking the stone floor on each step like flint against steel. But the sparks were in his incredible eyes. His emerald gaze held her, so she barely took note of his straight nose and full lips.

"Who are you?" he asked, his deep voice no louder than a whisper, but it rumbled through her like the distant memory of summer thunder. "What are you doing here?"

Lucinda tore her gaze from his enough so she could form a thought. "My name—"

"I beg you to keep your voice low, miss." His mouth worked, and his eyes grew hard. "Trust me that it is in your best interests."

"My best interests?"

"An explanation might be simpler if I knew your name, miss."

"I am Lucinda Hart, sir. Mayhap you would be so kind as to explain what is taking place that compels us to whisper. We were to meet my brother Terence here."

"Hart? Terence Hart?" He muttered something under his breath.

"Sir?"

A hint of a smile erased some of the strain tightening

his face. "Forgive me, Miss Hart. Circumstances have conspired to cause me to forget to send word to your brother that the gathering this weekend must be postponed." Again he glanced over his shoulder. "Mayhap permanently."

"So you know Terence?" Her forehead ruffled as she asked, "Who are you?"

"Lucinda!" chided her aunt, but kept her voice low.

His smile widened. "Do not give her a scold, madam, for she is right that I am quite bereft of my manners at the moment. Again I must ask your indulgence." Taking Lucinda's hand, he lifted it to his lips, but did not kiss it. Even so, her breath snagged sharply at the warmth of his rough skin surrounding her hand. He said, "Allow me to present myself in these somewhat awkward circumstances. I am Maximillian Loveland. Mayhap your brother has mentioned me."

Lucinda almost laughed. Nearly every other sentence Terence had uttered since his homecoming from Cambridge had begun with "Max did . . ." or "Max said . . ." Her eyes narrowed as she assessed him anew. She had to own that she had created a different image of Lord Loveland, for Terence had failed to mention the golden hair and those catlike eyes which made his expression as mysterious as any feline's. Nor had anything Terence said suggested Lord Loveland had a sense of humor. She had thought Maximillian Loveland might provide a good example of dignity to her often frivolous brother.

But this man was smiling as if he did it often. Had she misunderstood Terence?

"My lord," she said cautiously, "this is indeed a pleasure." She hoped the trite words would cover her hesitation.

Before he could reply, Mrs. Chaplin gasped, "My lord, I thought—"

He put his finger to his lips and glanced back over his

shoulder. Mrs. Chaplin nodded, then scurried away into the back of the house.

Aunt Jennie tapped his arm with her cane and said, "I think the explanation you promised us, young man, is long overdue."

"This is Lady Jennie Benedict," Lucinda said, when Lord Loveland regarded her with hooded eyes. "She is my and Terence's great-aunt."

"And very anxious for that explanation," Aunt Jennie added.

His smile grew taut. "I would be most pleased under other circumstances to offer it, Lady Benedict, but now, if you will excuse me, I must take my leave of this house before the gentlemen in the other room carry out their plan to kill me."

Two

"Kill you?"

Lucinda was glad Aunt Jennie spoke the words that were stuck in her own throat. She stared at her great-aunt in astonishment, when Aunt Jennie added, "What do you suggest we do, my lord?"

"I suggest," he said quietly, "that we make our plans with speed if we wish to escape. These owlers will not want us to be able to point them out to the authorities."

"Smugglers?" Aunt Jennie shuddered. "Loathsome creatures. I wish the constable would put an end to their dirty enterprise."

"Aunt Jennie!" Lucinda cried, finding her voice. "We cannot do anything against smugglers. We must get help."

"Hush, my dear. You do not want to draw unnecessary attention to ourselves." She tried to peer around the corner into the passage. "There is no telling what these beasts might do if cornered."

Lucinda's face grew as cold as the wind beyond the stone walls. "Are you suggesting they might slay us as well?"

"You can never be certain with this low type."

Maximillian Loveland folded Miss Hart's trembling hand between his. "Fear not, Miss Hart. The brute's anger is focused on me. I suspect even he is not churl enough to hurt as much as a wisp of your ebony hair."

When he forced a smile, he thought his consoling

words—no matter how false they might be—would return color to her cheeks which had been dusted such a charming shade of pink. He had not guessed Terence's younger sister would be such a delight on the eyes, for Terence had yet to outgrow his adolescent gawkiness. The enticing curves beneath Miss Hart's cloak showed she did not share her brother's awkwardness.

"My lord," she said, her husky whisper a pleasure on his ears, "there must be a way we can help save you from this unkind fate." She drew her hand out of his. "This is absurd. Come with us in our carriage. We will leave posthaste."

He shrugged, the cape of his greatcoat flapping on his shoulders as he went to the door and peered out the window beside it. "Dash it! There are more of them out there." Turning back to the women, he said, "I have discovered the leader of this pack of rabid dogs has a temper of unprecedented proportions. Disregarding that fact, Miss Hart, was my first mistake."

"The constable would—"

"The constable is paid well to look the other way when these owlers bring their illegal cargo ashore."

When she stepped forward and put her hand on his sleeve, Max was astonished by her boldness until she urged, "Go, my lord! You have lingered here too long."

"Go? And leave you here with these beasts?" He shook his head. "I think not."

Lady Benedict leaned on her cane and said, "I see the obvious solution is for the lot of us to take our leave with all due haste."

"As I said, the front door is guarded," he answered.

"And the back?" she asked.

"The beasts, as you call them, stand between us and the door, even if it were unguarded, which seems unlikely." He smiled coldly. "Mayhap through the cellar with Mrs. Chaplin's help in creating a diversion." He opened a door beneath the stairs. "Stay close. If they were to find us, I have no idea what they might resort to."

Lady Benedict hurried to his side, then looked back. "Lucinda? Child, come quickly!"

"But we cannot go. Terence might walk blithely into this bumble-bath," Miss Hart argued, taking a single step, then pausing. "If he were to come here without knowing what awaits him—"

"We wondered what had delayed you, Loveland."

Lucinda glanced back at the voice which was as cultured as a vicar's. A pinch of dismay taunted her. Mayhap the vicar *was* a part of this gang of smugglers. It was impossible to know. Rumors floated about the shire of those who had joined the interlopers, but she did not know which were true.

The dark-haired man walked to where Lord Loveland stood. With a triumphant smile, he slammed the cellar door. He twisted a key in it. "Thank you for reminding me of the one thing I forgot, Loveland."

He strode back closer to Lucinda, and she cowered away from him. He was as tall as the marquess and much of an age, although she could only guess at his years, for his features were half-obliterated by a thick brush of beard. Rough clothes gave off the scent of brine and other less pleasing odors. Mud was caked on his heavy boots, and she noted a bottle protruding from the pocket of his dirty coat which once might have been light brown.

"More guests?" the man asked into the strained silence. He bowed his head toward Aunt Jennie. "Good afternoon to you, madam." His eyes lit with more than amusement as he turned to Lucinda. He made no effort to hide his lascivious appreciation, and her cheeks grew hot. "This is, indeed, an unexpected pleasure. You did not tell us, Loveland, that you were awaiting the company of such lovely guests."

"Dayton, there is no need to detain the ladies," Lord

Loveland said as he drew off his greatcoat and folded it over his arm, blocking the man's view of Lucinda. "They realize the gentleman they sought is not in this afternoon."

"That is a shame." Dayton hooked his thumb in the waist of his filthy breeches, drawing back his coat.

Lucinda could not silence her gasp when she saw the pistol he wore beneath it. She had seen a similar one in her father's book room, but that was kept in a locked case on the uppermost shelf. Easily she recalled his warnings of the peril of being at the target end of such a weapon. Although the long-barreled pistols were not easy to aim, the damage they could do was horrifying.

Lord Loveland stepped between the smuggler and Aunt Jennie. He reached out and grasped Lucinda's arm, pulling her behind him as well. "You are frightening the ladies needlessly, Dayton."

"Nay, I would say you have done that." He smiled as footfalls sounded from the passage. Although Lucinda hoped Mrs. Chaplin would return with a few strong lads, a dozen men dressed as poorly as Dayton crowded the doorway, but did not push past the man who was obviously their leader. "I will do no more harm to these ladies just now than to ask them to speak their names, so I might greet them properly."

"I am Miss Hart," said Lucinda, forcing the words past her fear which threatened to strangle her. Mayhap if they were allowed to leave, they could meet Terence on the road and halt him from becoming mixed up in this shocking mull. But if they left, what would happen to Lord Loveland? To leave might mean to condemn him to death.

Dayton stepped forward and reached for her hand. She pulled it back. He snapped his fingers. One of his men drew a sword from behind him.

When he raised it toward Lord Loveland, the marquess

said, "Dayton, no gentleman would use such means to threaten a lady who has made every effort to cooperate."

"Has she been cooperating?" His dark eyes aimed at Lucinda, and he smiled coldly. "Have you, Miss Hart?"

"Do leave off, sir!" snapped Aunt Jennie, striking her cane on the floor. "Lucinda is trying to cooperate with you, so say what you have to say, and stop toying with my grandniece. You shall frighten her nigh to death."

Dayton bowed his head toward them. " 'Tis not my intention to *frighten* her to death, madam."

Aunt Jennie's eyes widened with horror. "Pray release Lucinda from this madness. She is young, but she knows how to hold her counsel."

"Does she, Mrs. . . . ?"

"I am Lady Benedict. I implore you to release all of us unharmed." She slipped her arm through Lucinda's and leaned heavily on her. "Please."

The smuggler took Aunt Jennie's hand and bowed over it. "I am sorry you have entered this house at this point, my lady. It is very difficult for us to have callers right now."

"Because you intend to slay Lord Loveland? How can you kill a man who has done you no wrong?" Lucinda clamped her hands over her mouth when she realized the words were hers.

Lord Loveland put his hand on her shoulder. "I thank you for your defense, Miss Hart, but that sordid business is solely between Dayton and me." His eyes narrowed to emerald slits. "You have had your introductions, Dayton. Now bid the ladies farewell, so we might return to the matters that do not include them."

"That may no longer be true." He snapped his fingers again.

Lucinda gasped in horror as the men behind Dayton stepped aside. A man was shoved forward.

"Brooks!" she cried.

The coachee did not look up. His shoulders shook, and she feared he was weeping in pain.

"What have you done to him, you beast?" she shouted.

Lord Loveland's hand on her shoulder became a clamp to keep her from stepping forward. In a near whisper, he said, "Beware his temper, Miss Hart. Your man clearly made the same mistake I did. I would not wish to see Dayton's fury turned on you or your great-aunt."

"Your man, Miss Hart," snarled Dayton, all bonhomie vanishing from his face, "has, indeed, made a mistake. If he had had the sense of a goose, he would not have poked his nose into the stables behind this cottage and tried to satisfy his curiosity about what was stored there in the crates. On your orders, Miss Hart?"

"Do not be ludicrous," Lucinda said, raising her chin. "Why would I give him such an order when I had no reason to suspect anything was amiss here?"

"Your father is Jerome, Lord Hart, is he not?"

"Yes," she answered with a shaky voice.

Max wondered why she was so hesitant to answer. Everything he had heard of the baron was admirable. The man was devoted to his wife and his family and his duty to his country. He seldom missed being seated in the House of Lords. For a few brief months, he had worked in one of the government ministries as all of England bent to the task of protecting their homeland when Napoleon's war swept outward to swallow half of Europe.

He absently rubbed his upper arm. Even the thought of Boney and his frogs brought back the memory of the ball that had smashed into his shoulder. Dash it! This was not how he had wanted to spend the weekend. Terence had promised a diversion to keep Max from remembering the nearly forgotten foray over two years before on Valentine's Day that had taken place in the wake of the Battle of Corunna. He had not thought to spend this one fighting once again.

"Lord Hart might be willing to pay well for the return of his youngest and his aunt," Max said quietly. "Well enough so you might retire from your crimes against the crown."

Dayton stroked his beard and grinned. "That is a thought. 'Tis a shame you chose to be a milord, Loveland. You have the wit to be a damned good smuggler."

"Chose to be a lord?" asked Miss Hart, confusion again in her blue eyes which changed shade with every emotion flashing across her face.

"He can," growled Dayton, "choose to remain a live milord or—"

Lady Benedict shrieked as he ripped the sword from his man and raised it toward Max. No one moved as the old woman collapsed to the floor, her cane dropping from her fingers to strike the stones with a thump. Her bag of embroidery flew across the foyer.

"Dayton, you . . ." Max bit back his words as Miss Hart pushed past him to kneel next to her great-aunt. "How does she fare?"

"Stay back!" Lucinda cried as she chafed Aunt Jennie's wrists. The pulse beneath her fingers remained strong and steady. "Have the decency to give her enough air so she might regain her senses."

"She fainted?"

She aimed her most fierce glower—the one which usually daunted even Terence—at Dayton. When he mumbled something and stepped back, she did not pause to be amazed. To Lord Loveland, she asked, "Do you have *sal volatile* here?"

"It is a hunting lodge," he said, as he squatted beside her, being careful not to step on her cloak.

"Are there hunting trophies here?"

He regarded her in confusion. "I saw a few stuffed beasts in the other room."

"Just beasts, or did you espy birds among them as well?"

A slow smile spread across his face, and Lucinda was overmastered by the flush of warmth flowing over her with the sweetness of spring's first breeze. Her first impression returned doubly strong. She had seen a cat smile with this same self-satisfaction while it cleaned its whiskers in the aftermath of a feast.

"A worthy idea, Miss Hart," he said, "but I suggest we get your great-aunt off this cold floor before we think of plucking and burning feathers to bring her back to her senses." Setting himself on his feet, he added, "Dayton, allow me to take the ladies to the left front bedroom upstairs. I trust you will keep your henchmen away until we are assured Lady Benedict is unhurt."

Lucinda was astonished when the smuggler nodded. She tensed as he said, "But if you try to escape, my lord, 'twill be the ladies who pay the price of your folly."

"I understand," Lord Loveland said grimly.

The men stared as Lord Loveland bent and lifted Aunt Jennie into his arms with an ease that suggested she weighed no more than one of the flakes of snow drifting lazily past the window. He carried her toward the stairs at the back of the entry.

As she gathered up her aunt's cane and bag and was about to follow Lord Loveland, Lucinda paused and said, "I trust you will, in addition, Dayton, refrain from doing anything to harm Brooks. My father would not look kindly upon such an act."

Again he nodded, but his smile became as vicious as the glitter in his eyes. "And I trust you will not forget the warning I gave to Lord Loveland, Miss Hart, or you shall share his fate."

She feared her heart had forgotten how to beat as she stared at his delight at her fear. Gathering up her skirts and cape, she hurried up the steps after Lord Loveland.

The soft light from a single lamp drew her into a room that was not much larger than the entry. The sloped roof rose to the stones of the fireplace where a fire burned to take the chill from the room.

Lucinda closed the door and pushed forward as Lord Loveland put Aunt Jennie on the simple rope bed set in the corner by the door. She leaned on the iron footboard. "How is she?"

Her great-aunt sat up, smiled, and asked, "Did I do well?"

"Do well?" choked Lucinda.

Lord Loveland laughed, adding to Lucinda's bafflement. "You have proved you are a worthy adversary for those below, Lady Benedict."

As Aunt Jennie's smile widened, Lucinda asked, "Are you intimating, dear aunt, that your swoon below was feigned?"

" 'Twas a performance," Lord Loveland said, his grin broadening, as Aunt Jennie retied her bonnet, "as fine as any I have enjoyed in Town. Congratulations, my lady. You have saved my neck for the moment as well as yours."

"I wish to know more of these fellows who have apparently taken us prisoner."

"Not apparently, I fear," he answered. "They were here when I arrived. They took me quite by surprise."

Lucinda rubbed her cold hands together as she hung her cloak over the footboard. "You were traveling alone, my lord?"

"My servants showed better sense than I and fled, save for Mrs. Chaplin." He smiled again as he tossed his greatcoat on the bed. "I can only hope my diversion in the front allowed her time to escape out the back. I offer my apologies, Lady Benedict, Miss Hart, that my scheme unfolded moments too late to keep you from becoming involved in this."

"Nonsense," Aunt Jennie said, standing. "If you had

left, my lord, we would be facing these brutes alone. What do you suggest?"

Lucinda watched his face as he weighed the options he must have in his mind. She wished he would speak them. When he went to stand before the hearth and gazed down into the fire, she went to stand beside him. "My lord?"

"Yes," he whispered.

"Is there a chance we might escape alive?"

"We must believe that or we are lost even now." He cupped her chin in his hand and smiled, but she saw no amusement in his eyes. "Terence has never turned away from any challenge. Neither have I. Neither must you."

"I own to being scared."

"You would be a widgeon not to be, Miss Hart." Releasing her, he strode back to the center of the room. "We must devise a plan to escape. Something simple that will be flexible so we can counter every move they make until we are free of their heinous clutches."

Lucinda went to the small window overlooking the garden below. "But what of Brooks? What will they do to him?"

"You may find your coachman is more resourceful than you give him credit for," he said. "I met him on several occasions when Terence had him driving for him in Cambridge. The man is good and loyal. After all, Dayton gave you his word nothing would happen to him."

"For now."

"You seem unduly distressed, Miss Hart. We remain alive, thanks to the splendid resourcefulness of your aunt."

"Alive, that is true." She turned to face him and realized he had to bend his head to stand beneath the slanted ceiling. He was leaning toward her, his face only inches from hers. "But for how long?"

"Mayhap for a short time; mayhap for many years."

His finger twisted a strand of her hair which had come loose to fall along her shoulder. "If I were no gentleman, and your aunt was not here as a watchdog, I could suggest several other ways to pass the hours until our executions."

"You are no gentleman, my lord, even to give voice to such thoughts."

He leaned his other hand on the ceiling above her head. "The flush in your cheeks intrigues me, Miss Hart. Of what did you think I spoke?"

"You know quite well."

"If I knew, there would have been little reason for me to waste what might be my last moments quizzing you. Don't you agree?"

Lucinda wanted to put her hands up to cover her cheeks which must be glowing bright red with her embarrassment. She could not remember the last time she had blushed, but now she had twice in this handsome man's company.

"I no longer wish to discuss this," she said in the prim tone she borrowed from her cousin's wife Constance.

His brows rose, and he smiled. "Now, now, Miss Hart. I did not mean to put you so delightfully to the blush. You cannot fault a man for being so honest when the minutes of his life are ticking swiftly away."

"You seem very serene in accepting this death sentence."

"Aye, there is the devil to pay and no pitch hot." He sighed. "I collect I shall soon be able to lament that to the Black Prince face-to-face." Gazing past her out the window, he smiled with regret. "I have long known such a meeting is inevitable, but I did not anticipate it coming today when I was looking forward to the chance to play host to my tie-mate Terence and his lovely sister."

A loud clatter sounded from beyond the cottage. Lucinda whirled to the window just in time to see her father's carriage driving neck-or-nothing toward the main road. When a trio of the smugglers erupted from beneath the trees, she gripped the sill. She moaned when guns fired. The smugglers raised them in the air and shook them, their words sifted out of their shouts by the thick stone walls.

Lord Loveland tried to turn her away, but she refused to move. She searched the shadows beyond the trees. Had one of the smugglers hit the carriage?

Her heart leapt with joy when the carriage emerged from beneath the trees and raced along the road back in the direction of Hart's Priory. Clapping her hands, she crowed, "Brooks got away! He will bring help!"

"Do not pin all your hopes on that," Lord Loveland said darkly. "This may make our captors even more anxious to be done with the burden of three witnesses to their dirty tasks."

Lucinda stared at him in horror, then turned back to the window. His fingers stroked her bare arm, and she raised her eyes to his. As their jade glow invited her even closer, she forgot about Aunt Jennie, Brooks, and even the smugglers waiting below. She noted a shadow of a scar along his jaw. She wondered how he had gotten the pale crescent which marred the otherwise straight line. His hand grew more brazen as his fingers closed around her wrist, drawing her closer. She knew she should push him away, tell him he was being too impertinent, remind him of how a marquess should treat a baron's daughter.

She whispered, "You should not—"

"Do not deny me this innocent pleasure when I might soon lose every chance to touch a lady's soft hand," he answered as lowly.

"I know nothing of you."

"Nor I of you." He raised his hand toward his lips. "But, my dear Miss Hart, I would wish to learn more in the scant moments we may have left."

Unsure what to say, she watched as he bent to press

his mouth to her fingers. He froze and cursed. She stared at him in the second before the door crashed open.

As Lord Loveland turned, still holding her hand, Lucinda saw a cold smile curl along Dayton's lips. The disdain in Lord Loveland's voice was as frigid.

"What do you want, Dayton? I thought you would give Lady Benedict a chance to recover from her frightening experience before you intruded."

He sneered as Aunt Jennie clutched the bed, her mouth nearly as round as her eyes. When Lucinda rushed to her, handing her the cane, Dayton said, "She clearly has had enough time. She is back on her feet. Too bad, my lady, you did not stay senseless, for now you must hear as the others will that I shall see you all dead before we meet our incoming cargo at midnight."

Three

Lucinda caught her great-aunt just as Aunt Jennie swooned . . . for real, this time, she feared when she felt the rapid pace of her great-aunt's pulse. Raising her eyes, she spat, "Have you no decency? Can you not find it in your heart to spare an old woman who may not have many more years left?"

"Mayhap," Dayton drawled, "if you have something to offer me in return."

Lord Loveland strode to put his hand on the foot of the iron bed, again standing between her and the smuggler. "Now see here. That suggestion goes beyond decency, even the questionable decency of an interloper."

"Shall you demand for me to name my friends, my lord?" He snickered.

"You would be a paper-skull to do that." Lord Loveland's voice was taut with fury. "If I let fly the pop, you would without question find yourself put to bed with a shovel. I assure you I am slashing with a pistol at ten paces."

Dayton's lips twisted. "Mayhap, or mayhap not, but we shall not know, my lord, for I would be from a windmill to let you have a popper." He put his hand on the pistol at his waist. "And I can assure *you* I am no addle cove."

Lucinda knelt next to the bed and her great-aunt. Raising her gaze to the crude man in the doorway, she whispered, "I beg you to free my great-aunt from your death sentence."

"And you, pretty miss?" He leaned toward her, but Lord Loveland put out his arm to keep the owler from coming too close. "Don't you wish to have your death sentence revoked?"

"Do you enjoy tormenting us like this?" she asked, letting her frustration overmaster her common sense. "If you plan to call old Mr. Grim upon us today, you need not parade that endlessly before us." Slowly she came to her feet. "Your voice suggests you come from gentle stock, Mr. Dayton, and I would ask that you remember how to be pretty-behaved for the short time you have granted us left to live."

Astonishment wiped the taunting expression from Dayton's face. It returned to tighten his lips when Lord Loveland smothered a chuckle. She glanced from one man to the other, but their eyes were locked.

"Well said," Lord Loveland murmured, "although I question your temerity at such a time, Miss Hart." Stepping forward, he raised his voice. "I ask again, Dayton, for you to reconsider. These ladies have done you no wrong."

"Save for being witnesses to your demise."

"Not yet." He held up his arms. "I remain alive, as you can see and as Miss Hart will confirm." Taking Lucinda's hand, he pressed it to the center of his chest. "Do you feel my heart beating, Miss Hart?"

"Yes," she whispered, glad he could not feel hers, for it raced like a storm-lashed wave toward the shore. The firm muscles of his chest beneath her fingers were like a stone wall, unyielding and strong.

At her soft answer, he looked at her. He splayed her palm over the sleek brocade of his waistcoat, drawing her a half step nearer. His fingers laced through hers as the green mysteries in his tantalizing eyes warned her to decipher them only if she dared to risk the truth. She suspected it was as dangerous as Dayton.

"Lucinda?"

She pulled away from the marquess and rushed to where Aunt Jennie was struggling to sit. Putting her arm around her great-aunt's shoulders, she assisted the old woman to swing her feet over the edge of the bed.

"No, you should remain sitting," Lucinda chided when her great-aunt tried to push herself to her feet.

"Why?"

"You could hurt yourself."

"More than he shall hurt me?" Aunt Jennie grasped her cane and pointed at Dayton, who was watching with his sly smile. "I think not. Forgive me, my lord, for such feminine vapors. Thank goodness Lucinda is stronger than I. She has not succumbed to any female weaknesses."

"Thank goodness," Lord Loveland answered.

Lucinda heard his smile, for she dared not look at his face. She could not bear to see him grinning at Aunt Jennie's words that were an unwitting falsehood. How easily she had been about to surrender to the feminine fantasy of Lord Loveland's arms around her, protecting her from the evil Dayton! Mayhap Aunt Jennie was right. Mayhap she read too many novels, for she was uncertain if Lord Loveland would be the brave hero who put her reputation above fulfilling the passions she had seen in his eyes . . . and he had unleashed within her mind.

"Are you done?" asked Dayton, impatience filling his voice.

"That is what you seem in the position to decide," fired back Lord Loveland. "It is not late, and you have given us until midnight to live."

He chuckled. "No, my lord. I said you must be dead so we may meet our cargo at midnight."

"At the very least, give us the customary last meal."

"How can you think of eating?" Lucinda gasped.

Lord Loveland waved her to silence. "What do you say, Dayton?"

"And what can I get for your lordship and your fine ladies? I doubt if anything we low smugglers would eat is fit for your cultured palates." His eyes twinkled maliciously. "I do know where I can obtain some excellent vintage to wash the taste away."

With a diffident wave of his hand, Lord Loveland ordered, "Bring us whatever swill your men will be eating tonight, and a bottle or two of that vintage. I collect you will allow a finer palate than yours to decide its quality."

Lucinda thought Dayton would retort to such insult, but he simply closed the door. Her shoulders sagged as she heard his heavy steps going down the stairs. Dropping to sit on the bed, she shut her eyes and sighed. Nothing had changed. They were still due to topple heels in whatever way the smugglers had devised.

"Miss Hart?"

She raised her eyes to Lord Loveland's. Seeing his concern there, she straightened her shoulders and said, "We cannot waste our reprieve. Do you have any suggestions for a way out of this situation, my lord?"

"One or two."

"Which is less dangerous?" She stood and took her great-aunt's hand. "I do not wish to do anything that might harm Aunt Jennie."

"When the alternative is death," the old woman said tartly, "I am willing to chance a turned ankle or a few bruises."

"You may prove a better trump than I, Lady Benedict," he answered with a chuckle. He went to the window and raised it. Icy wind speared its way into the room, blowing honed snowflakes to cut into their skin. "No roof here to assist in our escape. If we use the bedding and—"

Aunt Jennie shook her head. "You ask too much of

these old bones, my lord. Is there a tree, mayhap, that might give me an easier route out of here?"

"Not close."

"Can you bring a branch closer, so I may grasp it?"

Taking the poker from by the fire, he stretched to hook one end over the nearest branch. When the branch snapped and twigs cascaded to the ground, he drew the poker back into the room. "Not strong enough, I fear, even for your slight weight, Lady Benedict."

Lucinda frowned as she listened to them debate other ways out the window. Walking to the door, she lifted the latch. "Why not go out this way?"

"It is unlocked?" asked Aunt Jennie in amazement. "Dayton has grown careless."

"Unless he hopes to lure us out that way," Lord Loveland said. "I warn you not to underestimate our foe. He has stayed alive through his wits."

"So must we," Lucinda answered.

The marquess smiled at her, and she could not help returning it. "You are plucky, Miss Hart. For that we may be grateful before this is over." He pushed the door aside slowly and motioned them to silence.

From the floor below, the voices of the men reached them. She tensed when she heard a guffaw. No doubt the amusement was aimed at the expense of the prisoners in this room. Pushing aside her fury, she tried to think clearly. Escaping and sending the authorities to capture these smugglers would be the sweetest vengeance.

Lord Loveland slowly closed the door. "They remain in the entryway. There is no escape in that direction."

"Do any of the other rooms on this floor have windows that open over a roof?" Lucinda asked.

"That is a smasher of an idea, Miss Hart." He scowled as he tapped his finger against his chin. "It has been a while since I was last here, but I believe there is a small roof over the door from the kitchen."

"Wonderful!"

"Do not celebrate our escape yet." He drew open the door again and whispered, "Even if we can reach the room and raise the window and slip out of it without being noted, we must still get away from here and find shelter, for the wind is growing stronger."

She turned and clasped her great-aunt's hand. "Dear aunt, do you think you can manage such a route?"

"You may be surprised." With a smile, she added, "I was quite the hoyden in my younger days, my lord."

"If both of you are willing, so am I." He gathered up his greatcoat. Picking up Lucinda's cloak, he frowned. "This is strangely heavy."

"I keep a book within a pocket underneath it." Lucinda opened the cloak so he could see the sagging pocket.

"An ingenious idea. Yours, Miss Hart?"

"Yes."

"As I said, most ingenious." He held up the cloak. "May I?"

"Thank you," she murmured as he settled it over her. "I think . . ." She forgot what she planned to say when his fingers lingered on her shoulders, gently massaging the tightness of fear from them. His breath warmed the back of her neck in a hint of the fire she had seen glowing in his eyes. At her sides, her fingers curled into fists as she fought the craving to turn and beg him to put his arms around her to keep her safe from Dayton.

There would be no safety within his embrace, she realized, as his finger boldly caressed the curve of her ear. So easily she could have swayed back against the hard strength of his chest. His arms would sweep up around her as he turned her to meet his mouth. He would . . .

With a gasp, Lucinda pulled away from his teasing touch and the images that should not be in her mind when death might come at any moment . . . or to own the truth, she should not be thinking of this pleasure at any time. What did she really know of Lord Loveland, save that he was Terence's tie-mate? He might be a rogue, little better than Dayton. His brazen caresses suggested that, for a gentleman should not take advantage of this situation and her unremitting terror to practice his seductive wiles.

She bumped into Aunt Jennie, who put out a hand to steady her. "Child, are you too frightened to try this?"

Not willing to own to what unsettled her, Lucinda forced a smile. "Of course I am frightened, but what choice do we have?"

"Exactly," the old woman said. "Do show us the way, Lord Loveland."

Lucinda urged her aunt to lean on her and hold her cane up off the floor so the sound of it striking the boards would not betray them. Lord Loveland paused only long enough to collect the poker; then with him assisting the old woman on the other side, they inched along the narrow hall to a door in the shadows. He pushed it open, holding the iron poker high. Nothing but more shadows and an unmade bed waited within.

"This way," he whispered.

Steering her great-aunt toward a draped window, Lucinda wanted to sob when Lord Loveland shoved aside the heavy green velvet. The window was smaller than the one in the other room. Although Aunt Jennie and she should be able to squeeze out with only a bit of difficulty, she doubted if the marquess's wide shoulders would fit beneath the narrow panes, even if it was raised to its utmost.

"My lord—"

His smile was not dimmed by what he must see as clearly as she did. "As we are now confederates on a most dangerous adventure, why don't I call you 'Lucinda' and you call me 'Max'?"

"Not Maximillian?"

He shuddered, then chuckled lowly. "A family curse handed down to me from an uncle who had the good sense to die young and rid himself of the name. Only my nurse and my grandmother were granted leave to use Maximillian. I prefer my friends to call me 'Max.' "

"Max, the window—"

"Trust me, Lucinda," he said with a grin. "I have gotten myself out of tighter spots."

He raised the window. It creaked, and she held her breath. If Dayton or one of his cronies were to come back now and find them here, he would have no choice but to slay them instantly.

She edged forward when he motioned to her. They did not dare speak loudly now that the window was open, for Dayton might have posted a guard within earshot. Her smile returned when she saw a nearly flat roof just a hand span beneath the sill.

"Let me go first," she whispered.

"If a guard sees you—"

"It will matter little," she argued, "if you or I or Aunt Jennie is the one spied. Our fate will be the same." She patted her cloak. "This is dark, and so is my hair. I fear you, Max, or Aunt Jennie with your light hair will be more visible."

"Aye, and for that reason alone, we must be grateful the weather is unfavorable. Mayhap that one thing in our favor might be our salvation." He bent and locked his fingers together in front of him. "Allow me to assist you."

Aunt Jennie said, "A moment." Putting her hands on either side of Lucinda's face, she whispered, "Be careful, child. I had not thought this would lead to you cavorting about on the roofs like a common chimney sweep. My lord, mayhap we should reconsider."

"There is no other way."

"But there is. If we were to—"

Max put his finger to the old woman's lips to silence

her. No careless words must give them away. As he heard bare branches scraping in the wind, he bent again and held out his hands.

Slowly Lucinda raised her foot to set it on his palms. She put one slender hand on his shoulder and the other on the sill. The soft scent of her perfume washed over him, intoxicating and intriguing, just like the woman who wore it. Although he had never imagined meeting Terence's youngest sister in this manner, he had to own it was a most unforgettable introduction to a woman he would not soon forget.

He swallowed his gasp when her soft breast brushed his arm. This was a torture as exquisite as any Dayton could conceive. When she whispered, "Now!," he did not move, reluctant to release her. Her face turned toward his, and her mouth was temptingly close to his. As her lips parted in a breath of astonishment, he had to fight himself to keep from covering them with his.

Blast it! This was his tie-mate's sister, and he was supposed to be thinking only of saving her life, not of the flavors he might relish on her soft mouth.

With a low curse, he lifted her from the floor. She scrambled through the window, giving him an enticing view of her slender ankles. Snow struck him as the wind rose to a howl. He grasped her arm through the window, not wanting her to be swept from the roof by the capricious weather.

"I am fine," she whispered. "Help Aunt Jennie now."

Max turned back and held out his hand to Lady Benedict. "My lady?"

"Do not waste your charm on me, young man." She tapped him on the shoulder with her cane. "Nor on my grandniece, for I have heard enough tales of your escapades with young Terence to be wise to your ways."

"And he has told me much of you, my lady."

"Then you are aware that I might allow my grandniece

to enjoy a conversation with a witty rake, but nothing more."

"I take the warning in the manner in which you have given it." He took her hand. "I trust we may continue this brangle at a later time."

"If we can."

He chuckled as he assisted her out through the window. He heard Lucinda's soft voice helping her great-aunt in the thickening darkness.

Pulling off his greatcoat, Max dropped it out the window into Lucinda's hands. Then he tried to follow it. The opening was a dashed tight fit, but, with the tearing of his favorite riding jacket, he squeezed through and clambered onto the roof. Dash it! He hoped his valet could mend it, although he dreaded telling his man how it had been ripped. Hammond would find this all amusing, as Max hoped he would—once it was over.

"Now down from here and to the stable. I suspect—" A threatening creak silenced him.

" 'Tis the roof!" Lucinda gasped. "It cannot hold the lot of us."

Four

Before anyone could halt her, Lucinda slid to the edge of the roof.

Max called, "What are you doing?"

"The roof will collapse if we all stay up here."

"Lucinda, no!"

She pushed her feet over the edge and jumped down. Pain careened up her right leg, but she ignored it as she pressed back against the wall, not wanting to give the smugglers inside a hint of their escape. She gasped when she heard another ominous creak from the supports of the small porch.

"Hurry!" she called in a low whisper.

Max peeked over the eave. "Are you all right?"

"Yes," she lied.

"Then look by the door. Is the bench still there?"

She risked a look around the edge of the porch. "Yes."

"Good." That was his only warning before he jumped down beside her as lightly as a cat leaping from a wall. Brushing snow from his greatcoat as he pulled it on, he skulked to the short wooden bench that would hold no more than a single person.

He set it beneath the porch, then climbed onto it and held out his hands to her great-aunt. When it wobbled, Lucinda rushed to steady it. Another stab of pain along her leg nearly undid her, but she silenced it. She must focus only on saving Aunt Jennie now.

When she looked up to see how her great-aunt was managing, snow struck her face. Not gentle flakes, but snow mixed with sleet that stung before clinging icily to her.

"Careful," she heard Max whisper.

"Just hold on to me, young man," Aunt Jennie replied, "and refrain from dropping me. I am not as young as Lucinda."

His rumbled laugh was too low to betray them. The bench settled more deeply into the snow; then Max stepped down and set Aunt Jennie on her feet.

"Well," said the old woman, rearranging her cloak about her and gripping her cane, "I did not expect I would be doing this today. I am surprising even myself."

"Let us hope we shall be surprising Dayton and his gang as well." Max pointed toward a stand of trees. "The stable is in this direction."

Lucinda hooked her arm through her great-aunt's, but stumbled on her first step. "I shall be fine," she whispered when Aunt Jennie glanced at her in consternation.

"You are hurt," her great-aunt gasped. "Oh, my!"

Max knelt. He touched her right ankle, and she moaned. He glanced up. "I believe it is not broken."

"It simply feels that way."

"Can you walk on it?"

"I have no choice."

"There are always choices, Lucinda."

Before she could ask what he meant, he lifted her in his arms as easily as he had Aunt Jennie. She grasped the front of his coat as he strode through the thickening sleet. When she strained to see past him, he murmured, "Lady Benedict is right behind us."

"I can walk. There is no need to—"

"Do be silent, Lucinda," he hissed. "We have come too far to have your injured sensibilities expose us to Dayton."

She nodded and tried to relax. It was impossible, for

then her cheek would rest against the damp wool stretched across his chest. When his boot caught in a rut, she grasped his shoulders.

His low chuckle resounded through him and her as he tightened his hold. "Fear not, Lucinda. I have no plan to send you sailing into a snow drift."

"If you wish to put me down—"

"That thought has not crossed my mind." His fingers stroked her side where her cloak had fallen back with the weight of her book.

Aunt Jennie's sharp question halted Lucinda's retort at his audacious caress. "What is that?"

Lucinda squinted through the snow to see a bulky shadow beneath the trees. Too large for a hedge, it was too small for a shed.

"It looks like a phaeton," Max said.

"Why would they leave a carriage out here on a night like this?" Lucinda gasped.

"They must have some use for it when they collect their illicit wares."

"A phaeton?"

"It is fast when the government's men are close on one's heels." He lengthened his stride. "However, now we have a more urgent use for it."

"But a carriage—"

Aunt Jennie chided, "Look neither a gift horse nor the carriage it can pull in the mouth, child. Just be grateful for whatever Providence put it in our path."

"More likely, one of those fools did not obey orders to get it out of the storm," Max said with a chuckle. "They do not have a brain among the lot of them." He settled Lucinda on the snowy seat, then handed Aunt Jennie up next to her. With quick competence, he raised the top to protect them from the icy rain. "Wait here."

"Where are you going?" Lucinda asked.

"We have a carriage, but it is of little use with no horses." He vanished into the night.

Rubbing her gloved hands together, Lucinda hunched down into her dark cloak. She feigned a smile when her great-aunt asked how she did. She was scared and cold and injured and tired and . . . "Terence!" she gasped.

"Here? Where?"

"Not here yet, but if he does come here, he could take our place in Dayton's game of murder."

Aunt Jennie patted her hand. "I suspect your brother found something to delay him at Lord Kenyon's house."

"Why would he stop there?" She wrinkled her nose. "Terence has less tolerance for Constance's boasting than I do."

"I asked him to pick up the listings for the Valentine's Day lottery and take them to Constance." Aunt Jennie folded her hands over the top of her cane and peered into the storm. "Your brother has more sense than those within the cottage, so he will let the storm keep him from traveling here this evening."

Lucinda never had expected to appreciate the Valentine's Day lottery, but if it kept her brother from this nest of thieves, she must be grateful to the odious tradition. Vowing not to complain about having to participate in it next time— if she survived that long—she scanned the empty yard.

Max's low whisper identified him as he led a horse across the frozen earth to the carriage. He put steaming bricks in the metal box near Lucinda's feet. "I hope this helps with the chill."

She did not have a chance to answer before he went to hitch the horse. Climbing up to sit next to her, Max grasped the reins. He clucked to the horse.

"Quietly," she urged. "If we go off to the left there, we might be able to reach the road without being seen."

He nodded. "You are becoming quite the competent

conspirator, Lucinda." Winking at Aunt Jennie, he said, "I do not know what I would have done without the two of you to help me in this escape."

"You shall learn," the old woman said in her tartest tone, "if you do not manage to get us away from here in our skins."

"I shall be as quiet as a morning sneak on his way to relieve you of your valuables."

Lucinda tensed as he slapped the reins on the horse's back. The horse strained, but the carriage did not move.

"Damn," Max said without apology. "Frozen in place. What a blasted time for an ice storm!"

"Can you loosen it?" she asked.

"I can try."

He slid off the seat and kicked at the wheels. Lucinda stared at the cottage. If even one of the blackguards chanced to hear the dull thud of his boots on the iron-rimmed wheels, all might be lost.

Quickly he swung back up to sit beside her. "Shall we try again?"

"Still quietly?"

"Most definitely quietly," he said, smiling. When he raised the reins, the wheels broke free with the sound of shattering crystal. They rolled slowly forward and clattered on the stones in the frozen dirt as the iron horseshoes clicked on each step.

Max kept the horse to a sedate walk as he drove the carriage under the trees. Gripping her great-aunt's arm, Lucinda held on to the seat and breathed shallowly. Could a single breath betray them? She did not dare to find out. They bounced from side to side as Max tried to find the quickest route down the steep hillside and through the wall of shadows.

She looked through the storm toward the road leading back up the hill. The lights from the cottage were still too close. Hunching her shoulders again, she prayed no ball would be aimed at her back.

"By Jove!" came a shout from near the cottage. "Dayton, they are getting away!"

Max muttered something under his breath before he slapped the reins on the horse and shouted. The horse sprang forward. Aunt Jennie gasped and clutched onto Lucinda, who threw her arms around her great-aunt. Snow and mud sprayed up from the horse's hoofs to pelt their faces.

Something exploded behind them. She started to look back, but Max's hand pressed her toward the seat.

"Stay down!" he shouted. "Stay down before you are hit."

Leaning over to protect Aunt Jennie, Lucinda bit back language that would be too despicable even for her outspoken great-aunt. Aunt Jennie was quaking as if with the highest fever.

More shots sounded, and Max bellowed a command to the horse. Branches broke across the top of the phaeton as they careened down the hill. She feared they were out of control, but what did it matter if they died in the crushed carriage? To survive now would gain them nothing but death.

The carriage tilted as they burst out onto the road. Max propped his boots against the dash and fought to keep the phaeton from flying onto its side. His victorious shout spurred the horse, and they raced along the road at a dangerous pace.

"Try not to kill us with your driving, my lord," Aunt Jennie said as she straightened and grasped the side of the rocking carriage. "We have endured too much to die in such a commonplace manner."

"How do you fare?" he asked, glancing from the road to Lucinda.

"Grateful."

When her great-aunt chuckled, Max said, "That I can understand very well."

"I hope Terence is safe."

"I am certain he is. From what I have seen, he is at least as resourceful as his baby sister, who sprinted as spryly as a monkey across the roof."

"And ended up with a twisted ankle."

His smile faded. "That is my one regret through all this. How does it do?"

"Much better. I suspect it will be fine by morning." She wiggled her foot cautiously. "It feels better already."

"Good. We may need to run if we are followed."

Her relief vanished. "Followed?"

"Did you think Dayton would give up so easily?" He scowled at the rain which was freezing each branch into an icicle. "This night must be his favorite element, cold and stormy and keeping decent folk within the walls of their homes."

The carriage abruptly lurched, and the horse whinnied a warning. Lucinda grabbed for her great-aunt as the old woman shrieked. Strong arms surrounded both of them, pinning them to the seat. The carriage wheels struck a snowbank on the side of the road, then came to a stop.

Max shoved the reins into Lucinda's hands. He jumped to the road and ran to grasp the horse's head as it pranced nervously.

"What is it?" called Aunt Jennie. "Is there a bridge out?"

"No, thank goodness, but the road ahead has flooded and is now frozen," he shouted back. "I shall have to guide the horse until we have cleared this mess."

"Do you want my cloak?" Lucinda asked.

The glitter of his smile was nearly as bright as the sheen on the ice. "Nonsense! You need it, or you could freeze."

"I can share Aunt Jennie's." She smiled genuinely for

the first time since they had arrived at the cottage. "She is so little, she will take up scarcely more room than I do."

Undoing the cloak, she pulled the book out of the pocket and stretched to hand the cape to him. She could not keep from laughing as he tossed it over his greatcoat. It fell no farther than his knees, for his broad shoulders and the cape on his coat bunched the material around his arms. When he pulled the hood over his head, he laughed as well.

"I shall not be mistaken for a fashion plate," he said, as he grasped the horse's halter. "Let us go before Dayton finds us. I would not wish to meet my end dressed like this. Think how mortifying that would be to my family."

Aunt Jennie swept her cloak over Lucinda's shoulders and bent to whisper in a conspiratorial tone, "You are doing admirably, dear child. You have shown a rare courage in the face of incredible odds."

"Do you think we can flee those curs?"

"I trust Lord Loveland will keep us from being slain by them." Her eyes twinkled with merriment. "He seems quite taken with you, Lucinda, and this opportunity to play the hero straight out of one of your novels. Who would have guessed you would meet a gentleman in this manner?"

Lucinda clenched the seat as the carriage inched forward. The wheels skidded on the ice, and she knew the horse had been wise to refuse to cross this frozen pool at a breakneck speed, for all of them could have been killed.

"Aunt Jennie, can't you leave off from playing the matchmaker even now?" she asked, trying to see through the curtain of sleet that was turning back to snow. "Max is being kind to his friend's younger sister in an intolerable situation. Nothing more."

"Dear me, where did we go wrong with your education?"

She pulled her gaze from the road to regard her great-aunt in bafflement. "That tact will not work either. I am as familiar with the skills of flirtation as I am with how to calculate the grocer's bill. My education has not been neglected."

" 'The skills of flirtation'?" She sniffed. "Listen to yourself. You approach matters of the heart as if they were a craft, when I can assure you they are an art." Shaking her head so her bonnet brushed Lucinda's hair, she sighed. "How many times have I told Jerome he should insist you spend more time with the caper-merchant and less with your books?"

"I hope it will be many more times."

Aunt Jennie squeezed her hand. "Do not be frightened. I think we shall succeed in putting this incident behind us. We are fortunate to have Lord Loveland here to assist us."

As if his name were a cue, the carriage slowed and Max walked back to them. He was smiling, but Lucinda saw the lines of strain carved by the wind into his face. When he clenched and unclenched his fingers stiffly, she realized he had no gloves.

She seized his hands and rubbed them between her smaller ones. "Max, you shall suffer frostbite on your fingers if you do not take care."

"What alternative do you suggest?" His smile broadened beneath his brows which were frosted with the storm. "Your ministrations are delightful, but will do us little good, for I cannot lead the horse and enjoy this at the same time."

"Why must you continue to lead the horse?" Aunt Jennie asked, fear suddenly sifting into her voice.

"The road ahead does not look promising. Half of it is filled with ice, the rest with snow." He kicked at a clump of ice which had fallen off the carriage. "To make the horse pull this carriage along closed roads with all of us riding would be cruel."

"There must be a house nearby," Aunt Jennie said.

Lucinda released Max's hands, and he clamped them under his arms as she asked, "How can we be certain which house offers a haven? If we were to seek shelter at a house where one of the smugglers lives, we could be right back where we started."

"I think we shall have to take that risk." He sneezed, then smiled. "Pardon me, ladies. If we stay out here much longer, I suspect all of us shall be suffering from more than a ticklish nose."

"We cannot be far from Rexleigh-on-Sea," Lucinda said. "If we find a crossroad heading toward the water, we might find the village."

"Or Dayton and his boys."

"You said we must take a risk. I think that is our best gamble. If—"

"What is it?"

She would have answered Max's sharp question if she had been able. All she could do was clasp his hand and Aunt Jennie's and stare at the form coming out of the storm. The only prayer she had left was that their deaths would be quick and merciful.

Five

Max pulled away from Lucinda and seized the whip on the dash. He raised it as the shadow emerged from the storm.

"Terence!" Lucinda cried and caught Max's arm before he could swing the whip. "What are you doing out here in this storm?"

"Terence!" Aunt Jennie's gasp rose over Max's shout.

Terence Hart, his mother's crowning glory for having given her husband a son after two daughters, and his father's despair in the wake of too many of his antics, strolled toward them, his horse in tow as if it were the sunniest of days. Snow pocked his dark hair, and his coat of the same ebony was lacquered to his lanky body. Shorter than Max, he possessed an aura of good humor that drew both men and women to him.

Tipping his tall beaver toward them, he grinned. "Well met, although this is a surprise. I had thought you would be wise enough to remain at the cottage until the roads were cleared."

"We found it expedient to leave earlier than I had planned when we last spoke," Max answered, setting the whip back in its stand.

Terence reached up and took Aunt Jennie's hand. "You look well, Aunt."

"I have had a most interesting day." Her eyes twinkled like moonlight on snow. "It is good to see you, my boy, although I must own that the sight of my own hearth will be the most welcome I can imagine now."

"Not likely," Terence said. "The roads in the direction of the Priory are in a worse state than this one. I think we should return to the cottage posthaste."

Max shook his head, then, with a low grumble, pulled off Lucinda's cloak when a laugh bubbled from Terence. Wadding it into a ball, he tossed it into the carriage. "We are not going back there tonight."

"But it is not far, and we can—"

Lucinda angrily gripped her brother's lapels and leaned toward him. "Thunder, Terence. Will you listen to Max? We cannot go back there."

His dark brows shot toward his hair as he crowed, " 'Max'! Friend, you have inveigled your way into my sister's good graces with extraordinary speed."

"Terence, will you stop talking fiddle-faddle and listen?" Releasing his coat, she took a deep breath to steady her voice. She did not need to scold her brother as if she were a fishwife. "We have narrowly escaped the deadly nevergreens at the hands of smugglers who have taken over the cottage."

"Is that so?" He rested one elbow on the side of the carriage. His brow furrowed. "This is not our phaeton, and I recall you sent yours home to Sussex, Max."

"We stole it." Aunt Jennie chuckled. "Let those wicked blokes take the shin-stage to the coast to do their evil work."

Max held up his hands when Terence started to ask another question. "We must get the ladies out of the storm. It shows no signs of easing."

"We are wet and cold," Lucinda added in a calmer tone, "and Max is about to catch his death. Once we get out of the night, I swear we shall share with you every detail about our adventures, Terence."

Terence's smile did not waver. "I know of a place not

far from here. It is not grand, but it should hold us for
tonight."

"Lead on," Max said.

Mounting, Terence motioned for Max to get back in
the carriage. "I can ride by the horse's head and guide it
through the snow. You look as if you could use a chance
to rest."

"I had not planned to climb across a roof this evening," he said, as he sat next to Lucinda.

"A roof?" He laughed. "I can hardly bear to wait the
telling of this story."

His smile vanished when an ear-splitting crack filled
the night. He shouted a warning. Max threw himself
across the seat, pushing Lucinda and Aunt Jennie down.
The carriage shook, and something slapped Lucinda's
leg as fabric tore. Renewed pain scored her.

With a shaky laugh, she looked down to see broken
twigs littering the carriage. She raised her eyes, and her
breath caught to discover Max's face only a finger's
breadth from hers. Not even the shadows could conceal
the emerald fire in his eyes.

"Are you hurt?" he whispered.

She longed to close her eyes and savor the warmth of
his breath upon her as well as the steel-strong grip of
his arms surrounding her, protecting her . . . endangering her by creating thoughts she must not let tempt her.
The golden caress of his hair falling against her face
urged her to let the storm winds sweep all caution away
as she tangled her fingers in it.

"Just scratched," she answered as softly. She reached
up to brush his hair back from her face.

"And Lady Benedict?"

Lucinda started at his question, her fingers halting a
bare inch from his face. How could she have forgotten
Aunt Jennie?

"I am fine," grumbled her great-aunt. With another

mutter, she pushed Lucinda aside and sat. "This is becoming more of a trial than a diversion. Terence? Boy, where are you?"

As Max assisted Lucinda to sit in the carriage that was strewn with broken twigs, her brother peeked around the side. His grin was dimmed as he said, "That might not be the only branch to fall beneath the weight of ice on it. We must find shelter immediately."

"Just as I told you," Lucinda retorted. When he stared at her, clearly astonished at her acerbity, she started to apologize.

Her words melted as Max bent down to draw aside her skirt which was torn from just below her knee. A rush of pleasure seared her, and her skin tingled in anticipation of his touch. She gasped as the delight became a piercing pain.

Pulling a handkerchief from beneath his coat, he shook it open. Water splattered them both. He smiled ruefully as he dabbed it against where blood stained her white stocking.

"It is nothing," she said, drawing his hand away. "Just a scratch. Terence will assure you that I have suffered worse when I tried to race him to the top of the trees in the orchard."

"You are brave." He did not let her pull her hand out of his. "If I could have had your rare courage among my men, things might have been very different two years ago."

"Two years ago? What took place two years ago?"

Max did not answer and instead reached for the reins, calling to Terence to lead the way. Dash it all to perdition! This weekend was supposed to help him forget Spain and Boney and everything to do with mud and blood and war. Instead events were conspiring to resurrect those memories. He rubbed the scar on his chin, then frowned. He would forget it.

He found that easier than he had expected, for all his concentration was needed to guide the carriage behind Terence. As if the storm could not make up its mind, first snow, then sleet raged at them. He glanced at his passengers. Lucinda was hunched over her great-aunt, trying to keep the old woman as dry as possible. He had never guessed this weekend would be so miserable when Terence first suggested he come to the cottage.

Looking again at Lucinda, he had to smile to himself. This weekend was not totally miserable, for Miss Lucinda Hart was a pleasant surprise amidst the insanity of these adventures. And a most pleasant armful. He could not be oblivious to the concerted matchmaking of Lady Benedict and her grandnephew, but he already had discovered Lucinda possessed a mind that was decidedly all her own. Now he needed to discover if her lips were as sweet as he suspected.

He nearly laughed aloud in spite of the cold rain. Lady Benedict might allow—in fact, she would most likely encourage—a flirtation, but he could not imagine that strong-willed lady sanctioning any untoward behavior by her grandniece. It was quite acceptable for Lucinda to scamper down a roof with him as long as she was not in his arms, her soft mouth against his.

When Max saw a glow through the darkness, he squinted. It must be their destination, for Terence turned toward it from the dim outline of the main road between the snow-covered stone walls. He hoped Terence would have the good sense to recall his great-aunt needed a solid roof over her head and walls to keep out the wind.

He drew in the reins as Terence raised his arm and slowed. "I suspect we are here," he said, not sure what would happen now.

"Here?" Lucinda peeked out from beneath the cloak. "Here where?"

Her eyes widened when she saw the unmistakable out-line of a trio of wagons in the small clearing. As branches crashed together overhead, she could only stare and whisper, "Gypsies?"

Terence had swung off his horse and knocked on the door of the closest wagon. When a man opened the door, she could hear the rumbled voices. Terence handed the man something and stepped aside as the man rushed past him to the next wagon.

Coming back to the carriage, Terence grinned. "We have a place to spend the night. We are welcome to use anything within the wagon."

"We are staying here?" Lucinda choked.

"I apologize for any damage this might do to your reputation, Lucinda, but . . ."

She sighed and glanced at Aunt Jennie, who was asleep as comfortably as if she had been in her favorite chair in the Priory's solar. " 'Tis not my reputation that I fear for. I doubt if she will agree to such lodgings."

"There is no other choice." Max swept snow off his shoulders and shook his head, sending more cascading onto both of them. "The storm is not lessening. I am not sure how much farther the horse can drag the carriage through the snow."

"Listen to him, Lucinda." Her brother shivered. "After all, you have both Aunt Jennie and me to guard your reputation."

"And me," Max added with a smile. He jumped out of the carriage as Lucinda woke her great-aunt. When Terence assisted Aunt Jennie down from the seat, Max held out his hand to Lucinda. "Let's get you inside; then Terence and I shall see to the comfort of the beasts."

Lucinda hesitated. *Gypsies?* Could this day take a worse turn? As much a part of the shire as the smugglers, Gyp-sies were even more untrustworthy. The man might take Terence's money, then slay them while they slept.

"Lucinda?" Max prompted.

She took a deep breath and squared her shoulders. She was rewarded by cold water dripping down her back. With a shiver as she pulled on her own damp cloak, she said, "I see we must be reasonable, although, Max, I would have preferred nearly any other quarters."

" 'Tis better than having Dayton as our host," he grumbled, and Lucinda feared she had hurt his feelings by not being grateful for his assistance. She dared not think what would have happened to her and Aunt Jennie if Max had not been there when they entered the cottage.

Aunt Jennie chuckled as she picked her way through the snow that reached high on her calves. "You made a doodle of that catoller Dayton. No question of that, my lord."

" 'Twas with the aid of two very lovely, resourceful ladies." Holding up his arms, he said, "Lucinda, you shall be mistaken for a snow-creature if you remain much longer on that seat."

"I think I can walk that short distance."

"As you wish."

Surprised he did not argue, she wondered how long he had been a captive of the smugglers. He had not said. It was possible he had arrived at the cottage yesterday and had spent the night waiting for his destiny to be decided. If so, he must be exhausted. She should not add to his fatigue with her petulance.

Her steps were tentative as he handed her down from the carriage. The cold burned against her scraped leg, and her ankle threatened not to hold her; but she refused to surrender to the pain. She took another step and gasped.

With a laugh, Max swung her up into his arms. Her cloak flared out, then dropped back, the side with the book striking him on the leg.

He grimaced. "You present a danger to all of those around you, Lucinda."

"You might have asked before grabbing me."

"If you keep wiggling about like a young pup," he murmured, his voice lowering until it was as deep and lush as the snow, "you shall have other concerns than me picking you up."

"Lord Loveland!"

With another laugh, he said, "Simply an honest warning."

She was not sure how to answer, so she remained silent as he climbed the steep steps to the open door. Warmth struck her like a blow, but it was a most welcome one. Pushing back the hood of her cloak, she looked about as Max set her on a bench by a table in the middle of the wagon.

With the four of them, a small stove, the table, the bench, and a bed built against one wall where what paint that remained was peeling, there was no room to do much more than catch her breath. Aunt Jennie drew off her cloak and sat on the bed, her short legs hanging over the doors that opened beneath it. Her nose wrinkled as a stale smell rose from the coverlet.

"Our circumstances could be more appalling, I suspect," Aunt Jennie said, patting her white hair back behind her ears, "although I would not want to witness that."

When Max and Terence went back out into the storm, Lucinda rose gingerly. She smiled. Here, where the snow did not try to snare her on every step, she could walk more easily.

"Are you hungry, Aunt Jennie?" she asked as she peered at the sacks on a shelf in the shadow of the stove.

"Famished. Is there something worth eating in this hovel?"

"I believe I can manage something." She smiled as

she lifted a small package. "There is tea, at least. That will take the chill from our bones."

By the time the door reopened and the sound of Terence's laugh reached into the wagon, Lucinda had found plates and cups. She tried not to think how long it might have been since they had been cleaned. Instead she toasted bread on a griddle and put the steaming slices and a cup of jam on the table.

The two men wasted no time sitting at the table, once they were certain Aunt Jennie was seated comfortably. Lucinda set cheese before them and turned to cook a pot of the oatmeal that had been in the largest sack. It would not be the grandest meal any of them had ever eaten, but it would be filling. Setting the pot on the table, she ladled out four bowls and sat.

"You are an excellent cook, Lucinda," Max said as he reached for another slice of toast and cheese.

"Terence and I often went for al fresco lunches along the shore." Her smile faded as she glanced toward the door. "Do you think those beastly creatures will follow us here?"

"The snow should hide our tracks quite effectively." He stabbed another piece of cheese with his fork. "The storm that keeps us here will keep them far from us. I think you can sleep without a care tonight."

"On that matter," Aunt Jennie interjected, "we must be candid, my lord."

"My lady, I appreciate your insight into this unforeseen situation."

"Unforeseen?" She chuckled. "My lord, you honestly did not think we would reach the Priory before nightfall, did you?"

"I must own that at the inspired moment when we left the cottage I was more concerned with keeping my neck its current length than endangering your great-niece's propriety."

Lucinda put her spoon on the table. "Do not chide him, Aunt Jennie. I doubt if any of us will find sleep easily tonight, and, to own the truth, I share Max's opinion. I would gamble my reputation at this point to stay alive."

"Do not let Father hear you say that," Terence said as he rose. Searching the shelf, he held up a dusty bottle. He pulled out the cork, sniffed the bottle, and then, with a smile, poured wine for each of them. "He will not be pleased by this turn of events."

"Once we tell him the truth—"

"Yes, Lucinda," he said, folding his arms on the table, "tell me all that has chanced to happen to you today."

Although she did not want to relive the events of the day, she began to relate them. Max and Aunt Jennie interjected comments occasionally as her brother listened intently. He gave a low whistle when she spoke of their hasty escape out the window.

When she finished, Max paced the pair of steps from the door to the table as he kept her brother busy with dozens of questions about the countryside and the possibility of travel at dawn. Lucinda cleaned the dishes and set them back on the shelf. Exhaustion weighed heavily on her. They had thought only of fleeing, and now that they appeared to be safe, every muscle within her throbbed with pain and fatigue.

She sat on the bench by the table. When her great-aunt handed her something, she took it silently.

"What is that?" Max asked.

Looking at what she held, she said, "A book." She opened it to the page where she had left off. How could she have guessed such perilous circumstances would delay her from finishing the passage? She whispered a mild oath.

"Lucinda!" chided Aunt Jennie. "Do refrain from speaking with an adder's tongue. You will have to forgive her, my lord. She has lived a very sheltered life. I had hoped a Season in Town would teach her to curb her thoughts before she gives them voice."

Dropping to sit cross-legged beside her, he rested his elbow on the low bed. "It is refreshing to meet a woman who is not afraid to avoid the polite talk of the Polite World. I salute you, Lucinda, for being so candid."

"I am trying to read, Max," she murmured, not raising her gaze from her page. She did not dare, for every inch of her was aware how near he sat. A heat, which was more pleasurable and sought much deeper within her than the flames in the stove, oozed outward from where his sleeve brushed her tattered skirt.

His fingers slipped over her arm. "Tell me about this book. Mayhap I have read it, too."

"I doubt that for it is a romantic tale." She fought to keep her eyes focused on the book. If she were to look in his enigmatic eyes which had showed no fear in the face of death, every bit of her own residual fright might be unleashed to disgrace her.

"Terence mentioned often your love of reading."

"She reads too much," said Aunt Jennie, threading her needle anew as she pulled her embroidery out of her bag. "She always has a book propped in front of her face."

"Either that," added Terence, "or she is out riding along the shore, imagining she is the heroine of some such silly story. My baby sister has a very fanciful nature."

Lucinda expected Max to laugh, but as lief he said, "A noble use of your time, in my most humble opinion. I can imagine nothing more delightful than to think of myself as the hero of one of Sir Walter Scott's grand romances. 'Tis much the pity I am not, for such a hero would not have sat quietly as a captive of these owls."

"You did not sit quietly," Lucinda argued. "You saved our lives."

"Or, to be more honest, you saved mine." He clasped one hand between his and lifted it to his mouth.

Her lips parted in a soft breath when he pressed her palm against his face, his kiss as fervent as his touch. Sweet fire blazed through her when his mouth grazed each finger. Slowly he drew back and curled her fingers closed within his. She leaned toward him, wanting more of this incredible splendor.

"Lucinda?"

Aunt Jennie had to call her name again before Lucinda rose and went to where her great-aunt was trying to pull out another blanket from the cupboard beneath the bed. Bending to help, Lucinda glanced back at Max.

His green gaze caught hers, and her hand tightened on the open door as a slow, promising smile spread across his stern lips. Her breath came fast over her rapidly beating heart. True, they had escaped from the smugglers, but she wondered if she had traded that prison for a very different, but equally dangerous captivity in her longing for his kisses.

Six

Lucinda's hope that the morning would bring pleasant weather came to naught when dawn arrived with the steady clatter of icy rain against the roof of the wagon. Standing and rubbing the middle of her back which ached from a night of sitting propped against the end of the bed where Aunt Jennie slept, she sighed.

"What a dolorous sound!" The whisper was followed by a low chuckle.

She gave Max a weary smile, but looked hastily away before her gaze could linger on his tousled hair and his loosened shirt which revealed his strong chest. Such images had filled her dreams during the brief moments she had found sleep. To see him like this now . . .

She hurried to say, "Nothing is as sad as the noise of that storm. I do not look forward to traveling in that cold rain half the day to Hart's Priory."

"Kenyon Hall is not far," Terence said as he sat, clasping his arms around the knees of his breeches. "Yesterday Constance was lamenting how long it had been since she last saw you, Lucinda. Think how delighted she would be if we gave her a look-in."

"In this state?" She stared at her tattered dress and poked at her hair which refused to remain in its chignon. "She will have a paroxysm if we deposit ourselves at her door looking like this."

Terence jumped to his feet and drew on his jacket. "I know you are not overly fond of Constance."

"An understatement, if ever one was spoken," Aunt Jennie said, sitting up on the bed. "However, I think stopping at Kenyon Hall is a famous idea, Terence. I had half-thought to spend this weekend with Constance as it was." She flashed Lucinda a triumphant smile. "Just think, we can be there for the Valentine's Day lottery and dance."

Lucinda shook her head. "Dear aunt, you know my feelings on that subject."

Beneath Aunt Jennie's chuckle and her brother's guffaw, Max asked, "A Valentine's Day lottery? What is the prize?"

"A young woman's company," Aunt Jennie said with another smile, "and a chance to win that young lady's hand."

"A most disagreeable, archaic custom." Lucinda swept her cloak over her shoulders. "If we start now, we might be able to reach Hart's Priory before sunset. What do you think, Max? Should we hook Terence's horse to the carriage as well?"

Max drew on his greatcoat and followed Lucinda as she rushed out. Cold rain slid down his collar, and he resisted cursing. Why was Lucinda being so blasted prickly this morning? She should be pleased with the way matters were going.

He watched as she led the two horses from the shelter beneath the trees toward the drenched carriage. Icy water oozed into his boots, adding to dampness which made a nearly obscene sound with every step. Moving to block her way, he held out his hand.

"You would show more sense to have stayed inside while we hooked up the horse," he said.

When she bristled at his condescending tone, he almost laughed. How seriously she took every word and motion! If her brother had half her fire, he would have finished Cambridge just in time to be appointed to a cabinet post. Instead of spending her time seeking ways to amuse herself and those around her as Terence did, she concerned herself with their well-being. Only the mention of the Valentine's Day lottery had altered that and he was curious why.

"Can both horses be hitched to the carriage?" she asked, her voice as cold as the rain pelting them.

"Not easily." He lashed the reins of Terence's horse to the dash as he led the other horse to the front of the carriage. "Why are you in such a rush?"

"That is a silly question! I wish to put as much distance as possible between those smugglers and us. They are the most disagreeable men I have ever encountered." She shivered and whispered, "I hope never to see their like again."

"Odd, you did not mention the owlers inside. One would think you were more anxious to avoid Lady Constance than the smugglers."

She rubbed her hands together and avoided meeting his eyes. "Max, you do not understand."

"Clearly. That is why I am asking."

"I have been able to keep myself free of being entangled in that dashed lottery so far."

"Miss Hart, your language!" When she smiled at his easy imitation of her great-aunt, he walked back to where she stood. He took her hands in his and said, "If it troubles you so deeply, do not take part in it now."

"I shall have no choice if I am at Kenyon Hall." She sighed. "You would comprehend the depths of the humiliation it can bring if you had to participate. Of course, as a gentleman, the choice is yours."

"And that is part of the humiliation?"

"Yes."

He chuckled. "Then count me in the lottery, Lucinda."

"What?"

"I shall throw my name in among the other young blokes who hope to gain the attention of a young lady."

He was not certain what she mumbled, but it sounded remarkably like her brother's favorite curse. Most remarkable, for Miss Lucinda Hart had been the pattern-card of decorum, save for their ignoble journey across the porch roof. There might be more to this lady than first met the eye, even though, he had to own, she possessed enough pleasurable sights to draw his eyes from the onset.

Handing her into the carriage, he said, "You look down-pinned at my gallant suggestion."

"Not as down-pinned as you shall be by half when you find yourself mixed up in that intolerable muddle."

He laughed, but, when she did not as much as smile, he wondered what he had volunteered for now. He should have learned his lessons about volunteering two years ago. Now only one thing was certain. However this lottery played out, it would be interesting as long as Lucinda Hart and her family played a part.

Lady Constance Kenyon flowed into the small blue sitting room at the front of Kenyon Hall in a cloud of smuggled perfume and silk. Her cheeks were dusted to the palest pale, then rouged to give them a girlish color. With her hair nearly the shade of holly berries, she wisely had chosen to wear a sedate white.

She was as squarely built as the hulking house her husband had inherited along with his father's generous bequest of blunt. In the gray light trickling through the arched windows at one end of the room, she could not hide her smile as she surveyed her drenched collection of guests.

Rushing forward, she grasped Aunt Jennie's hands and crooned, "Oh, my poor, poor dear! To have to suffer such a fate at your advanced years."

"It would be enough to kill some old toughs," Aunt Jennie said as she withdrew her hand from Constance's grip. She fired a warning to Lucinda to keep her smile hidden when she added, "And think where that would leave this family with your husband at its head."

"That would be so, wouldn't it?" She purred. "I had not given that a thought in my concern for you."

"I bet," Terence muttered under his breath.

"What did you say, young man?"

"I said, 'I bet you were deeply concerned,' " he said so smoothly Lucinda was not surprised Constance believed him. Or mayhap it was as simple as her father's cousin's wife could not imagine anyone not thinking she was the pick of the Polite World. "Dear cousin Constance, have you had the pleasure of meeting Lord Loveland?"

She held out her hand and cooed, "Terence has told us all so much about you, my lord. Trust a bird-witted bulchin like him not to reveal how handsome you are." She barely paused before hurrying to say, "Lucinda, you are fortunate to have such a dashing blade escorting you about the shire."

"As lief," Max said before Lucinda could imagine what she could say without putting herself to the blush, "I would say I am the fortunate one, my lady, for Miss Hart has proven her wit and courage in the past day."

"Thank you," Lucinda whispered beneath Constance's gasp of alarm as Aunt Jennie related the tale of their escape from the smugglers. "I am sorry, but Constance has never learned to think before speaking."

"You warned me."

When he smiled, she did as well. She might look a complete rump, and he little better if the truth be told, but she appreciated his honesty. She could be nothing less with him.

Constance bustled toward them, her bosom bouncing on every step. "After your trials, my lord, you must consider staying with us here until you have rested yourself from this ordeal."

"If I am to agree to such a generous proposition to join you *en famille,* I hope you will feel comfortable to call me 'Max,' " he answered.

She batted her ruddy lashes at him. "You must stay with us, Max."

"Then I would be honored to accept your kind invitation, Lady Constance, for I had hoped to spend more time with your charming family."

A flutter in Lucinda's center urged her to give Max a smile as warm as his. Here, where they were safe from those evil creatures, he had not lost a smidgen of the sense of strength and will she had seen while they escaped from the cottage. Yet, she was curious why he urged, with all alacrity, each one he met to dispense with his title. He seemed to want no label, save his own name.

She was given no time to ask. With Constance on one side of her and Aunt Jennie on the other, both chattering like a pair of African monkeys, she was herded up the stairs to clean herself and change into something that did not make her look like an urchin on London's bleakest street.

She looked back to see Max and Terence walking in the opposite direction. As their laughs drifted to her, she wondered why her spirits were suddenly so low. She should be delighted they were warm and safe, but a peculiar urge to cry gripped her. She could not understand it . . . not at all.

* * *

"Is it interesting?"

Lucinda glanced up from her book and smiled, closing the book over her finger. As Max crossed the book room where the afternoon sun inched across the Persian rug, sparkling on Lord Kenyon's collection of dueling swords, his steps were as smooth as the floor beneath his feet. He was dressed in riding clothes, and his greatcoat struck his perfectly polished boots on every pace.

"I see your coat has managed to dry," she said, standing and putting her book on the table by the chair. She would get back to the adventures within its covers later.

"Constance's household arranged for that in bang off time." He plucked at his sleeve. "Not a bit of dampness left in it, and it does not smell scorched either." He held it up toward her.

Knowing she should be more circumspect, she stretched to smell the wool. "Yes, they did an excellent job." She drew back far enough so she was not overmastered by his smile. "Are you going out?"

"I thought I might wander about the grounds." He took her hand and led her to the window. "I love snow, although I suspect you have had quite enough after our journey."

"Not really," she said, struggling to keep the tremor from her voice. It did not matter, for he could not be unaware of how her fingers quivered within the strength of his hand. His skin was a rough caress against her which urged her to think of delights best left to dreams, because she knew so little of him.

"Remarkable." Leaning one hand on the sill, he said, "Each time I think of you, Lucinda, that is the word that springs into my head. I shudder to think of what would have happened if you had been as delicate as a hothouse flower when we faced such a challenge yesterday."

She traced the contorted pattern of frost along the window, watching it vanish beneath her fingertip. Deciding it would be best to change the course of the conversation back to something less personal, she whispered, "I love the snow, too. It makes the whole world look like a gift waiting to be opened. We cannot guess what might lie beneath the white cover, and we are anxious to discover the flowers soon to be reborn."

"Then shall we?"

"Shall we what?"

He crossed the room and reached around the corner of the door. Lifting her cloak, he said, "Take that walk."

"Now?"

Coming to stand beside her, he settled the dried cloak on her shoulders. When she looked up at him, astonished, he said, "I suspect it is not much more chilly out there than it was this morning. I miss seeing your cheeks that charming shade of red."

"But we only have gotten warm."

He ran his finger along her jaw, and she closed her eyes, savoring the restrained passion in his touch. How she longed for him to unleash it! Knowing she was mad, she put her hand on his arm and turned to face him. His arm slipped around her waist. With a sharp tug, he brought her tight to him. When he bent toward her, she closed her eyes again, aching deep within her for his kiss.

Her eyes popped open as, instead of brushing his mouth against hers, he whispered, "Wouldn't you prefer a bit of frost to being roasted?"

"Roasted?" she asked, trying to convince her mind to work. She had been so certain—she had been so hopeful—that he would kiss her.

"Even now, Constance is planning a tea for all of us within the hour."

Lucinda smiled as a wicked glint brightened his eyes. She had suffered through enough of Constance's teas, which Constance considered her prime chance to interrogate each of her guests about what gossip they might have heard. If Constance even suspected that Lucinda was dreaming of Max's kiss, there would be no halting Constance from probing until she obtained every detail. "Did Terence warn you?"

"No need. I have met Lady Kenyon's like before. She is a generous soul, but her prattle explains why Lord Kenyon prefers the company he keeps in London."

"He is very busy in the government, not with mischief."

"If I suggested that, Lucinda, I apologize for any insult I may have given your family."

She laughed at his attempt to look properly apologetic. She could not imagine Max being anything but honest, and for that she was grateful. With her mind in such a jumble, she did not want to watch every word she spoke. She, too, could be candid.

He offered his arm, and she let him draw her hand within it. When he said nothing else, she was oddly pleased. Other men had tried to lather her with compliments and keep her ears buzzing with their endless parade of words. Max did not seem to fear the silence.

After pausing only to get her boots and a pair of thick gloves, Lucinda walked with Max through the snow along the drive. The wind had vanished to leave the flakes falling in a silent quadrille, spinning around each other, apart and together, in a pattern she could not discern.

When he turned toward the lane leading through the topiary garden to the river farther down the hill, Lucinda warned, "It shall be colder by the water."

"Do you think the river will freeze?"

"Only at the edges, for the water runs too quickly."

"Hard enough to skate on?"

She shook her head. "If you wish to skate, you will have to settle for one of the ponds. First you will need to remove the snow stacked upon the ice."

"Do you skate?"

"Of course." She smiled as she glanced back at the house which was nearly shrouded by the storm. "In spite of Terence's attempts to trip me up each time we went out on the ice when I was trying to learn."

"Siblings can be a trial." He laughed as they followed a stone wall toward the river. "I have to own to gratitude that mine are far away in Sussex."

"You have many?"

"Siblings?" He arched his brows which were powdered with snow. "An embarrassment of riches, I believe is the most polite term I can use. Like your brother, I have three sisters, but I also have a like number of brothers."

"And you are responsible for the lot?"

He paused by the wall as the land swept down across the lea to the river. "As their brother, it behooves me to find them proper mates and establish their futures. Thea is the eldest, and she is about your age, I suspect. If I were a doting brother, I would be concentrating on finding her a match as lief enjoying this sojourn in grassville."

"Have you considered my brother?" She shot him a challenging smile and continued down the hill.

"Terence?" he called after her.

Stopping, she turned to face him. "He will have a title and the Priory, and he is not completely intolerable. Mayhap we should send for your sister to join us for the Valentine's Day lottery. We could delay it a day or two to give her a chance to travel here."

He shook his head and grinned as he strode to where she stood. "You Harts enjoy playing pranks on each other, don't you?"

"If I need be miserable with this lottery—"

"You wish my sister to be miserable as well?"

Lucinda sighed. "There is that to consider, so I should abandon the idea."

"Actually it has some merit. Thea found your

brother's company very pleasing last time he called, but he teased her unmercifully."

"As he does anyone he cares for, a trait I fear all the Harts have inherited."

"Odd, for he has seemed most solicitous of you and your great-aunt."

When he took her gloved hand in his, she could sense the tantalizing warmth of his skin even through the layers of leather. She did not dare to look at him, for he might discern the yearning she could not govern to be even closer to him. Staring out at the river which snaked through the fields, she said, "Father always insisted that we Harts pull together when someone else taunts us. Only we are allowed to taunt each other."

"Much like England as a whole."

She stopped, surprised at his abruptly grim tone. "What do you mean?"

"We English enjoy insulting one another," he said, folding his hands behind his back, though he did not lessen his long strides, "but let another nation threaten us—"

"Please do not talk about the war!"

"Ignoring it will change nothing," he fired back, still walking away from her.

"Max?"

When he did not turn, she was torn between following or returning to the house. The idea of Constance's scan-mag urged her feet forward, even though she did not like this sudden change in him. One moment, he had been teasing her with the ease of Terence or Father. The next . . .

She was not sure how to describe him. Mayhap like a turtle, for he had drawn back within himself. Something she had said must have distressed him, but what?

Her steps slowed as she stared at the back of his great-coat which flapped against his strong legs with every pace.

Max must be on the shady side of Terence, mayhap by as many as a half dozen years. His sharp wit would have endeared him to his teachers at the university, and he would have advanced with all due speed. He must have delayed going to Cambridge. Again a question: But why?

An icy chill far colder than the snow raced down her spine. Max must have fought in the war. She shivered and raced to catch up with him. He said nothing when she drew even with him, but held out his hand. She slipped hers in it, wanting to give him the solace he had offered her so often since they met at the lodge.

They paused in silence by the riverbank. Listening to the hushed song of the water, Lucinda tried to think of something to say, some question to ask, that would break the wall between them as readily as she could have broken the wafer of ice on the water.

"Rip me!" Max rushed to the edge of the water. Bending, he pulled something out of the half-frozen mud. "This is most unsettling."

"What do you mean?"

He held up the iron hook. "Do you recognize this, Lucinda?"

"I do not know if—"

"It is used to wrestle boxes of illegal cargo to shore." He glanced along the river. "It would seem that our friends from the cottage are not willing to give up on their plan to stretch my neck." He straightened and brushed mud from his gloves. "I fear, Lucinda, we have let them tighten the net around us. Our escape may be only temporary."

Seven

"This is beneath contempt," announced Constance as her abigail stood over her, wafting her with a befeathered fan. Constance waved her own pudgy hand before her face and clutched a glass of brandy.

Lucinda watched without comment. It was easier to say nothing when her mind was a-jumble.

Leaning toward Lucinda, Max whispered, "How long do you think she will carry on like this until she decides to swoon and we shall have to burn those hideous feathers on that fan which is ugly as bull-beef?"

"Do not put thoughts into her head," she said, as lowly, a smile tugging on her lips.

"Much better." He put his hand over hers as they sat together on the window seat. "If I had guessed the sight of a smuggler's hook would have such a muting effect on your family, you can be sure I would have presented it to yon lady."

"But if they have followed us here—"

"We cannot be certain, for it might have been discarded when the owlers were about their dirty business some other night than the one they tried to put an end to our lives."

She shifted so she could meet his gaze. "Do not coddle me, Max. I am not as skimble-skamble as Constance nor would I want to set a trap for them as Terence shall once he learns of this."

"You are clear-thinking. I am most grateful to you and to Lady Benedict." His eyes crinkled as he leaned toward her again. "You have given me yet another smasher of an idea."

"What sort of good idea?"

"We shall not have a moment's good rest until Dayton and his tie-mates are caught. If you will excuse me, Lucinda, I think I shall find out where Terence has taken himself." Setting himself on his feet, he did not release her hand.

"Do not be queer in the attic!" She lowered her voice when Constance glared in her direction. Gripping his hand within both of hers, she whispered, "They intend to kill you! Do not give them the opportunity. We can continue to Hart's Priory and—"

"We must not lead them to the heart of your family." When she gasped, he knelt before her. "It is as I told you. If we do nothing, we shall be haunted by these devils. Take courage, Lucinda."

"From knowing that you are well-acquainted with battle?"

He flinched, and she knew her words had struck a true target. His smile grew brittle. "I see Terence has told you more about me than I had suspected."

"Terence has told me solely about the studies you shared along with the jests you succeeded in perpetrating on your long-suffering teachers." Her fingers quivered as she brushed his hair back from his forehead. "I was only guessing."

"Guessing very well." He shook his head, making the hair fall across his brow again. "I suspect it is because of that time that I have been as uncomfortable with the title 'Lord Loveland' as I was with 'Lieutenant Loveland.' I have come to prefer simply 'Max.' "

"I am sorry the memory distresses you so." Her finger sifted through the thick hair along his temple. The coarse, gold silk slid across her skin, inviting her to be more bold, as emerald fire burned in his eyes.

The fire of a battle long past, she realized when he murmured, "Distresses me? As lief you could say it obsesses me. My final meeting with Boney's men was in Spain two years ago tomorrow." He caught her wrist between his thumb and forefinger. Tilting her hand toward him, he looked over it to capture her gaze as completely. "I came here to escape its memory on this anniversary, hoping events would distract me."

"Have they?"

"Better you should ask if you have distracted me, Lucinda, for I vow you have . . . until now."

"I am sorry. I did not mean to disturb you."

"But you have disturbed me from the moment I first saw you." He pressed his warm lips against her palm.

She gripped the cushion on the window seat as she fought not to melt into the flame he sent blazing across her skin. When he curved her fingers along his face, his wind-roughened cheek teased them to caress him with the passion she could read in his eyes.

He stood. She opened her mouth to speak, but all words vanished when he bent toward her. Brushing the back of his hand against her cheek, he released her hand. He turned on his heel and left her to stare after him, not sure what she would have said if he had given her a chance. She was not sure of anything at all; most especially she was not sure of the longing for him to kiss more than her fingers.

"Lucinda?"

Setting her book on her lap, Lucinda wondered if she would ever reach the part where the hero and heroine finally were reunited. Terence was the third person to interrupt her in the past ten minutes. Was he conspiring with Aunt Jennie and Constance to keep her from reading?

He dropped to sit on the light blue settee next to her chair. Propping his chin on his fist, he said, "It is too nice a day to be inside."

"It appears to be cold and windy." She pointed to where the tree branches were rocking beyond the window.

"Would you as lief be chilled or be waiting here when our sisters arrive with all their plans for the gathering tonight and the lottery?" He gave her a wicked grin. "With all their plans for you, sister dear."

"Edna and Verna are coming for the lottery?" She rolled her eyes and rose. "And whose idea was that? Yours, mayhap?"

"Why are you accusing me?" His expression of feigned innocence was marred by his twitching lips. Standing, he surrendered to the smile. "All right, 'twas me, for I sent word to Father and Mother that you and Aunt Jennie were unharmed by your traumatic sojourn at the hunting lodge. No doubt, our family saw your survival as a sign to involve you in the lottery."

"Both of us."

"I do not have to—"

"Verna told Aunt Jennie at Christmas that she was going to be certain your name was included this year."

"Blast!" He shook his head. "I have to own, Lucinda, their meddling is much more entertaining when it is focused exclusively on you."

She slapped his arm and chuckled when he frowned. "It is about time some of their considerable energy in matchmaking was turned on you, big brother. Now that you are finished with school, you need to settle down, buckle yourself to a wife, and prove you can fill Father's shoes at Hart's Priory. If you want to listen to what *I* heard, Father has made no secret of the fact he expects you to assume more responsibility now that you have completed your schooling."

"Egad, what a horrible reward for all my hard work at Cambridge." He suddenly chuckled and grabbed her hands. "So are you coming with us, Lucinda?"

"Where?"

"Ice skating."

"Ice skating? We have no skates here."

"Constance has a full box in the stable. I am certain we will find something that will fit on our shoes. Come along." He tugged her toward the door.

"But if the smugglers—"

"Fear not, Lucinda." His smile broadened. "That matter shall soon be laid to rest."

"What do you have planned?"

"Ice skating at the moment." When she frowned, he chuckled. "After all, Max said it was your suggestion."

"I merely mentioned—"

"Your wish is his command, it would seem."

Lucinda planted her feet, pulled her hand out of his, and crossed her arms over her chest. Giving him what she hoped was a withering glower, she said, "You shall embarrass your friend with such talk."

"Embarrass Max *and* you?" He swept his arm over her shoulders, steering her toward the door. "Little sister, Max is my tie-mate. I would not do anything to injure him in any way, although you and Max would be wise to put a goodly distance between yourselves for the rest of our stay here. One look at the two of you making calf eyes at each other, and Verna and Edna will have you within ambs ace of the altar." He paused at the top of the staircase and motioned to the floor below. "So will you come with us?"

She did not have to ask who "us" was. The bright light bouncing off the snow and through the windows in the foyer glistened on Max's hair, turning it into molten gold. When he looked up the stairs, his gaze caught hers as if they stood only a breath apart. He smiled and held up his gloved hand. She thought she heard a low laugh behind her, but she did not lash out at her brother for his crude behavior, for she could not escape the enchanting thought of Max's touch. She wanted to watch her fingers disappear within his again and be immersed in the green depths of his fathomless eyes.

She descended the stairs and slipped her fingers into his, and he gave them a slight squeeze. Even that motion, which was as chaste as her brother's touch, sent a flush of pleasure through her. How right Terence was! She must be careful not to divulge her nascent feelings in front of her sisters.

"You are joining us?" he asked, his low voice resonating within her as if she were a harp and he the musician who knew exactly which string to pluck.

"I have been told I would be wise to disappear until my sisters arrive and get themselves settled this afternoon."

"And I thought you were coming along because you enjoy my company."

"I do. That is—" When both men laughed, Lucinda did as well. She was acting as witless as a debtor with the sheriff pounding on the door.

Quickly, she pulled on her long, dark red spencer and hooked the frogs at her throat. Her heavy bonnet was lined with silk, and a thick scarf tied beneath her throat. Wiggling her toes into her heaviest shoes, she pulled on wool gloves to keep her fingers warm.

Or so she hoped when she went out into the bone-gnawing wind. She followed her brother along the drive toward the stable. Although Max walked by her side, he said nothing, pulling his green scarf up over his chin as he settled his beaver more firmly on his head.

He expelled his breath in a gust as they entered the

stable and gave a broad shiver. She smiled at him and said, "I believe it was your idea to go on this outing today."

"I must have taken a knock in the cradle." He rubbed his hands together. "I hope you will acquaint me with my folly in the future instead of being a good hostess."

Terence disappeared into the back of the stable, but Lucinda stopped by the stalls, taking a chance to admire the horses which were waiting for spring and the chance to return to the fields. She reached over one door and patted a chestnut.

"A good horse," Max said, resting his elbow on the door. "It has strong lines."

"He is very strong." She smiled. "I rode him last summer and beat Terence by more than a length in a race up the drive. Constance wasted no time spreading the word to half the shire that I had bested him in a race, much to his irritation." Glancing toward where her brother should be collecting the skates, she added, "Of course, it helped to have arranged for his horse nearly to be cut off by one of the gardeners."

"You did that?"

"Yes. Does that surprise you?"

He chuckled. "Nothing you Harts do surprises me any longer. Your brother must not have taken that well."

"Terence does not like being the butt of a jest, but I like to turn the tables on him once in awhile." Laughing, she said, "He was still smarting from that prank when he returned to Cambridge."

"I recall him mentioning something of it."

Lucinda's next question went unasked when Terence appeared with three pairs of skates draped over his shoulders. Walking with them out into the windy afternoon, Lucinda was happy to put her hand on Max's arm. Not only could she walk more closely to him, but his broad shoulders lessened the power of the wind.

She was glad, too, that Terence had chosen a pond on the opposite side of the Hall from the river. To go back there could mean finding another clue that the smugglers were seeking them . . . or they might meet the criminals themselves.

The snow had been swept from the pond and a fallen log dragged close to the shore. Sitting on it, she tied on her skates, making sure they were snug. Last winter had been milder, and she had had no chance to enjoy gliding across the ice.

"I believe I shall need some assistance," Max said as he stood and walked with careful steps toward the pond.

"Assistance?" Lucinda put one foot on the ice and coasted across the milky-colored surface. Turning, she held out her hands to him. "You have never skated before, Max?"

"It seldom gets cold enough in Sussex for the ponds to freeze." He seized her hands, nearly upsetting her.

"Slowly," she urged.

She drew him out onto the ice. His ankles wobbled, the motion reverberating up his legs and across his body. She laughed and gripped his elbows. His arms swept around her, just in time to knock both of them to the ice.

"Forgive me," he said, trying to untangle his legs from hers.

With a laugh, Terence skated over. "Do you two need some help?"

"*One* of us does." Max gritted his teeth as Lucinda, laughing, stood. When Terence took one arm and Lucinda the other, he managed to scramble to his feet. "Thank you."

"Here," Lucinda said, holding out her hand. "Let me help you."

"I do not want to send you crashing to—" Max yelped as his feet slipped.

She grasped his windmilling arms and wrapped one around her shoulder. "Terence, take his other arm."

"He is gone," Max said.

"Gone?" She tried to look past him. Hearing the sound of skates cutting into the ice farther along the shore, she said, "Blast him!"

"I suspect he thinks I should be able to stand on my own two feet after all this time."

"Can you?"

His folded finger tilted her chin up. Smiling, he murmured, "I doubt if I would own to that at this moment, Lucinda, for holding you like this is most pleasurable."

All sounds vanished into the thud of her heartbeat as she stared into his eyes. Even the thickness of their coats could not dampen the firm lines of his chest which was pressed so closely to her. Each breath he took stroked her until she matched the rhythm, which was growing more swift and shallow. In a whisper, she managed, "We should—"

"What?"

"We did come here to skate," she said lamely. His smile suggested other pleasures more intriguing than standing like this, but she knew the danger of letting her imagination guide her. "We should skate before we freeze."

"Then help me skate, if you will, before we are both frozen."

Trying to ignore how perfect his arm seemed around her shoulder, she guided him along the ice. She struggled to keep her glides as short as his, but it was nearly impossible. When Terence sped past them, laughing at their labored progress, she could not help laughing as well. Max began to chuckle, and his chest grazed her arm on each motion.

"We are a pitiful pair," she said, hoping her teasing

would defuse the emotions that refused to lie quiescent within her.

"You looked quite graceful on your own," Max replied. " 'Tis I who is as clumsy as a lad in short coats."

She gasped as his feet betrayed him. He fell to the ice, and she stayed on her feet only by luck. "Are you hurt?" she asked.

"Help me up." When she did, he growled, "Let me try on my own, Lucinda."

"Do you think you are able?"

His eyes narrowed as Terence went by in a blur again. "If your brother can master this skill, I daresay I shall." He took a small step away.

"Be careful," she said, as he inched out farther onto the ice.

"You fret too much." Holding out his gloved hands, he smiled. He tried another step, then a glide. Grinning as brashly as a young boy, he said, "Mayhap it is not so hard."

"Not bad," Terence announced as he came over to them. "If Max can manage to stay on his feet a moment, how about racing me along the pond, Lucinda?"

She shook her head. "You are a head taller than me, big brother, and your legs are half again as long as mine. I would be at a true disadvantage."

"I will give you a head start." He squinted across the ice. "It is about forty yards out and back. What if I give you a five yard head start?"

"Ten."

"Eight."

With a smile, she nodded. "Eight it is, and Max will decide the winner."

"Aye," Terence said, frowning, "and there will be no dashed gardener today to get in my way."

"When will you put that behind you, old man?" Max slapped him on the back, then nearly collapsed. "You had better make haste quickly, or I may not be able to stand long enough to laud the victor."

Lucinda checked her skates to be certain they were secure, then glanced at her brother. He bowed and motioned for her to start. With a shout, she dug into the ice and sped away.

The wind sang against her face and soared past her ears. Through the whistle, she heard Terence's bellow and bent to add speed to her feet. Her breath caught beneath her ribs, but she would not slow. Terence was determined to defeat her in the wake of the last race, so she must not give up.

He called again. What was his ploy? If she looked about, she would slow.

"Lucinda!"

Her eyes widened. That deep voice was unquestionably Max's. She glanced over her shoulder. Max stood by the shore, and Terence was—Where was Terence?

She screamed when she saw a dark wound in the ice. It must have broken. Terence must have fallen into the water. Spinning, she skated back toward the hole.

"Not too close!" shouted Max.

Dropping to her knees, she inched forward. The ice creaked a warning. She shouted, "Terence!"

A hand reached over the ice. She saw his head bob up. He gripped the ice. It broke, and he vanished beneath the inky water.

She slid on her stomach toward the hole, calling to him. His head popped out of the water again. Stretching, she grasped his wrists.

"Don't let go!" His voice was choked, and she guessed he had swallowed more than a mouthful of the cold water.

"I shan't!"

"Pull me out!"

Lucinda tried to inch back. Pain erupted across her

shoulders when his weight refused to move. "Can you help, Terence?"

"Nothing to push against." His answer was weak.

Clenching her teeth, she fought the slippery ice to move backward. She gasped in horror when the ice cracked beneath her elbows. Water scored her sleeves, seeping through the wool. If she did not get him out within seconds, she would be in the water, too.

Hands grasped her ankles. Every muscle protested as she was pulled back. Tightening her grip on Terence's wrists, she watched as he was drawn out of the water. The ice chipped off under him, but they slid away from the hole. A button on her spencer caught on the ice and flew into the hole.

"This should be safe." Max's voice broke as he panted with exertion.

Lucinda sat and stared at him. Only his thick socks covered his feet. "Where are your skates?"

"On shore somewhere. Pulled them and my shoes off and tossed them without looking." He sank to the ice. "Terence, are you all right?"

"I am now." He wrung water out of his coat which was already stiffening in the wind. "I should have known better than to try to take a shortcut over the spring. The ice is never safe there."

"A shortcut?" cried Lucinda. "How could you be so cockle-brained? If Max had not been able to help me, you would have—you would have—" She covered her face with her hands. She would not let them see her silly tears. Strong hands drew her against Max's broad chest. Clinging to him, she whispered, "I have never been so afraid."

"Nor have I." He tilted her chin up so her face was close to his. His fingers uncurled along her cheek. "I thought I would lose both of you. I have never seen such foolish bravery."

Slowly her hand rose to his face. His wind-worn skin would be as rough as his fingers which brushed her hair back from her tear-dampened cheek, lingering along her chin. A rush of warmth erupted from beneath his touch and roiled through her, exhilarating and undeniably baffling.

"You are freezing."

She nodded, not sure how she could tell him the shivers had been of anticipation of his lips against hers. To be so bold . . . No, she could not say those words, not even to Max, who dared her to speak her mind. She should be honest with him as he was with her, but this precious secret within her, this joy that might be love, could not be shared. Not even with the man who made her heart leap with ecstasy each time he smiled at her.

"Let us get Terence back to the Hall," she said, standing.

"Yes," said her irrepressible brother, "you want plenty of time so you can look your best for the lottery tonight, Lucinda."

"And if you think you're going to avoid the lottery because of this, you—"

"Have sympathy for your only brother. I could have drowned."

"You didn't." She shivered. "You are a complete chucklehead, Terence. If you had tried that when we weren't here, you—"

He interrupted with a laugh. "I could have waded ashore."

"What?" She stared at him, sure she had misheard him. "You could have *waded* ashore?"

"If you didn't spend all your time with a book, Lucinda, you would have heard Constance lament about how this pond needs to be dredged next summer." Terence held his hand up to his waist. " 'Tis no deeper than this where I was."

His laugh vanished as Max seized his lapels. Lucinda watched as her brother's face went as gray as the ice when Max half lifted him off his feet.

"Your pranks go too far," Max snarled through clenched teeth. "Look at your sister. She was soaked in cold water, and she was frightened nigh to death by your prank."

" 'Twas just a jest." Terence drew away and scowled. "Max, you know you enjoy a joke as much as I do. As much as Lucinda did when she fixed that race last summer."

"But where do you draw the line?"

He shrugged. "No one got hurt." His eyes twinkled again with mischief as he winked. "And you can keep my baby sister warm on the way back to the house." Crowing another laugh, he strode away from the pond.

Lucinda sighed. Trust Terence to repay her like this! "I am sorry, Max. I should have known better."

"Than to try to rescue your brother when you thought he might drown or freeze to death?" Taking her hands, he drew her a step closer. His green eyes glowed like twin gems as he whispered, "He has no idea how precious your courage is. If any of my men had had half your courage . . ."

"Max?" she asked when he turned away.

"You need to get back to the house before *you* freeze."

She grasped his shoulders and looked up at his face which was as frozen as the pond. "Max, it is over. What happened then will never happen again. Forget it."

He touched the scar on his jaw. "I wish I could." Suddenly he smiled. "And I shall while I give your brother the dressing-down he deserved years ago." Holding out his arm, he asked, "Do you wish to be a witness to my lengthy outlining of his shortcomings?"

"I would be delighted." She put her hand on his strong arm.

When his smile grew gentle, the fire in his eyes threatened to scorch her. "It shall give both of us something to do to while away the time until the gathering this evening."

"That blasted lottery. How can you be anticipating it?"

"Your brother will be involved in it, and I suspect there must be a way to make his evening miserable with a match who has enough tongue for two sets of teeth and will make Constance look like a shy wallflower." He squeezed her hand as he led her toward the house. "I cannot help but think that will be entertaining. Mayhap it will be entertaining enough to make you glad you did not avoid this lottery."

She looked away. He must not suspect she had a new reason for hating that hateful lottery. If another lass were matched with him. . . . She did not want to think of that, but it could happen.

Tonight was going to be absolutely horrid. She was sure of that as she was of nothing else.

Eight

Lucinda stared at a spider making slow progress across the ceiling of the bedchamber as her sisters inspected her. She wondered what they could find fault with as they clucked about her. Edna had supervised Constance's abigail doing Lucinda's hair. Swept back into a bun which was entwined with pearls, only a few curls curved along her face which was encircled by a bandeau of the same black velvet as her gown. Verna had chosen the ear-bobs and necklace of twisted silver matching the tassels on the vandyked hem which revealed her silver satin slip.

Edna shook her head, threatening the curls piled on top. She wore the garish colors of her husband's crest, which pleased the earl, but succeeded only in making her look sallow. "I wish the gown had short sleeves. Long sleeves are so unflattering."

"Nonsense." Verna lowered herself to the chaise longue by the dressing table. Even pregnant, Verna still had the faery-like charm which had, from childhood on, labeled her the prettiest of Lord Hart's three daughters. "Lucinda, I do believe you have turned out quite well this evening."

"Thank you."

"How wondrous you are here for the lottery!" Verna continued. "Remember our first one, Edna?"

"I had the good fortune to have my name drawn with Lionel's, but you were matched with that horrible Mr.

Appleton." She fluttered her yellow fan in front of her face, but her eyes crinkled in a smile.

"You were matched with Mr. Appleton, as I recall, and I introduced you to your husband, who was my escort."

Stepping in front of the cheval glass, Edna smoothed the short sleeves of her bright yellow satin gown. "So true, and he could not wait to call upon me once the Season began." She turned. "Don't you see, Lucinda? Such joy awaits you tonight."

"Mayhap."

Verna smothered a laugh. "It is possible you may be matched with Lord Loveland. He is in prime twig, I must own, although I prefer darker hair on a gentleman. He does cut a fine figure."

"And such a nice title," cooed Edna, handing Lucinda her gloves. "I understand the family seat in Sussex is lovely, just waiting for the lord to bring a lady home."

"Leave off," returned Lucinda. "Max and Terence are in good pax, which is the reason Max is calling here. You know as well as I how men wish to enjoy a bachelor's fare after their time at their studies. Did you see the flowers Constance had brought from the hothouse?"

"But," Edna said, refusing to let Lucinda change the course of the conversation, "Lord Loveland is not a young man who has never experienced life. There are tales of how he bought a cousin's commission and spent time on the Continent."

The door from the hall opened just as Verna added, "Just the perfect, storybook hero for you, little sister. Too bad Father is not—"

"Hold your jaw!" Aunt Jennie fired into the room. Her short legs beneath her gown, which was as white as her hair, made quick work of the breadth of the carpet. When she focused her coldest stare on Verna and Edna, Lucinda was grateful not to be standing in its way. "Can you not see that Lucinda is nervous enough about this

evening without you two twittering around her?" She
motioned toward the door. "Do go and be certain your
husbands are ready to come down. The first guests will
be here soon."

When the door closed behind her sisters, Lucinda
sighed and smiled. "Thank you, Aunt Jennie."

"I suspected you would need some assistance from
their combined teasing." With a warning wag of her finger, she said, "You younger generations of Harts shall
be the death of my old heart with all your jests and
pranks." Her smile faded. "Are you certain you feel hale
enough to take part in this evening?"

Lucinda longed to use her near-dunking in the pond
as an excuse to be absent from the lottery this evening,
but Terence would be certain to reveal the truth. She
did not hesitate to say, "I am fine, dear aunt. After all,
it was Terence who suffered the brunt of the cold."

"Young moonling! I have half a mind to tell him exactly how jobbernowl he was."

"Come along, Aunt," she said, holding out her arm.
"I would not want you to waste even a smidgen of your
mind on telling me what you think of Terence's escapade. They—he should be in the parlor now."

Aunt Jennie took Lucinda's arm. " 'They'? You need
not try to hide the truth. I may be getting weaker, but
not my eyesight, my child. It is clear you enjoy Lord
Loveland's company very much."

"As I told my sisters, he is Terence's friend, and it
behooves me to be hospitable to him."

"Is hospitable what you call glowing like a lightning
bug when he glances in your direction?"

As heat climbed her cheeks, Lucinda listened to her
great-aunt's chuckle. Mayhap she should just own to the
truth of how easily she could free her heart to belong
to Max. He was everything she had dreamed of in a
hero—brave, trustworthy, and undeniably handsome. He

had been honest with her from the beginning, and she should be as honest . . . if only she dared.

Her resolve wavered when shadows at the end of the hallway became her brother and Max. As Aunt Jennie greeted them, Lucinda hoped nobody noticed her staring at Max's coat which was the same black velvet as her gown. The silver buckles on his shoes complemented his white breeches and the silver threads in his forest green waistcoat. The lion had become a panther.

She managed to mumble something that must have made some sense when Max took her hand and brushed his lips against it. Her kid glove threatened to melt away beneath the heat, and she fought to keep a vague smile in place.

When Terence offered his arm to Aunt Jennie, they led the way to the grand room where the Valentine's Day lottery and party would be held. Lucinda listened to their jovial voices as she let Max draw her hand within his arm.

"Where is your heart, Miss Hart?" he asked, chuckling.

"Heart?" She dared not speak the truth that she wanted it to be in his possession.

He pointed to the piece of red velvet secured to his lapel. "I have been informed everyone taking part in the lottery should be so festooned."

"Must there be no end to this silliness?"

"Apparently not."

Lucinda laughed at his grim tone. When he smiled, she walked with him to the room where Constance would greet her guests.

Their hostess was buzzing about the room like a bee in a field of flowers. She went from the dais where the orchestra was readying themselves to the trio of tables burdened with food and wine. Her housekeeper and butler followed like drones, nodding to each question she fired at them. Their drawn faces were reflected in the mirrors along the gilt and walnut walls.

Constance rushed across the room. "Dear friends, how wondrous you look!" Her powdered face creased in a frown. "Lucinda, where is your valentine brooch?"

"With Terence's, I suspect."

Her brother groaned. "Lucinda, I told you—"

"Wonderful idea! Mayhap both of you will be winners in this evening's lottery." She picked up two pieces of felt from the table closest the door and, with a pair of pins, dropped them into Lucinda's hand. Then she grasped Aunt Jennie's hands. "Think how grand that would be. We could arrange for a double wedding by spring."

Terence pulled Lucinda aside. "Now see what you have started."

She smiled as she watched Max rescue Aunt Jennie from Constance's enthusiasm by escorting the older woman to a chair not far from the door. "It is no more than you deserve." She pinned one piece of felt to his navy lapel.

"Deserve?" He motioned for her to pin the other to her dress. "After all I have done for you?"

"And what exactly have you done for me lately except try to scare me half to death at the pond today?"

Terence bent to murmur, "Things are working out very nicely, little sister."

"With the assembly tonight?" She glanced about the room as her sisters entered on the arms of their husbands. Both men wore the expression that suggested they would prefer to be almost anywhere else. Mayhap they were recalling the lottery that had introduced them to their wives. "Yes, I think Constance has surpassed herself tonight with—"

"Not with this gathering, but putting an end to the menace you and Max and Aunt Jennie have been fleeing."

She spun to face him. Putting her hands to her cheeks

which were suddenly as cold as the water in the pond, she whispered, "The owlers? You have set a trap? Terence, you need to be cautious."

"Caution is what I have preached to Max."

"Max?" She frowned. "I can imagine no one more prudent than Max. You would be wise to heed his counsel on this."

"Which is that he cannot leave you and Aunt Jennie here until he is certain you are in no danger."

"Leave?" She almost choked on the single word.

His eyes narrowed to dark slits. "You didn't think he was taking up permanent residence in Kenyon Hall, did you? I suspect he will be departing on the morrow or shortly thereafter."

"Oh." She knew she should think of something else to say, something witty or caustic or teasing, but nothing formed in her deadened mind, save the thought that Max would be gone so soon. Of course, he had his own family to concern him. He had paid this call on his friend for the weekend, and now that soon would be past. She would be left with nothing but her dreams of a storybook hero.

"That is why we cannot delay in settling this matter. Will you help?"

"Help?"

"Lucinda, what ails you? You are repeating everything I say."

Shaking herself mentally, Lucinda squared her shoulders. "Of course I shall help. What can I do?"

"Nothing right now, but I shall let you know when the trap is set to be sprung. Just be ready for anything."

Max appraised the room and the assembly of the Polite World that Lady Constance Kenyon had persuaded to come to this snowy country house. Although he could name few of the women, he knew most of the men in the room. This party would celebrate more than Valentine's Day, for it was a last chance for friends to gather together in comparative quiet before the swirl of the Season.

He needed to thank Terence later. This weekend had proven to be just the balm he needed to forget the pain of his past when his men had left him for dead in a Spanish field. Although he would not have arranged for a weekend complicated by the addition of a Valentine's Day lottery, he could not doubt Terence had arranged for everything to be perfect.

Perfect . . .

His gaze settled on Lucinda's slender form. The red heart pinned to her bodice drew his eyes to those appealing curves. With her hair swept up and the silver chain accenting the column of her neck, he was tempted to press his mouth to that skin which had been so soft beneath his fingers. Who would have guessed gangly Terence Hart's sister would be so utterly enticing?

Stopping a passing servant, he collected two glasses of champagne. He went to where Lucinda was speaking with her eldest sister and another young woman. Edna, if he recalled the garrulous woman's name correctly, mumbled something and disappeared into the crowd, dragging the other woman with her, as he nodded a greeting.

He smiled. He recognized the work of a matchmaking sister, for Edna was not the first to set her cap on him as a match for a younger sibling. When he turned to Lucinda, a pretty blush brightened her cheeks, highlighting her wine-warm lips. He looked at the champagne he carried. It would taste bland in comparison. Of that he was certain.

He offered Lucinda the glass of champagne. "Have I met your friend previously and offended her?"

"Do not mind them." She gave him a smile that tickled every muscle in him. "Judith Tracy has been asking Edna to introduce her to Lord Cosgrove all evening."

"Is *he* here?"

With a shrug, she answered, "I do not know the man, so I cannot say. Do you know him?"

"He was at Cambridge while I was." Raising his glass, he added, "This party is a fitting ending to a most unusual weekend."

She took a sip. "You should know by now that anything Terence is involved in will prove to be unusual. He does not like the commonplace."

"Your brother has proven he is a resourceful and entertaining host." Looking across the room, which was growing more crowded, he mused, "I had no idea there would be so much interest in this Valentine's Day lottery. Your comments had led me to believe it was something to be avoided."

"Like Terence, I find my opinions do not always agree with others'." Lucinda hesitated, running a finger along the top of the glass, then said, "Max, Terence suggested that the threat from the smugglers might come to an end this evening. Do you know what he is speaking of?"

He put his finger against her lips. When her eyes widened in shock, he grasped her hand and drew her out of the parlor. She started to ask a question, but he motioned her to silence as he led her along the passage to where an arched window filtered moonlight through stained glass. Cold inched out from the panes, and she shivered.

Placing his arm around her shoulders, he drew her closer to him. Again she shivered, but this time from the slow caress of his leg against her on each step. His fingers toyed with the curls draped along her ear, and she feared her trembling legs would forget how to walk. She wanted to forget everything, save the fascinating pattern he was etching with sweet fire into her skin.

"Forgive me for bringing you so far from the hearth," he whispered as they paused in the shadows, "but this is for you alone."

"What madness do you two have planned?"

He took their glasses and set them on a table near the window. "I know not what Terence has planned. *This* is what I have planned."

His hands framed her face, and his lips captured hers. No gentle kiss wooed her, for his mouth was as demanding as his wit which had challenged her. When his arm slid down her back to tug her against him, she slipped her arms around his shoulders. He pressed her to his chest as her breath grew swift. When she gasped against his mouth, his tongue probed within hers. Her fingers clenched on his velvet coat which could not disguise the iron muscles beneath it.

Slowly he lifted his mouth from hers. When she moaned a soft protest, wanting more of the indescribable delight, he grazed her lips with his. He murmured her name, and she opened her eyes to stare up at him. His green eyes glowed like a cat's, with the same self-satisfaction at having caught his quarry. Yet, there was one difference. She had wanted to be enfolded in his arms like this.

"You are bold," she whispered.

"To kiss you when I met you only a pair of days ago?" He laughed lowly. "We have faced death together, Lucinda. Such an experience creates a bond between two people."

"Does this mean you soon will be giving Aunt Jennie a chaste salute?"

"Chaste, mayhap, but not like this."

Her lips welcomed his again as her fingers combed up through his golden hair. Freeing her dreams to become verity, she dared to be as brazen as he was. The slick warmth of his mouth, the hard line of his arms, the brush of his collar against her chin as he bent to trace her fevered pulse along her neck. Her breath strained as she drew his mouth back to hers.

A throat cleared behind Lucinda. Wide-eyed, she whirled to see her brother's grin.

"I don't have to ask if I interrupted," he said, laughing.

"Terence!" She stepped away from Max.

Max's arm brought her back to him. "Watch the rough side of your tongue, old man."

"The rough side? Is that—?" He gulped and flushed, something she had never thought to see. "Sorry, Lucinda. I need to recall my manners."

"Not a bad idea," she said, glad the twilight hid the fire blazing on her cheeks. "Did you need something, Terence? It cannot be time for that blasted lottery yet."

"I must speak with you, Max," he said, looking past her.

"Lucinda and I were—"

"I saw what you were doing, but I must speak with you. Now!"

Lucinda frowned. "Terence, what is wrong?"

"I need to speak with Max, little sister," he said with a grin. "He is my friend, so you should not monopolize his company all evening."

The cold seeped back into her again. "Is this—?"

"Say nothing here of what I spoke of earlier."

"Be cautious of the danger of what you have planned," she pleaded.

"I know it very well."

"Danger?" Max asked. "What danger? I thought we were going to wait until after the lottery drawing to—"

Again Terence interrupted him. "I need to speak with you *now*, Max."

With Lucinda's confusion mirrored on his face, Max said, "As you wish. Will you excuse us, Lucinda?" His fingers brushed her face, and she closed her eyes to savor their enticing touch. Lowering his voice, he whispered, "Shall I meet you in the book room as soon as Terence is done explaining his crude manners? We shan't be long. You can acquaint me with what I should expect with this absurd lottery, and I can acquaint you with . . ."

"Perfect." She ignored her brother's laugh. Picking up the glasses, she hurried along the corridor.

She set them on a table by the ballroom door and eased back out of the room which had become even more crowded. Constance must have invited every unmarried person in the shire. As she went along the hall and up the stairs, the pressure of dozens of voices vanished into serenity.

Yet there was nothing serene about her throbbing heart. With every breath, she imagined Max's arms around her and his mouth over hers. Could anything be more wondrous?

The book room was dimly lit, which suited her well. Walking through the maze of leather-bound chairs, she let her fingers linger on their backs. For the first time, she did not rush to the shelves to discover what book might open a new world of fantasy to her. Tonight, she had no need for anyone else's dreams. Her own were coming true.

The door opened. She turned, about to greet Max. In shock, she locked eyes with a man she had seen only once. She never could forget the man who had stood behind Dayton and drawn a sword while the smuggler announced their death sentence.

And now that smuggler was within Kenyon Hall!

Nine

The man in the doorway took a pair of steps forward. "Miss Hart—"

Lucinda twirled and grasped one of Lord Kenyon's swords. Lifting it, she leapt forward to keep him from escaping.

His eyes widened as he gasped a curse. "Miss Hart, in the wrong hands that is a most dangerous weapon."

"It is in the *right* hands, but you can be assured it is still dangerous to you. Do not let my feminine appearance bamblusterate you into believing I am unable to use this effectively." She pointed the tip at his chin. "Even a novice could cause much damage from this distance."

"Miss Hart, listen to me." His face was a sickly shade of gray.

"I shall listen to you tell me how you managed to sneak into this house and where you condiddled a gentleman's clothes."

"I have stolen nothing. Miss Hart—" He gulped as she tilted the sword when he tried to move. "You must listen to good sense. You are making a horrid mistake."

" 'Twas you who erred when you thought you could perpetrate your heinous crimes in this house."

Footsteps resounded along the hall. Lucinda's palm grew clammy with sweat. If it were another of the smugglers, she might not be able to flee to warn the others.

She should toss aside the sword and seek out Max. Yet the owler in front of her would escape. If . . .

"Max!" she cried when he paused in the doorway, staring at her and the interloper. "Be careful! That man is one of the smugglers who would have killed us." The sword wavered, and she tightened her grip on it. "Send for the constable before he escapes."

The man tried to edge away. She pressed the tip of the saber to the top button of his gold waistcoat. Horror filled his eyes. "Loveland, do something before this misguided woman skewers me!"

"Why should he do anything for you? You would have slain him," she retorted. "Max, send someone for the constable."

"Lucinda—"

She did not dare look at Max, but realized he was in the room. Why was he coming in? Why wasn't he going for the constable? "I can keep him here. Go!"

Broad hands covered hers on the hilt. When her fingers were peeled from it and the sword lowered toward the floor, she stared at Max in astonishment.

"He will escape!" she cried. "He will—"

"Lucinda," he said quietly, "I thought you knew. I would have disabused you of your misapprehensions if I had had any idea you did not know."

"Know what?" She glanced at the interloper, who was edging once more toward the door, his face still colorless. "Max, he is escaping."

"John Cosgrove is just returning to the ballroom where Miss Tracy is awaiting him."

"John Cosgrove? *Lord Cosgrove?*"

The man in the doorway paused, guilt lengthening on his face, and bowed toward her. "Miss Hart, I beg your forgiveness for the misunderstanding. When we met at the cottage—"

"Allow me to tell her," Max said quietly. "You have left Miss Tracy to her own company long enough."

Gratitude replaced the guilt as Lord Cosgrove smiled and left as swiftly as a lad seeking to avoid a lashing.

Lucinda stared after him in disbelief, then turned to see Max putting the saber back into its resting place by the hearth. When he lit another lamp, its glow accented every plane of his taut face.

He did not look at her as he said, "Please sit, Lucinda. This explanation shall not be simple."

"I am not want-witted." She went to stand in front of him so he could not avoid her. Seeing the pain in his eyes, she whispered, "I can see what is before me."

"And what is that?"

"You are protecting your friend who has involved himself in a sport that does not belong to a gentleman." She lifted her arms to curve along his shoulders. "Max, you are so magnanimous, for I do not recall him speaking in your defense when Dayton would have left you as raven's meat beyond the cottage."

He drew her arms from around him and folded her hands between his. When she regarded him in bafflement, for she had not expected him to push her away, he said, "Sit down, Lucinda. I need to explain."

Unsettled by the tension in his voice, she lowered herself to one of the leather chairs. Dozens of thoughts raced through her head; none of them made sense. Was Max a part of the smugglers and a falling out between him and Dayton had led to the scenes she had witnessed at the cottage? Was he a part of another gang? Was he—and she prayed, of what she had envisioned, this was so—here on government business to put an end to the crimes?

He sat in a chair beside her, still holding her hands. When she saw how dim the glitter was in his expressive eyes, she bit her lip. Something was wrong, horribly wrong.

"Max," she whispered, "please believe that whatever you have to tell me makes no difference. My affection for you will not change."

He winced as if she had snarled an insult at him. "I fear it may."

She drew her hand out of his and curved it along his cheek. "Max, how can it? I love you."

"Don't say that until you know the truth."

"That is the truth." She smiled. "How could I not love a man who has saved my life so many times in the past two days?"

He shook his head. "Not once, I must own."

"Not once? But, Max, you saved me from the smugglers."

"Not once." Standing, he muttered, "Damn your brother! I should have known better than to trust him."

"Terence?" She wished he would say something that would make her less confused as lief adding to her bafflement. "Max, please explain."

He whirled and gripped her shoulders. "It was nothing but a game."

"What was a game?"

"The whole of these past two days, save when I fished you and your blasted brother out of the pond." He laughed coldly. "No, even that was a game, but one I was not privy to until Terence nearly stole a year from your life with his prank." His voice softened. "Lucinda, the whole of the past two days has been a game."

She stared at him, opening her mouth and waiting for words to come from her frozen brain. Nothing emerged. A game? This had been all a game? No, that was not possible, for then Max had been false with her. In a choked whisper, she asked, "The smugglers weren't real?"

"They are comrades from Cambridge whom your brother invited here for the weekend as he invited me."

"Even Dayton?"

"Even Dayton."

"And the Gypsies?"

He shrugged. "Real enough, I suppose, but Terence had arranged for them to be there in case we devised an escape from the fake smugglers. If I didn't know better, I would believe he had devised even the storm to maroon us in the middle of the shire, so we had no choice but to stay in that wagon."

"Blast Terence!" She put her hand on his arm. "Max, please accept my apology on his behalf, because I doubt he will think he did a thing wrong. If—"

His hands framed her face, and he slanted his mouth across hers. Slowly she raised her fingers to cover his, wanting to be enfolded within his embrace, to melt against him, to explore every pleasure until she had sampled each one.

He raised his mouth away. When she started to draw it back, he shook his head. "Listen first to what I must say, Lucinda."

"I know you are exasperated with Terence."

"No, I am not."

Lucinda frowned in bafflement. "But why not? He has bamboozled you along with everyone else."

"You were the only one bamboozled, sweetheart."

She stared at him. No, she must have heard him wrong! She shook her head as she saw the truth in his eyes. Or was it the truth? She had believed him from the moment they met, and he was saying everything had been a lie. With a moan, she whirled away.

He put his hands on her shoulders and brought her to face him. No sparkle brightened his eyes as he whispered, "Until a few minutes ago, I had no idea you did not know the whole of this was part of the game Terence had devised for our entertainment this weekend. If I had had any idea—"

"You wish me to believe you would have altered your sport, my lord?" She blinked back tears. What a moonling they all must think her to be! "I daresay you enjoyed your rôle as my dashing hero far too much to forsake it. I congratulate you, for you have proven yourself worthy of walking the boards on Drury Lane. Such a performance I have never seen! Pity me who simply played a part in your great production."

"But that was what I thought, Lucinda." He grasped her hands. "I thought you were enjoying the game as much as I. In our invitations, each of us were given our rôles by your brother, and I could only guess he had selected for you the damsel I should rescue from her distress."

She drew her hands away. That he did not try to hold on to her fingers added to her pain. All of this had been a game? Even his heart-teasing kisses? She longed to ask, but did not need to add to her humiliation. There was only one question she could ask. "Why?"

His hand went to the scar on his chin, and his lips became straight. "Your brother is a good friend, Lucinda. He knows how the memory of the day two years ago today haunts me. He wished only for me to forget it this year."

"I can tell you, my lord, that *I* shall never forget this day." She blinked back her tears and walked toward the door.

"Lucinda, do not leave like this," he called to her back.

In the doorway, she turned. She kept her chin high so he would not see the tears burning in her eyes. "What? You wish me to ruin my glorious exit from your little production, my lord? I bid you *adieu* and the best of fortune with whatever other rôles you choose to play in the future, but I wish you to know I shall be neither participant nor audience for your acting talents." She swallowed roughly, but her eyes hardened. "I do not think I could endure watching you speak your court-promises so sincerely to your next leading lady."

"Lucinda!"

When she strode away, Max slammed his fist into the leather chair. By Jove, how was he to guess Terence Hart's grandest prank would be on him and Lucinda? Blast Terence!

He rushed out of the book room. Where would she go? To her bedchamber? If he followed her there, he could ruin her reputation, but he could not let her walk out on him like this. A prank! That was what Terence had called this. A way to forget the past. Mayhap the day would come—sometime—when he could think of this weekend and smile.

A hand caught his arm. He shrugged it off and snarled, "Damn you to perdition, Terence Hart!"

Terence frowned. "By your words, I assume Lucinda did not take the truth well."

"Is that all you have to say?"

"What would you wish me to say? That I am sorry?" He shook his head. "I am not. I thought this would help you escape your dreary spirits."

"So you thought to grant me a few laughs at your sister's expense?" He forced his fingers to uncurl from the fist that ached to teach his friend's chin a lesson. "Are these ongoing pranks at her expense the price she has to pay for besting you in one silly race?"

Terence's eyes widened. "I never meant—that is—"

"I hope you enjoy your vengeance, for you have broken your sister's heart."

"I have? Or was it you?"

Before Max could answer, Constance twittered, "Here you are." She grasped both of them by the arm and steered them toward the parlor. "The lottery is about to be held, and I know neither of you want to be late for your first drawing."

Max said quietly, "I believe it would be better if I withdrew."

"Nonsense!" Constance gave them both a shove into the room. "The fun is just beginning."

Terence clasped his hands behind his back and started to turn around. He paused when Lady Benedict greeted both of them. Hearing him mutter something, Max remained silent. How could the lottery be any worse than seeing the pain on Lucinda's face?

By the platform where the band had been playing, Constance called for her guests' attention. "There is no need to wait any longer! When your name is called, please come forward." She laughed and motioned to the man who was introduced as Dr. Wood, the vicar. He was frowning as if he were taking part in the Black Prince's work. "Dr. Wood, will you bring forth the names?"

Max ignored the laughter around him as he scanned the room. He caught a motion near the door. Lucinda! She was here. But why? He had thought she would avoid this horror in the wake of his revelation. He took a step in her direction, but Lady Benedict slipped her arm through his.

"Listen," the elderly woman said. "They are about to announce the first name."

"Terence Hart!" called the vicar in his grating voice. She chuckled. "Go, boy!"

"Blasted tradition," he growled, but stepped forward.

Max did not watch or listen as Terence drew a slip of paper and gave it to the vicar so Dr. Wood could proclaim the name of his match. He could not brush Lady Benedict aside, but he needed to speak with Lucinda alone. There must be a way to sort out this bumble-bath. How was he to guess she would speak of love? That complicated everything more than he wanted. This weekend was supposed to be fun, but it had become anything but.

Lady Benedict's elbow poked him in the ribs, and Max

looked back at her as she said, "Dr. Wood just called Lucinda's name."

"Excuse me." He did not wait for her answer as he slipped through the press of the crowd who were gathered around the platform.

Freeing himself of the other guests, he stared at Lucinda. She was standing an arm's length from Constance. She glanced at him, and the pain in her eyes nearly undid him. He recognized that expression, for he had worn it himself the day his men had fled. It was of trust betrayed.

"Pardon me," said a deeper voice.

Max looked over his shoulder to see a grin on Jonathan Dayton's face. Without a week's growth of beard and with his clothes and hair neat, Jonathan bore little resemblance to the smuggler who had threatened them with death.

"Why?" Max asked.

The vicar leaned forward and held out a piece of paper for Max to read. "Mr. Dayton had the good fortune to draw Miss Hart's name."

Max bit back the words that would have had no place in a clergyman's ear. Through clenched teeth, he said, "Dr. Wood, I believe Miss Hart might be uncomfortable in Mr. Dayton's company."

"Nonsense," the vicar said.

"Nonsense," echoed a lighter voice.

When Lucinda pushed past him and held out her hand to Dayton, she smiled as he bowed over it. "Good evening, Mr. Dayton. 'Tis very different from the last time we met."

"I trust this evening will not end with you climbing out a window as you did last time we met." He flashed Max a triumphant smile as he offered his arm to Lucinda.

Max put out his hand to block it. He heard a collective gasp from the guests, but ignored their whispers. "Miss Hart, I beg a moment to speak with you."

"I am sorry, my lord, but Mr. Dayton has drawn my name and—"

"Blast the lottery!" He gripped her hands and pulled her closer. In a husky whisper, he said, "You have to accept the truth, Lucinda."

"That you all lied to me?"

"I have told you I thought you knew the truth."

"Did you?" Her lips remained straight, but he saw that appalling pain of betrayal dimming her lustrous eyes. "I was frightened as I never have been."

"By our smugglers or—" He grasped her arms and spun her against him. His fingers cradled her nape as he bent toward her. "Or is this what frightens you, Lucinda?"

His mouth over hers refused to be denied. With slow intensity, he enticed her lips to soften. Her sweet breath caressed his mouth as he swept his hand down her back, pressing her closer until her softer curves molded to him. He ignored the gasps from the other guests as he delighted in her eager response to his kiss. Lightning flared through him, starting at the spot where her breasts brushed his chest. When he teased the crescent of her ear with his tongue, she clutched his shoulders. Shaping his hand to her nape, he guided her mouth back to his.

Lifting his mouth from hers, he whispered, "Tell me the truth, sweetheart."

Something flashed in her eyes, but he feared it was fury, for she eased out of his arms. "You overstep your welcome in this house, my lord." She held her hand out. "Mr. Dayton?"

As Dayton drew her hand into his arm, Max waited for her to glance in his direction. No one spoke when she swept by him on Dayton's arm. Pulling the red heart off his lapel, he crushed it into a ball and threw it to the floor before striding out of the room.

Ten

"Lucinda, be sensible!"

With an icy laugh, Lucinda closed her book and looked up at her brother. "Odd that you should suggest that to me, Terence, when it was your absurd idea to instigate this dashed charade."

"Mother would be furious to hear you use such language," Edna said, her hands waving to accent each word. She frowned at Terence. "Not that I fault you, Lucinda. This has been a frightful prank to play on her, Terence. How could you risk her heart like this?"

"How was I to know she would develop a calf love for Max Loveland?"

"He is a dashing blade and titled and plump in the pockets," Verna replied as she patted at her eyes with her soggy handkerchief. "Even you, Terence, should have been aware of how dangerous that combination is for a naïve girl barely out of the schoolroom like Lucinda."

Setting herself on her feet, Lucinda snapped, "I am neither naïve nor a schoolgirl any longer. I do not need you protecting me, sisters. Nor do I need your silly games, Terence, to keep me entertained." She held her book close to the blue ribbons beneath the bodice of her white gown. "If you all will excuse me, I would like to enjoy my book in peace and quiet."

Lucinda hurried down the hall and into her own bed-

chamber. Closing the door behind her, she leaned
against it and stared at the moonlight coming through
the red velvet drapes on the tall window on the opposite
wall. A dull ache as bitter as wormwood thudded through
her with every beat of her battered heart.

Knuckles rapped against the door. She half considered
not answering, but opened it.

Aunt Jennie bustled into the room. Grasping Lucinda's arm, she herded her grandniece across the room.
She sat Lucinda on a bench by the dressing table and
then lowered herself to the chaise longue. "How long
do you intend to remain here in your room and continue
in this?"

"I just came in here. I—"

"You know what I mean. You have avoided everyone
all day. Constance has been pacing the floor, wondering
what she has done to offend you. Carriages have come
and gone, and you did not come to enjoy some scan-mag
with any of us. I thought you had better manners than
that."

"I had no interest in listening to a rehashing of last
evening's ignoble events with Constance's neighbors."

"How do you know her neighbors were the callers?"

When Lucinda looked at her, baffled, Aunt Jennie
smiled with triumph. "I thought you were so lost in your
own woes that you would not have noticed who came or
went. When you did not come down to join your family
at supper, I sent your siblings into that musty book room
to talk to you, and you scurried away. They are upset,
thinking they have added to your distress. That is exactly
what you wish, isn't it?"

"Aunt Jennie—"

"Let me finish. I watched you at the party last night.
You barely could tolerate Mr. Dayton's company once
Lord Loveland took his leave after that very public dem-
onstration of affection. Anyone who witnessed that can

be certain of one thing: You welcomed Lord Loveland's kiss."

"Aunt Jennie—"

"Child, do not interrupt. Don't you know how rude that is?" Folding her arms over her chest, she asked, "How long will you continue to act like this? Just until Lord Loveland takes his leave, or will you shut yourself away from the rest of your life?"

"I honestly do not know." Rising, she clasped her hands, then flung them out. "I trusted Max, and look what he did to me!"

" 'Twas not Lord Loveland who devised it. I as lief thought it was Terence Hart's game." She arched a single white brow. "And it was a splendid one."

Lucinda rounded on her. "You knew it was nothing but a game, too?"

"Yes."

"So you thought I knew the truth, too?"

Aunt Jennie smiled. "No, my dear, I knew you did not know."

Lucinda dropped to sit on the window seat as she stared at her great-aunt. She could not think of a single word to retort.

There was no need, for Aunt Jennie said, "When Terence mentioned it to me one afternoon while you were lost in one of your books, I asked him if we could be a part of it."

"You *asked* him to involve us in his moonshine?"

"I thought you would enjoy it." A sly smile brightened her face. "And you did."

"I did not."

"But you did. My dear, we gave you an adventure of your own—no book could better it. I have seldom seen you so animated as you were when you debated with Lord Loveland about the best way to flee from our make-believe smugglers, and, as I have already said, no one could doubt the affection that has developed with such speed between the two of you. My dear child, I believed it was the only way for you to leave the world of your books and look about you to see the fine gentleman who was making you smile as no man had before." Her satisfied smile broadened. "You must own I picked exactly the right match for you."

Lucinda refused to acquiesce so easily. Her fury remained too strong. "You picked a man who prefers to live a lie as lief face the truth."

"The truth?" Aunt Jennie's smile vanished. "What do you know of the truth Maximillian Loveland keeps hidden? Has he spoken to you of that frightful day when his fellow officers ran in the face of an enemy ambush, leaving him to die alone?"

"Alone?"

She nodded. "Have you given thought that he would wish to spare you from the appalling truth of war? By all that's blue, Lucinda, only in your books will you find glorious battles with the hero escaping unscathed. This is the truth. Lord Loveland has stared down the maw of death, and yet he is learning to set it behind him and get on with life."

"But why did you go to this elaborate scheme, and why did you involve me?" Lucinda asked.

Aunt Jennie took Lucinda's hands in hers. "Dear child, no matter what you may think at this juncture, you are very dear to me. I knew how desperately you wished to avoid the Season. Yet I could not allow you to remain here and molder away with your books. If I could not persuade you to go to Town, I thought the best alternative was to bring the gaiety of Town to you."

"You are a wicked old woman," Lucinda said, unable to keep from smiling.

"Wicked for the very best of reasons." She patted Lucinda's cheek. "You remind me much of myself at your tender years, and I wish to see you happily settled before I go to Rot-my-bones."

"Aunt Jennie! Such language!"

The old woman laughed at Lucinda's easy copy of her scold. "When you have as many years to your credit as I, my child, I trust you will speak the truth as freely." Aunt Jennie's face grew serious again. "You censure your brother for his ingenuity and Lord Loveland for his part in the prank which was meant to hurt no one, but, Lucinda, ask yourself this question: How many of us can claim to be unstintingly honest?"

"I try to be."

"Did you try last night?"

Lucinda flinched. "I can own the truth now when I say that I wished him to see how lies can hurt."

"I would say you succeeded beyond your expectations. Lord Loveland has ordered his carriage, which has been delivered from the hunting cottage, to be brought around first thing in the morning." Aunt Jennie put her gnarled hand on Lucinda's shoulder as she stood. "Lord Loveland did as he did for the past few days because he thought you were playing a part in the game. He wanted you to have a grand time, and you did. Why are you trying to wound a man who went out of his way to give life to the fantasies you have enjoyed in your collection of books? If you wish to fly off the hooks with anyone, it should be me, child, for I thought Terence's ideas for this whole weekend would give you a taste of the stories you love."

"Love . . ." she whispered.

"What did you say?"

Sitting straighter, Lucinda asked, "Do you know where Max might be?"

"When I came to speak to you," Aunt Jennie replied with a smile, "he and your brother were going down to the river to gather up the so-called clues they left as part of their sport."

"At this hour?"

"Lord Loveland told me earlier he wanted some fresh air to clear out his head of all that had happened."

Lucinda stood.

"Where are you going?" her great-aunt asked.

"For a walk."

"Do not go as far as the river. They should be on their way back even now. Terence said it would take but a minute."

"I shall stay in the garden."

Aunt Jennie held her cheek up for Lucinda's kiss. "Dress warmly, dear."

Her satisfied chuckle drifted out of the room as Lucinda rushed down the stairs to the front foyer. Lucinda pulled on her cloak and bonnet before being sucked out into the brisk night wind. As she hurried down the path toward where she would have a view of the river, the wind threatened to peel her hood back from her head. Her hair whipped her face as she tried, futilely, to push it back beneath the dark wool hood. Along the shore, water threw itself upon the mud, leaving a glittering band of frozen foam like the fur on a lady's cloak.

She owed Max the duty of an apology. If he did not agree to forgive her, she could not blame him. Aunt Jennie was right. All he had done was out of kindness and fun. She had been spiteful and hurtful.

Something moved in the shadows to her right. "Max?" she called. "Terence?"

"Lucinda?" came back a shout, but from farther along the path.

She looked from the shadows to where she could see her brother and Max striding up from the river. The flash of moonlight off Max's hair was unmistakable. Waving, she called, "Did you find all the smugglers' tools?" She gathered up her skirt and cloak and rushed toward them.

"No!"

She faltered at Max's shout. Mayhap his earnest words as he had tugged her into his arms last night had been nothing but another aspect of the game. No, the game was over. It was over for both of them. It was time to be honest.

She took another step, and he surged forward. He halted, an expression of horror twisting his lips. Her arm was seized. Something hard pressed through her hood against her temple.

"Let her go!" he snapped.

"First, we talk, milord, then yer fine lady goes free."

Lucinda strained to see past her bonnet. When she saw the narrowed eyes of a man who wore a handkerchief over his mouth and nose, her hands clenched at her sides. He was barely taller than she, and what she could see of his hair beneath the broken rim of his hat was gray. She reached up and knocked away his hand. "This has gone on long enough," she said, exasperated. "Max, if this is your idea of a way to apologize—"

Max grasped her and pushed her behind him. "This is no game."

"Hush, Lucinda," whispered her brother, putting his arm around her shoulders. "You have no idea what is going on."

She looked past Max to see a half-dozen men all dressed as poorly as the one who had grabbed her and all wearing cloth covering their mouths. Her eyes widened when she saw bare knives and pistols in the men's hands. When she realized the one who had held her carried a pistol, she grasped Max's sleeve. "Who are these men?"

"That is what I would wish to know," Max said coldly. "Gentlemen, I would appreciate an answer to Miss Hart's question."

The leader raised his gun. "Shouldn't need one, milord, when ye was puttin' yer nose 'bout our business down by the river.''

"They are real owlers!" choked Terence.

She put her hand on his arm. It quivered beneath her fingers. Even Terence was not such a good actor to feign this fear. Raising her eyes to Max's face, she saw his mouth was in a taut line. His hands curled into fists at his side as he stepped forward to stand between her and the smugglers. She almost laughed, for, if she had seen this real anger before, she would have known he was only acting in the hunting lodge. Yet she had never felt less like laughing. Terror swirled around her, tying her in its invisible bonds.

Holding up his hands in which he held the iron hook and an empty bottle, Max said, "Gentlemen, if you saw me and Mr. Hart by the river, it was to gather up these things.''

The man who apparently was the leader peered over his handkerchief. "Trash."

"Exactly."

"What's a milord want with trash?"

Terence interjected, " 'Twas nothing but a part of a game.''

"Game?" The smuggler spat on the ground. "Ye shouldn't be nosin' 'round our place. Can't 'ave ye goin' to t'authorities with yer tale of what ye might've seen."

"We saw nothing," Max said quietly.

"Can't be sure of that." He raised the gun. "Know only one way to keep a milord quiet tonight."

Lucinda cried, "Don't kill him!"

The smuggler laughed. "I've no plan to kill just 'im, milady." He pointed with the gun toward the shore. "C'mon."

Lucinda tensed, but Max whispered, "Cooperate, Lucinda." He put out his hand to halt Terence from surging forward. "We would be wise to keep in their good graces."

Terence hissed, "But you were a soldier. You must be able to figure out something to do."

"I have. I suggest we cooperate." Max put his arm around Lucinda and turned her toward the river. "There is no point in being a hero if your sister ends up dead." He added softly, "Watch for an opportunity to run, Lucinda. We shall try to cover your escape."

"With what?" she asked as they went down the path to the river. "You have no weapons?"

"I shan't let them kill you."

She started to argue, but the leader snapped an order for them to be silent. Cold crunched on her bones as the wind off the water struck her. She paid it no mind. What did it matter if she suffered this slight chill when soon the cold of death could claim all of them? She reached out to take Terence's hand and squeeze it.

The moonlight on the shore revealed a small boat set in the shadow of a cairn of huge boulders. When the leader called for a halt, Lucinda gripped Max's arm with both hands.

The leader motioned with the pistol. "C'mere, milady."

"Stay where you are, Lucinda!" Max again took a step forward.

The smuggler drew back the hammer on his gun. Lucinda feared her heart had stopped as surely as if a ball had been fired into it.

"No!" she cried, pushing past him. "Don't kill Max!"

"Ain't that charmin'?" crowed the smugglers' leader. "Sounds like true love, don't it, m'lads?"

His men laughed along with him.

"Don't want to separate lovers, do we, lads?" he continued. His tone suddenly changed as he spat, "Tie up the other one."

Terence raised his fists, but, with quick efficiency, he

was tied and propped against the boulders. He opened his mouth, and a cloth was stuffed in it.

"Lucinda," Max whispered as the men laughed and pointed at Terence's fury, "when they tie me up, I shall cause such a ruckus, you can—"

"I shan't leave you." She leaned her cheek against his shoulder. "I love you."

"In spite of everything?"

"Because of everything. You've given me fantasy and true love together." When Max looked at her, his eyes glowing as brightly as a cat's, she said, "You tried to escape from the past by hiding in Terence's game. I tried to escape from the future by hiding in my books." She smiled sadly. "Then I tried to escape from the love which frightened me by pretending to hate you. It was as useless as hiding in my books."

He was given no chance to answer. The leader stepped forward and raised his gun. "Milord, brin' yer lady with ye."

Max nodded. Keeping his arm around Lucinda, he stayed close beside her as they were herded around the boulders to the far side. He ignored Terence's muted frustration as he gauged his enemies. They formed a half circle around him and Lucinda. He drew her back against the rocks. If he could distract them for a second, she might be able to flee around the cairn.

He knew that was a futile thought when he looked down into her face. She would never leave him to face death alone. Here, where he had least thought to look for it, he had found a courage and a loyalty beyond any he had imagined.

When she gasped and stiffened, he scowled at the leader, who was pointing the gun at them again. He watched as the interloper slowly drew back the hammer.

His finger tipped her chin toward him. "If it is with

my last breath, sweetheart, I want you to know I love you, too."

"Perfect!" cheered the smuggler. "The very perfect ending! Just what Aunt Jennie would wish."

Max stared at him in astonishment as the leader raised the pistol and fired it into the sky. The man's words were as cultured as a lord's. What in the name of perdition was going on?

When the man drew down the kerchief to reveal a broad grin, Lucinda pulled out of his arms. Max reached to halt her, but she raced to throw her arms around the smuggler's neck.

"One moment," the man said as he disentangled himself from her embrace. Taking a pistol from one of the other men, he fired that one skyward, too. "Don't want Terence to take comfort from the fact I let either of you survive. By now, he should be shaking in his boots and feeling more than a morsel of guilt about his prank on you."

"Who are you?" Max asked bluntly.

Lucinda smiled and reached out her hand to him. "Max, I thought you would know Papa. This is Jerome, Lord Hart. Papa, this is Lord Loveland."

"Lord Hart," he said in the same rigid tone.

"No need for such ceremony on this meeting that has been delayed too long, my boy," Lord Hart said with a smile that pulled his gaunt face, which, upon a second look, resembled Terence's as closely as if they had been made of the same mold. "Such a heartfelt declaration to my daughter as I just witnessed suggests you soon will be due the informality of family."

Lucinda glanced at Max. She did not want to hold him to words that he may have said only because he thought they were about to die. No, she did not want to hold him to those words; she wanted to hold him to her as his mouth tantalized her with promises of delights still undiscovered.

"You need to excuse Papa," she said quietly. "I am afraid both Terence and I inherited our love of pranks from him."

"As I inherited them," Lord Hart interjected, "from your great-aunt, who was determined that your brother, Lucinda, would be repaid in kind."

"*This* was to repay Terence?" she asked.

"I think it shall be a while before he plays such a prank on you again." He patted her shoulder. "When I arrived this morning—"

"You arrived this morning?" she gasped. Now she understood what her great-aunt had meant by Lucinda missing family at dinner. She wondered if her mother was here as well.

Papa continued as if she had not interrupted, "Aunt Jennie told me how Terence had frightened the two of you at the pond. That was beyond the limits of a jest, even for a Hart." Looking past her, he held out his hand. "I assume you agree, Max."

Lucinda held her breath as she looked from her father's outstretched hand to Max's stern face. When Max slowly raised his hand to shake her father's, he said, "I agree, sir. I trust we shall eventually untie him and explain the truth."

"Before he freezes to death would be a good idea. He is, after all, the only heir I have to my title, and I cringe at the thought of one of my lackluster sons-in-law passing it on to one of their sons." Papa laughed and motioned to the other men. As they came closer, she recognized them all as retainers of Hart's Priory. Only her fear must have blinded her before. "Back to the house, lads, before you freeze. I'll let my pride and heir loose after he promises to think more thoroughly before he designs his next prank."

Lucinda's smile wavered as she watched Max watching her father walk back around the pile of rocks. Quietly she said, "We should return to the house, too."

"Not yet." He caught her shoulders and brought her to face him. "Lucinda, I owe you an apology as well."

"You did not know I did not know. Aunt Jennie explained it all to me." She could not help smiling. "I believe she hoped to teach me a lesson."

"This certainly taught me one, for I vow to you I have learned well the danger of playing this game of hearts with you."

"And what danger was there to you?"

"Losing mine." His mouth brushed hers before tilting in a smile. "And winning yours. Shall we recall this Valentine's Day holiday from now on as the day when you told me you would marry me?"

"Yes," she whispered, "I will marry you, Max."

She heard Terence shout his outrage and knew Papa had revealed the truth, but she paid him no mind as Max claimed her lips as the sweetest prize ever won in any game of Harts'.

The Unwilling Bride

Lois Stewart

Prologue

The carriage lurched and skidded to a stop. Lucinda's abigail squealed in apprehension. Roused from her thoughts, Lucinda glanced out the window and noticed with considerable surprise that a heavy snow was falling. Only a short time before—not so much as an hour, surely?—when they'd made their last change of horses in Aylesbury, she'd observed only a few stray flakes falling. The temperature had dropped, too. Her feet and hands felt stiff and chilled.

In a moment the door opened. Her coachman, his hat and clothing thickly encrusted with snow, his face crimson with cold and exposure, peered in at her.

"What is it, Hawkins? Why have we stopped? And how long has it been snowing so hard?"

"Started pouring down like a white curtain a mile or so out of Aylesbury, my lady. Never saw a storm come up so fast. I cain't hardly see more'n a foot or so ahead o' the horses, and the road's gitting right slippery. A real nasty blizzard, that's what it be. Wi' yer permission, my lady, I'd like to stop fer the night at the next posting stop. I reckon as how Sturbridge Village in't more'n a mile or so farther along."

"Oh, but—my grandmother is expecting me to arrive this afternoon." Then Lucinda took a closer look at the coachman and felt a pang of guilt. Hawkins' eyebrows were frosted with rime, and his ears looked frostbitten.

The two grooms perched at the rear of the coach must also be perishing from the cold and exposure.

"However, I expect you're right, Hawkins. Better to arrive at Marshfield Court a little later than I'd planned, but all in one piece! We'll stop at Sturbridge for the night."

"Yes, my lady."

The coachman closed the door, and soon afterward the carriage started up again, inching along at a snail's pace and occasionally making an alarming sideways slither to the opposite side of the turnpike road.

"Oh, my lady, I'm so glad ye decided not to go on," gasped her nervous abigail. "The snow's coming down heavier'n ever."

Unfortunately, when the carriage rolled into the courtyard of the Sturbridge Arms a short time later, Lucinda discovered that her coachman's scheme to take refuge from the storm had been far from an original one. The courtyard was crowded with carriages, the owners of which, Lucinda learned when she entered the vestibule of the inn, apparently having had the same idea: to spend the night and resume their journeys on the following day.

After some delay Lucinda finally located the harassed and apologetic landlord, who shook his head regretfully, saying, "I'm that sorry, ma'am, but I can't help ye. I've jist now rented out my last available room. The best I could offer, mayhap, after all the dinners have been served, is to put a cot into one o' the private dining parlors fer the night."

"Such a ramshackle arrangement won't do for Lady Brentford, Landlord," said a crisp voice. "She may have my bedchamber, of course. And speaking of private dining parlors, Lady Brentford will be my guest for dinner. Pray send in a menu and a waiter as soon as possible."

Before a dumfounded Lucinda quite knew what was happening, she was whisked into a private dining room, with the door firmly shut against the tumult in the vestibule, staring incredulously at the husband from whom she'd fled six months previously on her wedding day, even before her marriage could be consummated.

Jonah Leighton, Marquess of Brentford, hadn't changed one iota. He needed only to enter a room to dominate it with his charm and good looks: his tall, graceful figure in its exquisitely tailored clothes, the handsome lean face with the sensual quirk of the lips, the waving tawny hair and the silvery gray eyes that were now boring into hers. Doubtless, Lucinda thought resentfully, he'd barely had to exert himself to obtain the last available bedchamber and the last available dining parlor from the landlord.

He pulled an armchair closer to the roaring flames in the fireplace, saying, "Here, Lucinda, warm your bones. It's perishing out there tonight." Drawing up a chair for himself, he sat down, eyeing her purposefully. "I daresay, under these crowded conditions, that we won't enjoy an epicurean supper in this establishment tonight, but by God, I'll accomplish one thing: I'll make you talk to me. Lucinda, why did you leave me, practically at the altar, without a word of explanation?"

Lucinda stared back at him, her lips firmly clamped together against an inadvertent reply. She'd rather rip her tongue out than reveal to Jonah why she'd run away. During these past few months she'd learned to live alone, wretched, unfulfilled, but growing ever more sturdily nondependent on Jonah's quicksilver charm for her psychic survival. Perhaps, in a few more months, she could revert to the kind of comfortable, happy existence she'd known with her grandmother, before the Marquess of Brentford had disrupted her life. . . .

One

Lucinda scampered into the dining room of Mansfield Court, saying breathlessly, "I'm sorry I didn't stop to change my riding habit, Grandmama, but I didn't like to keep you waiting for your luncheon."

Lady Cardew peered at her over the rims of her eyeglasses. "My dear child, you're not only late for luncheon, but you look positively disgraceful. There's a long rent in your skirt, for one thing."

Looking down ruefully at her dusty and torn riding habit, Lucinda sighed. "Oh, dear. I hate to admit it, but Caesar brushed me off his back when I tried to make him jump the fence into the south paddock. The railing must be a mite too high." She sat down at the table, shaking out her napkin.

"Caesar? Isn't that the new stallion? Didn't you tell me that our head groom advised against buying the animal, on the grounds he was too strong to be a lady's mount? And now I see that Higgins was right."

"Oh, Higgins is a worrywart," rejoined Lucinda unconcernedly, as she helped herself to the lamb chops being served to her by the footman and began to partake of her usual hearty meal. "Caesar was simply a trifle fresh today. He and I will deal excellently with each other before very long, you'll see."

Lady Cardew shook her head. "Sometimes I think I'm

rearing a hoyden instead of a proper young lady," she said ruefully.

Lucinda grinned at her grandmother. The pair understood each other very well, and they were very fond of one another. Lucinda was an only child and an orphan. Her parents, the Earl and Countess of Thornton, had died in a carriage accident when she was very small. The title had passed to a distant cousin, but Lucinda had been left a substantial heiress in the care of her maternal grandmother.

"What's that you're studying?" Lucinda inquired, motioning to the slip of paper in the countess' hand.

"Oh, that. It's the menu for the Valentine's Day supper. Much the same as last year's menu, except the chef wants to bake some kind of fancy French *gateau* that he's heard has caught the Regent's fancy at his pavilion in Brighton."

Lady Cardew set the menu on the table beside her plate. "I've been thinking, these past few days," she said with an unwonted seriousness. "Perhaps it's time to discontinue these annual Valentine's Day balls for the county. Oh, it's true my birthday falls on Valentine's Day, and your grandfather always insisted we celebrate the occasion in a lavish way . . . but I'm getting to be an old lady now, and Valentine's Day should be for young lovers."

"Grandmama!" Lucinda exclaimed in horror, dropping her fork. "Don't say such things. You, an old lady? You're one of the youngest women I know. You should go on celebrating your Valentine's Day birthday until you're a hundred!"

It was true, Lucinda reflected. If she'd exaggerated, it wasn't by much. Emily Cardew's eyes were still as bright and sparkling blue as her granddaughter's, her porcelain skin nearly as unlined, her figure as trim as it had been in her youth, and, if her auburn locks showed not a trace of gray and were, indeed, even a richer red than Lucinda's, that was a secret between her and her abigail. Before her husband's death she had been one of the great beauties and one of the great political hostesses of English society. She still opened her town house every year during the Season, and the *ton* still flocked to her entertainments.

"Well . . . I expect it would cause quite a social void here in Oxfordshire in the dead of winter if I discontinued the event," the countess agreed without any further argument. Lucinda suspected that her grandmother had never had any real intention of ending the custom. Lady Cardew went on, "We'll plan to carry on, then, at least for this year." She frowned. "Speaking of making plans, we ought to decide soon on a date for going to London in the spring. Your wardrobe is in a frightful state. We'll need several weeks—a month—to fit you out properly for your come-out."

Lucinda pushed her plate away from her. Slowly she said, "I've been thinking about my come-out, Grandmama. I'm not sure . . ."

The countess sipped her tea. "Oh? Not sure about what?"

"As a matter of fact—and I do hope you won't be overset, grandmama—I've decided I'd much rather *not* have a come-out."

Lady Cardew's cup clattered in her saucer. "Not have a come-out? What kind of balderdash is that? You're eighteen years old. Time, and past time, to take part in a London Season. Perhaps you'll be so kind as to explain yourself."

Looking uncomfortable, but determined in her views, Lucinda said, "Let us be honest. What's the purpose of a come-out? To give unmarried females the opportunity to meet eligible suitors, isn't that so? Well, I'm in no need of an eligible suitor. I don't wish to be married."

Every reddish curl on Lady Cardew's head seemed to bristle with a life of its own. "Nonsense," she snapped. "Every woman should be married."

"Why? In my opinion, if a female has sufficient income to live comfortably, and has respectable family connections to bolster her reputation, like you, Grandmama, she has no need for a husband. You'll admit, I trust, that I have a sufficient income? Papa left me his entire personal fortune."

"What about your social responsibilities?" demanded Lady Cardew. "With your looks and fortune and ancestry you could take a prominent place in society. And if *that* doesn't interest you, what about children?"

"Oh, children. Well, of course, some day I'd like to have children. But what is the hurry, Grandmama? I'm only eighteen. Why shouldn't I wait a few years to marry?" Lucinda paused a moment. "Do you know what I'd really like to do for a time? I'd like to manage the stud farm that Great-uncle Horatio left me in Cambridgeshire."

Throwing up her hands, Lady Cardew said in annoyance, "That brother of mine! I might have known that no good would come of his leaving a stud farm to a female!" Her expression softened, and she began to laugh. "On the other hand, Horatio always said that you were the only person in the family besides himself who really understood horseflesh."

Her spate of ill humor vanishing, Lady Cardew leaned forward, resting her elbows on the table. "Darling Lucinda, consider the matter. Tongues will certainly wag if you go off to the wilds of Cambridgeshire to manage a stud farm, and *I* should be deprived of the pleasure of your company during the Season. Shall we make a bargain? Oblige me by going through the motions of a come-out, and I promise I won't pressure you to accept any hopeful offers for your hand. I agree with you, you have plenty of time to find a husband!"

"Done!" said Lucinda promptly. She and her grand-mother grinned at one another, once more in their customary harmony with each other.

Two

As Lucinda cantered slowly down Grosvenor Place in the direction of Hyde Park Corner, she lifted her head appreciatively to allow the rays of the early May sun to warm her face. It was a perfect spring day. The Season was about to start.

She and her grandmother had been in London for three weeks, staying in Cardew House in Grosvenor Square. Until now Lucinda had been enjoying herself. Her objections had never been to visiting London itself, but rather to her grandmother's matchmaking plans. She had a healthy feminine appreciation for pretty new clothes, she was a tireless sightseer, she'd had the opportunity to ride every morning in Rotten Row and in the afternoons to drive in the Park, and she was honestly looking forward to parties and balls, now that she was relieved of the necessity of choosing a husband from among the young men to whom she would soon be introduced.

Just behind St. George's Hospital, Lucinda prepared to turn off into a narrow lane. Her groom muttered uneasily, "I do wish ye'd reconsider going ter Tattersall's, my lady. Higgins will have my hide if he finds out ye went there."

Lucinda said impatiently, "Nonsense, Roberts. Higgins is an excellent head groom, but, as I've told him often enough to his face, he's a worrywart. He's heard some vague rumor that Tattersall's is out of bounds to respectable females, and he's bound and determined to protect my reputation. Which is nonsense. Why should it be scandalous for me to select my own horses? I've bought a new phaeton, and I have no intention of allowing anyone but myself to choose a team. Of course, I'm told there won't be any sales today—they take place only on Mondays in the summer—but the horses will be on display."

The groom subsided into a resigned silence, and Lucinda continued down the lane to the entrance to the Repository, as she was informed Tattersall's was generally known to the public. She entered a large, circular enclosure surrounded by a gravel path bordering a grass plot, on which a number of horses were being exhibited. Ahead was the subscription room, and to the right a passage led to another enclosure where the actual sales auctions took place.

The enclosure was crowded with fashionably dressed men who were inspecting the horses and exchanging gossip of the racing world. As Lucinda entered the enclosure and dismounted, handing her reins to her groom, a brief, pregnant silence descended on the crowd. Conscious of the surprised, decidedly disapproving stares directed her way, Lucinda felt a moment's qualm.

Perhaps, she thought, she *had* made a mistake in entering what was obviously an all-male bastion. To a logical mind, it would seem petty, indeed picayunish, to exclude females from Tattersall's, but then Lucinda had decided that many of the rules governing a fashionable female's conduct were based on equally groundless prohibitions: no lady who valued her reputation could be seen walking down Bond Street or St. James's Street in the afternoon, for example, and she could never go out unless she was accompanied by a maid, footman, page, or groom.

Lucinda tossed her head. She was here, and she might as well make the most of it. Ignoring the stares, she was soon absorbed in her examination of the horses being offered for sale. She quickly located a pair of matched bays, in whom, try as she might, she could not discover a single flaw.

"Ye'll not go wrong if ye buy this pair, ma'am," offered the groom who was showing the horses. "Near broke Lord Broadhurst's heart ter part wi' 'em." The groom sighed. "Poor gentleman. Gone to pigs and whistles, ye understand—ruined hisself on 'Change, or so I hear say."

"Well, I'm sorry for Lord Broadhurst," declared Lucinda, "but his misfortune is my good luck. These bays will be a perfect team for my new phaeton. I'll be here bright and early next Monday to buy them."

"Can I be of any assistance, ma'am? I fancy I've a good eye for horseflesh."

Lucinda looked up to find a weedy-looking young man standing beside her, smiling at her ingratiatingly. He had spots on his face, and obviously belonged to the Dandy set, since he was wearing a spotted handkerchief instead of a cravat, and sported a small, round porkpie hat.

Giving him a long, raking glance from head to toe, Lucinda said coldly, "No, thank you, sir. I'm quite capable of choosing my own horses."

Unabashed, the man said, "Well, then, if I can't assist you to buy a team, perhaps we could become better acquainted socially? Today, for example, we might jaunt out to Richmond Hill for a gala luncheon at the Star and Garter." He put out his hand to caress her cheek. "Dashed if you aren't the prettiest filly to grace these parts in ages."

Her cheeks flaming, Lucinda brushed aside the young man's hand. "Pray have the courtesy to leave me, sir. I have no desire to know a niffynaffy, vulgar person like yourself."

The man flushed. "A mite high in the instep for a ladybird, aren't you, my girl?" He pasted the ingratiating smile back on his lips, placing his hand on her arm and drawing her closer to him. "Come along now, I'll over-look your little spell of rudeness. We'll have a splendid time at the Star and Garter."

Lucinda pulled away from him, at the same time giving him a sharp slap on his face. With an angry growl he sprang at her, but before he could lay a finger on her, he was stretched flat on the ground, limp and vacant-eyed.

Lucinda stared in surprise at the man who had appeared out of nowhere to come to her rescue.

"I trust this loose screw didn't injure you, ma'am?" the stranger asked politely, massaging the knuckles of the hand that had just planted a facer on her tormentor.

"No, not at all, thanks to you, sir."

Lucinda studied her rescuer. He was a man of almost thirty, tall and well-proportioned, dressed in the height of fashion, with a lean handsome face, curling tawny hair and eyes of a piercing silvery gray hue.

Lucinda's attacker began to stir. He sprang to his feet, staring in consternation at the man who had knocked him down. "Lord Brentford!" he gasped. "I had no idea this—this lady was a friend of yours. I assure you, if I had known . . ."

"Well, now you do know, Gifford," said Lord Brentford coolly, "and I suggest that you relieve the lady of your company."

His face a bright red, the man bent to pick up his obnoxious hat, which had fallen from his head, and shambled off.

Striving to appear collected and dignified, Lucinda said to Lord Brentford, "I thank you, sir, for coming to my aid." Nodding, she moved off toward her waiting groom.

"One moment, ma'am, if you please."

Lucinda turned to find Lord Brentford examining her closely. She flushed slightly. His gaze was so intense that she fancied he could not only describe every article of her clothing, but could even guess the name of her modiste.

"Yes?" she said stiffly.

"Correct me if I'm wrong, ma'am, but may I hazard a guess that you are a newcomer to London?"

There was an edge to Lucinda's voice as she replied, "You're quite right, sir. For whatever interest it may be to you, I've come here to make my come-out."

He seemed unperturbed by her hint of annoyance. "As I suspected. Being a newcomer, then, you were doubtless not aware that ladies customarily do not frequent Tattersall's."

Lucinda ground her teeth. The implication was urbanely polite but unmistakable. The gentleman was telling her that she herself was partially responsible for the unspeakable Gifford's assault on her because she had breached one of the rules of etiquette. Before she could reply, Lord Brentford walked over to her horse and extended his cupped hands to help her into the saddle.

"I suggest, ma'am, that it might be wise for you to quit the premises." He added kindly, "Your groom can always return to represent you if you wish to purchase a horse."

Drawing a deep breath, Lucinda said, "Thank you for your advice, sir. I'm sure you mean well." She allowed him to assist her to mount. "Good day, my lord."

As she rode through the portico of Tattersall's, Lucinda struggled to repair her battered feelings. She'd been determined to prevent Lord Brentford from realizing how much he'd mortified her, but the fact was that his condescending kindness had made her feel like a chastened and not overly bright schoolgirl. At least he'd recognized her as a person of quality rather than the ladybird that the miserable Dandy, Gifford, had mistaken her for, but that was small comfort.

* * *

Lady Cardew's eyes twinkled as Lucinda's partner escorted her off the ballroom floor and deposited her respectfully at her grandmother's side.

"It's easy enough to see why come-outs are reserved for the very young," said the countess with a smile. "Only the young have the energy to participate in an entire Season. Here you are, Lucinda, for example, at your first formal ball. You've danced every dance, and I'm sure you'll have partners for every remaining dance. And you'll be attending a ball or a rout or an affair of some kind every night for the next three months. It makes me weary just to think of it!"

Lucinda laughed. "You know you'd be disappointed, Grandmama, if nobody asked me to dance. And I'm not tired in the least."

"Good evening, Lady Cardew. What a great pleasure to see you again. Won't you introduce me to your charge?" said a familiar voice.

Lucinda's heart sank at the sight of the tall, elegant figure bending over her grandmother.

"Lord Brentford," exclaimed the countess in delight. "Lucinda, I'd like you to meet a very old friend of mine. Lady Lucinda Vernon, may I present Lord Brentford. Jonah, do sit down. We'll have a comfortable coze about the old days."

"A little later, Countess? First, however . . ." The orchestra had started up again, and Brentford extended his hand to Lucinda. "May I have this dance, Lady Lucinda?"

"Well . . . I believe I promised it to a Mr. Lucas . . ."

"More fool he, then, to be so laggard in claiming it, don't you agree?" said Brentford cheerfully.

"Jonah is quite right, Lucinda," said Lady Cardew. "Go along with you."

As she took his arm, trying not to show her embarrassment at seeing him again after the episode at Tattersall's, Lucinda seized on a topic of conversation. "So you and Grandmama are very old friends?"

Brentford chuckled. "Lord, yes. When your grandfather was still alive, and a power in Parliament, I was one of the young blades who congregated in the drawing room of Cardew House. We were all half in love with Lady Cardew, even though she was more than twenty years older than most of us. But then, her charm is ageless."

As they met in the various figures of the dance Lucinda's sense of awkwardness decreased, although she took the first opportunity to say, "May I ask a favor? Please don't mention to Grandmama that we met at Tattersall's."

"Of course. We didn't actually meet, you know. You'll recall that I carefully refrained from asking for an introduction!" He smiled. "I attended the Monday sales at the Repository yesterday. That superb pair of matched bays sold immediately. Someone was acting as your agent, I presume."

Lucinda nodded. "Yes, that was my head groom. I *had* to have those horses." She looked at Brentford challengingly. "And whether or not it was proper or improper for me to go to Tattersall's, you must admit that if I *hadn't* gone there, I would never have known of the existence of those bays."

"Touché." He looked at her keenly. "Was acquiring the bays a lucky choice on your part, or are you really a good judge of horseflesh?"

"Better than most," flashed Lucinda. "As a matter of fact, I inherited a stud farm in Cambridgeshire. Some day I'd like to manage it personally."

Brentford raised an eyebrow. "Not a usual occupation for a young lady of quality, surely? What does your grandmother think of your ambition?

"Not very much," admitted Lucinda candidly. "Grandmama would much prefer that I emerge as the belle of the Season and receive an offer of marriage from the most eligible bachelor in the *ton*. So we compromised. I agreed to put off any plans to manage my stud farm and come to London for my come-out, and she agreed not to press any unwelcome suitors on me."

Brentford burst out laughing. "You must surely be the most refreshingly original candidate on the Marriage Mart this Season. You're truly Lady Cardew's grand-daughter. As I remember, she never hesitates to say exactly what she thinks."

Biting her lip, Lucinda said vexedly, "My wretched tongue. I do hope you won't repeat any foolishness you may have heard me say, Lord Brentford."

"I make it a point not to gossip," Brentford assured her. But a smile of amusement wreathed his mouth as the dance ended and he brought her back to her grand-mother's side.

Later that evening, as Lucinda and Lady Cardew drove home to the house in Grosvenor Square, the countess remarked, "I do believe you were partnered by the most eligible bachelors in the *ton* this evening. Lord Cathcart, Sir Beverly Waring, Mr. Adams, Lord Bruce. Truly an opening triumph in your come-out." She added dryly, "Not that it matters, since you've already made up your mind not to consider any advantageous offers, but still . . ."

Lucinda grinned at her grandmother in the darkness of the carriage. "I thought all of the gentlemen were most charming," she said demurely. After a moment she added casually, "You didn't mention Lord Brentford. Isn't he an eligible bachelor? Or is he already married?"

"No. Well, I'd have to give you both a yes and a no to your question. Strictly speaking, there's no more eligible bachelor in all of England than the Marquess of Brent-ford. As you've seen for yourself, he's young, handsome, charming, wealthy, and he comes from one of the oldest and most prominent families in the kingdom. However, he's definitely not on the Marriage Mart. For almost ten years now he's been the property of Lady Melling. He met her shortly after her father had married her off to the Earl of Melling, an immensely rich and powerful man many years older than Daphne. Brentford fell madly and instantly in love with her, and she with him. They've been very discreet. By this time, I'm told, society has accepted their relationship as practically legitimate."

"Oh." In her own ears Lucinda's voice sounded flat.

Lady Cardew added guiltily, "Oh, dear, I daresay it was indelicate of me to mention Brentford's romantic arrangement to an unmarried female. It's your fault, Lucinda. You've gotten me accustomed to saying the first thing that enters my mind!"

Lucinda chortled. "Most people would say that I acquired the habit of being plain-spoken from *you!*"

"Don't be impertinent, my girl," said Lady Cardew with a pretended severity. She went on, "Oh, well, I fancy you'd have heard about Brentford and Daphne Melling at some point. All these young girls appear to be so mealy-mouthed, but seem to hear all the gossip."

"Lord Brentford feels no need to marry and provide an heir to the title?" Lucinda inquired, rather proud of her disinterested tone, though why she should have felt any need to be disinterested she could not have explained.

"Oh, Brentford has an heir, his younger brother, Lord Harry Leighton. Harry married several years ago—she's a most charming girl, Lord Evesham's oldest daughter— and no doubt we'll be hearing an interesting announcement before long. I don't think Jonah has any need to fear for the succession."

* * *

Lady Cardew looked up from her desk as Lucinda entered the morning room, dressed for an afternoon drive. "Well, my dear Lucinda, we're only some three weeks into the Season, and already I've received a second application to pay addresses to you."

Lucinda grinned. "And who is my new admirer?"

The countess frowned. "Don't be vulgar, my girl. It doesn't become you. Sir Vincent Maynard left me, not an hour ago, after protesting his undying regard for you. I presume you didn't wish me to encourage him? As I thought. I told him we couldn't begin to make any decision about your future until at least the end of the Season."

"Thank you, Grandmama. You always know what to say."

Lady Cardew put down her pen, giving Lucinda a long, examining look. "You're looking very handsome today. Your pelisse and the blue feathers on your bonnet are almost the same shade as your eyes. And so, you're off to drive your phaeton in the Park." She pursed her lips. "You know, when you first broached the idea of driving a phaeton in London, I was a bit dubious. It's quite different in the country, of course. Many females drive a phaeton or a gig on the quiet country roads. Here in London I was afraid you might be considered a little fast for doing so. However, I was talking to Lady Jersey several days ago, and she informed me that you were much admired as a whip. So that's all right. Well, be off with you, my dear. Enjoy your drive."

During her scant few weeks in London Lucinda had met a large number of people. As she guided her phaeton along the Carriage Road she found herself continually waving at acquaintances, and often she had to stop by the side of the roadway to chat with friends.

At one point she spotted a tall, elegant figure on horseback paused beside a fashionable barouche.

"Lady Lucinda," called Lord Brentford. "Will you allow me to present you to an old friend?"

Lucinda wasn't in the least surprised to learn that the lovely woman in the barouche was Lady Melling. The lady had spun gold hair and Dresden-like features of a fragile beauty. Lucinda had to acknowledge that it wasn't hard to understand why Lord Brentford had remained attached to his mistress for so many years.

"Lord Brentford tells me that you are the granddaughter of a lady he much admires," said Daphne Melling graciously.

His eyes twinkling, Brentford said, "Lady Lucinda, I've confessed to Lady Melling that your grandmother was my first love!" He gave a long look at the phaeton and its team. "Will you take me up in your phaeton? I don't believe I've had the pleasure of being driven by a lady. Will you excuse us, Lady Melling?"

After a short drive along the Ring, Brentford looked sideways at Lucinda, saying, "I'm ashamed of myself for having any doubts about your driving ability. I thought the bays might be too strong for you. But you're a superb whip. A perfectly matched driver and team."

Lucinda felt her cheeks growing warm. She couldn't explain her feelings, but she knew that Brentford's praise meant more to her than any other compliments she'd ever received on her driving ability.

"Thank you, Lady Lucinda," said her partner as he brought her off the dance floor at Almack's.

She smiled and nodded. He was a nice young man, so ordinary, however, that she wasn't sure she would recognize him at their next meeting. She glanced around the ballroom. She was under no illusions about the glamour of Almack's. The Wednesday sessions there were sedate and rather boring, under the gimlet-eyed surveillance of the watchful hostesses; but Lady Cardew considered it important for Lucinda to have the entree there, so she had at least always managed to enjoy the dancing.

"Good evening, Lady Lucinda. I hope you'll allow me to have at least one dance."

Lucinda looked up with a welcoming smile. She wondered why it was that Brentford looked so much more impressive than the other males in the room, even though he was wearing the same uniform of dress coat, white breeches and hose and polished slippers. No doubt it was because he wore his perfectly tailored clothes with a supremely indifferent grace.

"Oh, I think I can find a dance for you. Although," she added with a grin, "Almack's is almost the last place I would have expected to see you."

He returned her smile. "It's true, a very small dose of Almack's suffices for a considerable time." He glanced at her gown of sheer apricot-colored aérophane crape over a slip of white satin. "You look enchanting tonight. I would have thought that the color of your gown was so close to the color of your hair that the two would eclipse each other. I was wrong."

"Why, thank you. It's all Grandmama's doing. She has an infallible eye for color." Before Lucinda could stop herself she blurted, "Have you been away? I haven't seen you for several days," and then wished she could bite off her unruly tongue.

Apparently he didn't notice anything untoward about her remark. "Yes, I've been out of town, visiting my stud near Epsom. I have a horse entered in the Derby, and I wanted to check on his progress in training."

"You have a horse entered in the Derby?" Lucinda's face glowed. "Oh, how I envy you. I think I could die happy if I owned a horse that had raced in the Derby."

Brentford's lips twitched. "I sympathize with your am-

bition, but I fear it's impossible. To enter a horse in the
Derby, one must belong to the Jockey Club. Unfortunately, ladies are barred from the Jockey Club."

"Oh, of course, ladies are barred from the Jockey
Club," said Lucinda bitterly. "One more instance of the
unfair, arbitrary rules governing a female's conduct."
She brooded for several moments, then said impulsively,
"Well, supposing I had a likely candidate for the Derby.
Couldn't I persuade a member of the Jockey Club to
enter the horse in the race under his name? You, for
example."

Brentford burst out laughing. "Good God, Lady Lucinda, what will you think of next? Yes. If the occasion
ever arises, and you acquire a horse of Derby caliber, I'll
consider entering the animal in the race under my
name." He paused, sobering. "Were you and Lady
Cardew planning to attend the Derby? I've invited a
small group of friends to join me at my stud farm in
Epsom for the race. I'd be delighted to welcome you and
Lady Cardew also. Shall I extend an invitation to your
grandmother?

Flushing with pleasure, Lucinda said, "Oh, yes, please
do. Of course, Grandmama isn't a racing enthusiast, but
I think I can persuade her to accept your invitation."

Brentford put out his hand and brushed his forefinger
lightly along her cheek. "Oh, I have no doubt you can
persuade Lady Cardew," he said smilingly. "I think
you're probably the most persuasive female I've ever met!
Good, we'll consider it settled. You and your grandmother will arrive at Woodbury Park on the Saturday or
Sunday, attend the running of both the Derby and the
Oaks, and stay on to celebrate Whitsuntide with me."

He held out his hand as the orchestra started up.
"Shall we?" They walked out on the dance floor just as
the man to whom Lucinda had originally promised the
number appeared hopefully on the scene.

When the dance was over, and Brentford was escorting Lucinda to her grandmother's side, Lady Melling appeared unexpectedly beside them. Smiling brightly, she said, "I haven't had a moment to exchange a word with you tonight, Lady Lucinda, and here I'd been promising myself the opportunity to get to know you better. Lord Brentford, you'll excuse us, won't you?"

Looking faintly puzzled, Brentford bowed and moved away.

Glancing down the crowded expanse of the ballroom, Lady Melling said, "It's such a squeeze here tonight. Shall we go to the card room where we will have more privacy?"

A vaguely bewildered Lucinda nodded her assent. Why had Lady Melling made it a point to seek her out? Their only common point of reference was their acquaintance with Brentford. Improbable as it seemed, Lucinda had to assume that Lady Melling was simply being gracious out of deference to him. Lucinda was the granddaughter of a woman whom he had admired years ago.

Seated opposite Lady Melling at a table in the card room, Lucinda studied the woman covertly. Close up, Daphne Melling was even more beautiful than she remembered from their one previous meeting. The lady was an ethereal vision in misty blue gauze.

"I hear you're one of the great successes of the Season, Lady Lucinda," Daphne Melling observed with a smile, a smile that appeared to Lucinda to be rather forced.

"Thank you," Lucinda replied. "But I fear you've been listening to exaggerated rumors."

Lady Melling shook her head. "Oh, I hardly think so. The *on dit* is that you're besieged by every eligible bachelor in the *ton*, that your social calendar is filled until the end of the Season, that universally you're considered to be one of the great originals who has come along the pike in recent years."

Lucinda could feel her cheeks growing warm. "I repeat, you've been listening to exaggerated rumors."

Giving her a long look, Daphne Melling observed, "I'll confess, I did hear one report that disturbed me. Lady Lucinda, as an older woman with a great deal more social experience than you can possess, may I offer you some advice?"

Completely nonplussed, Lucinda gaped at her companion. "Er—certainly."

"Well, then . . . It is understandable that you should wish to make the best marriage possible. That is why you've come to London for your come-out, after all. However, it has come to my attention that you've been setting your cap for a gentleman who is not a candidate for the Marriage Mart. If you persist in your ill-judged pursuit of this gentleman, you risk damaging your reputation and put in jeopardy your opportunities to make a suitable match."

Stiffening, Lucinda said coldly, "I must ask you to explain your remarks, Lady Melling. Who is the gentleman to whom I'm presumed to be casting out lures?"

With a sweet reasonableness that somehow was more annoying to Lucinda than an angry response would have been, Lady Melling said, "Really, I think you know quite well that I'm referring to the Marquess of Brentford. You must know—or your grandmother should have told you—that Jonah has no intention of marrying. That being the case, you only demean yourself by flirting with him, by trying to take advantage of the friendship he felt for your grandmother years ago, by attempting to become closer to him by trading upon your common interest in horses."

Trying to keep her calm, Lucinda declared, "You're quite mistaken, Lady Melling. For your information, I am *not* on the catch for Lord Brentford, nor have I any intention of doing so."

Rising, Daphne Melling said with an indulgent smile, "There now, you're very young, aren't you, and I've embarrassed you. The truth does that sometimes. I felt an obligation to give you a little warning in this matter, since your family and Jonah's are such old friends, but . . . We'll say no more, then. Please believe I meant my remarks kindly."

"Thank you for your concern, Lady Melling. Will you excuse me, please?" Lucinda stalked out of the card room. Outside the entrance of the ballroom she paused, drawing a deep breath to compose herself. Could Daphne Melling be correct? Was it possible that her friendship with Jonah had led the *ton* to suspect her of matrimonial designs on him? What did Brentford think of the friendly overtures she had made to him?

Lucinda drew another deep breath as her native common sense took over. Perhaps Daphne Melling was simply jealous, unlikely as it might seem. Perhaps the superb poise and self-confidence she always displayed in public had cracks in the facade. She was human like everyone else, after all, and perhaps she'd magnified Brentford's small, platonic attentions to Lucinda into a danger to her hold on her long-time lover's allegiance.

Deciding to put the incident out of her mind, Lucinda walked into the ballroom. Brentford hurried over to her, saying with a smile, "I'm going to be selfish and claim another dance."

Out of the corner of her eye Lucinda glimpsed a graceful figure in blue entering the ballroom behind her. She placed her hand on Jonah's arm. "I should be delighted, Lord Brentford," she said, raising her voice slightly so that Daphne Melling could hardly fail to hear her.

Three

As the carriage drove across Westminster Bridge, Lucinda began to feel a sense of great exhilaration. Of all the social events she'd attended during the first part of the Season, the opportunity to view the running of the Derby was easily the most exciting to a confirmed horsewoman like herself.

"We'll be a small but very select company these next few days, I believe," Lady Cardew observed as they began the fifteen-mile journey into the lovely rolling countryside of Surrey's North Downs. "Lord and Lady Jersey will be there, among others. Lord Alvanley, I hear. Lord and Lady Melling, of course. Jonah's younger brother—he manages the stud at Woodbury Park—and his wife. I look forward to a very agreeable weekend."

Lucinda gave a little bounce of excitement. "I, too. When we were planning our trip to London I never dreamed I'd have the opportunity to attend the Derby."

The countess gave her an amused smile. "Oh, you. Do you ever think of anything except horses?" She lapsed into a pensive silence, from which she emerged to murmur, "I wish . . ." Her voice trailed away.

"What, Grandmama?"

Lady Cardew tossed her head. "I'm a foolish old woman, so I fancy I'm at liberty to entertain any ideas I like. I was wishing—oh, confound it, I'll come right out with it. I wish Jonah wasn't entangled with Daphne

Melling. I think you and he would make a splendid couple. I can't think of anyone I'd prefer to call my grandson-in-law."

"Grandmama!" Lucinda flushed crimson.

Lady Cardew bit her lip. "I'm sorry, Lucinda. My wretched tongue is growing as unruly as yours! Brentford's relationship with Daphne is most certainly permanent, so it makes no difference. Oh, well, he's probably a little too old for you, in any event."

To her granddaughter's relief, the countess dropped the subject of Lord Brentford. In the deepest privacy of her own thoughts Lucinda had admitted to herself that she was attracted to the marquess more than to any other man she had met in London. If he were free, unencumbered romantically . . . But he wasn't, and Lucinda also had to take into account the contrariness of human nature in general, and her own in particular. She'd come to London determined to reject any suitor who might offer for her. Brentford *hadn't* offered for her because he was firmly attached to another woman. Could Lucinda be drawn to him simply because he *wasn't* available as husband material?

Lucinda put the marquess out of her mind and tried to concentrate on the gentle Surrey scenery. She wasn't impressed by Epsom itself. It was a large, ordinarily quiet town, its streets and hotels bustling and crowded now with visitors for Derby week. However, after she and the countess had passed through the town, she was thrilled to drive along a road on Epsom Common, a broad open heath, covered with furze and bisected by a myriad of roads, where the running of the Derby and later the Oaks would take place.

After a time the coachman turned the carriage onto a narrow side road, nearly overshadowed by arching hedgerows. Soon they entered a long drive leading to a large group of buildings dominated by an extensive group of paddocks and stables. Servants swarmed out of the house to help Lucinda and Lady Cardew out of the carriage, take their luggage and escort them into comfortable though simply furnished bedchambers. Lucinda was to decide later that Woodbury Park was certainly not a typical pretentious country house. It had obviously been designed and built with its owner's stables and racing interests as its primary focus.

After Lucinda and Lady Cardew had changed from their traveling clothes and had enjoyed a restorative cup of tea, they went down to join their fellow guests in the drawing room before dinner. The first person they encountered was Daphne Melling, who, after greeting Lady Cardew, favored Lucinda with what could be termed a rather lukewarm smile. Her husband, an elderly, rather decrepit-looking gentleman, who had naturally been included as a member of the house party out of respect for the proprieties, was his usual vague self. He had been known to fall asleep in public.

"My dear girl," Lady Cardew murmured as they sat down, "have you contrived to offend our Daphne? She seemed a little cool to you."

Trust Grandmama to be awake on every suit, Lucinda reflected. Did she ever fail to notice anything?

"Perhaps Lady Melling is just a trifle out of sorts," Lucinda said. "Perhaps she doesn't care for racing, or for country life."

Lady Cardew looked unconvinced. "Daphne's famous for her aplomb, her exquisitely correct manners. I do hope you haven't unwittingly offended her. She carries a great deal of social weight in our circle."

Lord Alvanley came over to them, his face wreathed in its usual genial smile. "Well, Lady Cardew, I hear you have a notable whip in your family. Lady Lucinda, you've been much admired." His eyes crinkled in amusement.

"Tell me," he teased, "have you ever considered driving a high perch phaeton?"

"Lady Lucinda is far too intelligent to attempt such a thing," declared Brentford as he joined them. "She leaves such idiocies to Prinny, though heaven knows even he's acquired some common sense of late." He nodded to the young couple who had accompanied him. "Lady Cardew, may I present my brother, Lord Harry Leighton, and his wife, Cassandra? Harry, Cassandra, this is Lady Cardew's granddaughter, Lady Lucinda Vernon."

Lucinda looked with interest at Harry Leighton, who appeared to be a less vivid, less forceful version of his older brother. Cassandra was a pretty, shy-looking girl without a great deal of personality.

Probably because she and Lucinda were closer in age than the other guests, Cassandra devoted herself to Lucinda in the interval before dinner. She was, in fact, quite talkative, almost as if she hadn't had much opportunity for social conversation of late.

"I'm so happy you and your grandmother, and indeed, all the other guests, have joined us here at Woodbury Park," Cassandra remarked with a shade of wistfulness. "I daresay you're wondering why we haven't met before, Lady Lucinda. Of course, Harry and I normally spend most of our time here at the farm—we prefer country living—but the fact is, I've been more or less in seclusion recently." She blushed faintly. "You've doubtless guessed that I'm increasing, and my doctors have advised me to rest as much as possible." Her face clouded. "Several times recently I've had such great hopes, you see, and then I've been—disappointed. So I must be extra careful now to follow the doctors' orders."

Lucinda remembered that Harry Leighton was Brentford's heir, and only a son born to him and Cassandra would guarantee the continuance of the title and estates

in the immediate family, since Jonah had decided not
to marry. She said gently, "I'm confident that this time
you'll have a happy outcome, Lady Harry."

Cassandra's eyes filled. "Thank you. You're very comforting."

Lucinda made up her mind to spend as much time
with Cassandra as possible during her stay at Woodbury
Park, to take the girl's mind off her terror of losing her
baby. They could go for easy walks together in the gardens; they could sit together while Cassandra embroidered or practiced the pianoforte; they could go for quiet
drives in Brentford's phaeton or gig.

During the next several days before the running of
the Derby on the Wednesday before Whitsuntide, the
guests at Woodbury Park pursued a leisurely schedule
of activities: inspecting Brentford's stables, going shopping in the town, taking pleasant walks on the Downs to
nearby villages, visiting several of the larger estates in
the area. And, true to her resolve, Lucinda was a great
deal in Cassandra's company, and the girl was almost
embarrassingly grateful for the attention.

During the course of her visit, though she did her best
to put the subject out of her mind, Lucinda was both
fascinated and chagrined to observe the discretion with
which Brentford and Daphne Melling conducted their
affair; in public their relations were so impeccably correct
that no outsider would have suspected they were lovers.
In fact, Lucinda guessed that Jonah spent rather less
time with the Mellings than with his other guests.

One morning, shortly before race day, Lucinda came
down to an early breakfast to find Brentford in the dining room ahead of her. He raised his coffee cup to her
in a kind of salute. "Everyone else in the house must be
a lazybones this morning." He grinned. Sobering, he
added, "I never seem to see you alone, so I'd like to take
this opportunity to thank you for being so friendly to

Cassandra. She's been a little lost of late, I think. I fancy she's felt lonely here at Woodbury, almost as if everyone has abandoned her, though Harry's done his best to keep her mind occupied."

Lucinda said simply, "I like Cassandra, and I enjoy being with her. I don't deserve any special credit for keeping her company."

Brentford flashed her a warm smile. "Permit me to disagree with you." He cocked his eyebrow at her. "I can't allow you to spend all your time playing the good Samaritan. Look, I rose at an ungodly hour this morning to accompany my training groom to the Downs to give Caesar a long workout. Would you care to go with us? I'll drive you in my curricle."

"Now? Oh, yes, I'd love to watch your horse run," said Lucinda eagerly. "Wait one moment. I'll just get my pelisse and bonnet."

As she and Brentford left the dining room, they met Daphne Melling, who was just descending the stairs. "Oh, Jonah, I trust you haven't forgotten our engagement to join the Ashfords at Slean House for a late breakfast?"

Brentford looked guilty. "I'm afraid I did forget, Daphne. I've already breakfasted. In any event, I'd made plans to go with my training groom for a workout session on the Downs—the race is two days from now, you know—and I've just invited Lady Lucinda to join me."

Lady Melling's face turned wooden. "I see. Lady Lucinda is such a racing enthusiast that I wouldn't for the world wish to deprive her of an enjoyable experience." She turned to go back up the stairs.

Brentford said contritely, "Wait, Daphne. I'm truly sorry for my forgetfulness. But then, it's no great thing, is it? We can visit the Ashfords on the weekend, after all, at the end of the racing meet."

Daphne looked at Brentford without any softening of

her expression. "We can only hope that dear Mrs. Ash-
ford won't be offended. I'll send her our regrets."

Watching Daphne Melling's figure walk stiff-backed
up the stairs, Lucinda said, aghast, "Lord Brentford,
since you had a prior engagement with Lady Melling,
perhaps you should keep it."

Staring after his mistress, Brentford looked puzzled.
"I wonder if Daphne has the headache. It's not like her
to be so thin-skinned." He shook his head. "Oh, well, it
can't be helped. I'll speak to her later . . . Time is growing very short, unfortunately. As a responsible owner I
need to know exactly how my horse is progressing in his
training." He gave Lucinda a quick grin. "Besides, the
Ashfords are pudding-headed bores, and I'd as lief not
spend any time with them! Go along and fetch your bonnet and pelisse. I'll meet you at the stables."

Leaving the house a little later, Lucinda was still feeling uncomfortable. On the one hand, as a fellow horse
enthusiast, she understood Brentford's all-absorbing interest in his Derby entry, which he had allowed to take
precedence over his mistress' purely social engagement.
However, it was obvious that Daphne Melling was furious
over the incident. If she had any tendency to be jealous
of Lucinda, or to resent the time Brentford spent in her
company, this morning's confrontation could only in-
crease her sense of injury. It would be much wiser for
Lucinda to withdraw from the training session and to
avoid being alone with Jonah for the rest of the day, but
somehow she couldn't bring herself to do that. She told
herself that this was her sole opportunity to share in the
activities of a Derby race, and she was loath to give up
the privilege.

At the stables, Lucinda found Brentford and his
trainer, a man named Osborne, conferring with serious
faces, while a young stableboy walked the Derby entry,
Caesar, around the vast courtyard, which was sur-

rounded by the loose boxes of the horses composing the stud. Lucinda studied Caesar admiringly. He was a large, strong black stallion marked with a white star on his nose, a handsome animal, although a nervous one. To-day he appeared unusually skittish, attempting to pull away from his young groom, who could barely control him.

Brentford turned away from his trainer. "I'm sorry, Lady Lucinda, but I fear we'll be obliged to cancel the training session."

"Really?" Lucinda said in disappointment. "Is there a problem?"

"Yes. Caesar's regular jockey, Sam Grayson, ate something that didn't agree with him last night. He's sick today, and in no condition to ride Caesar."

"Will this jockey be well enough to ride Caesar in the Derby?" she inquired anxiously.

"Oh, I think so. This isn't the first time that Sam has made himself ill from overeating. He tends to be a glutton. We're always after him not to gain too much weight. I'm sure he'll have recovered by the day of the race."

"One of your regular grooms couldn't ride him today?"

"I'm afraid not. As I think I've told you, Caesar is a difficult horse. Sam Grayson is the only jockey who's ever succeeded in riding him."

The trainer nodded. "Indeed, my lady. In fact, until Sam came along his lordship had about given up on the notion of racing Caesar. The animal's even a problem with the stableboys and grooms who look after him. Well, just look at him now."

It was true. The black stallion was rearing so energetically that he was practically tearing the arms off the slight lad who was attempting to hold him.

Impulsively Lucinda walked to the horse, took the leading reins from the surprised groom and, before

Brentford and his trainer quite realized what she was doing, stepped close to the animal and began to stroke his velvety black nose.

"Lady Lucinda," exclaimed Brentford in alarm, "move away from Caesar. You could be badly hurt."

"I don't think so," said Lucinda matter-of-factly. "Most horses like me. I think Caesar does." Indeed, as she continued to stroke his nose and murmur to him soothingly, the horse became visibly calmer.

"My God, my lord," said Jake Osborne, taking off his hat and beginning to mop his brow. "I wouldn't have believed this if I hadn't seen it with my own eyes."

After a short pause, Lucinda began to walk the horse slowly and then asked, "Lord Brentford, these training sessions are important to prepare a horse for a race, aren't they?"

"Yes, of course. However, I'm not the stickler some owners are. I think some of them overtrain their horses, but a certain amount of good hard exercise is essential."

"Well . . . supposing *I* ride Caesar today?"

"What . . . ?" Jonah's voice sounded strangled. The trainer and the stableboy stared at her mutely, their mouths agape.

Recovering his poise, Brentford chuckled. "For a moment I thought you were serious."

Lucinda halted the horse, though she continued to pat his neck gently. "I *am* serious. Caesar needs exercising, and at this moment he has no rider. I know I can ride him. Fortunately, I'm as light in weight as your usual jockey. Even lighter, probably. Well?" Lucinda gazed at Jonah expectantly.

Obviously torn between a mixture of annoyance and amusement, he retorted, "You're funning, I trust. For starters, Caesar has never worn a sidesaddle. How would you ride him?"

"I don't propose to use a sidesaddle. But somewhere

in your stables there must be a suit of racing silks that would fit me."

"You are serious." Brentford frowned. "Tell me this, then. Supposing, just supposing, I allowed you to ride Caesar, and you were able to do so successfully without breaking your neck? What if the story then got around the *ton* that the fashionable Lady Lucinda Vernon had been seen cavorting on Epsom Downs in male riding gear? What would happen to your reputation?"

"Why should anyone in the *ton* discover that I'd ridden Caesar? You wouldn't tell them, would you, Lord Brentford? Or you, Mr. Osborne? Or the stableboy? And certainly *I* wouldn't tell anyone!" She gazed at Jonah rather pugnaciously.

Suddenly he started to laugh. "You're a very persuasive woman, Lucinda. I have an idea I may regret this escapade, but yes, you may ride Caesar, provided you prove to me you can do so without breaking your neck." He spoke to the trainer. "Sam Grayson and Lady Lucinda appear to be of about a size. Find her some of his racing silks."

A little later, having changed in the trainer's quarters from her pelisse and bonnet to white breeches and boots, a white stock and a shirt in Jonah's yellow and blue colors and a billed cap into which she'd tucked her bright hair, Lucinda walked out into the stableyard rather self-consciously. She'd never appeared in public before with her legs exposed, and suddenly she wasn't so sure of what she was doing.

Resolutely she walked over to Caesar, who was becoming restless again under the uncertain hold of the stableboy. Standing next to the horse, Jonah looked pale and decidedly apprehensive, as if he, too, had been having second thoughts.

"Do you really want to do this, Lucinda?" he asked in a low voice.

"Yes. Will you mount me, please?"

He cupped his hands to help her into the saddle. Caesar reared sharply as he felt her unaccustomed weight.

Jonah exclaimed, catching his breath, "God, Lucinda, I should never—"

In the next moment Lucinda had the horse under control, patting his neck and leaning over to murmur softly in his ear. She relaxed the pressure on the reins slightly, booted Caesar with her heel and put him to a slow walk. On the opposite side of the courtyard she eased him into a trot, rocking gently in the saddle. Slowly she circled the courtyard, coming to a halt in front of Jonah and the trainer.

"Well?" she said, smiling.

"You've convinced me, my dear Lucinda," said Brentford with a relieved grin. "Yes, you have my permission to ride Caesar."

"Oh, but you can ride, my lady," exclaimed the trainer, his eyes wide with admiration. "You were posting beautifully."

"Let's saddle up, Osborne, and escort our new jockey to the Downs," said Jonah, the signs of strain fading from his face.

They rode out of the courtyard, down the long driveway bordered with thick hedgerows, to the heath. Caesar lost more and more of his nervousness, until, by the time they reached the Downs, he appeared eager for a strenuous run.

On the windy, crisscrossing roads of the heath, redolent of wild thyme and juniper, a large group of other jockeys and horses were taking part in training sessions, but their numbers were small in comparison with the roaring crowds that would compete for standing room on race day. Most of the jockeys were training furiously, reducing their mounts to sweating jelly.

"Look at those idiots," said Brentford disapprovingly.

"They're killing their horses. Now look, Lucinda, I want you to take Caesar at a slow trot over the entire course, and then, at the end, run him full out for one complete turn around, beginning at the Steward's Stand, then on to Tattenham Corner and thence along to the winning post. That will give Caesar enough exercise for today."

Lucinda felt like a free soul as she skimmed over the fragrant grass, the wind threatening to blow her cap off, thrilling to the rippling muscles of the superb horse beneath her. When she returned to Brentford and the trainer, who were waiting for her near the last uphill stretch at the finish line, they were both smiling at her in pleased satisfaction.

"Well done, Lucinda," said the marquess. "Now let's go home."

In the courtyard of the farm Brentford helped Lucinda down from the saddle. "Go and change quickly before someone sees you in those clothes," he told her. "I've been on pins and needles since you mounted Caesar, for fear you'd be caught out in male costume." To his trainer he said, "Osborne, I depend on you to be discreet about Lady Lucinda's little impersonation, and to keep that stableboy quiet, also."

"Not to worry, your lordship," Osborne assured him. "The lad and I are prepared to swear that Lady Lucinda never stepped foot in the stables this morning."

"Heavens, Mr. Osborne, I hope you won't find it necessary to perjure yourself," Lucinda laughed as she started for the trainer's quarters. At that moment Daphne Melling entered the courtyard.

"Oh, good, Jonah, I'd hoped I'd find you returned from your horse training session," Daphne said with a bright smile. Lucinda suspected that Daphne regretted her peevish outburst of the early morning and had determined to make amends to Jonah. "It's such a lovely day, Jonah," Daphne continued. "It seems a shame to stay indoors. Do you think we might have time for a short drive before luncheon—?''

She choked, staring at Lucinda in her racing silks. "Lady Lucinda?" she inquired incredulously.

Lucinda was tongue-tied with embarrassment. Osborne, was mute also, rolling his eyes helplessly. Only the marquess had the self-possession to reply. Or to attempt to reply.

"Er—Daphne—I think you'll find this amusing," he began. "Lady Lucinda kindly offered to exercise Caesar when his jockey fell ill, but of course she couldn't ride astride in her gown and pelisse. So I suggested she borrow the jockey's breeches and shirt. As a matter of fact, Caesar had a very successful workout. I'm much indebted to Lady Lucinda."

Daphne's features were frozen with disdain. "Actually, Jonah, I fear I see nothing amusing about the situation. In my opinion, Lady Lucinda has behaved in an extremely hoydenish fashion. I shudder to think how society will view her conduct. In fact, I daresay she's in great danger of losing her reputation."

Jonah's expression had been hardening as Daphne spoke. "Lady Lucinda is in no danger of losing her reputation over an insignificant incident like this," he said sharply. "Not, that is, if she isn't the object of malicious gossip. Therefore I want your promise, Daphne, that you won't mention a word to anyone about her masquerade in my jockey's racing silks."

Daphne put up her chin. "Why, pray, should I protect Lady Lucinda from her own indiscretions?" she inquired in a brittle voice. "You'll surely agree that most well-bred young women don't find it difficult to conduct themselves like ladies of quality. Nor do most *gentlemen* of my acquaintance encourage such behavior."

Obviously controlling himself with an effort, Jonah said, biting off his words, "I feel sure that you spoke too impulsively about Lady Lucinda's trifling escapade, and that you have no intention of spreading the silly story. I know I needn't remind you that I abhor personal gossip, and I don't willingly associate with people who traffic in it."

Lucinda gasped inwardly. Jonah had as much as told Daphne—surely he couldn't really mean it—that she would have to choose between him and her desire to gossip about Lucinda.

Daphne looked stricken, and Lucinda wanted to sink through the ground in embarrassment. In the next moment, however, a thoughtful expression came over Daphne's face, and she said with a rueful smile, "Can you forgive me, Lady Lucinda? Jonah is quite right. This—prank—of yours, disguising yourself as a jockey, might have been foolish or ill-advised, but it certainly wasn't immoral! I simply overreacted." She smiled again. "And perhaps, as an older and more experienced woman, I couldn't resist the impulse to give you a little scold! But let me assure you that I wouldn't dream of discussing your little escapade with anyone else."

"Thank you, Lady Melling. You're most kind," Lucinda murmured.

Out of the corner of her eye she caught a glimpse of Jonah's relieved expression. He smiled at Daphne, saying, "I knew we could depend on you to be understanding."

"Well, I hope I have at least a modicum of sense and a touch of common charity," Daphne replied graciously. She turned to Lucinda, saying, "All's well that ends well, but, just to be on the safe side, may I suggest that you change out of those racing silks as soon as possible?"

"Good God, yes," Jonah exclaimed. "As few people who see you in that costume, the better."

As Lucinda went off to the trainer's quarters, she was puzzled. Daphne Melling had *sounded* sincere, as if she

truly regretted her outburst against Lucinda. In the light
of her initial scathing disapproval, though, it seemed to
Lucinda that Daphne had had a suspiciously abrupt
change of heart. Had she apologized to Lucinda in order
to keep her image bright with Jonah? If so, she'd succeeded. Jonah was obviously very pleased with her. And
Lucinda ought to be happy for the lovers. She *was* happy.
In any case, she told herself firmly, she was glad that her
impulsive impersonation of the jockey hadn't resulted in
damage to Jonah's love affair with Daphne.

Derby Day dawned bright and cool, a perfect day for
the most important event on the English racing calendar.

Jonah's guests traveled out to the track in several elegant landaus. Cassandra Leighton didn't accompany
them. "The doctors thought the excursion might be too
much for me," she told Lucinda rather forlornly. "The
crowds, and the excitement, you know. I daren't take any
foolish chances with this babe. Dear Harry offered to
stay at home with me, but I couldn't have deprived him
of the pleasure of seeing the Derby. He's such a keen
horseman."

"We'll be returning to Woodbury Park very soon after
the race is over," Lucinda comforted Cassandra. "You
can help us celebrate your brother-in-law's great victory!"

Cassandra managed a wan smile.

Jonah rode to the track in a landau with Daphne
Melling, her husband, and Lord Alvanley. As far as Lucinda had been able to judge during the past two days
since their near-quarrel, Jonah and Daphne were on
their old terms with each other, pleasant and politely
formal and exquisitely discreet to each other in public.

Lady Cardew's experienced old eyes, however, had detected something. "Have Brentford and Daphne Melling

quarreled, to your knowledge?" she inquired of Lucinda on the day before the Derby.

"I don't think so," Lucinda replied, startled. "Why do you ask?"

"I'm rarely wrong about the progress of a love affair," declared her grandmother. "In this case, I sense a slight constraint that wasn't there before. More to the point, I've noticed that Jonah hasn't been taking Daphne for long drives in the countryside, and he doesn't stay glued to her side every evening in the drawing room, as he was wont to do."

"Grandmama, Lord Brentford has a great deal on his mind these days, namely preparing for the biggest race of his life. He hasn't time to play the gallant," said Lucinda, exasperated.

Lady Cardew, however, merely looked thoughtful. "Now, I wonder what they could have quarreled about?" she conjectured.

Lucinda made her escape from her grandmother's inquisitive presence.

On Derby Day Jonah had made sure that he and his guests not only started for the Downs in good time, but that they had procured good viewing places next to the finish line. Her grandmother, though probably the least enthusiastic racegoer of them all, had one of the best seats; she was an old friend of the Regent and had been invited to sit with him in the Prince's Stand.

Having taken her place at the finish line, Lucinda gazed wonderingly at the vast sea of people who crowded the Downs. The numbers were in such contrast to the scattering of horses and riders that had been the only occupants of the lonely stretches of the heath several days before, when she'd ridden Caesar on his workout.

The track was all ups and downs and sharp curves, and was, indeed, a temporary affair, occupying a cleared space bounded by rope barriers through the very middle

of the crowd, with just enough room for the horses to
run. Most of the spectators would actually have no opportunity to view the race, except for those few fortunate
enough to obtain places next to the rope barriers or the
guests of the Regent in the Prince's Stand. Lucinda
didn't bother to conjecture how Jonah had arranged to
have his places held for him at the finish line. He was
simply an efficient man.

At one point, while they were waiting for the start of
the race, Daphne exclaimed in amused surprise, "My
dear Lady Lucinda, what has happened to your gloves?
They're positively in shreds."

Equally surprised, Lucinda stared at her gloves, in
which she'd absentmindedly chewed small, neat holes in
most of the fingertips. "Good God, what a ninnyhammer
I am," she said, laughing. "It's all your fault, Jo—Lord
Brentford. I'm in a state of nervous suspense about the
outcome of the race."

"My dear girl, there's no need to be nervous, surely.
Everyone tells me that Jonah's entry is the best horse in
the race, and should win easily," said Daphne, taking
Lucinda's little joke literally, as she so often did the remarks of her friends. Lucinda had decided some time
ago that Daphne had no sense of humor.

Jonah shook his head. "Thank you for your confidence, Daphne, but I assure you that luck is as important
to a horse as ability in a race. Caesar could easily stumble,
or another horse could run into him and knock him off
stride."

A loud roar of sound from the crowd announced that
the official starter had arrived at last. Waiting until the
jockeys had aligned their mounts with the starting post,
he shouted, "Go!" only to have one of the horses bolt
out of position at the last split second. The starter repeated the procedure three more times before the crowd

thundered, "They're off!" Lucinda settled down tensely to watch the running of the race.

It was one of the closest finishes in Derby history, she learned later. At the end of the first steeply rising half mile of the left-handed course, the horses began to bunch together. Several were neck and neck as they reached the head of the long, sweeping descent to Tattenham Corner and made the abrupt turn at the Corner. On the last fifty uphill yards of the course, two of the lead horses appeared to be in a dead heat. At the finish line Lucinda's heart was in her mouth as she watched Caesar flash by the post a fraction of a nose ahead of his next competitor.

"We won, we won!" she shrieked, grabbing at Jonah's arm and dancing up and down in joy.

Daphne's expression was pained. "My dear girl, do compose yourself," she said, casting a wary glance around her to observe whether the people in the crowd around them were looking disapprovingly at Lucinda.

"Oh, come now, Daphne, I think a little excitement is warranted," observed Jonah indulgently. "We won the Derby, after all." He glanced at his arm, where Lucinda's fingers clutched the fabric of his sleeve in a convulsive grip. "However, I draw the line at ruining my new coat, Lady Lucinda," he added dryly. "Please release my arm, though I doubt that my tailor will ever be able to remove these wrinkles."

Feeling impossibly gauche and young, Lucinda snatched her hand away. She couldn't imagine Daphne Melling being so overcome with excitement at the outcome of a horse race that she lost her air of elegant self-possession.

The crowd was so tremendous that it took Jonah and his guests almost two hours to regain their carriages and fight their way out of the Common along the congested roads. Lady Cardew arrived at Woodbury Park just ahead of them from her engagement with the Regent in the Prince's Stand.

"My dear Jonah, congratulations on your splendid victory," said the countess as she stepped down from her carriage. "The Regent sends his congratulations also. He's very pleased with you. I gather he won an enormous sum betting on your horse. It seemed to console him for the disappointment of not having a Derby entry himself this year."

As Lady Cardew was speaking a footman dashed out of the house to speak to Harry Leighton. "Please, my lord, Doctor Loman wishes to see you immediately in her ladyship's bedchamber."

"My wife is ill?" Cutting himself short, his face drawn with worry, Jonah's brother scrambled out of the landau and ran into the house. The other house guests gathered in the drawing room, speaking in low tones. The high excitement of the Derby triumph faded away.

"I hope this isn't what I think it is," murmured Lady Cardew to Lucinda. "Lady Harry is in her fourth month, I believe."

Lucinda nodded, feeling apprehensive. Cassandra Leighton had had several unsuccessful pregnancies in the past few years. Each time she had lost the babe in the fourth month of conception. Was history going to repeat itself?

Harry Leighton appeared in the doorway of the drawing room. "Lady Lucinda, will you come with me?"

The occupants of the drawing room seemed to draw their breath collectively, but no one spoke. They watched Lucinda in silence as she walked out of the room with Harry Leighton.

"Is something wrong?" Lucinda asked in a low voice as she walked up the stairs with Harry.

He nodded. "She's lost the baby," he said, his face drawn with misery. "Her abigail told me that she began feeling ill shortly after the rest of us left Woodbury Park to go to the Downs for the race. Cassandra wouldn't allow the abigail to call a doctor. It was her way of denying what was happening, I daresay. She probably believed that if she wasn't ill enough to call in a doctor, then she wasn't ill enough to lose the baby, either. But eventually she had to let the abigail summon the doctor. He arrived an hour ago. He couldn't save the baby."

Lucinda made a little sound of pity. "Is Cassandra in any danger?"

Harry shook his head. "The doctor isn't concerned about her physical condition. Mentally, however, she is in a very bad state. I'm hoping you can help her, comfort her, improve her spirits. She has taken a great fancy to you these past few days, you know. She is very shy, and I've rarely seen her as attracted to another person as she is to you."

"I'll do what I can, of course."

But Lucinda's heart sank when she entered Cassandra's bedchamber. Desolate sobbing rocked the girl's slender frame in a paroxysm of grief.

"Her ladyship will fall ill if she doesn't stop this dreadful crying," fretted Cassandra's anxious abigail.

The elderly doctor, standing on the opposite side of the bed, nodded his assent. Upon being introduced to Lucinda, he said, "Her ladyship needs rest and peace of mind, not medicines. I've done all I can for her. Perhaps you can do better, my lady."

The doctor and the abigail withdrew quietly. Harry Leighton stood silently in the shadows of the bed hangings. Lucinda drew up a chair and sat down beside the bed, holding Cassandra's hand and talking to her in a low, soothing voice. At first Cassandra was unresponsive. Discouraged, Lucinda doubted that the girl heard and understood much of what was being said to her. The hopeless, abandoned sobbing continued. At this rate, Cassandra would soon make herself ill.

Lucinda tried a new tack. Suddenly she exclaimed sharply, "Now, see here, Cassandra, admittedly, you have a reason to be in the mulligrubs, but you're carrying the matter much too far, feeling sorry for yourself like this. I'm out of all patience with you."

Cassandra choked in the midst of a sob. Lord Harry lifted his head abruptly and stared at Lucinda in angry surprise.

Pretending not to notice the reactions of either husband or wife, Lucinda went on matter-of-factly, "You'd think from the way you're acting, Cassandra, that it was the end of the world, when actually you have a great deal to be optimistic about."

Her tears ceasing, Cassandra gaped at Lucinda. "Optimistic?" she repeated.

"Yes, optimistic. I know it must have seemed to you, just at first, that your hopes of having a family had been completely dashed. But think about it: you're young, you're healthy, you've never had any difficulty becoming *enceinte* previously, you have excellent doctors. There's good reason to believe, in other words, that you'll find yourself increasing again in a very short time."

Cassandra gave Lucinda a long, intent look, her agitation perceptibly decreasing as the seconds ticked by. "I hadn't thought of it like that," she said slowly. She sat up, reaching out her hand to her husband. "Harry, I've been so spineless. Lucinda is right. It's far too soon to give up our hopes for a baby. Now that I think about it, I recall that my Aunt Caroline tried unsuccessfully for more than ten years before she produced an heir to the Seagrave estate. Who knows, we may be parents before another year goes by!"

Harry's strained expression relaxed. "I'm sure of it," he said tenderly, smoothing Cassandra's hair away from her face. He grinned, teasing her. "However, we can't begin the process immediately. Certainly not tonight, at any rate! You must get some rest now. Lady Lucinda and I will leave you so you can sleep. Good night, my dearest."

As he walked into the corridor and down the stairs with his companion, Harry said, "Thank you, Lady Lucinda. I fear Cassandra was very close to a breakdown when you finally managed to reason with her. I think she'll recover her spirits now." He grimaced. "I must say, though, that I was tempted to lay rough hands on you until I realized you weren't being cruel to her, merely trying to shock her out of the near-hysterics that had her in their grip."

Lucinda said with a shiver, "I don't deserve any thanks. Fortunately, my method worked, but it occurred to me, when it was over, that I could easily have made the situation worse. Cassandra was in a very unstable, delicate frame of mind. I might have pushed her too hard."

"But you didn't, and I'll be forever grateful to you," exclaimed Harry.

That evening, during dinner, Harry said very little about Cassandra's miscarriage, other than to reveal that it had taken place, but evidently he had a long talk with his brother, for Jonah sought out Lucinda while the others were playing cards.

"Harry tells me our family is in debt to you, Lady Lucinda."

Shaking her head, she replied, "As I told Lord Harry, no thanks are due to me. What I said to Cassandra to rouse her out of her grief could easily have been the wrong thing. As Grandmama keeps telling me, I'm too fond of managing other people's affairs, and I'm frequently wrong!"

"Oh, I suspect that Lady Cardew exaggerates. You

seemed to know exactly what to say to Cassandra. Harry and I are very grateful to you."

He rose politely as Daphne came over to them and sat in a chair beside Lucinda.

"Jonah told me how kind you were to Cassandra," Daphne said pleasantly to Lucinda. She gazed at Jonah. "If you think it might be helpful, I could speak to her tomorrow," she offered. "She needs a woman's attention at this time, I think, and she has no close female relatives. She lost her mother so many years ago, and she had no sisters."

Jonah said warmly, "Please do that, Daphne. I'm sure Cassandra will appreciate a visit from you. She should be alone as little as possible during these next few days, so that she won't have the opportunity to brood."

Lucinda privately doubted there would be much rapport between shy, stricken Cassandra and the more worldly Daphne, but she kept silent. It was only natural, she supposed—and rebuked herself for being catty—that Jonah should believe that his beautiful mistress could be a comfort in any situation!

The house party at Woodbury Park ended several days later, with attendance at the running of the Oaks on the Friday and at church services on the Sunday. During the interval Lucinda spent most of her time sitting with Cassandra. Thus it was on the following Monday Lucinda and her grandmother decided not to return to London with the other guests.

"No, really, Lady Lucinda, you're very kind, but I can't allow you to inconvenience yourself and Lady Cardew in this way," protested Harry Leighton when he heard Lucinda's proposal at breakfast on Sunday morning to remain at Woodbury Park for at least a week to keep Cassandra company while she recovered her strength and spirits. Lady Cardew, of course, would also remain to play the duenna.

"You and Lord Brentford are staying," Lucinda pointed out.

Daphne intervened, saying quickly, "Oh, but Lord Harry is Cassandra's husband, and Jonah is family. Quite a different situation, entirely. And this is already the month of June, recall. Dear Cassandra was probably being a trifle forgetful—understandably so, under the circumstances!—when she asked you to stay on. Ordinarily she would hardly expect a young woman who was making her come-out to sacrifice several weeks of her time in the middle of the Season!"

"Daphne is quite right," Jonah said firmly. "We can't impose on you, Lady Lucinda. Not to speak of also interfering with Lady Cardew's plans."

"Ah, well, the older I become, the less inclined I am to make hard and fast plans," said Lady Cardew. "Missing a week of the Season won't ruin my summer." She chuckled. "As a matter of fact, I welcome the excuse to miss old Lady Messenger's dinner party next week. The woman is such an insufferable bore!"

Giving her grandmother a grateful look, Lucinda said to Harry, "In another week or ten days Cassandra should be feeling much stronger, and then she can return to London with the rest of us to take part in at least some of the events that will occur during the remainder of the Season. And certainly it won't be any great hardship for me to miss a ball or a dinner or two."

Daphne gazed from Lucinda to Jonah, an oddly calculating expression on her face. After a moment she addressed her husband. "My dear, I think it might be more pleasant for Lord and Lady Harry if we stayed on, too. What do you think?"

Before Lord Melling, a hearty trencherman, could swallow a mouthful of steak and kidneys and make his reply, Jonah said, sounding somewhat impatient, "Good

God, Daphne. Have you forgotten you're giving a ball in honor of the Regent next week?"

Chuckling, Lord Melling set down his fork and wagged his finger at his wife. "Caught you out that time, m'dear. A fine how d'y'do if the Regent were to arrive at our house and find his hostess missing!"

"Oh. Yes. I don't know how I could have been so forgetful," Daphne muttered, looking distinctly ruffled. It was one of the few times that Lucinda had ever seen her lose a shred of her self-possession.

Four

Lucinda clapped her hands delightedly as Cassandra Leighton walked out of the dressing room of Madame Bernadin's dress shop in Bond Street and preened herself in front of her friend.

"Cassandra, the gown is even more beautiful than I thought it would be," breathed Lucinda, gazing in admiration at the dress of sheer rose-colored Indian muslin, worn with a striking stomacher composed of double rows of gold lace.

"It *is* becoming, isn't it?" Cassandra murmured, turning slowly around and around in front of the cheval glass to see her reflection from all angles.

She and Lucinda had arrived in London after departing Woodbury Park several weeks before. Lady Cardew, Jonah and Lord Harry, of course, had accompanied them. Cassandra and Harry were staying with Jonah in his town house on Bruton Street.

It was now the first part of July. Cassandra was no longer the apprehensive waif whom Lucinda had first met. The girl was a changed person, trim and healthy-looking, vibrant with life, doing her best not to brood over the loss of her baby. Increasingly fond of Cassandra, Lucinda didn't begrudge the hours she was spending in her company, to the exclusion of other friends and acquaintances, but occasionally she did wonder if the girl was growing a little too dependent on her.

"Thank you for going shopping with me today, Lucinda," said Cassandra as they drove to Leighton House from the modiste shop. "I'd forgotten what an uncommon pleasure it is to shop for new clothes. I had absolutely nothing remaining from last Season that still fit me. And naturally I had to have a very special gown for tonight."

"Indeed, yes," Lucinda agreed. "It isn't every evening, after all, that we have the privilege of being fellow guests of royalty."

"And not every evening, either, that we'll have so many hosts. Harry tells me that we've been invited to a gala given by Lord Alvanley, Sir Henry Mildmay, Mr. Pierrepoint *and* Beau Brummell."

Lucinda began to laugh. "Yes, I fancy it will be an unusual evening in a number of respects. Grandmama is one of Lord Alvanley's oldest friends and is quite looking forward to the occasion. Did Lord Harry tell you how it came about? It seems that the four men were gambling together at Watier's not long ago, and each of them won a great deal of money. They decided to celebrate their good fortune by inviting their friends to a ball at the Argyle Rooms. They also decided it would be ungentlemanly not to invite the Regent. So they did. Grandmama thinks it was a muttonheaded notion."

"Oh? Why is that?"

"Well, as I'm sure you know, the Prince and Mr. Brummell were thick as glue for many years, but in recent months they've had a falling-out. In fact, they no longer speak, and the Prince isn't friendly anymore with Sir Henry, either. Grandmama fears there may be an unpleasant scene. That is, if the Regent even attends the ball, which Grandmama considers doubtful."

That evening Lucinda and Lady Cardew stepped out of their carriage on the northeast corner of Little Argyle Street, joining a stream of people who were entering the

Argyle Rooms, which for some years had been a popular gathering place for public balls, masquerades and plays. The four hosts, splendidly turned out, as might be expected in any group that included Beau Brummell, were standing at the door of the ballroom to greet their guests.

Giving Lord Alvanley her hand, Lady Cardew said dryly, "Well, my lord, I anticipate an interesting evening."

Alvanley grimaced. "We'll soon see, won't we? I fancy Brummell agrees with you."

The Beau's face was expressionless. He shrugged, saying, "Dear Lady Cardew, all I can say is that dealing with royalty is often very unpredictable."

Since the ball had not yet officially started, Lucinda and her grandmother joined a group of familiar acquaintances—Jonah, Harry and Cassandra Leighton, and Daphne Melling and her husband—who were standing near the door of the ballroom, not far from the receiving line.

"Good evening, Lady Cardew, Lady Lucinda," Jonah greeted them, his eyes twinkling. "Like me, I gather you wouldn't have missed this occasion by any manner of means. Anything might happen. That is, if Prinny condescends to accept the invitation."

"I don't think he will," said Lady Cardew. "The Prince avoids unpleasant situations whenever he can."

Jonah lowered his voice. "His Royal Highness has accepted the challenge," he said, nodding toward the door.

A hush descended on the ballroom as a very large, unwieldy figure, splendidly dressed in gold-laced military uniform, entered the room, followed by a retinue of attendants.

"Evening, Alvanley, Pierrepoint," said the Regent, extending his hand to the two men in turn. Completely ignoring Beau Brummell and Sir Henry Mildmay, the

Prince walked past the pair as if the men were invisible.
A dead silence enveloped the ballroom.

Brummell broke the silence by exclaiming in a loud,
clear voice, "Alvanley! Who is your fat friend?"

Checking himself in midstride, the Regent paused for
a split second, his face and the back of his neck turning
a bright red, then continued walking into the ballroom,
where he began greeting his numerous acquaintances.

"He'll never forgive the Beau, never," murmured Lady
Cardew. "This is the most humiliating thing that has
ever happened to him. In recent years he's been *so* sen-
sitive about his weight."

"Mr. Brummell was monstrously insulting to the Regent," declared Daphne severely. "It was practically *lésé
majesté*. The Prince is Mr. Brummell's sovereign, or as
near as makes no difference, now that the poor old king
has gone out of his mind."

Daphne paused, staring at Lucinda, who was holding
her reticule in front of her face to conceal the amusement that was destroying her composure.

"You're laughing, Lady Lucinda," said Daphne accusingly. "I must tell you that I disapprove heartily of such
disrespect to the Regent."

Jonah had also turned a bright red, and he, too, was
having difficulty controlling his hilarity. At last, taking
a deep breath, he said, "Come now, Daphne, aren't you
refining over much on the matter? Oh, I admit that
Brummell has pulled the wrong pig by the ears this time,
but it's on his own head, after all. It's no skin off our
backs, and you can't deny that the Beau's remark was
excessively funny."

Daphne sniffed. "Funny! I'd call it vulgar, demeaning.
Mr. Brummell should be ostracized from polite society.
If a bit of advice would not come amiss, Lady Lucinda,
I'd suggest that you restrain your ill-considered amuse-
ment about the Regent's affairs. I daresay you'd agree

that it is surely unwise for a young lady making her come-out to offend the leader of society."

Jonah exclaimed on a note of exasperation, "Really, Daphne, don't you think you're being a bit of a high stickler?" Noting the quick look of displeasure on her face, he added hastily, "But there, I'm sure we're all weary of Prinny and the laceration of his tender feelings. The ball has started, Daphne. Do you care to dance?"

Stiffening, Daphne hesitated just long enough to make Lucinda suspect she might refuse Jonah's invitation to dance. Then, evidently taking second thought, she smiled thinly and placed her hand on Jonah's arm.

Watching the pair move out onto the ballroom floor, Cassandra murmured with a giggle, "For what it's worth, Lucinda, I agree with you that Mr. Brummell's remark was very amusing." She sobered. "Daphne is so charming and kind, but I suspect she's seriously lacking in a sense of humor. Mind, I shouldn't want you to think I was criticizing her—I realize how important a part she plays in Jonah's life, and how sad it is that they can't marry—but I've often thought they were poorly matched in some respects. Jonah is such a vital person. He's never high in the instep; he always sees the humorous side of what's happening." Cassandra's eyes widened. "He's so much like *you*, Lucinda." A fond smile curved her lips. "I should have told you this before: I feel so fortunate, so blessed, in having you for a friend. You've helped me over such a difficult time in my life."

Cassandra's heartfelt remarks more than compensated Lucinda for the many hours she'd spent with the girl, trying to keep up her spirits. In the following days the two continued to be a great deal in each other's company, until one afternoon, while waiting for Cassandra to come by to drive with her to the latest showing at Somerset House, Lucinda received a terse note crying off from the engagement, pleading a headache.

During the next few days Cassandra broke several more engagements, each time with the vague and unconvincing excuse of a slight illness. Lucinda began to feel apprehensive. Finally she ordered her carriage and had herself driven to Leighton House in Bruton Street, where an apologetic footman informed her that Lady Harry was not at home.

"Fiddle-faddle," said Lucinda crisply. "I fancy Lady Harry is at home to me." She brushed past the discomfited footman into the entrance hall and went up the staircase to the first floor and Cassandra's bedchamber. Opening the door without knocking, she burst into the room to find Cassandra lying facedown on the bed.

"Well, now, so you really are ill, are you?"

Hearing Lucinda's voice, Cassandra sat up, turning a dull red. "Yes—I told you . . . I have a headache."

"Do you take me for a gudgeon? A young and healthy girl like you down with a headache for a week? Devil a bit, Cassandra. What's wrong?"

Bursting into tears, Cassandra covered her face with her hands. "It's too terrible . . . I can't talk about it . . . Oh, Lucinda, my life is over," she wailed between sobs.

Lucinda sat down on the bed and put her arm around Cassandra. "Come now, you mustn't talk such fustian. Tell me what's happened."

"Oh, Lucinda . . . Dr. Blair finally told me what he'd suspected from the beginning. Something dreadful happened when I lost my baby. I'll never be able to have another. There won't be any heir to Brentford Abbey, since Jonah won't marry and have a son of his own. The title and the estate will go to a distant cousin who they tell me is a cad and a vulgarian."

Cassandra's face deepened in misery. "And even worse, I've lost Harry, too. The moment he heard the news he went off by himself, to his club, I suppose, to gamble and drink and try to forget. He comes home at dawn, when he comes home at all, and then he doesn't talk to me."

Holding Cassandra more closely, Lucinda tried to reassure her. "It may not be as bad as you think. The doctor could be wrong, you know. And even if the doctor proves to be correct, why, your husband will come out of the doldrums and be more supportive, you'll see."

Cassandra shook her head. "You mean to be kind, Lucinda, but you're wrong, you're wrong. I told you, my life is over."

Rising, Lucinda paced across the floor several times. At length she said, "How did Jonah react to the news?"

Cassandra gave her a vague look. "Oh . . . I don't know. I haven't talked to him. I've stayed in my room here for a week, not seeing anyone. I don't know what Harry told him." She burst into a renewed storm of tears. "Just go away, please," she sobbed. "You can't help. No one can help." She threw herself down on the bed again, hiding her face in the bedclothes.

Hesitating only briefly. Lucinda shrugged and left the bedchamber. For the moment, at least, Cassandra was too overset to be comforted.

When she returned home to Grosvenor Square, her grandmother greeted her with surprise. "I thought you were planning to visit Somerset House with Cassandra Leighton."

"Cassandra isn't feeling quite the thing today."

"Still in the dismals, is she?" Lady Cardew cocked her head at Lucinda. "You've received another offer, my girl. Mr. Gilbert Draycott. Needless to say, I discouraged him." The countess' gaze sharpened in a mixture of amusement and disappointment. "Do you know, when we arrived in London, I honestly thought you might change your mind about looking for a husband, but you've certainly stuck to your guns. I was so sure there

must be at least one gentleman in the *ton* who could
attract your interest!"

Feeling depressed and more concerned than she cared
to admit about Cassandra, Lucinda said suddenly, "Actually, Grandmama, I'm growing a trifle weary of this
constant round of balls and parties. Couldn't we go
home soon?"

"Not before the end of the Season," said Lady Cardew
firmly. "A bargain's a bargain. You promised to take part
in your come-out *if* I refrained from forcing a husband
on you."

Lucinda's worries about Cassandra came to a head several days later when she received a barely decipherable
scrawl from her, which read, "I've gone to Woodbury
Park. At least I feel at home there."

The message worried Lucinda. On the whole, she approved of Cassandra's move to the country. But, on the
other hand, she couldn't think it a good idea for Cassandra to be entirely alone except for servants at this
time. And, in the back of her mind, she couldn't entirely
dismiss a foreboding sense of tragedy.

After a few moments of thought she sent for her carriage and drove to the Leighton residence in Bruton
Street, where she learned, as she had anticipated, that
Lord Harry was not at home. Next she ordered her
coachman to drive to St. James's Street. The carriage
stopped in front of an Adam-style mansion, the stately
style of which had prompted some people to describe
Brooks's Club as a "country house in the city."

Instead of sending a footman into the club to make
inquiries, she caused a minor commotion by going up
to the door herself. Several gentlemen passing by on the
street stared at her in frozen disapproval, and she remembered belatedly that gentlewomen did not walk on
St. James's Street in the afternoon. The porter at the
entrance gasped when he saw her. "I beg your pardon,

ma'am, but ladies are not permitted to enter the premises."

"I wish only to inquire for Lord Harry Leighton," began Lucinda impatiently. At that moment a rough hand seized her elbow from behind, and a voice growled, "Good God, Lucinda, what are you doing here? Is that your carriage in front of the club? Come along, before anyone else sees you!"

Before Lucinda quite realized what was happening, she was sitting in her carriage beside Jonah, who had given hasty instructions for her coachman to drive away up the street.

"Well, what's this you're up to?" she declared, glaring at him in high dudgeon. "What have you to say for yourself, my lord?"

"Don't you be in a pet with me, my girl," Jonah retorted. "Rather you should thank me for saving you from likely disgrace. My dear pea-goose, please allow me to warn you that *ladies do not risk ruining their reputations by attempting to visit a gentleman's club.*"

Lucinda eyed Jonah defiantly. "Your brother wasn't at home, and I had to see him immediately. A matter of—of life or death, possibly. I couldn't think where to look for him, except perhaps at one of his clubs."

"Life or death?" Jonah looked nonplussed.

"Did you know that Cassandra has gone off to Woodbury Park?"

"No . . . Harry didn't mention—"

"I don't think Lord Harry is aware of it." Lucinda hesitated. "Did he tell you the doctor has informed him and Cassandra that she will never be able to have children, as a result of losing her baby?"

Jonah's expression turned to stone. "No. Harry didn't say a word."

"I'm worried about Cassandra. She's deep in the megrims, at least partly because—" Lucinda looked accusingly at Jonah— "at least partly because your brother has been leaving her to rattle about by herself in that big house and mope about her sorrows, while he apparently spends his time swilling down wine and attempting to break the faro bank. And now she's gone off to the country. I think Lord Harry, or someone, should join her. She shouldn't be alone now. She might—she might do herself some harm."

"Nonsense! She's far too sensible . . ."

"All the same, someone should be with her. If you or your brother won't go to Woodbury Park, I'll go myself."

Looking chagrined, Jonah retorted, "It's very kind of you to take such interest in my family affairs, Lady Lucinda, but I trust that my brother and I can take care of any problems that may arise in respect to Cassandra."

"Very well, Lord Brentford. Don't say I didn't warn you." Her face cold, Lucinda tapped on the roof of the carriage to signal the coachman, and, as the vehicle came to a stop, she said, "You'll want to go about your affairs, my lord, and I have matters of my own to attend to."

Jonah opened the door of the carriage and stepped down to the pavement. "Thank you, Lady Lucinda. Goodbye." He was equally cold.

"Goodbye, Lord Brentford."

Enjoying the sensation of defying Jonah, Lucinda stopped at several other clubs situated on St. James's Street, yet not finding Harry Leighton at either Boodle's or White's, before returning home. There, even after a reviving cup of tea, she became increasingly burdened by a dragging sense of foreboding. Abruptly she called her abigail and told her to order the traveling carriage. Then she wrote a note to her grandmother, who was out paying calls, and started off for Epsom Downs.

She drove through the town, arriving at Woodbury Park in late afternoon. At this time of year the late twilight would not settle in for some time, so the skies were still bright.

The housekeeper at the stud farm was obviously relieved by her arrival. "I'm that happy to see you, my lady," said Mrs. Peyton. "I've been a mite concerned about her ladyship."

"Is Lady Harry ill, do you think?"

"N-n-no, not to say ill, exactly. Not in her body, leastaways. She seems very down, howsoever. She does nothing except take long walks about the estate, coming back to the house so tired she can scarcely stand. She doesn't eat enough to keep a mouse alive. She doesn't rest. I go past her bedchamber late at night, and I hear her pacing up and down the floor. I hope you'll be able to make the poor child feel more the thing, my lady."

"I hope so, too. Where is Lady Harry at this hour? Out on the grounds?"

"Yes. She allowed as how she'd walk to the lake, mayhap take a boat out."

"I'll join her. The exercise will be good for both of us."

Lucinda walked briskly through the kitchen gardens and around the stable area to the rear of the property, where there was a pretty little lake, with several boats moored at the dock. During their childhood, Jonah had told her, he and Harry had been enthusiastic boaters and fishermen.

When Lucinda arrived at the dock, she could see Cassandra sitting in a boat in the middle of the lake, gazing into the water, grasping a pair of oars but making no effort to row.

"Cassandra," called Lucinda. "Come fetch me. We'll go for a boat ride together."

Raising her head, looking startled, Cassandra stared without speaking at Lucinda for a long moment. Then, abruptly, unexpectedly, she stood upright in the boat and leaped into the lake.

"Oh, no, oh, heavenly father, no!" Lucinda raced down to the dock, released the rope moorings of a boat, jumped into it and began rowing frantically toward Cassandra's boat, which had capsized. Cassandra was nowhere to be seen. By the time Lucinda reached the other boat, Cassandra had surfaced several times, blowing and spluttering, but obviously making no effort to save herself, if, indeed, she could swim at all.

Leaning over the side of her boat, Lucinda grabbed for Cassandra the next time the girl surfaced, succeeding in catching her, and holding on to her briefly. Almost immediately, however, arms and legs flailing, Cassandra was able to wrench herself from Lucinda's grip, and in the process pulled her rescuer into the water.

Catching hold of Cassandra again, Lucinda soon realized she wasn't strong enough to lift both the girl and herself out of the water into a boat, and so she began swimming toward the shore, towing Cassandra behind her. Though Cassandra had ceased to struggle, Lucinda found it almost impossible to swim one-armed, and her waterlogged clothing began to wear her down. Halfway to shore her faltering strokes became slower and slower. Just as her strength gave out completely she touched bottom, and, with one last Herculean effort, she was able to drag Cassandra onto the beach. Completely exhausted, she collapsed on the sand, where she lapsed into unconsciousness for at least a few moments. The next thing she was aware of was Jonah's voice.

"Lucinda—Oh, my God."

He sank down beside her, brushing the wet hair away from her face. "Open your eyes, Lucinda. Are you all right?"

Lucinda stared up at him. "Yes, I'm fine. Please see to Cassandra. She tried to drown herself."

In a few moments Jonah bent over her again. "Cassandra nearly drowned—she swallowed a lot of water—but she'll recover. We should get her to shelter, though, before she catches a chill. Can you walk? I'll have to carry Cassandra to the house."

Feeling as drained and tired as she knew she must look, Lucinda trailed slowly into the morning room and sank gratefully into a chair in front of the brisk fire in the grate. Her damp hair was drawn away from her face into a knot on the top of her head, and she was wearing some garments of Cassandra's that the housekeeper had found for her. She hugged a warm shawl tightly around her shoulders as she was still suffering chills from her immersion in the lake. Mrs. Peyton bustled in with a tray containing a teapot and cups and buttered scones.

"I've been praising the good Lord for a miracle, my lady," said the housekeeper fervently as she deposited the tray beside Lucinda. "His lordship told me that both you and her ladyship could easily have drowned. You're a real heroine. You saved her ladyship's life."

"How is Lady Harry?"

"Tolerable. I've got her tucked up in bed, surrounded by hot bricks, drinking a steaming tisane like the ones my dear mother used to make." The housekeeper shot Lucinda a meaningful look. "Her abigail is sitting with her. Dr. Morton says her ladyship is not to be left alone."

Lucinda nodded. It was a wise precaution.

Jonah walked into the morning room, looking wan and depressed. He sat down opposite Lucinda, saying, "I'll have a cup of that tea, Mrs. Peyton, and one of your delicious scones."

After the housekeeper had left, Jonah sipped his tea and munched at a scone in silence for a few moments. At length he said, "I owe you an apology—and an enormous debt of gratitude. You saved Cassandra's life. I feel so guilty. Why didn't I listen to you when you tried to warn me about her state of mind? Dr. Morton's just told me that many women who lose a child sink into a temporary decline, and that suicide attempts are not unusual."

"You couldn't know. You weren't even aware until today that Cassandra had discovered she couldn't have any more children. In my case, it was just a vague sense of danger that alerted me. I could easily have been wrong."

He shook his head. "Still, I should have listened to you. Thank God I came to my senses, if not in time to help you rescue Cassandra, at least in time to be of some support to you here, I hope. I've sent for Harry. I'll see to it that he stays with Cassandra every moment until she recovers, however long it takes."

He smiled at her, lifting his cup in an informal toast. They sat in silence for some time, drinking their tea, until Lucinda murmured, "I'm falling asleep sitting up. I must see if my clothes are dry, so that I can start back to London. Grandmama will worry about me."

"You'll stay the night here, of course. I'll send a message to Lady Cardew."

"But won't there be gossip if folk hear I spent the night at Woodbury Park . . . ?"

"Of course not. You're more than adequately chaperoned. Your hostess, Cassandra, is here. And so is Mrs. Peyton, who I assure you is known to all my friends as a dragon of propriety!"

Setting down his cup, Jonah rose and walked over to Lucinda's chair. He extended his hands, saying, "Come along. I'll help you up the stairs to your bedchamber."

Lucinda allowed him to pull her to her feet. She was conscious suddenly of painful muscle strains and a bone-deep weariness from her exertions in the water, and made no further protests about staying the night. The prospect of sinking into a soft, warm bed was infinitely inviting. Jonah adjusted the shawl more closely around her throat and shoulders and slipped his arm around her waist. "Just lean on me," he said at her startled look. "I'll have you in your bedchamber in a trice."

Jonah's arm tightened at her waist for added support as they began to climb the stairs, and Lucinda let herself relax against him. In the upper hall he paused in front of one of the bedrooms, releasing his arm and placing his hands on her shoulders. Smiling down at her, he said, "I hope you'll feel much more the thing in the morning. I've asked Mrs. Peyton to bring you some supper. Is there anything else you'd fancy? A hot bath, perhaps? I have some premium champagne in the wine cellar . . ."

Lucinda smiled back at Jonah. "No champagne, thank you. A bit of supper and a good night's rest will make me a new person."

She couldn't explain it, but as she stood there her breath began to quicken. She was acutely aware of the slight, brush of his tall, muscled body against hers. His eyes, those cool, silvery gray eyes, always so observant and dancing with life, had softened, gazing into her eyes as if they would see deep into her soul. He put his hand up to her hair, ruffling the drying curls that had escaped from her prim topknot.

"Your hair is so lovely," he murmured, as if mesmerized. "The color of corn silk, deepening into red. It clings to my fingers and won't let go . . ." Slowly he bent his head, pressing his lips against her mouth in a kiss that deepened and lingered until Lucinda felt as if she were sinking into a bottomless abyss of pleasure.

The clinking of china brought her back to herself. She pulled away from Jonah as Mrs. Peyton rounded the curve of the stairs with a supper tray.

Stepping back with a jerk, Jonah muttered, "God, Lucinda, I didn't mean . . . Forgive me."

"Good night, Jonah," Lucinda said hastily, and bolted into the bedchamber before Mrs. Peyton could see her flaming face.

Five

"Not feeling in prime twig today, my dear?" inquired Lady Cardew, who had swept into Lucinda's bedchamber after the briefest of knocks. "You had breakfast in your room, you didn't go out for your morning ride, and it looks very much to me as if you had no intention of taking your phaeton to the Park. If you're not well, perhaps I should call Dr. Monroe."

Lady Cardew sat down in a chair near the bed, where Lucinda was reclining, an unlikely position for her, at least at this time of day, reading a book. The countess gazed at her granddaughter with a look of acute curiosity, mingled with another expression that Lucinda could not decipher.

"I'm not ill, Grandmama. A trifle bored, perhaps. You recall, I told you I'd as lief go home soon, before the Season ends." Lucinda glanced down at the book she was reading. "Actually, I'm quite fascinated with this novel. I can't seem to put it down. *THE LOST HEIR*, it's called. The author is anonymous, but they do say it's a *roman à clef*, written by a prominent lady of the *ton* who wants to ruin the reputation of the Marquess of Innsbrook. According to the rumormongers, Lord Innsbrook jilted this woman, after seducing her and breaking her heart. She gives him an assumed name, of course, in the book, but everyone knows his identity."

Lady Cardew made a perfunctory protest. *"THE LOST*

HEIR's a disgraceful novel, not at all suitable reading for refined young ladies.''

"Nonsense! I may be 'refined,' but I'm not missish. And I'll wager *you've* already read the scandalous thing, Grandmama.'' Lucinda's eyes twinkled with momentary amusement at her grandmother's discomfiture, but in truth she didn't feel very lighthearted. Since her return from Woodbury Park she had been in the dismals, keeping mostly to her bedchamber, rarely venturing out lest she encounter Jonah.

Jonah. What had possessed him to kiss her? What had it meant to him, if anything? Had he simply been carried away in a sudden burst of gratitude for her rescue of Cassandra? And wouldn't he now be so embarrassed by his impulsive act that he would simply avoid her in future? How could he look her in the eye the next time they met, with the memory of that kiss between them? What could he possibly think to say to her that wouldn't remind him of that searing moment?

Still with that odd expression on her face, Lady Cardew said, "I wonder if you'll still want to leave London so soon when you hear my news.''

"Oh? And what news is that?'' Lucinda crinkled her nose. "Don't tell me you've received another offer for my hand.''

Lady Cardew's face beamed with triumph. "As a matter of fact, yes. Lord Brentford just left me. He wants to marry you, and as soon as possible. Lucinda, you've made the conquest of the Season. And this time—this time I'm sure of it—you won't ask me to refuse the offer. I've suspected for weeks that you're not indifferent to Jonah. What I *wasn't* sure of were his feelings toward you. Now we know. My dearest girl, I wish you happy!''

"No!'' Lucinda jumped off the bed and faced her grandmother with clenched fists. "No, and no again! Jonah's the last man in the world I'd wish to marry. I've told you, more times than I can remember, that I don't want to marry *anyone*. Tell Jonah I don't wish to see him again under any circumstances. And I want to go home as soon as we can make the arrangements. I hate London. I hate this whole meaningless parade of anxious mamas and eager would-be brides and hopeful heiress hunters!"

"Well!" exclaimed Lady Cardew. "You don't have much of an opinion of the Marriage Mart, do you? Perhaps you're right. But you and Jonah are a different matter. You have a special relationship. You get along so well together, and you can't hide the friendliness, the fondness you feel for each other. In fact, as far as Jonah is concerned, in all the years I've known him, I've never seen him so at ease with, so taken with a young woman."

Lucinda's lip curled. "With the exception, of course, of Daphne Melling."

"Oh, Lucinda, you refine too much on that situation. Yes, Jonah's been having an affair with Lady Melling for some years now, but surely you'll admit the possibility that feelings do change, people do tire of each other. And from what you tell me about Cassandra Leighton's barrenness . . ."

"Grandmama, you know I swore you to secrecy about Cassandra—"

"Not to worry. I assured you that wild tigers couldn't lure the truth from me. I won't say a word. But still, you must admit that poor Cassandra Leighton's misfortune has altered Jonah's situation. He can't depend on his brother and sister-in-law for an heir now. It's only natural that he should think of getting married himself."

"But not to me, never to me. I don't fancy the thought of being married as a source of baby fodder. I'd much rather breed champion colts!" Tossing her head with a mulish stubbornness, Lucinda sank back down on the bed and picked up *THE LOST HEIR*. "Now that we've settled this matter, Grandmama, would you mind leaving me? I want to finish this book so I can return it to the circulating library."

"Lucinda, I must insist you come down."

Lucinda sat in an armchair in her bedchamber, arms folded over her chest, staring defiantly at the door, on the other side of which her grandmother stood, alternately pleading and commanding that Lucinda descend to the drawing room to speak to Jonah.

"Lucinda, you're being unconscionably rude to Jonah. The least you can do is hear him out."

"Why am I rude? You didn't think it necessary for me to refuse the offers from my other suitors in person."

There was an audible sniff of disdain from the other side of the door. "None of your other suitors was important enough to require a hearing. Jonah most certainly is. As we've both agreed often enough, he's the prime catch on the matrimonial market!" After a brief pause, Lady Cardew continued, "You may as well give in. That, or stay cooped up in your bedchamber, unable to see anyone for fear of encountering Jonah. Today, for example, he vows he won't leave the house until you agree to see him."

Throwing up her hands, Lucinda exclaimed, "Oh, very well. Tell him I'll be down directly."

A little later, she strode into the drawing room, head held uncompromisingly high, her back stiffly erect. Jonah, who had been impatiently pacing the floor, swirled to face her as she entered. She noted unwillingly that he looked more impossibly handsome than ever in his meticulously tailored town dress. She also noted, with more satisfaction, that he seemed quite subdued, and displayed less self-confidence than usual.

"Good afternoon, Lucinda. Thank you for seeing me."

"It seems I had little choice. I didn't relish the thought

of staying a virtual prisoner in my own bedchamber in order to avoid your company."

He reddened. "I had no intention of coercing you. . . . Lucinda, be frank with me. You don't dislike me, do you?"

"No." Biting her lip, she admitted reluctantly, "Actually, I've always liked you very well."

His face brightened. "Well, then, why won't you marry me?"

All of Lucinda's pent-up resentment came boiling up. She glared at him. "Do you take me for a ninnyhammer, my lord marquess? I may be a mere female, but I have good health, a respectable social position, a supportive family, and a fortune of my own. Regardless of what society thinks, I've no *need* for a husband. I've no need to be married simply for the sake of being married, especially not to oblige you by providing an heir to the marquessate of Brentford."

"Good God, Lucinda," he gasped, "is that why you think I offered for you? Just to provide me with an heir?"

Lucinda tossed her head. "I didn't notice you making an offer of marriage until you learned that poor Cassandra was barren."

Striding over to her, Jonah seized her by the shoulders. "Lucinda, listen to me . . ."

"Let me go," she exclaimed, trying to release herself.

"Not until you've given me a hearing, you little peagoose," he snapped, digging his fingers more sharply into her shoulders. "Lucinda, my darling, for weeks now I've been falling in love with you, *but I didn't know it.* I only knew that I liked being with you, that you made me feel vibrant and alive and amused and interested in life, as I hadn't felt in years. It wasn't until the other day, when I kissed you, when I realized I'd almost lost you forever in the depths of the lake at Woodbury Park, that

I *knew.* I knew I wanted to spend the rest of my life with you."

Looking up into Jonah's eyes, which were alight with a hot flame that kindled an answering heat in her own, Lucinda hesitated. "What about Lady Melling?" she asked. "You've loved her for years. Everyone in the *ton* says that you've sworn off marriage because of her."

A muscle twitched in Jonah's cheek. He released her, backing away slightly. "I've been blind," he muttered. "The months and the years went by, and I never questioned my feelings for Daphne. Now I know that the passion we had for each other—the passion I had for her, at any rate—had subsided into a pleasant habit." He turned red. "At the risk of sounding like a cad . . . the fact is, except for sharing intimacies occasionally, Daphne and I have very little in common anymore."

"Is that Lady Melling's opinion, too?"

"No." Jonah looked uncomfortable, as if he was recalling an unpleasant memory. At length he said, "Daphne and I had a frank discussion. She was quite satisfied with our arrangement. She was surprised, shocked, that I wasn't equally satisfied. However, being a civilized person, she's accepted that my feelings have changed. She's agreed to join with me in ending our—our relationship. I'm free to ask you to marry me, if that's what you're really asking."

Jonah edged closer to Lucinda, saying pleadingly, "I love you. You're the only woman I will ever love. Children—heirs—have nothing to do with the way I feel. Even if you were barren, like poor Cassandra, I'd still want to marry you. So—will you? Will you make me the happiest man on earth?"

Lucinda's bitterness dissolved in a great burst of happiness. All her doubts faded away. She threw her arms around his neck and pressed her body close to his, as she'd been longing to do for so many weeks—and had not only stubbornly resisted the urge to do so, but had refused to admit that she felt any desire to do it.

The last month of Lucinda's first Season was pure delight, one she could never have imagined when she'd so unwillingly set out for London with her grandmother. The very skies seemed bluer, people's faces were kinder and happier, ordinary meals tasted like ambrosia, and dancing in a ballroom was like floating on air.

With her usual shrewdness, Lady Cardew recognized the change in Lucinda's attitude at once. Entering the drawing room of the house in Grosvenor Square one morning to find Lucinda standing at a window, peering out on the street, the countess said, laughter in her voice, "Expecting Jonah, are you, my love?"

Turning away from the window, Lucinda said, "He's coming to take me to luncheon with Cassandra and Harry at Woodbury Park."

"And you're so eager to see him, even though you've been separated for less than twelve hours—he was your partner for virtually every dance at Lady Wiggins' ball last night—that you've been standing impatiently at the window, waiting for a glimpse of his carriage!"

Lucinda colored. "Grandmama, you're teasing me."

"So I am, and with good reason," the countess retorted. "When I think how I had to argue and plead with you to persuade you to come to London for your come-out! You didn't want to get married, you said, at least not for a long time. You didn't care that you risked being left on the shelf. You thought balls and dinners and routs were a dead bore, compared to the pleasures of managing your own stud farm. You considered most men uninteresting fortune hunters, considerably less intriguing than your favorite horse. You—"

"Stop, Grandmama," said Lucinda, laughing. "You've made your point."

Sobering, Lady Cardew said, "I hope you know your betrothal has made me supremely happy. You're my only family. You're all I have, and I want you to be happy. And I know I'm an old lady and not always right, but I'm convinced a woman needs to be married to be happy. With Jonah, I'm sure you will be."

Blinking away the two large tears that had gathered in her eyes, the countess changed the subject. "I meant to ask you last night—what were you and Daphne Melling talking about at the Wiggins' ball? I haven't heard any gossip—well, naturally, my friends are too well-bred to discuss my granddaughter's fiancé's former mistress with me!—but I *have* been wondering about Daphne's reaction to your engagement."

Lucinda frowned. "She puzzled me. She was most pleasant, most charming. She wished me a lifetime of happiness. But—it's hard to describe—there was a sort of stiffness beneath all that charm. She also mentioned how much she was looking forward to the wedding. Grandmama, have you really invited her and Lord Melling to my wedding?"

"Yes. Why? You don't approve?"

"You don't think the invitation is a—a little vulgar? That it might cause gossip? It's well-known that she and Jonah were lovers for years."

"Ah, but you forget, my dear, that they were completely discreet. For me to remove Lord and Lady Melling's names from my guest list would be the height of indiscretion. It would merely call attention to the liaison."

Lucinda felt dissatisfied. She disliked the idea of having Daphne Melling's eyes on her back as she walked up the aisle of the church. Nor did she relish the thought of having to make polite small talk with the woman on the happiest day of her life. Then she shrugged. There was nothing more to be said. They could hardly withdraw the invitation.

Jonah was announced just then, and on the drive to Woodbury Park Lucinda forgot about the vexing little problem of Daphne Melling's attendance at her wedding.

The drive to Epsom was delightful. The sun was shining and the temperature balmy, though in truth the lovers were less engrossed in the weather than in themselves. Though he managed to drive his curricle with his usual expertise, Jonah's attention was all on Lucinda, and hers on him.

"Do y'know what Alvanley said to me last night?" said Jonah with a sideways grin, as he drove the curricle over Westminster Bridge. "He told me I looked like a lovesick calf. He said I was acting like an eighteen-year-old in the throes of his first love."

"Well?" Lucinda returned his grin. "*I* don't mind if everyone is aware of how much you love me."

His eyes twinkling, Jonah replied, "Alvanley also says that such an open display of affection on my part is positively ill-bred! We members of the *ton* are expected to make polite, suitable marriages, not runaway love matches!"

Lucinda put her hand on his sleeve and squeezed his arm. "I don't care a fig what the *ton* thinks. Don't change one iota of your courtship, Jonah. I like it just the way it is."

As she and Jonah continued on their drive to Woodbury Park, Lucinda marveled at the open, affectionate, bantering tone of their relationship. It was so unlike the usual proper behavior she'd observed in other betrothed couples, and so much like what she had always dreamed would be the course of her own engagement.

At Woodbury Park Lucinda was happy to observe that the atmosphere was considerably brighter than it had been on the occasion of her last visit, when she had narrowly averted Cassandra's suicide. Cassandra, though still wan and thin, was herself again.

"I'm reconciled," she said quietly to Lucinda during a brief private talk before lunch. "It wasn't meant for me to have children. It would be fruitless for me to spend the rest of my life in remorse."

"And Harry? How does he feel?"

"Harry has been wonderful. No reproaches, no bewailing what might have been. In fact, in an odd sort of way, I think he may even be relieved. He never liked the idea that Jonah, the firstborn son, had renounced his duty of carrying on the family line. Now Jonah will have a son of his own, as it should be."

Cassandra pressed Lucinda's hand. "Harry and I want you to know that we're happy Jonah is marrying the woman he loves." She shot Lucinda a questioning glance. "We're so isolated down here, we don't hear gossip or rumors. . . . Tell me, have there been any repercussions about Jonah's broken off affair with Daphne?"

"No. Not really. Jonah calls her reaction 'civilized.' "

Looking thoughtful, Cassandra said, "Yes, 'civilized' is a word that comes to mind about Daphne. Yet—now I can say this, since she's no longer practically a member of the family—I've always thought that still waters ran very deep in Daphne. Perhaps, she's not as 'civilized' as she looks. She hasn't—well—she hasn't been spreading rumor or gossip about you, has she? Some years ago, when Lady Inwood was in such difficulties, I recall that Daphne made some very unkind remarks."

"No, she's been utterly friendly and charming to me."

"I'm glad to hear it." Cassandra's voice was expressionless. But it was obvious, Lucinda thought, that Cassandra was relieved to be free of the necessity of being enamored of her brother-in-law's mistress.

After lunch, when Cassandra went to her bedchamber

for her usual afternoon nap, Jonah and Lucinda went
out to inspect the stud before starting back to London.
The stableyard was momentarily empty of grooms when
they entered, and Jonah, giving a swift glance around,
drew Lucinda into an empty loose box. He crushed her
in his arms, bending his head to claim her lips in a bruis-
ing kiss.

"I've been aching to do this for hours. Days. We're
never really alone, curse it," he murmured, lifting his
head between kisses only long enough to draw breath.
A tremor shook his body, and his arms tightened. "My
darling, my own love, you feel so wonderful against me.
Your lips taste so wonderful . . ." He looked down at
her, his eyes molten with a hot gray light. "I'm so glad
you're not making me wait until autumn, or Christmas,
or even the spring, perish the thought, to get married.
I'm not sure I *could* wait. Think, my love, in two short
weeks I'll never have to leave you again."

Voices sounded in the stableyard, and Lucinda quickly
withdrew from Jonah's arms. He opened the half door
of the loose box, and they walked into the courtyard.
Jonah greeted his trainer. "Afternoon, Osborne. How's
our Derby champion?"

"In fine fettle, your lordship. As evil-tempered as ever,
which with him is a very good sign, I do believe."

Osborne's face and voice were respectful, but Lucinda
felt the color mounting into her cheeks. The trainer was
a shrewd observer. He could hardly be unaware of what
she and his master had been up to in the empty loose
box!

They spent an absorbed half hour inspecting the
horses in the stud, with Lucinda asking as many questions and making as many knowledgeable comments as
Jonah. At one point Osborne said admiringly, "Dashed
if I've ever met a lady who knew as much about Thor-

oughbred horseflesh as you do, Lady Lucinda. You and his lordship will make a good pair."

Lucinda smiled her thanks at the compliment. Jonah looked thoughtful. Later, on their way back to London, he said, "Cassandra and Harry enjoy living at Woodbury Park, wouldn't you say?"

"Why, yes. Harry is as interested in raising horses as you are, and I think Cassandra prefers country living to the city. She's no social butterfly."

"Well, then . . . what would you say to my deeding Woodbury Park to them as their permanent residence? It's quite a large establishment, with a number of good farms. You see, the Brentford estate was so thoroughly entailed that my father wasn't able to leave Harry much in the way of real property."

"I think that's an excellent idea. But Jonah—what about your stud? It's your greatest interest in life."

"Not anymore," he said, giving her a meaningful glance. At her quick blush, he chuckled, then he went on, "The fact is, I'm considering transferring my horses to your stud farm in Cambridgeshire. We could manage the place together. We would be partners."

"Oh, Jonah." Lucinda's heart was too full for her to say any more. How close she'd come to missing this wonderful moment. If she had been adamant in refusing to come to London for her come-out, she would never have met this man who was at once fascinating companion, sensual lover, and partner who treated her as his equal in all things.

Lucinda's wedding day coincided with the end of the Season. In fact, the wedding was the last great social event of the year.

The previous two weeks had been hectic and tiring. Many of Lady Cardew's friends had insisted on hosting last-minute parties for her granddaughter. Lucinda had to spend hours at the modiste shop, being fitted for the voluminous trousseau the countess had ordered. She suspected that most of the trousseau would prove superfluous, since she and Jonah intended to leave immediately after the wedding for her stud farm in Cambridgeshire, but she said nothing to spoil her grandmother's pleasure in providing and supervising the making of the wardrobe.

In order to accommodate her legion of friends, Lady Cardew had decided not to have the wedding at the Grosvenor Chapel, which, though closer to her house, she considered too small. Instead, she arranged for the ceremony to be held at St. George's, Hanover Square, where she, and later Lucinda's own mother, had both been married.

As she stood in the vestibule of St. George's on the morning of her wedding day waiting for the organist's signal, Lucinda wasn't the least bit nervous. However, standing near her, Cassandra betrayed her tension by her spasmodic grip on her nosegay. And beside Lucinda, Lord Alvanley, who, as one of Lady Cardew's oldest friends, had claimed the honor of giving Lucinda away, slipped a betraying finger inside his cravat to relieve the pressure of his high shirt points. "Are you feelin' all right and tight, m'girl?" he muttered. "Not faint, or anything of the sort?"

She smiled at him. "Not at all, Lord Alvanley. I'm perfectly calm. See?" She held out her hand, which was without a tremor.

She saw no reason to be nervous. She knew she looked well in the gown of sheer apricot-colored *crêpe lisse*, looped at the hem with knots of pearls and tiny bouquets of field flowers, and with the wreath of delicate yellow rosebuds in her hair. She felt nothing but eagerness to take part in the ceremony so that she and Jonah could belong entirely to each other.

The strains of the organ changed to a processional, and Lucinda nodded to Cassandra, who swallowed spasmodically and then started out of the vestibule into the tunnel-vaulted nave. Lucinda took Lord Alvanley's arm to follow her down the aisle.

The big church was full, from the side aisles to the galleries with their square pillars and Corinthian capitals. Exchanging a last look with a teary-eyed Lady Cardew in the front pew, Lucinda released Alvanley's arm to stand beside Jonah before the minister. She had to repress a strong desire to laugh. *She* wasn't nervous, but Jonah was decidedly pale, and she caught Harry's furtively anxious look at his brother.

Jonah had recovered his composure by the time the wedding party and their guests entered the ballroom of the Cardew house in Grosvenor Square, where an elaborate breakfast was about to be served.

After the ritual toasts at the end of the meal, Jonah and Lucinda walked about the ballroom, greeting their guests and thanking them for coming.

"Well, my dear," Lady Jersey said to Lucinda with an arch smile, "you certainly took the town by storm. When I first saw you at Almack's I never dreamed you would climax your Season by capturing England's most eligible bachelor!"

Mr. Brummell was more restrained but equally complimentary. "My dear lady," he pronounced languidly, "you and Lord Brentford share such perfect taste that you can't fail to be happy."

Bright-eyed and smiling, Lady Melling appeared to be in the highest of spirits. "Dear Lucinda, I was just agreeing with Lord Melling that yours was the prettiest wedding of the Season, or, indeed, of many Seasons. We're longing to entertain for you—as soon, that is, as you two can bear to tear yourselves away from the pleasures of your honeymoon."

Lucinda felt gauche and ungrateful that she couldn't thoroughly appreciate Daphne's charm and social skills. Jonah seemed more impressed. He gave both Daphne and her husband a beaming smile and a warm handshake.

As they completed the circuit of the ballroom, Lucinda murmured, "I'll go up now to change, Jonah."

His eyes kindled. "I thought the time would never come. Lady Cardew tells me that your abigail has your luggage packed and ready for our departure." He consulted his watch. "I'll meet you in half an hour in the mews." His voice deepened. "Come even sooner if you can manage it, darling. I'm aching to be alone with you."

Lucinda's abigail, who was a country girl from Lady Cardew's estate and who had never really become accustomed to London ways, began to chatter enthusiastically when her mistress entered the bedchamber, followed shortly by Cassandra.

"Oh, my lady, such a lovely wedding, and her ladyship made sure I had such a fine seat, almost like one o' the gentry. And Paul—that's Lord Brentford's valet, you know, and a genteel person he is, too, almost like a real gentleman himself—well, Paul and I will be following right behind you and his lordship in a fourgon, so's we'll be in Cambridgeshire as soon as you be, like as not, or even before . . ."

Clearly rattled by the unaccustomed excitement of the day, the abigail wasn't her usual efficient self. She dropped the pins from Lucinda's hair when she removed the bridal wreath, and fumbled with the fastenings of the gown as she attempted to undo them.

Impatiently Cassandra exclaimed, "Run along, Sarah, and make sure the luggage is properly stowed. I'll help Lady Lucinda change into her going away clothes."

A little later, as she held out to Lucinda the new muslin

pelisse in a tender shade of spring green, Cassandra said, "You're the calmest bride I've ever known, Lucinda. On my wedding day I was a candidate for Bedlam. In fact, I can't remember a single detail of that day, from the time I left my father's house until I emerged from the church!"

Lucinda looked in the mirror as she adjusted the smart straw bonnet with its green ribbons and yellow roses. Her smiling, exuberant face looked as happy as she felt. "Why shouldn't I be calm?" she said to Cassandra. "Why would I be overset? I've married the man I love, and who loves me, and I know we'll live happily together for all the rest of the days of my life."

A knock sounded, and a moment later Daphne Melling peered around the half-opened door of the bedchamber. "Could I see you for a moment, Lady Lucinda?"

Daphne walked into the room without waiting for an answer. She raised a questioning eyebrow at Cassandra, saying, "Would you mind . . . ?"

Looking faintly puzzled, Cassandra shrugged, saying, "Of course. I'll leave you then, Lucinda, so that you can talk to Daphne."

After Cassandra had gone, Lucinda said, "Will you sit down, Lady Melling?" She kept her voice as polite and expressionless as she could, though she was genuinely perplexed by Daphne's visit. What could Jonah's ex-mistress want of her on her wedding day?

"Thank you, I won't sit, nor will I stay long."

"Actually, I cannot give you much time," Lucinda went on, still in that polite, artificial tone. "Jonah and I are leaving for Cambridgeshire in a few minutes. What did you wish to speak to me about, Lady Melling?"

Most people in her circle—including Cassandra, Harry, Jonah, her grandmother—used Daphne's Christian name, but Lucinda couldn't bring herself to the intimate usage.

Smiling thinly, Daphne said, "I'll be brief. I considered it to be my duty to point out to you a truth that everyone is keeping from you."

Lucinda gave her a startled look. "What do you mean? What truth?"

"The truth that Jonah isn't marrying you for love. He still loves me, my dear, and but for two recent developments he would have remained unmarried, very satisfied with the arrangement he and I have been sharing happily for these many years."

"And what are these 'recent developments'?" Lucinda's lips felt stiff.

"The first, and most important, is Cassandra Leighton's barrenness. The second is Jonah's recent discovery that his brother Harry has brought the family to the brink of financial ruin at the hazard tables by losing fifty thousand pounds. Faced with this double disaster, Jonah realized that he'd been deceiving himself in thinking that he could permit the Brentford title and estates to devolve upon an undistinguished distant cousin, and certainly he couldn't allow his brother to go to debtors' prison. Because, of course, he never entertained the possibility that Harry could refuse to repay the fifty thousand pounds."

Daphne's lip curled bitterly. "A debt of honor, you know. Don't pay your tailor, or the grocer, or your estate agent's salary, but never, under any circumstances, fail to pay a debt of honor." She shrugged. "So Jonah decided to marry you. It was a perfect solution to a two-pronged problem. At one and the same time he could enable himself to procreate an heir of his own body, *and* avoid family disgrace and ruin by using your fortune to pay Harry's debts."

Giving Lucinda a straight gaze, Daphne went on: "There was only one difficulty. He still loved me. But he solved that easily enough. He proposed that he and

I simply continue our affair. What you didn't know wouldn't hurt you, as he put it."

Lucinda flinched. She had turned very pale.

Her lips set, Daphne nodded. "I agreed with the proposal, God help me. After all, my husband, though elderly, is quite healthy. He'll probably live for years. It's not likely that Jonah and I would have been able to marry in the foreseeable future. Meanwhile, he needs an heir, and he must repair the family fortunes. So yes, I agreed that we should continue our relationship."

Clenching her hands into fists so tight that her fingernails dug into her palms, Lucinda said in a voice she didn't recognize as her own, "May I ask why you decided to tell me this?"

Daphne's eyes, at once angry and tormented, bore into hers. "I don't pretend to have perfect morals. I've never felt guilty about my association with Jonah. Frankly, I see no reason why females shouldn't be allowed to live by the same moral code as men, provided they go about it discreetly. I do, however, have a sense of justice." She paused.

"Yes?"

"The more I thought about it, the more I came to believe that Jonah was treating you very unfairly by concealing from you his decision to continue his affair with me after his marriage. I never tried to hide my liaison with Jonah from my husband. He chose to overlook the affair. In other words, he had a choice. You had none. I've observed that you're a very independent young woman, and I suspect you wouldn't have married Jonah if you'd known the truth. Simple justice seemed to indicate that I should tell you the truth, even so late in the situation. I've done that, so I'll take my leave. Goodbye, Lady Lucinda."

Turning on her heel, Daphne Melling walked quickly to the door and left the room. Shortly afterward Cassandra came into the bedchamber, saying, "I stayed in the corridor, waiting for her to go. That was the strangest thing, Lucinda. Why did Daphne come here?"

Making a supreme effort, Lucinda said airily, "To give me her best wishes, why else? You know how Jonah describes Daphne Melling as 'civilized.' "

Cassandra shook her head. "Daphne's behavior still seems strange to me." She hugged Lucinda. "Goodbye. You look beautiful. I needn't wish you happy. I *know* you'll be happy. Go along, now. You mustn't keep your bridegroom waiting."

"No, indeed, I mustn't do that. Goodbye, Cassandra. Thank you for your friendship."

With a wave and a smile Lucinda went out the door and walked down, not the back stairs exiting to the stables, but the front staircase leading to the street entrance of Cardew House. She didn't meet anyone. Servants and guests alike were elsewhere in the house. She stepped into the square, walked past the endless line of carriages waiting for her wedding guests to depart, into Duke Street and thence into Brook Street, where she hailed a hansom cab.

"Lombard Street," she instructed the driver. "Cameron and Sons."

A little later, in the heart of the City, she sat across a desk from the distinguished head of one of London's most prominent banks.

"Lady Lucinda!" said Mr. Cameron in surprise. "That is to say—er—Lady Brentford. May I offer my felicitations? I believe today was your—er—"

"My wedding day. Quite right. Mr. Cameron, I require some money. How great a sum, I'm not sure. How much, offhand, would you say it will cost me to hire a post chaise to carry me to Cambridgeshire?"

His eyes bulging, Mr. Cameron said weakly, "I'm sorry, I really couldn't say . . ." He rang the bell on his desk. "Let me inquire."

At eleven o'clock that night, Luncinda stumbled wearily out of the post chaise into the courtyard of her stud farm near the village of Millbridge, seven miles out of Cambridge. The members of her domestic staff, their faces expectant and welcoming in the lantern light, piled out of the house to greet her. They gazed blankly at the hired carriage and its single passenger.

"Welcome, my lady," said the housekeeper. She peered past Lucinda into the empty post chaise. "His lordship isn't with you . . . ?"

"No. Nor will he be, at least for the time being."

As she entered the house, Lucinda reflected that there would be a considerable delay before Jonah caught up with her in Cambridgeshire. When she hadn't joined him in the stables of her grandmother's Grosvenor Square house after the wedding breakfast to begin their honeymoon journey, he would have instituted a search, of course, which would have consumed a great deal of time. Neither he nor her grandmother would be able to fathom the cause of her disappearance. They might even assume that she'd been abducted. But, even if he was successful in quickly tracing her escape route by hansom cab, from Grosvenor Square to the banker's premises to the posting inn in St. Martins-le-Grand, it would still be several days before he could arrive at the stud farm. She was sure of at least a short respite.

Six

At the breakfast table, Lucinda poured herself another cup of coffee and reread the two letters that had arrived in the morning post.

The first was from her grandmother.

> My dearest girl: I've tried repeatedly to make you aware of how grieved I've been by our estrangement. At this time I feel doubly grieved. Two weeks from today will be Valentine's Day, and Valentine's Day, as you know, has been the loveliest day of the year for me for most of my life. I was born on Valentine's Day, and my dear husband, your grandfather, from the time we were first married, always celebrated the occasion with a festive house party, culminating with a lavish combined birthday-Valentine's Day ball, to which everyone in the county and all my friends and relatives were invited. Over the years it became the most anticipated event of the winter season, which is why I continued it after your grandfather died. Dearest girl, this year will be the first year since you were born that you didn't attend my Valentine's Day gala. You came to your first one as a babe in arms! Won't you set aside your anger and resentment, at least for this

one day, and come to Marshfield Court to help
me celebrate my birthday? Your loving nana.

Tears came into Lucinda's eyes as she reread the letter.
For months her heart had been aching at the estrangement from her grandmother, who had reared her from
infancy with such love and devotion. But she couldn't
mend the rift with Lady Cardew without at the same
time welcoming Jonah back into her life. Lady Cardew
had been so adamant in her insistence that Lucinda return to her husband that she and her granddaughter
had quarreled violently.

Lucinda winced as she recalled the scene, the last time
she'd seen—no, heard—either her grandmother or
Jonah. As she had anticipated, Jonah had eventually
tracked her down to the stud farm. He'd arrived a scant
week after her runaway escape, in the company of Lady
Cardew. Lucinda had refused to see either of them.
She'd ordered her servants to show them off the property, and she'd prudently shut herself up in her bedchamber, where she'd had the foresight to order the
installation of a heavy bolt on the door.

Jonah, of course, had refused the servants' request to
leave. He had stationed himself in front of the bedchamber door, rattling the knob and shouting, "Open the
door, Lucinda. I insist that you talk to me. You owe me
an explanation. Why did you run off on our wedding
day?"

Standing near the door, to be sure that Jonah could
hear her clearly, Lucinda called, "I ran off because I discovered I didn't wish to be married to you. I still don't.
Go away and leave me in peace to lead my own life."

The turmoil and the rage in Jonah's voice were almost
palpable. "But why—why?" he gritted. "A day before
the ceremony—two hours *after* the ceremony at the

breakfast—you couldn't wait to be my wife. What caused you to change your mind?"

"I was mistaken, that's all. I don't love you. I don't wish to be married. Don't make this more painful than it already is, Jonah. Please, just go away."

There was a long silence on the other side of the door. Then Lucinda heard dragging footsteps fading away. A few minutes later her grandmother's voice said sharply, "Lucinda, stop playing the fool. Open this door immediately. I won't ask you why you abandoned Jonah, since you've already refused to tell *him*. But whatever your reasons for this foolishness, this *desertion* of your husband, you at least have the obligation to meet him face-to-face, to explain those reasons to him."

"I've already explained my reasons, Grandmama. I don't love Jonah. I don't wish to be married to him. Fortunately for both of us, I discovered my true feelings before anything of—of lasting consequence occurred."

The grimness in Lady Cardew's voice was plainly audible through the door. "Lasting consequences, is it? I daresay you're thinking of physical consummation, which has nothing to do with anything. My poor bird-witted child, your lasting consequences have already occurred. You're bound for life to Jonah. Oh, he *could* obtain a civil divorce from the House of Lords. You would never marry again, of course, though he would be free to remarry. Or you might arrange an ecclesiastical annulment, which would simply result in permanent separation for both of you. In any case, you've lost control of your money and your possessions, which now belong to Jonah to do with as he sees fit."

"You mean I no longer own *anything*? Not even my stud farm? That's not fair," protested Lucinda.

"Fair or no, that happens to be the case."

"And you approve?"

"What does it matter whether I approve? But yes, I do approve. A husband should be the head of his house."

Stung and bewildered, Lucinda snapped, "Then you're a fool, Grandmama. I thought better of you."

She regretted the remark immediately, but it was too late. Her grandmother snapped back, "And I of you. You're a bigger fool than I am, my dear. I didn't give up on my marriage on my wedding day. Goodbye, Lucinda. Enjoy your new life."

It had been her last meeting of any kind with either Jonah or her grandmother. Evidently regretting her spark of temper, Lady Cardew wrote, several times, deploring the estrangement, but she continued to urge Lucinda to reconcile with her husband. Jonah wrote, too, again demanding to know her reasons for abandoning him.

Lucinda didn't answer any of the letters. For some time she lived in a state of apprehension. If Jonah now owned all her property, he could lay claim to the stud farm and force her out of her home. For that matter, according to the solicitor she consulted in Cambridge, he could actually take possession of her person and hold her a prisoner. But the weeks passed, and nothing happened, and Lucinda gradually became relieved, convinced, for the time being, at least, that Jonah wouldn't claim his legal prerogatives.

But what was she to do about the problem posed by the letter that had come this morning? She sighed, taking a sip of her now cold coffee. Should she attend her grandmother's Valentine's Day-birthday celebration? Her first reaction to the invitation had been an automatic refusal. Much as she regretted being at odds with Lady Cardew, dearly as she loved, and felt obliged to her grandmother and still wanted to please her, she knew that a visit to Marshfield Court would subject her to repeated pleas to reconcile with Jonah.

However, her grandmother's letter wasn't the only one

she'd received that morning. The other was from Dr. Hemings, who had been Lady Cardew's physician for many years, and who regarded Lucinda with an almost paternal affection.

My dear Lucinda: No, I shouldn't be writing to you on the subject of your grandmother's health. I hope I respect the confidentiality of the doctor-patient relationship as much as anyone. However, I'm also her ladyship's friend, and *your* friend. Soon it will be Valentine's Day, always such a happy occasion in Lady Cardew's life, and I know she has invited you to celebrate the day with her. But you've quarreled—I won't pry into the reasons for that quarrel—and I suspect, in fact I'm certain in my own mind, that you've decided not to come to Marshfield Court for Valentine's Day. If I've guessed wrong, and you've accepted the invitation, then I've betrayed a professional confidence, but I must take the risk.

Lucinda, I beg you to visit your grandmother. It may be your last opportunity to see her alive. I've just diagnosed a serious heart problem. She could die at any time. She refused to allow me to tell you about her medical problem because she doesn't want to trouble you, and because she doesn't want you to make up your quarrel with her out of pity. So I leave the decision to you. I know you'll do what is right.

"My lady, ye haven't eaten a single bite."

Lucinda looked up from her letters into her cook's accusing face. "I wasn't hungry this morning, Mrs. Alcock. However, your coffee was superb, as always. Please tell the housekeeper I wish to see her immediately. I'm going on a journey today. To visit my grandmother, as a matter of fact."

The temperature had plummeted during the night, but the skies were clear as Lucinda started off that morning for Oxfordshire. She might have been alerted to what was coming by a raw, piercingly chilly wind, but she was too immersed in her worries about her grandmother's health to be concerned about the weather. Instead of warming up, it grew colder as she passed through Cambridge and continued on through Royston and Luton and Aylesbury, and an ominous gray veil began to appear on the horizon.

Wrapped snugly in lap rugs, her feet resting on the hot bricks renewed at each posting stop, and deep in her worrying thoughts, Lucinda remained oblivious to the deteriorating weather until her carriage nearly overturned in the heavily falling snow and her coachman advised her to seek shelter from the storm.

Thus it was that she now found herself sitting across from the angry visage of her husband and forced to answer his questions concerning their wedding day.

Lucinda clamped her lips together. The day of reckoning may have arrived, but she'd still rather rip her tongue out than reveal to Jonah why she'd really run away from him. After a moment she said, "Your memory is deficient. I told you months ago, when you invaded my privacy at my stud farm, why I ended our marriage. Or, rather, prevented it from ever beginning. I'll repeat what I said then. I don't love you. I don't wish to be married. I want to be free to live my life as I see fit."

"And I say you're a liar. Oh, I know you're an independent-minded female. You don't like to be dictated to by anyone, including your own husband. But I'll never believe you don't love me. Here, I'll show you . . ."

Rising, Jonah reached Lucinda in two long strides and

dragged her from her chair. He wrapped his arms around her and held her against him so closely that she had difficulty breathing. He crushed her lips in a hungry kiss that dissolved her bones and sent the blood rushing tumultuously through her veins.

"There," said Jonah, raising his head and looking down at her with a triumphant smile. "Do you still dare to deny that you love me?"

"I . . ."

A knock sounded at the door. Immediately afterward a waiter wheeled in a serving cart containing a large number of covered dishes. Respite, thought Lucinda, suppressing a sigh of relief.

With an apprehensive note in his voice, the waiter said to Jonah, "Master says ter tell ye, yer lordship, that he hopes the supper will be satisfactory, like. He's sorry aboot the stewed eels. We cain't serve ye any o' the critters. We got so many guests here tonight, and they've already ate all the eels we had in the kitchen."

"That will be all right," said Jonah. "I appreciate the landlord's problem. He has more than a full house tonight. Just set the food out on the table and then you can go."

A little later Jonah looked at Lucinda over the rim of his wineglass, saying, "A tolerable Burgundy. The Sturbridge Arms has always kept a good cellar." His gaze sharpened. "I didn't mean to offend you by forcing my attentions on you earlier, but I do not believe those attentions were unwelcome. You enjoyed that kiss as much as I did. Don't try to deny it."

Lucinda took a small sip of wine and put her glass down. "Of course I don't deny it," she said coolly. "I've always liked kissing you. But at the risk of sounding quite shameless, may I remind you that females may experience the same—er—physical excitement that men do, without at the same time having any strong romantic feelings?"

Jonah was clearly taken aback. "I see," he said after a short pause. "I was obviously wrong about your feelings toward me." He shrugged. "That being the case, I won't press you anymore." Showing no resentment, he calmly served himself a piece of ham and a spoonful of hothouse asparagus. After a moment he said, "I gather you're on your way to Marshfield Court to join with Lady Cardew in celebrating Valentine's Day, and her birthday."

"Yes." A sudden thought, and not a welcome one, occurred to Lucinda. "Marshfield Court is your destination, too?"

He nodded. "Does that surprise you? Quite apart from our mutual connection with you, Lady Cardew and I are very old friends, you know."

She knew that. She strongly suspected that her grandmother had invited Jonah to her Valentine's Day gala in order to exert pressure on Lucinda to make up her differences with her husband. It was an underhanded trick, but there was nothing to be done about it now. The only thing that concerned Lucinda was her grandmother's health.

Jonah flabbergasted her by his next remark. "Dr. Hemings wrote to me recently. I presume he wrote to you also."

Lucinda inhaled sharply. "Yes. Yes, he did. Then you know . . ."

"That Lady Cardew is dying, yes. Lucinda, I'd like to suggest something. Firstly, don't you think your grandmother would die happier, more at peace, if she believed you and I had reconciled?"

"Yes," Lucinda said unwillingly. She anticipated what he would say next.

"Then will you agree to pretend with me to Lady Cardew that you and I *have* reconciled, at least to the extent of giving our marriage another try? In all likelihood we needn't keep up the pretense for very long. Dr. Hemings says your grandmother could die at any time."

"No, oh, no. I couldn't live a lie like that," said Lucinda in a panic. "Not even for Grandmama's sake . . ." She paused, biting her lip. "This would be purely a pretense?"

"Merely a charade," Jonah assured her. "We'd be obliged to share a bedchamber, no doubt, but for a limited time, at least, I could sleep quite well in a chair, or even on the floor."

For several minutes Lucinda remained silent, wrestling with her feelings. She dreaded the thought of exposing her mind and her body to Jonah's unsettling sensual proximity. But could she live with her conscience for the rest of her life knowing she hadn't done everything in her power to make her grandmother's last days more peaceful?

"Very well," she said at last. "I'll play the part of your wife. I want your promise, however. At the first moment that this sham marriage is no longer necessary, we'll go our separate ways."

"Agreed." He gave her a wide smile. "You won't regret this. I know how close you and Lady Cardew have always been. And now, Lucinda, please eat something. You haven't touched the food on your plate. And then you must go to bed. You need your rest."

Sharing a bedchamber with Jonah proved easier than Lucinda had feared. After their supper he sent her upstairs without him, saying he wanted to sample the landlord's port. She had ample time to make her toilet, dismiss her abigail and climb into bed before Jonah entered the room.

Propping herself up on her elbow to speak to him, she said, "I sent my abigail to the housekeeper to ask for extra blankets." She didn't feel especially nervous at his presence in the room, because he'd promised not to attempt to share her bed. She went on. "Sarah put the blankets on that armchair in front of the fireplace. The chair looks tolerably comfortable."

"Thank you," he said pleasantly. "I daresay I'll need the blankets. It's a perishing cold night, and likely to get colder. Snow is still falling." He settled himself in the armchair, piling first his greatcoat and then the blankets around him. "Good night," he said, blowing out the candle on the table next to his chair.

Rather to her surprise, Lucinda fell asleep almost immediately. Some time later, however—she couldn't be sure how long—she awoke shivering with cold. There was no light in the room. The fire in the fireplace had burned completely out, and the bedchamber was frigid. Hearing a muttered curse in the darkness, she said softly, "Jonah? Are you awake?"

"Awake and turning into a block of ice," he replied grimly.

She made a sudden decision. "Bring your greatcoat and blankets and get into bed with me. We'll both be a little warmer, at least."

"Thank God, Lucinda, you may be saving both our lives!"

She heard the thump of boots being dropped to the floor, and then Jonah groped his way to the bed. He arranged his coat and blankets atop the coverings already there and slipped into the bed beside her with a sigh of relief. A moment later he put his arms around her and snuggled close. With a gasp of alarm she began struggling to free herself.

Jonah held her even more closely. "My dear girl, stop being a ninnyhammer. I'm not about to seduce you, merely trying to prevent us both from freezing to death!"

Feeling foolish, Lucinda relaxed. Soon she was almost comfortable beneath the extra blankets and with the added warmth generated by Jonah's body. But she wasn't sleepy. She was too conscious of Jonah's arm around her, and the taut muscled firmness of his body.

Nor was he sleepy, apparently. He shifted his position restlessly from time to time. At one point he murmured, "You're awake, too, aren't you?"

"Yes."

He burst out, "God, Lucinda, won't you tell me the truth at last? I haven't tried to force you to come back to me. I've never in my life taken an unwilling woman. But I'm going half out of my mind, not knowing *why* you suddenly stopped loving me, if that's what really happened. Lucinda, I love you. I'll never love anyone else."

Perhaps it was because her guard was down from so little sleep, or because she hadn't been with Jonah for six months and the unexpected meeting was a shock, or merely because the room was in total darkness and she couldn't see his face. Whatever the reason, Lucinda broke her self-imposed bond of silence and snapped, "On the contrary, you'll probably love dozens of women in your lifetime, one in particular more than most. And that one isn't me!"

Jonah said blankly, "What in heaven's name do you mean? I've never pretended to be a hermit, and there was Daphne, of course, but I'm no loose screw."

"*Was?* There *was* Daphne? Doing it too brown, Jonah," said Lucinda, her anger too exacerbated now for her to curb her tongue. "I'm not quite the bacon-brained innocent you take me for. I'm well aware that you planned to continue your liaison with Daphne after you and I were safely married and you had the use of my fortune to pay Harry's horrendous gambling debts. And as long as you had to marry me, an added bonus was the prospect of fathering your own heir."

"My God, Lucinda, is that why . . . ? It's not true, any of it. I broke off with Daphne before I asked you to marry me. I never planned to continue our affair with her after you and I were married. Even if I didn't care about humiliating you, hurting you, I couldn't have kept Daphne as my mistress. I told you, I no longer loved her. As for Harry's gambling debts, he has none. If anything, he's such an expert hazard player that he's ahead of the game. Moreover Cassandra came to him with a very large dowry, which is intact."

Jonah lapsed into a tense silence. After a moment he said, "What can I say to convince you how wrong you are? I haven't seen Daphne for months, and I certainly haven't touched her, though I suppose, without proof, I can't make you believe that. Harry's case is a different matter. You can contact his banker, who will reveal to you, I'm sure with Harry's permission, the state of my brother's account, which is flourishing. I had no need to marry you to rescue Harry from debtors' prison."

"But—Daphne told me . . ." Lucinda's voice trailed away.

Jonah stiffened. "Daphne told you these lies? When . . . ?" He drew a hard breath. "I know when. It was on our wedding day, wasn't it? After the ceremony, after the breakfast. Up to that point you were still blissfully happy, still madly in love with me. Then you went up to your bedchamber to change your clothes for our wedding journey, and Daphne followed you. Isn't that how it was?"

"Yes," Lucinda whispered. A painful lump in her chest was dissolving. Jonah loved her, had always loved her. Deep in the recesses of her bruised heart, she'd always known that. But Daphne, unhappy and tormented, so much a woman of the world, had been so convincing. Never reconciled to losing her lover, she'd tried with her poisonous lies to spoil Jonah's wedding day and his marriage, and she'd come very close.

Lucinda threw her arms around Jonah and buried her

face in his chest. "Darling, I'm so ashamed," she murmured. "I knew you. I should have trusted you. Can you ever forgive me?"

"Hush, my adorable bird-witted wife," Jonah exclaimed exuberantly. "What's there to forgive, now that I know you love me? And as soon as I can divest myself of these damned clothes I'm wearing—I don't care if I risk frostbite!—I'll prove to you just how happy I am. Tonight, my dearest love, is our wedding night!"

"Grandmama's outdone herself," said Lucinda, as she stood beside Jonah, gazing around the crowded ballroom of Marshfield Court. "The county will be buzzing about this ball for years. An imported orchestra from London. Cases of the most expensive champagne. Refreshments by a master chef. A guest list that includes everyone who is anyone from all over the kingdom."

"Yes, it's a gala affair," agreed Jonah. He smiled at Lucinda. "However, I daresay this Valentine's Day celebration would have been memorable for Lady Cardew in any event. You've come home to her, and you and I are happily married."

Lucinda nodded, her eyes tearing as she recalled the countess' reaction to the news that Jonah and her granddaughter had reconciled. "Oh, Lucinda, now I can die happy, knowing you have a husband to take care of you."

Lucinda's heart had contracted at the remark, though she knew it had been purely figurative. Her grandmother wouldn't have referred to her death if she'd realized that Lucinda had learned about her grandmother's heart condition.

Certainly the precarious state of her health hadn't precluded Lady Cardew from enjoying her elaborate Valentine's Day-birthday celebrations. She'd reveled in every pretty or frivolous or useless gift, from handkerchiefs daintily embroidered with hearts to countless boxes of chocolates and sweetmeats to enormous hothouse flower arrangements. During the days preceding the ball she'd enthusiastically hosted a series of dinners, routs, receptions and tours of the scenic attractions of the countryside.

Near midnight, Lucinda was walking off the dance floor with Jonah after a vigorous country dance when she spotted her grandmother's butler at the door of the ballroom, glancing about him as if he was looking for someone.

"Yes, Simmons, what is it?" Lucinda inquired, coming up to the butler on Jonah's arm.

"Have you seen Dr. Hemings, my lady? Her ladyship wishes me to inform him that supper is about to be served. He's to take her in to supper, you know. He's not in the card room, and of course he doesn't dance."

Lucinda laughed. Dr. Hemings was her grandmother's closest and oldest friend. It had never seemed to matter to her that he was considerably below her in station.

"No, the doctor doesn't dance. He comes to balls under protest," she told the butler. "I think I know where he is, Simmons. Lord Brentford and I will find him."

"Dr. Hemings doesn't dance, he thinks playing cards is a bore, he and doesn't hunt," Lucinda remarked as she and Jonah entered the conservatory. "Yet he and Grandmama deal famously. I think it's because she knows he would cut off his right hand to save her pain or discomfort. It will be a tremendous blow to him when she dies."

"You think the doctor may be here?" Jonah asked, gazing around the huge conservatory, seemingly empty of occupants. Not even a stray courting couple was in evidence.

"I *know* he's here," said Lucinda with a grin. She walked briskly to the end of the structure, where, in a dimly lit alcove, beneath a tropical flowering tree, an elderly gentleman sat at a table, peacefully sipping a glass of wine and smoking a pipe.

"Caught you out, Doctor," said Lucinda merrily. "Grandmama says to tell you supper is about to be served."

"Very well, my dear. For the sake of food I'm willing to leave this haven."

Dr. Hemings pushed his spectacles farther up his prominent nose and pulled himself painfully to his feet. "I'm happy to have this opportunity to say a private word to you, Lucinda, to tell you how pleased I am that you've mended your marriage." He glanced at Jonah. "I hope you know, my lord, how fortunate you are to have Lucinda for your wife."

"I'm well aware of that." Jonah cocked an eyebrow at the doctor. "Actually, we owe at least part of our happiness to you. I doubt Lucinda would have come here for the Valentine's Day party if you hadn't written to her about Lady Cardew's illness."

To Lucinda's surprise, the doctor chuckled. "That was a stroke of genius on her ladyship's part. She was sure Lucinda wouldn't refuse to attend the Valentine's Day gala if she believed it was the last such event that Lady Cardew would ever celebrate." He gazed at Lucinda, his eyes twinkling. "So, my dear, your grandmother was right. It went sorely against the grain with her to tell such a fib and to coerce me to do the same, but sometimes a lie is in the right cause."

Lucinda said stonily, "Are you saying there's nothing wrong with Grandmama's health? She's not going to die?"

"No, indeed. She'll outlive us all, thanks be to the Almighty," began the doctor, and stopped short. "You mean, her ladyship hasn't told you about her—er—little deception?" he faltered.

"No, indeed." She turned on Jonah. "Did you know that this report of Grandmama's illness was false?"

"I—yes. Wait, Lucinda," he exclaimed, putting out his hand to catch her arm as she whirled to go. "Doctor, will you leave us, please?"

As the sound of the doctor's footsteps grew fainter, Jonah said, "Don't judge Lady Cardew and me too harshly. We were desperate. You'd cut yourself off from us completely, refusing to give any reason why. We had to do something."

"Yes. Tell a lie. Get me here under false pretenses."

"Was that so terrible? Aren't you relieved now to know that your grandmother has years of life ahead of her? Aren't you happy that you and I have rediscovered our love for each other? If it weren't for the doctor's letter that might never have happened."

Lucinda stared at him, her anger and resentment beginning to soften. Was the lie, after all, so heinous? No one had been hurt. She and her grandmother were friends again, and she and Jonah were lovers at last. She shivered at the thought that their estrangement might have gone on forever. And finally, much could be made of the fact that it was Daphne's bile and her own stubbornness that made the estrangement possible in the first place.

She threw her arms around Jonah, clutching at him, rejoicing in the feel of his hard masculine body against her own.

"No, the lie wasn't so terrible," she murmured. "In fact, I'm glad that my husband and my grandmother and my family doctor are such skilled prevaricators!"

ZEBRA REGENCIES
ARE THE
TALK OF THE TON!

A REFORMED RAKE   (4499, $3.99)

by Jeanne Savery

After governess Harriet Cole helped her young charge flee to France—
and the designs of a despicable suitor, more trouble soon arrived in the
person of a London rake. Sir Frederick Carrington insisted on providing
safe escort back to England. Harriet deemed Carrington more dangerous than any band of brigands, but secretly relished matching wits with
him. But after being taken in his arms for a tender kiss, she found
herself wondering—*could* a lady find love with an irresistible rogue?

A SCANDALOUS PROPOSAL   (4504, $4.99)

by Teresa DesJardien

After only two weeks into the London season, Lady Pamela Premington
has already received her first offer of marriage. If only it hadn't come
from the *ton's* most notorious rake, Lord Marchmont. Pamela had already set her sights on the distinguished Lieutenant Penford, who had
the heroism and honor that made him the ideal match. Now she had to
keep from falling under the spell of the seductive Lord so she could
pursue the man more worthy of her love. Or was he?

A LADY'S CHAMPION   (4535, $3.99)

by Janice Bennett

Miss Daphne, art mistress of the Selwood Academy for Young Ladies,
greeted the notion of ghosts haunting the academy with skepticism.
However, to avoid rumors frightening off students, she found herself
turning to Mr. Adrian Carstairs, sent by her uncle to be her "protector"
against the "ghosts." Although, Daphne would accept no interference
in her life, she *would* accept aid in exposing any spectral spirits. What
she never expected was for Adrian to expose the secret wishes of her
hidden heart . . .

CHARITY'S GAMBIT   (4537, $3.99)

by Marcy Stewart

Charity Abercrombie reluctantly embarks on a London season in hopes
of making a suitable match. However she cannot forget the mysterious
Dominic Castille—and the kiss they shared—when he fell from a tree
as she strolled through the woods. Charity does not know that the dark
and dashing captain harbors a dangerous secret that will ensnare them
both in its web—leaving Charity to risk certain ruin and losing the man
she so passionately loves . . .

*Available wherever paperbacks are sold, or order direct from the
Publisher. Send cover price plus 50¢ per copy for mailing and
handling to Penguin USA, P.O. Box 999, c/o Dept. 17109,
Bergenfield, NJ 07621. Residents of New York and Tennessee
must include sales tax. DO NOT SEND CASH.*